RED CELL SEVEN

OTHER NOVELS BY STEPHEN FREY

The Takeover

The Vulture Fund

The Inner Sanctum

The Legacy

The Insider

Trust Fund

The Day Trader

Silent Partner

Shadow Account

The Chairman

The Protégé

The Power Broker

The Successor

The Fourth Order

Forced Out

Hell's Gate

Heaven's Fury

Arctic Fire

RED CELL SEVEN

STEPHEN FREY

 THOMAS & MERCER

Text copyright © 2013 Stephen Frey

Published by Thomas & Mercer, Seattle

www.apub.com

ISBN-13: 9781477809457
ISBN-10: 1477809457

Library of Congress Control Number: 2013906874

FOR LILY. I LOVE YOU VERY, VERY MUCH.
NONE OF THIS WOULD HAVE HAPPENED WITHOUT YOU.

PROLOGUE

MARCH 1973

"Hello, Captain."

The door clicked shut behind Roger Carlson. Shut by the same Secret Service agent who'd been shadowing him ever since he'd stepped onto White House grounds two hours ago.

Now that the agent was finally gone, a palpable wave of relief surged through Carlson. He had an intense aversion to being stalked. It was like claustrophobia in that it pushed him inexorably toward a state of extreme stress and a potentially violent reaction. He'd always been able to control the condition, though barely at times. And no military psychologist had ever diagnosed it despite the battery of skull-tests he was required to undergo once a year due to his highly classified missions.

Carlson was a Marine, but his orders weren't the normal "take the beach" type. He was an assassin, and he'd murdered four senior Soviet officials at close range in the last two years. He had all four of their cheap neckties hidden in a desk drawer at his small house in Alexandria. Trophies were important to him.

"We've been expecting you."

Before moving toward the three men who sat on the far side of the Oval Office as if in judgment, Carlson nodded subtly and respectfully to the presidential seal, which was woven into the dark blue carpet. Specifically at the thirteen arrows the eagle clutched in its left talon, while he deliberately avoided acknowledging the olive branch the magnificent bird gripped in its right.

"Come in, please."

After eleven years of military uniforms, the badly fitting three-button pinstripe suit, white button-down shirt, and plain blue tie Carlson wore today made him feel out of place, even a little vulnerable. But what made him most uncomfortable was that he had no idea why he'd been summoned here.

He caught a glimpse of himself in a large, gold-framed mirror hanging on the wall to his right. He was of average height and weight, but his jutting chin cut an impressive profile. Otherwise, he considered himself quite ordinary looking—though Nancy, his wife of seven years, disagreed. She always told him how handsome he was.

Nancy was a wonderful woman. She never asked what he did, even when he'd leave for weeks at a time with no account of where he was going or where he'd been. She was the perfect wife for him. She knew something unusual was going on, but she never pushed.

"Good afternoon, Mr. President." Carlson stopped a few inches shy of the wide desk and clasped his hands behind his back, standing ramrod straight with eyes ahead, just as he would if he'd been wearing his Marine uniform reporting to his superior officer. "How can I assist you, sir?"

"We'll get to all that."

"Yes, sir."

"At ease, Captain Carlson."

"Yes, sir."

"So, how are you today?"

"I'm fine, sir. Thank you."

"Any problem finding us?"

Carlson flashed a grin as the men sitting on either side of President Nixon eyed each other uneasily. Carlson figured Nixon was kidding. But he quickly masked his amusement when tiny beads of perspiration broke out on the president's upper lip.

"Um, no." Apparently Nixon's question had been sincere, and the president suddenly seemed mortified. Carlson had read about Nixon's intensity, but no newspaper article or book could have prepared him for this. "No problem finding you at all, sir."

"This is Mr. Haldeman." Nixon motioned stiffly to the right with his eyes down, apparently still recovering from Carlson's amused reaction. "He is the president's chief of staff."

Carlson had read how awkward Nixon could be in social situations. His superior had warned him about it, too. "Yes, sir."

"And to the left is Mr. Ehrlichman. He is counsel to the president."

Nixon had just referred to himself twice in the third person. It was a sign of delusion, Carlson figured. But with the Watergate noose tightening around his neck, perhaps the president needed delusion to stay in control.

The president nodded at a chair positioned in front of the desk. "Sit down, Captain."

As Carlson obeyed, he was struck by how dark Nixon's stubble was, the formality of his manner, and how stiff and clumsy the president's motions were. Nixon was no athlete.

"You are a Marine," Nixon stated.

"Yes, sir."

"You joined the Marines after graduating from Yale University."

"Yes, sir." Pride coursed through Carlson. The president of the United States knew the details of his life. "With loans."

"I was a naval officer, a lieutenant commander."

The physical rigors of boot camp must have been hell for Nixon. He could almost hear the RDC screaming. "Yes, sir, I know you—"

"Mr. Haldeman has done a great deal of research on you," Nixon interrupted, gesturing to the right again. "He's impressed with your record. We all are." The president's eyes flashed, regaining their intensity after the embarrassment of asking the awkward question about locating the White House. "Captain Carlson, we considered thousands of individuals for this mission, and we selected you."

"Thank you, sir." It seemed strange but somehow appropriate that Carlson should show appreciation for what remained an unknown. He'd heard people call Nixon a walking enigma. Now he understood why.

Nixon forced a smile to his lips. "I'm sure you're wondering why you were ordered to wear civilian clothes today, Captain Carlson."

Why would Nixon focus on that? There was a much-bigger-picture issue lurking in the shadows of this room like an eight-hundred-pound gorilla.

"Yes, sir, I am."

"The answer is because you're no longer a Marine."

"Sir?"

"You were honorably discharged from the Marine Corps this afternoon." Haldeman spoke up for the first time. "You will not return to the Pentagon today."

"All right," Carlson answered hesitantly, uncertain if the news was good or bad.

Nixon motioned to Carlson, then at Haldeman. "Mr. Haldeman has something for you, Captain Carlson. Take it, and protect it with every fiber of your being."

Carlson's heart began to thud as he stood up, moved to where Haldeman sat, took the large manila envelope the man was holding out for him, and returned to his chair. He could hear himself breathing deeply as he opened the envelope and pulled out two pieces of heavy paper. He was painfully aware of how the papers were shaking in his fingers even though he held them with both hands.

"I like it that you're affected," Nixon commented, acknowledging Carlson's visible anxiety. "Give him the details, Bob."

"Captain Carlson," Haldeman began in a somber tone, "you will found, organize, and run the most clandestine intelligence unit this country has ever operated. From now on you will officially be part of the Central Intelligence Agency, but you will report only to the president of the United States, and you will do that only when you decide a report to the Executive Branch is necessary. After today, you will have one meeting with the director of the CIA to obtain budget details for your cell, and that will be it. When that meeting is over, you are on your own to recruit agents, gather information on our enemies, defend this country, and even wage clandestine wars if you deem that course of action necessary. Your only mission will be to protect the United States in any way you see fit. Do you understand what your president is asking of you?"

Carlson gazed at Haldeman for a few moments then shifted his attention to Nixon. The perspiration on the president's upper lip had evaporated, and he looked like a black Lab on scent, completely focused and compelled by the subject at hand.

"It's beautiful, isn't it?" Nixon murmured breathlessly as he grinned at Carlson from behind the desk. "In fact, it's perfect."

Nixon's grin and his shifty little eyes seemed laced with a trace of evil. And somehow that seemed appropriate. "Yes, sir, it is."

How could it be that simple? How could Nixon create something as significant as this out of thin air? It was Carlson's dream job—executing global intelligence and waging a shadow war with no constraints. It was as if God had suddenly appeared before him and confirmed heaven's existence.

No, no, it was better than that. It was here, it was now. It was real. Heaven was off in the distance, waiting—maybe.

"How?" Carlson asked. "How does this happen?"

Haldeman motioned at the documents in Carlson's lap. "That is Executive Order 1973 One-E. It is signed by Richard Milhous Nixon, the thirty-seventh president of the United States of America. Under Article Two, Section Three, Clause Five of the Constitution, the president is empowered to take care that the laws of the United States are fully executed.

That is what President Nixon has just ordered you to do in his capacity as chief executive of this country and as the commander in chief of its military." Haldeman pointed at the documents again. "You have two originals of the Order. Those are the only two originals in existence, and you will keep both of them in your possession in case you ever need them."

"To demonstrate to agents I'm recruiting that my charge has complete credibility," Carlson surmised.

"The *ultimate* credibility," Nixon said firmly.

"I suggest," Haldeman continued, "that you conceal those two pieces of paper in separate locations; in addition, that you make one other person who you trust with your life aware of their existence as well as aware of at least one of the hidden locations. The Orders are genuine, they are legitimate, and they are completely enforceable as a matter of law. In fact, your name is written into the Order to completely protect you from any illegal prosecution and to assist you with that credibility you just mentioned. However, without them, you are vulnerable." Haldeman nodded to Carlson. "President Nixon empowers you to move forward with the Order, Captain Carlson."

The room went deathly still for several moments.

Finally, Carlson spoke up. "Thank you, sir."

"I expect your primary target will be the Soviet Union," Nixon said. Carlson had heard about Nixon's fear of the Soviet Union and its legendary Red Army. It wasn't a well-kept secret in the Pentagon. According to some he'd spoken to, Nixon's fear of the Soviets bordered on pathological paranoia.

"Of course, sir."

"But China and Castro will be of interest to you as well."

"Yes, sir."

"You'll call your new unit Red Cell Seven," Nixon directed, "and you'll subtly let the name filter out into the international intelligence community. It will drive Brezhnev crazy," he added, referring to the leader of the Soviet Union. "He'll have the KGB and others of his intelligence network search frantically everywhere for cells One through Six.

And he'll spend billions of rubles doing so. But he'll never find the first six cells, because they have never existed and they never will."

"Maybe we should call it Red Cell *Fifty*," Ehrlichman muttered.

They were the only words Ehrlichman would utter during the entire meeting, but they elicited the lone universal laugh.

When everyone's loud chuckles faded, the president took a deep breath, as if a weight had finally been lifted from his shoulders. "Do you have any other questions, Captain Carlson?"

"Does this Order give me license to kill?"

Nixon leaned forward, placed both elbows on the desk, and interlocked his fingers in front of his face as if he were praying. "After you leave this room, Captain Carlson, I want you to find a secure location to thoroughly read that Executive Order. When you've finished reading it twice, and I do mean twice, you will understand that you have the authority to do whatever you feel is necessary to keep this country safe. By that I mean absolutely *anything*. Kill, torture, steal, destroy—it's up to you. I don't care what it is as long as you in good faith and conscience can convince yourself that the action will be executed in the name of protecting the United States of America. Are we clear on that?"

Carlson nodded. He could barely control his euphoria. "Yes, sir," he managed to answer calmly for what he figured must have been at least the tenth time since he'd entered this room. "Crystal clear."

"This is the ultimate trust," Nixon said. "I can bestow no greater privilege on a United States citizen."

Carlson nodded again as the weight of the words cascaded down onto him like a powerful but incredibly pleasing waterfall. He cleared his throat softly to make certain his words came out firmly and without hesitance. "And I cannot possibly receive any greater privilege. Thank you, sir."

NOVEMBER 1983

"Hello, Captain."

The door clicked shut behind Bill Jensen. Shut by the same Secret Service agent who'd been shadowing him ever since he'd stepped onto White House grounds an hour ago.

The agent had been intense about his duties for the last sixty minutes, obnoxiously so. But that intensity hadn't bothered Jensen. The man was simply doing his job, and besides, Jensen made a point of getting angry only when exhibiting the emotion achieved a specific goal. Otherwise he considered anger nothing but negative energy that distracted the mind from rational and effective thought.

"Come in. We've been waiting for you."

Jensen nodded respectfully at the presidential seal, which was woven into the dark blue carpet of the Oval Office. Like Roger Carlson ten years before, he acknowledged only the thirteen arrows in the left talon.

As he moved across the room in his measured stride, Jensen felt great pride when he glanced at the president, who was sitting serenely behind the wide desk, and then at the chief of staff, who was relaxing in a chair to the left. In the last three years Ronald Reagan and James Baker had restored the country's respect on the international stage, after the Jimmy Carter debacle, by retooling the military and beating the hell out of interest rates. The country's economy was booming, and America's armed forces were once again feared throughout the world. Reagan and Baker were totally focused on maintaining the United States' role as a global superpower, and it was a pleasure to serve them as a Marine.

But Jensen still hadn't been told what he was doing here today.

He hadn't been told why he'd been specifically instructed to wear civilian clothes, either. Of course, it wasn't like he minded. Once in a while he enjoyed stepping out in his worsted wool charcoal suit, stylish blue Oxford shirt with white collar and French cuffs, and his favorite red silk tie, which was also imported from Paris. Today Jensen was wearing the uniform his father had worn every day. His father had been a prominent Wall Street rainmaker before an untimely death last summer had cut short his glittering career in Lower Manhattan.

Jensen caught a glimpse of himself in the gold-framed mirror hanging on the wall to his right. He was tall and slim with light blond hair, which was trimmed high and tight, and he cut a naturally aristocratic profile in the glass as he passed by. People had often described his look as presidential, too, and for a quick moment he wondered if someday this office would be his. It was entirely possible.

"Good morning, Mr. President." Jensen stopped a few inches shy of the desk and clasped his hands behind his back, standing ramrod straight, just as he would if he'd been wearing his Marine uniform reporting to his superior officer. "How can I assist you, sir?"

"You're a credit to our country, son," President Ronald Reagan said in his gravelly, naturally melodic voice. "A shining example of everything good our nation stands for. America is proud of you, son."

The president had been a B-list Hollywood actor in his younger days, so Jensen was fully aware that the short speech was technique driven. Still, it was difficult not to buy into everything the man was saying. The charisma emanating from the other side of the desk was undeniable and irresistible. The man with the rosy cheeks, perfect dark hair despite his advanced age, and electric smile had convinced an entire nation to follow him like puppies following their mother just by speaking to them through a television lens. So it was only natural that he could influence people even more readily in person at close range, even people who were ready for it and recognized it.

Now that was talent.

"Thank you, sir."

"You went to Yale before the Marines," James Baker spoke up in his soothing Texas drawl.

"That's correct."

"Sit down, Captain Jensen." Reagan motioned to a chair in front of the desk. "Please."

"And you graduated from Princeton before you went into the Marines," Jensen volleyed back in a friendly way as he eased into the chair and nodded respectfully to Baker. "After that you went to law school at UT."

"That's right, son." Baker glanced at Reagan and smiled. "He's exactly what we want, isn't he, Mr. President?"

"Um, yes . . . of course." Reagan had been looking out the window behind the desk, and Baker's comment had clearly caught him off guard. "Let's get to why you're here, Captain."

Reagan seemed distracted to Jensen, or maybe the president was just tired. After all, he was a relatively old man trying to execute the most challenging job on earth. "I'm obviously looking forward to that, Mr. President."

"You ever heard of Red Cell Seven?" Baker asked.

Jensen's eyes narrowed. On a dime this meeting had taken a compelling turn. "Just whispers on the wind," he responded, "but nothing definitive. Vague rumors about a hush-hush cell created by President Nixon to mess with the Soviets." He shrugged. "But I never buy stock in rumors. I short them."

"Well, you should have gone long this time. And though his main focus for the last decade has definitely been the Soviet Union, the man running RCS is about to significantly expand the cell's scope of operation."

Once more, Baker was doing the talking. Reagan was looking outside again, watching a robin that was sitting on a bush just outside the window. The bird was on late departure for its southern swing, as it had gotten quite chilly in Washington. As Jensen watched, a slight smile crept across the president's face when the bird began to preen itself.

"And you were right," Baker continued, "it is the most covert intelligence cell this country has ever operated. But now it's going even deeper into the shadows."

"How so, sir?"

"Up until now Red Cell Seven has been funded through the CIA. At this point RCS is only about thirty agents, and the man who runs it has been operating on a budget of less than ten million a year. So the 'miscellaneous' line item on the CIA books has been a rounding error. The opportunity for the unit's enemies to detect that line has been slight, and therefore the chance of being able to follow money trails and transfers has been negligible. Still, it has been and continues to be a risk." Baker held up a hand. "We don't like that. We want to make this cell completely transparent as it moves forward and takes on even more responsibility."

"*Completely* transparent," President Reagan echoed, again engaged in the conversation.

"Red Cell Seven has been a tremendous success," Baker said, "and success tends to attract attention."

Jensen nodded. "Of course."

"So we intend to switch funding for the cell from the government to the private sector."

Jensen gazed steadily at Baker for a few moments. "The private sector?" It was a fascinating idea. So simple but potentially so effective.

"That way there are no money trails that can lead to anyone inside the government." Baker hesitated. "We've all seen what can happen when money trails lead to the government. I'm sure former President Nixon still wishes he'd been more careful about that."

Jensen nodded again. "Yes, sir." A thrill surged through him. Now he was fairly certain of why he'd been invited to the Oval Office.

"We want you to lead the privatization effort, Captain Jensen."

The world blurred before Bill Jensen when the confirmation came. This could be the opportunity of a lifetime. He might be forever losing his chance to claim this office someday. But so what? This opportunity could prove infinitely more exciting—and more profitable.

"Your family is well connected financially," Baker went on. "And that puts you in a unique position to help us." A sad look worked its way into the COS's expression. "I'm sorry about your father, Captain Jensen. I met him several times. He was a good man who was taken before his time."

"Thank you."

"We know that you've kept in touch with his friends since he died last summer, and those connections could be very helpful to us."

Baker's condolence hadn't lasted long. Once more, the chief of staff's expression was flooded with anticipation.

"Further," Baker continued, "we intend to place you into a specific position on Wall Street that will enable you to quickly enhance your network of high-net-worth individuals. High-net-worth individuals friendly to our cause who can fund Red Cell Seven secretly out of their own pockets under your direction." Baker paused. "A friend of mine from Texas runs a firm in New York City called First Manhattan. Ever heard of it?"

"Yes, sir."

"It's not a bulge-bracket investment bank like Goldman or Morgan Stanley, but it—"

"But it's growing fast," Jensen broke in. Baker seemed miffed by the interruption, as though it had been a long time since anyone had been so brazen. But so what? They'd already selected him for the job, and they weren't going back on the offer now that they'd let the cat out of the bag. "First Manhattan has a white-hot technology group, and their M&A shop's a comer as well."

"That's right," Baker agreed. "In fact, you'll join that technology investment banking group as a vice president. Tomorrow morning you'll meet with the man who runs the group in Midtown Manhattan. If things go well with funding Red Cell Seven privately, one day I can see you running First Manhattan."

Everything was moving at light speed in exactly the direction Jensen wanted. "I assume I'm not going back to the Pentagon." The robin had flown from the bush, but Reagan was looking out the window again. This time the president's focus seemed to be on something in the distance. His fading smile seemed nostalgic, almost sad.

"You've already been honorably discharged from the Marines," Baker confirmed.

"What's next?"

Baker smiled thinly but appreciatively at the younger man's instant commitment and natural impatience. "As I said, you'll go to New York City this afternoon for a meeting with that First Manhattan executive tomorrow. At nine o'clock tonight you'll receive a call from the man who runs RCS. Make certain you're in your Manhattan hotel room at that time."

"What is the man's name?"

"Roger Carlson."

A powerful chill sprinted up Jensen's spine, and for several seconds he fought it for control of his body. He didn't want to exhibit any reaction the chill might induce. Jensen wasn't worried about Reagan noticing. The president was still staring off into the distance. But he didn't want Baker seeing it.

"I believe you know Mr. Carlson."

"I did," Jensen confirmed, fascinated by the fact that they knew of his connection to Carlson. Carlson must have had a hidden hand in today's meeting. "Roger was my mentor early on in the Corps. But he disappeared ten years ago." No one knew what had happened to Carlson. Now it all made sense. The same thing was about to happen to him. "I never heard from Roger again."

"Well, you'll be hearing from him again soon, after your New York trip."

"Are you prepared to do this job?" President Reagan asked solemnly as he reengaged. "It's one of the most important things I could ask of you, son. It will make Red Cell Seven untouchable, and that's crucial for the continued national security of this great nation. Do I have your commitment?"

Jensen nodded. It was interesting how Reagan went in and out of conversations so often. Interesting and a bit frightening, so thank the Lord for James Baker.

"Yes, sir, I'm absolutely committed to Red Cell Seven. Thank you for the opportunity. I'll make you proud."

"I know you will, Captain Jensen. I know you will."

PART I

CHAPTER 1

PRESENT DAY

"JACK'S GONE," Troy Jensen muttered to himself. "He's really gone."

Troy stared at the large photograph of his older brother, which was sitting on an easel in the middle of the church's anteroom. Cheryl, their mother, was standing a few feet away with another woman. They were crying softly.

"You okay, son?" Bill Jensen asked as he moved to Troy's side.

Troy cleared his throat. "Of course, Dad."

Troy glanced at the two FBI agents who were standing in front of the anteroom door in dark suits. They were here on direct orders from David Dorn, the president of the United States. More agents were outside this room, in the main part of the church. In their dark suits, they blended easily into the large congregation that had gathered to pay last respects to Jack Jensen. Even more agents formed a perimeter outside the church in the picturesque countryside west of Greenwich, Connecticut.

But Shane Maddux wouldn't have a problem getting through those defenses if he chose to, Troy knew. Maddux was eerily good at slipping through life undetected, like a specter, though he turned into a ferocious predator at the final, critical moment.

Troy had witnessed that fury firsthand, as well as Maddux's ability to glide through the world invisibly. All of which had Troy carrying a 9mm Beretta in a shoulder holster beneath his suit jacket. The first bullet was already chambered—a dangerous but necessary precaution. You could never be too careful if Shane Maddux had you in his sights. The coffin on the other side of the door was a testament to that harsh reality.

"It's hard," Troy admitted.

"I know." Bill shook his head sadly. "One second your brother is sitting with us on the porch. The next he's on the floor, dying." Bill gritted his teeth as he gazed at the picture of Jack resting on the easel. "So help me God, I'll find out who shot him. And no one will be able to help that person when I do."

The deadly shot had come from a tree line hundreds of yards away as the three of them were sitting on the porch together, from across the horse fields of the Jensens' sprawling property outside Greenwich. As Bill frantically called 911, Troy sprinted across the fields to chase down the shooter. But Jack's murderer was long gone by the time Troy made it to the trees.

"Come on, Dad. We both know who killed Jack. It was Shane Maddux."

"You can't assume that, son. We never saw the shooter. The bullet came from the woods. That tree line is a long way from the house."

"It was Maddux," Troy said confidently.

"If it was Maddux, wouldn't he have been aiming at you or me? That would make more sense. And if it was Maddux, we both know he hits his target. He doesn't miss."

"He was furious at Jack for saving President Dorn's life. It was a revenge kill for derailing the assassination in Los Angeles. For calling Rex Stein at the last minute so Stein could deflect the bullet. It was for saving me in Alaska, too. And for calling the Navy jets out on that LNG tanker Maddux had heading for Virginia. That bullet was for all those things."

"You knew Shane Maddux personally, Troy. I've only met the man a few times, and none of those meetings ever went long. But everything I've heard about him paints the portrait of an individual who takes emotion out of everything. And those meetings I had with him only reinforce my belief in that. His mind is so strong. Everything he does is motivated by purpose and objective, never by anger or retribution."

Troy nodded. "He's a focused son of a bitch."

"It's worse than that. He's obsessed. He's clinically insane."

"I don't know about that, Dad. If Maddux was insane, I don't think he'd be able to—"

Troy interrupted himself as Karen Morris, Jack's girlfriend, approached. She was a pretty brunette with a vivacious smile that wouldn't show itself today. She and Jack hadn't been together long, but they'd fallen deeply in love after surviving everything that had happened to them in Alaska and on the way there. Now their relationship was over before it had really gotten started.

"Hi, Troy."

"Hey." He slipped his arms around her and guided her cheek to his shoulder. She was trying hard to keep her emotions in check, but that wouldn't last. He could feel her shaking. "It'll be okay."

"I don't know," she whispered. "I can't stop thinking about him."

"Me neither," he agreed softly.

"I wish I could have seen him one more time. I wish I could have told him how much I loved him one more time."

"I know."

Karen gave Troy a gentle kiss on the cheek. Then she turned to hug Bill as a single tear rolled down her face.

Troy's gaze flickered back to the photograph on the easel. Jack had dark hair, brown eyes, and olive-hued skin. Troy, who at twenty-eight was two years younger than Jack, had blue eyes and dirty-blond hair that fell to the bottom of his collar in the back. They looked nothing alike, and there was a good reason for that. Both brothers had been told all along that Jack had been adopted just after birth—which was why they looked so different. But it was a lie, and the truth had finally spilled out into the open only recently. Troy loved Bill as much as a son could love a father, but he still hadn't forgiven him for the long-standing deception. He wasn't sure he ever could.

"You're sitting with us today, Karen," Bill said as he stepped back from their embrace.

"But I—"

"You're sitting with us," he repeated firmly. "You're family now."

She reached out and touched his arm gently in appreciation. "Thank you."

Bill patted Troy gently on the shoulder as Cheryl walked away. "We have to get down to Washington as soon as the funeral's over."

"I know," Troy said curtly.

"The plane's waiting for us at Westchester."

"*I know.*"

Bill exhaled heavily. "Are you ever going to forgive me, son?"

"I'm not sure," Troy answered honestly. "What you did was terrible. Telling everyone Jack was adopted for so long. It made him feel like an outsider for thirty years."

"I was a coward." Bill took another deep breath. "I'm sorry, very sorry. I wish I could say that to Jack, but I can't." His lower lip trembled slightly. "Will you help me bury him, son? I need to know you're in my corner today. I don't know if I can get through the eulogy if I look down at you from the pulpit and I see that same expression in your eyes I just did." He hesitated. "Are you there for me?"

Troy gazed at his father for a long time. Finally, he nodded. "I am, Dad."

"Thank you. I mean that."

"Are you sure you want to do this?" Troy asked as Bill started toward Cheryl and Karen.

Bill shrugged as he turned back around. "Do what?"

"Go to Washington."

Bill nodded somberly. "I'll be okay. But thanks for saying something. Your old man's not as tough as he used to be, but he's still—"

"That's not what I meant."

"Oh?"

"Are you sure you want to tell President Dorn everything?"

"Well, I gave him those files before we met with him at Walter Reed. I feel like I have to tell him everything at this point."

"Do you think he's told Baxter about Red Cell Seven?"

"I asked the president not to say anything to anyone about it. But I specifically asked him not to tell Stewart Baxter. In fact, I warned him not to." Bill paused. "Unfortunately, David Dorn is a stubborn man, and Baxter is his chief of staff."

"That's why it was such a risk to give Dorn all those files about what RCS has done in the last forty years."

"Of course it was a risk," Bill agreed. "But the fact is we knew Dorn was trying to shut down RCS before the attempt on his life. By the time we'd met with him at Walter Reed after the assassination attempt he'd had a change of heart. I think reading those files helped him with that change."

"I hope he still feels that way this afternoon, Dad. I hope he hasn't changed his heart or his mind back the other way."

"Me too, son." Bill put his hand on Troy's shoulder again. "Now help me bury your brother."

CHAPTER 2

"You can't be serious."

"I couldn't be more serious. *Decus septum.*"

"Whatever."

"Protect the peak," Agent Walker added tersely.

"'Protect the peak'?" Agent Beam spread his arms wide. "What the *hell* does that mean?"

So the kid hadn't heard that part of the greeting yet. Well, that was probably for the best, based on how he was acting. "Say what you have to say, Agent Beam. And do it before Santa comes with all your toys."

Of course, it wasn't like Walker knew what "protect the peak" meant, either. Agent Beam was a newbie, but Walker had been with Red Cell Seven for more than a decade. None of the other RCS vets to whom Agent Walker was close knew what it meant.

Supposedly, the words had been handed down as the second part of the cell's formal greeting since its founding, four decades ago. Just like *"decus septum"* had as the first part. *"Decus septum"* made perfect sense even though it was spoken in Latin. Translated, it meant "honor to the seven."

"Protect the peak" made no sense despite being spoken in English. No one knew what peak had to be protected—or why.

"We've gotta do the right thing here," Agent Beam spoke up. "And this isn't it, goddamn it."

"I don't know what you mean by that."

"Don't give me that. Don't act all innocent, Major Trav—"

"*What was that*, Agent Beam? There's *no way* I heard you right."

"Sorry, sorry." Agent Beam held up both hands, acknowledging his procedural blunder. Using real names in this situation was forbidden. "I—I mean, Agent Walker." The younger man took a deep breath and tried to calm down. "You don't have your go-ahead from COC. You've gotta wait. It's your duty as an officer, Agent Walker. It's your duty as a human being."

"My duty, Agent Beam, is to acquire information any way I can. Do you understand?"

"But you can't—"

"You heard the transmissions, Agent Beam. You read the transcripts."

"It could all be bullshit."

"You've been with us for six months and you're going to tell *me* what's bullshit?"

"Wait a little while. It might only be a few minutes before they call."

"And it might be hours."

"Have patience."

"I don't have time for patience, Agent Beam."

Agent Beam smirked at the play on words as though it was the dumbest thing he'd ever heard. "How could waiting a few minutes really matter, Agent Walker?"

Major Wilson Travers stared intently at the young man who was asking all the annoying questions. Travers was a tall, broad-shouldered African American soldier. He'd been protecting the United States for more than twenty years, invading Iraq as Marine PFC Travers in 1991.

Agent Beam barely needed to shave, and he'd never been close to a battle-field—except on his high school field trips. Even more aggravating for Travers, Agent Beam was acting like a battle-tested veteran. The arrogance of it all was absurd.

"Forget minutes," Travers said. "Seconds could make the difference in this—"

"That's ridiculous. You have no idea if seconds could—"

"Don't ever interrupt me again, Agent Beam."

When it came down to it, Travers didn't give a rat's ass what this kid thought. And seconds absolutely could make a difference.

"Something big is on the way," Travers said confidently. "I can smell it like a skunk in the woods, and we're running out of time to stop it." *Trust your instincts, trust your instincts.* "People are in danger, and my job is to protect them with any and all means at my disposal." He jabbed a thumb over his shoulder at the stone wall behind him. "Believe me. That man in the next room knows what's coming. Don't let him fool—"

"He doesn't know a damn thing, Agent Walker." Agent Beam sneered. "You're just manufacturing the situation out of thin air so you can—"

"It's coming at us like a thunderstorm on an August afternoon, Agent Beam."

"What you want to feel is your hands around his throat."

"Easy, Mister."

"You can't act on feelings, Agent Walker. Besides, that man in the next room, as you called him, is really just a boy. He's not even eighteen."

It was Travers's turn to sneer. "He's at least twenty-four."

"No way, Agent Walker. Those legendary instincts of yours are off on this one. You need to go on facts, not bullshit, especially when it comes to something like this. We're talking about a man's life here."

"I'm the ranking interrogator," Travers replied evenly. "I go on anything I want to, Agent Beam. I have that license and that privilege. And by the way, that is definitely a man in the next room, not a boy. I don't care how old he is. Ten, ninety, or anywhere in between, it doesn't matter. Age is defined by actions, not years."

"What if you were wrong for once in your life?" Agent Beam shot back. "What if he's done nothing? What if he *knows* nothing?"

"I'll take that chance."

"He's a United States citizen, for God's sake. I saw his birth certificate. I saw his social security card."

"So what?"

"*So what?*" Agent Beam looked to the ceiling and exhaled heavily so his aggravation could not be missed or mistaken. "Despite your job, don't you still have to remember little things like the Constitution and due process?"

"What I have to remember, Agent Beam, is that you probably still know the first song the band played at your high school prom."

Travers glanced down at the nasty scar that ran the length of his right forearm. He'd suffered the wound saving the life of a seven-year-old Afghan girl as a car bomb exploded on a crowded Kabul street. Just one glance into the eyes of the parked car's driver had told him what was coming. If not for his instincts working perfectly on that late afternoon half a world away, the eight-inch piece of metal that had impaled his arm would have sliced the girl's neck open instead.

"And that you've never been in battle," he added.

"You're worried COC won't give you the okay, Agent Walker."

"Oh, yes they will. This is just red tape. Someone's gone fishing in Montana, and I don't have time for them to catch their trophy rainbow."

"You're sick. You *want* to torture that boy. That's what this is really about."

"You're the boy," Travers retorted, tapping Kohler's chest hard. "*That's* what this is really about." He nodded over his shoulder at the stone wall. "I'm going in."

Kohler stepped boldly between Travers and the doorway leading to the interrogation room. "I can't let you do it, Agent Walker," he said firmly, raising his fists and squaring up. "Maybe that guy in there doesn't get due process in a court of law, but he's getting it from me. You're gonna wait for a call from the chain of command, even if it is a few hours away."

It took all of Travers's considerable self-control not to react. Kohler was a big blond kid who was only a year past starring in Ivy League football and dating its prettiest cheerleaders. But he wasn't nearly ready to swim in the deep end of this pool. "Get out of my way, Agent Beam," he ordered calmly. "You're making a fool of yourself."

"No, you bastard, I'm doing what's right, and you know it. You're the fool." Kohler stuck out his chin defiantly. "Do you know who my father was?"

Travers nodded deliberately. "I do know, and I don't care." That was a lie. The only reason he'd allowed Kohler this much leeway and disrespect was entirely wrapped up in who the kid's father was. "All I care about is keeping this country and its people safe. Nothing else."

"You don't get it, do you? You think you actually have a say in what goes on in the world. But you're just a pawn, you stupid nig—" Kohler caught himself but not nearly in time. It was a massive gaffe. Still, he managed a smug smile. "You better watch yourself, boy."

Travers stared into Kohler's arrogant eyes for several seconds. "I'll give you one more chance, Agent Beam. Step aside."

"Fuck you!"

Travers glanced over Kohler's shoulder at the stocky man standing in the corner, the only other person in this room. "Agent Smirnoff."

"Yes, Agent Walker?"

"Attack."

Agent Smirnoff raised a Taser gun and fired, sending 50,000 volts of electricity and 1.7 joules of power exploding through Kohler's body. The young man dropped to the cement floor like a sack of dirt the instant the charged projectile struck him and began convulsing and begging for help with barely intelligible moans.

Travers nodded grimly. "Nice shot."

"Thanks." Agent Smirnoff gestured at Travers. "Don't listen to that kid, Agent Walker. He doesn't get it. You're a good man."

"I'm not worried about him."

Agent Smirnoff's real name was Harry Boyd. Travers and Boyd had known each other for nine years, but they never called each other by their real names when an interrogation subject was in the area—only as "Agent" followed by the agreed-upon liquor brand code of the day. It was all for the benefit of the kid in the next room. Travers just hoped that kid hadn't heard Kohler call him "Major Trav." Even that partial mistake could turn out to be deadly with these people.

"Welcome to *my* chain of command, Agent Beam," Travers muttered as he leaned down and removed a small, clear plastic bag from Kohler's shirt pocket while the kid continued to twitch and spasm. "You'll be okay in an hour." He glanced at the turquoise-hued powder inside the bag, then rose back up and tossed it to Boyd. Inside Red Cell Seven the newly developed powder was known as TQ Haze. "Take care of that delivery, will you, Agent Smirnoff?" He gestured at the floor as Boyd caught the bag. "Take care of our dribbler, too." Travers's cop friends had nick-named what Kohler was doing "dribbling" because Taser victims resembled basketballs bouncing up and down on the hardwood. "Don't let him swallow his tongue."

"Like I said, Agent Walker, you're a good man. If it was me, I'd hope he did choke to death."

Travers patted Boyd on the shoulder as he passed. "We're all in this together. And there's good and bad everywhere."

"Bad everywhere I'll give you," Boyd replied stoically. "I don't know about good."

Travers grabbed a plain black ski mask off a hook on the wall, slipped it over his head, and pushed open the door. *Kohler was right,* he thought as he entered the interrogation room. He was worried about not getting his okay from COC. But he was more worried about his country.

The subject stood on his toes in the middle of the dimly lit room, struggling to ease his nagging physical discomfort as best he could by constantly changing positions and shifting his weight. His frail wrists were lashed together above his head and secured to a large silvery hook that hung from the ceiling by a shiny chain. He was skinny with a dark complexion, and he had a shock of thick black hair. It was cold here in the basement—on purpose—and he was naked from the waist up—on purpose—so he shivered as he twisted beneath the hook. Other than a plain wooden chair, a chest of drawers, and a bucket, which were all stationed in one corner of the room, there was nothing else within the four stone walls except Travers and the subject, whose driver's license claimed he was from Philadelphia—and more important, that he was seventeen.

"Hello, Kaashif."

"Hello, sir," the young man answered politely but miserably through his chattering teeth, watching Travers's every move as he held his head back to ease the intensifying ache in both shoulders.

"So, you are the discoverer."

"The what?"

"That's what your name means, right? The discoverer."

"I am not sure."

"You're not fooling me, you little son of a bitch."

"I am not trying to fool you, sir."

Travers moved across the room until he was standing directly in front of Kaashif. The young man was five-six, so at six-three Travers towered over him. "I'm going to ask you some very important questions this afternoon. I expect you to—"

"Why am I here?" Kaashif blurted out. "What have I done?"

"Easy."

"I am so thirsty," he gasped. "So thirsty. Please, may I have something to drink?"

They hadn't given Kaashif anything since yesterday afternoon, so it had been almost twenty-four hours. He had to be pretty well dehydrated at this point. "Agent Smirnoff," Travers called over his shoulder. "Can I have that glass of water for our guest?"

"Absolutely."

Nathan Kohler's ongoing agony from the Taser attack was still audible—which Travers liked. It made this situation even more frightening. He could tell by Kaashif's expression that he was hearing those sounds of suffering coming from the other side of the open door. He had no idea who was in pain or why—only that someone was.

"How old are you, Kaashif?"

"Seventeen," he muttered as he strained against the rope binding his wrists.

"That's what your driver's license says, but I don't believe it. I say you're at least twenty-four."

"I don't know why you are so hating me. It must be because I am a Mus—"

"Here you go." Boyd tapped Travers on the shoulder. He'd also donned a ski mask before entering the interrogation room. They always wanted to leave open the possibility of letting the subject go. That couldn't happen if the sub saw their faces. Then they'd have to kill him.

"We good?" Travers wanted to know.

"Oh, yeah." Boyd handed over the glass and then headed back out. "Very good."

Travers held the glass up to Kaashif's lips and tilted. He nodded approvingly as the young man drank every drop. When the water was gone, Travers turned and hurled the glass against the wall, shattering it into hundreds of pieces. Then he picked up the bucket in the corner—it was filled with ice water—and doused Kaashif.

He waited for the frigid liquid to have its effect. When Kaashif was shivering and sobbing uncontrollably, Travers grabbed the young man's chin and shook it hard. "What exactly do those transmissions mean?"

"I do not know what transmissions you are talking of. Please let me go home. I want to see my mother and father." Kaashif's sobs grew even louder. His trembling lips were turning dark blue.

"Why was your name mentioned in them?"

"It must have been someone else they were talking about. I am just a high school student."

"High school's your cover. You and I both know that."

"No, that is wrong."

"You started this year at this school, but there's no record of where you were before that."

"My parents moved down to Philadelphia from Toronto last summer. You can check it out."

"You're lying, you little bastard." Travers shook Kaashif's chin hard again. "When will the attack come?"

"What attack?"

"*Where* will it happen?"

"I do not know, I swear." Tears began to roll down Kaashif's face in fast-running torrents. "I told you, I am just a high school senior. How could I know anything?"

Travers grabbed a rope from one of the chest drawers and then moved back to where Kaashif was hanging. He tied the ends of the rope together so it formed a closed loop ten feet long, slipped one end of the loop over Kaashif's head so it rested on the young man's neck and shoulders, and then stepped back several paces. The rope sagged in the middle until Travers took a short piece of pipe he'd also snagged from the drawer, put the pipe into his end of the loop, and began to turn. The sag in the rope decreased as the head of the twist slowly approached Kaashif's vulnerable throat.

"Tell me about the attack," Travers demanded as the twist advanced. "That's the only way you live."

Kaashif turned his head slightly to the side as his upper lip curled, and he swallowed hard. "I do *not* know anything."

"Save yourself, son. Why die? What's the point?"

"I cannot save myself. I have no information. I should be taking a calculus test today. Please let me go."

"I don't have time for this. Tell me."

"I do not know anything," Kaashif repeated. His voice was shaking wildly.

"Tell me!" Travers roared. "Or so help me God I'll kill you!"

As the rope closed in on Kaashif's soft throat, he began to scream. Even through the screams, Travers could hear Boyd chuckling in the doorway.

Travers liked Harry Boyd. The man's honor, bravery, and commitment to country could never be questioned. He was a hero, a true patriot, though few people knew how many times he'd risked his life to keep America safe—how many times they both had. And they'd become fast friends along the way.

Travers grimaced as Kaashif continued to scream and Boyd continued to laugh. Harry Boyd was a good man, all right. But there was nothing funny about this.

CHAPTER 3

"IT'S THE best cell phone ever," the young salesman said confidently, smiling widely from behind the glass counter as he handed the young woman the device. "Fits perfectly in your palm, right? Screen's way cool. And what it can do is epic."

Jennie nodded. It *did* fit perfectly in her hand, and it *was* very cool looking.

"You're just lucky we've still got a few left over from the national roll-out last week." His smile grew even wider. "You must be a naturally lucky woman. Pretty, too," he murmured after a few moments. "Very."

"Thank you," she answered self-consciously at his forward compliment.

She had long jet-black hair, green eyes, light brown skin, and full lips that framed a high-cheekbone smile. Today she was wearing a low-cut blouse, snug jeans, and heels—edgy but not over the top. She'd caught the looks on her way through the mall to this store.

"Is this a last-minute Christmas gift for your boyfriend?"

Jennie recognized the intent behind the question—and the smile. She'd seen that smile many times from white boys. He was fantasizing about being with a Latina, but that was okay. She didn't mind. He wasn't being obnoxious about it, and guys were guys no matter the color of their skin. That was just the way of the world. She was only twenty-six, but she'd come to that conclusion long ago.

And she appreciated it when things were predictable. Predictability enabled one to prepare, and preparation was a key success factor in any endeavor.

"I'm getting it for myself, Chad." He wasn't bad-looking, either. "*If* I get it."

"I like the sound of that."

"I'm not sure yet," she cautioned, glancing at her watch. She still had time. "Don't count this thing in the sales column yet."

"I didn't mean that. I meant the part about you not having a boy-friend."

She grinned as she glanced at the camera in the ceiling corner, which seemed to be aimed straight at her, wondering. "Okay, I'll take it. It's a lot of money, but hey, so what?"

"Impulsive. Love it. What about dinner tonight? Can you be impulsive about a date with me?"

"Where are we going? Wendy's?"

The guy's happy expression disintegrated. "Is it that obvious I don't—"

"I'm just kidding. And I wouldn't care where we went. Besides, I like Wendy's."

"Hey, I can do better than that," he said confidently, looking relieved. "I think I've still got a hundred bucks left on my third Visa card."

They laughed together, and it felt right. A sense of humor, and he didn't take himself too seriously. Good, because both of those things were requirements in a man for her. Jennie tapped the phone's box as she gave him her sincerest smile. "Just ring this up, okay?"

"Sure."

She reached into her pocket and pulled out her old flip phone.

He shook his head and snickered when he saw it. "Dinosaur."

"I know, but can you transfer the numbers and the pictures over?"

"Absolutely," he agreed as he took the old phone from her. "Let me get the SIM card out and work a little magic in the back. Give me a minute."

When he'd returned and the new phone was ready, he started to hand her the plastic bag filled with all the ancillaries—case, cords, her old phone, receipt—but pulled it back at the last second as she went for it. "I should show you a few really cool apps before you leave."

She shook her head as she checked her watch again. "No time. Gotta go. And I'm busy tonight. Sorry."

"Come back tomorrow then," he suggested, relinquishing the bag. "Seriously, it'll save you a lot of time if I do it."

"Maybe."

"What's your name?" he called as she headed for the front of the store and the huge mall beyond.

"Jennie," she called back over her shoulder as she tossed her hair. "Jennie Perez."

"I like it."

"Yeah, yeah," she murmured as she moved into the mall and her heels began clicking on the tiles of the wide main corridor. "I know what you like."

The Tysons Corner Center, known in the area as Tysons One, was a sprawling, multilevel mall located in upscale McLean, Virginia, just outside the Capital Beltway, fifteen miles west of the White House. One of the largest malls in the region, it was anchored by the big names: Bloomingdale's, Lord & Taylor, Nordstrom. And with only a week to go until Christmas, the cavernous structure was jammed with shoppers searching for last-minute gifts.

"Wish I lived around here," Jennie murmured to herself as she admired the big diamond on the finger of a woman who was walking past. Jennie lived farther west, in Sterling. It was an okay area, but it wasn't anything like McLean. "Maybe someday."

As she hurried toward the south entrance, zigging and zagging through the crowd, she took a few random pictures with the new phone. She had to admit the definition and color were much better than the old flip phone she'd been using. She tapped the reverse camera option on the touch screen and took a picture of herself.

"Ugh," she moaned softly as she looked at the photo. "Do I really look like—"

Jennie stopped abruptly as she neared the entrance—six doors across, which led to the buffer lobby beyond, and then six more doors beyond that leading to the outside and a cold, gray December afternoon. Three men were just entering the mall from the buffer lobby. They were dressed in matching long black overcoats, and they wore baseball caps with the brims pulled low over their eyes.

Her gaze flashed right when something else caught her attention. For a few critical moments she was distracted from the entrance by a beautiful little girl who was coming out of a store. She couldn't have been more than seven years old. She had long, shimmering blond hair and gorgeous eyes, and she was carrying a new doll in a large box. She was being followed by a man who was slipping a credit card back into his wallet and who must have been her father, given how proudly he was watching her.

As the three men at the entrance lifted guns from beneath their coats, Jennie spotted a security guard running toward them. Her eyes raced back to the little girl, who was clutching her new doll and smiling at it, unaware of what was about to happen.

Jennie wanted to run; every instinct inside her was *screaming* for her to get away and save herself. But she couldn't. She had to help that little girl. She'd hate herself for the rest of her life if she didn't. She'd never been a coward, and she wasn't going to start being one now.

THE BLACK VAN pulled to a quick stop in the deserted Philadelphia alley. This location was twelve miles from the address on the driver's license, and that was exactly how Travers wanted it. He wanted the young man to have a long way home—if that address on the license really was his home.

Travers glanced at Boyd from the back of the van. "Ready, Agent Smirnoff?" he called.

Boyd nodded. "Yeah, good to go. Nobody around, Agent Walker. You're clear."

Travers leaned over so he was close to the young man, whose hands were secured tightly behind his back. "We'll be watching you, Kaashif," he whispered through the heavy dark blue T-shirt, which was wrapped around Kaashif's head so it covered most of his face. "You understand me?"

"Yes, sir," Kaashif murmured fearfully.

The young man still wasn't sure he was going to be set free. Travers could tell by the frightened tone of his response. "I'll be watching you, but you'll never know when." Kaashif probably thought that was an idle threat, but it wasn't. "You understand?"

"Yes, sir."

"Guess you'll have to make up that calculus test."

"I shall."

"Liar."

"I am not a—"

Travers reached for the handle, yanked the van's side door open, and pushed Kaashif roughly out onto the broken glass strewn across the pavement. "Clear!" he yelled to Boyd as Kaashif tumbled out.

Three minutes later Boyd pulled to a stop in another alley not far from where they'd ditched Kaashif. They needed to put plates back on the van so they wouldn't arouse suspicion from local law enforcement. They'd removed the plates in case Kaashif had somehow gotten his blindfold off quickly once he was out of the vehicle.

Travers leaned back in the seat and rubbed his eyes as Boyd climbed out of the van. He still had that terrible feeling they were running out of time and that an attack was imminent. He grimaced as he listened to

Boyd reattach the plates. Would the plan work before the attack went down? That was the key question now. Because his instincts told him the moment was at hand, and hell would rain down on the country if they didn't do something soon.

CHAPTER 4

WITH A quick burst of automatic gunfire, the three men wearing long black coats murdered the security guard racing toward them. The older man tumbled to the mall floor on his stomach with his arms outstretched as the hail of bullets shredded his body.

Two of the men turned their weapons on the crowd while the third destroyed the security cameras overlooking the area. Then he turned his gun on the crowd, too.

Calm turned to chaos in a heartbeat. People in front of Jennie shrieked and raced past her or darted into stores for cover as the sound of the guns peppered the air. But for a few seconds, all she could do was gaze straight ahead. Her shoes seemed cemented to the floor as the terrible scene erupted in front of her.

At that point everything seemed to slow down, so she could see every detail of what was unfolding.

The father coming out of the store to Jennie's right lunged for his daughter. But a bullet tore through him just as he reached his little girl, killing him instantly as the storefront glass shattered behind him when another bullet blew through it. The little girl screamed as her father tumbled to the tiles in front of her.

Jennie had been about to turn and run. But she couldn't leave the little girl out there alone, helpless. So she raced the few steps to her and grabbed the girl's tiny wrist.

As she did, she locked eyes with the assassin on the right. She'd heard the term "killer instinct" so many times, but she'd never actually seen it. Until now. The man had cold, dark shark eyes. And yet, as lifeless as they seemed, she could still see passion burning in them. "Come on!" she urged the little girl as the man pointed his gun at her. "Run with me! *Run!*"

As Jennie turned to flee, a bullet tore through her shoulder from behind. It sent her tumbling to the floor and the new phone spinning from her hand. She came to rest on the glass-strewn tiles exactly as the security guard had, on her stomach with her arms outstretched. And the little girl came down right beside her.

Jennie had never been to Alaska. In fact, she'd never been anywhere near it. But she'd read an article on the Internet about a man who'd survived a grizzly bear attack on Kodiak Island by playing dead even as the huge animal toyed with him. The awful pain in her shoulder spread quickly through her body, but somehow she managed to stay still and not moan.

"Close your eyes," she whispered to the little girl as they stared at each other. She tried not to show any fear. The little girl was obviously terrified, and if Jennie showed fear, the little girl might start screaming. Then she wouldn't have a chance. "Don't move. Don't even breathe. You must listen to me."

"Okay," she whispered back, closing her eyes as she'd been told.

She was terrified, all right, Jennie could see, but she was listening. Jennie shut her eyes and went perfectly still, too.

"Shoot her," someone yelled from the distance.

"She's already dead" was the response of the deep voice, from very close.

Even as the cold barrel of a gun brushed her cheek, Jennie didn't flinch. Even as she smelled the leather of his shoes and the awful pain coming from the wound knifed through her body, she kept still. She just hoped the little girl could, too.

"Shoot her anyway. Make sure she's dead. Come on!"

The cold metal withdrew from her face as the screaming in the mall faded and the awful sounds of the dying and the wounded rose. For a moment Jennie believed she was safe, that whoever was standing over her wasn't going to obey the command.

But then the barrel of a gun pressed firmly against her back, slightly off-center to her spine. Somehow she fought the urge to scream.

CHAPTER 5

"A FRIEND of mine told me it looked like a war zone outside with all the military personnel," Bill said quietly to Troy as they entered the Oval Office. They'd been escorted by two Secret Service agents every step of the way since arriving on White House grounds. "And like Walter Reed Hospital in here."

The level of security around President Dorn had been ratcheted up dramatically since the assassination attempt a few weeks ago in Los Angeles. Before the shooting Dorn was constantly complaining to the Secret Service that they were getting in his way and not letting him be himself by wading into crowds to shake hands and kiss babies. But those days were gone for good now, by the president's own admission. The assassination attempt had affected him profoundly. For the first time in his life Dorn had met his mortality face-to-face, and he'd never again allow himself to be so vulnerable.

"Your friend was right," Troy muttered back as the two agents who'd been tailing them finally turned around and left them alone.

To the right was a long table covered with medical devices and boxes of all shapes and sizes. Beside it was an adjustable bed, raised so whoever was in it would be sitting up.

"Come in, Jensens," President Dorn called to them weakly.

He was sitting behind the desk across the room, in a wheelchair. The assassin's bullet had barely missed his heart on that outdoor stage in L.A. It had been off target a critical fraction of an inch only because Rex Stein, Dorn's former chief of staff, had lunged in front of Dorn at the podium just as the shot had been fired from a building across the street. It had killed Stein, but he'd saved the president's life by deflecting the bullet with one of his ribs before it tore out of him and into the president.

A sturdy-looking nurse wearing a white uniform stood behind the president with her arms folded tightly across her chest. She looked uneasy to Troy, like she hated that, against his team of physicians' stern advice, the president had still deemed himself well enough to leave Walter Reed two days ago and return to work in the West Wing. More to the point, he guessed she was worried that Dorn might keel over and die at any moment—on her watch—and that she'd be blamed.

Before following his father's footsteps across the royal blue carpet emblazoned with the seal of the president, Troy subtly saluted the arrows the eagle clasped in its left talon.

"It's good to see you again, Mr. President," Bill said respectfully as he stepped behind the desk and shook hands with Dorn. "You're looking much better, sir."

Troy took his turn to shake hands, making certain to ease off on his normally firm grip. Bill, Jack, and Troy had met with President Dorn at Walter Reed after the shooting. Though he was obviously still weak, Dorn looked in much better shape and spirits than he had that day. He'd looked pretty close to going flatline then, but now he was getting back to being the "presidential floor model," as Bill had always called him because of his dark good looks and commanding charisma. As liberal and dovish as Dorn had proven to be, Troy still had to respect the man's courage and dedication to country. The nation had gotten a tremendous emotional boost watching him walk back into the White House two days ago on television, even if it had been slowly and with the help of an aide on either side.

The president had been in the process of shutting down Red Cell Seven before the assassination attempt, but that and the massive explosion of a huge liquefied natural gas tanker only ten miles off the coast of Virginia at almost the same moment as the shooting had apparently changed his thinking. If the tanker had reached the shoreline, countless thousands in Norfolk and Virginia Beach would have died. Thankfully, two Navy fighter jets scrambled out of the Norfolk naval base had destroyed the ship before it churned close enough for the terrorists commanding the craft to blow it up and inflict their devastation.

Thanks to Jack, Troy thought. Jack was the one who'd uncovered the LNG plot, and a lot of people had him to thank for their lives—though they didn't know it. Then Maddux had taken his revenge, the bastard.

"Hello, Mr. President."

Though Dorn looked better to Troy, his breathing was still measured and a little shallow. His movements were deliberate, and though he was trying hard to seem energetic, it was obvious that he was tired— physically and emotionally.

"Hello, Troy." Dorn smiled up warmly as they shook hands, then he gestured over his shoulder. "Guys, that's Connie. She's here to take the reins of power in case I expire unexpectedly."

Connie nodded stiffly to Troy and Bill, obviously not enjoying her momentary celebrity status or the president's remark. "Hello."

Dorn grinned wryly. "She thinks I came back to the White House too soon."

He waved to her and then at the door. "Give us a few moments, please."

Connie glanced nervously at the bed and the table beside it. "Mr. President, I'm not supposed to leave you at any—"

"Connie, if I collapse these men will get you back in here very quickly. They don't want my death on their shoulders either, okay?"

"Yes, sir."

"But don't go far."

"No, sir."

"And over there," the president went on, pointing at the man who was sitting in a wingback chair a few feet away, "is Stewart Baxter, my new chief of staff."

"We met Stewart at Walter Reed a few weeks ago," Bill reminded Dorn. "He was there that day we came to see you."

"Oh, right, of course." Dorn's grin faded as he watched Connie leave the Oval Office. "Stewart is replacing Rex Stein, God rest his soul."

Baxter had a full head of snow-white hair, but other than that and a few shallow lines at the corners of his thin-lipped mouth, he looked extremely fit for a man who was almost sixty. His skin had a healthy glow to it, and there was no paunch above his belt.

"Hello, Stewart," Troy said in a friendly tone as they shook hands. Baxter's expression was locked in an arrogant smirk, as it had been at the hospital. "Good to see you again." Baxter had a reputation in Washington as a man who got things done. Still, not many people liked him. Troy understood why. He gave off a very negative vibe. "I trust you've been well."

"Did I meet you that day?" Baxter asked as if he wasn't really interested, not bothering to get up from his chair to shake hands. "I remember your father but not you."

Impossible, Troy figured. It hadn't been that long since they'd met, and an Oval Office chief of staff was trained to remember everyone. Baxter was simply trying to establish dominance. It seemed like everyone in Washington was always doing that. Like everyone here was part of some inept wolf pack. It was one of the main reasons Troy hated this city. Everything here was about image, not results.

"I want to thank both of you for coming all the way down here today from Connecticut." The president pulled the jacket he was wearing tighter around his thick sweater as he glanced out the window behind the desk into the cold, gray afternoon. "I know this is a sad day for you two. For me, too," he added. "I'm sorry for your loss."

Bill nodded solemnly as he and Troy eased into the two chairs positioned in front of the big desk. "Thank you, Mr. President."

"It was Jack who called Rex Stein on the platform in Los Angeles. That's why Rex ran to me at the podium. Jack called him just in the nick of time." The president glanced from the window to Troy. "Right?"

Troy nodded. "And if it weren't for Jack, that LNG tanker would have made it all the way to Virginia. And I mean all the way to the beach."

"So many people would have died," Dorn murmured, looking past Troy.

"Including a lot of military personnel at our naval base there," Bill said.

"Rex and Jack are heroes." Dorn pointed at Troy. "You are, too, son."

"Thank you, sir, but I—"

"I should have been better to Rex," Dorn said. "He was right all along about me needing to be more careful, but I ignored him. I should have given him more credit. If I had, he might still be alive. I'll have to deal with that for a long time."

Troy glanced at Baxter, who didn't seem swayed at all by the emotion in Dorn's voice. He was picking at his fingernails and didn't seem at all interested in his boss's sentiment.

The president grimaced. "I learned a great lesson." He held up a hand. "I'm not trying to say I'm turning into Ronald Reagan, George W. Bush, or Attila the Hun. But maybe there's more of a place for Red Cell Seven in our intelligence structure than I thought. In fact, maybe it should be one of the cornerstones from now on." Dorn took a deep breath. "Jack was an inspiration for me in terms of changing my thinking on that."

"And with all due respect, sir," Troy spoke up, "the ironic part about what you just said is that Jack might have been even more liberal than you."

"You're the hawk," the president spoke up, nodding at Troy. "Don't think I didn't spot that salute to the arrows."

"Of course I am." Troy had thought the president was looking at Baxter when he'd saluted the arrows. "You know that." He glanced at

Baxter. Dorn had mentioned Red Cell Seven by name a few moments ago. He wasn't supposed to have told Baxter anything about the files Bill had given him. But he must have broken that promise. "And you know why, Mr. President."

"Yes, I—"

"Jack wasn't actually your son, was he, Bill?"

Troy's eyes raced back to Baxter. It was the first time Baxter had spoken, other than to greet them. In his peripheral vision, Troy saw his father's posture go defensive.

"What are you talking about?" Bill asked. "He was absolutely my son. He *is* my son."

"He wasn't your *natural* son," Baxter went on. "He wasn't your blood. See, that's what I'm getting at." The chief of staff gestured at Troy. "Not like Troy is. Jack was your wife's natural son, but not yours."

"No. He wasn't," Bill agreed tersely.

"And what ever happened to Rita Hayes?" Baxter continued. "She was your executive assistant at First Manhattan for so many years. Why'd she quit so suddenly, and where did she go? No one can seem to find—"

"What's your point, *Stewart*?" Troy interrupted. When they'd shaken hands, Baxter hadn't reacted well to a man thirty years his junior addressing him by his first name. So Troy did it again, this time loudly.

"Yes, Stewart," President Dorn echoed. "What is your point?"

"We did background checks on you two before you came down here today," Baxter answered, as though none of this should be a big deal and he didn't see why everyone was getting so irritated. "Thoroughly, I might add." He shrugged. "I'm just making certain we're all on the same page, okay?"

"Okay," Bill snapped. "Let's do that. Let's make certain we're all on *exactly* the same page." He gestured at the president. "Sir, Mr. Baxter should not be in here while we discuss Red Cell Seven. And this is nothing personal. This is not because of what he just said."

"I'm the president's chief of staff," Baxter countered, glaring at Bill. "I'll stay in here if I choose to. And in this case, I do. In fact, it's critical that I stay, given the subject matter."

"Then Troy and I are leaving, Mr. President," Bill stated, starting to rise from his chair. "I will not discuss this topic in front of anyone but you, sir. It's that simple."

"No, no," Dorn spoke up quickly. "Sit down. Please, Bill." He glanced at Baxter. "I'm sorry, Stewart, but you'll have to leave."

"*What?*"

"I have to trust Bill on this."

Baxter clenched his jaw as he stared back at the president. Finally he stood up and stalked across the carpet.

When he reached the door, he turned back and pointed at Troy. "Don't let these cowboys put on their Red Cell Seven Stetsons any time they want to, Mr. President. Rope them in, like you were going to before you were shot. We can't allow RCS to keep operating without putting some significant constraints on it. If we don't, these guys will get this country in a lot of trouble."

"THOSE PEOPLE are idiots," Kaashif said. "They couldn't interrogate their way out of a paper bag."

"Don't be so sure," the man driving the pickup truck warned.

"One of them was so stupid he used a real name during my interrogation."

"How do you know?"

Kaashif rubbed his stomach. It was bothering him a little. "The other one became very angry when the name was spoken."

"What was the name? Do you remember?"

"Uh, I think it was Major Trav."

"That sounds like a partial."

"Perhaps."

"Could it have been Travers?"

Kaashif shrugged. "It could have been."

"Think back. It's important that you—"

"They have too many rules," Kaashif interrupted, "too many regulations. They have chains of command and due process. They think their

Constitution is so grand and so much better than the founding principles of all other societies. They think it makes them invincible." He laughed confidently. "But what they think makes them so strong is precisely what makes them weak. They cannot react quickly because of their rules and regulations. They cannot be agile like we can, because their Constitution weighs them down. In time it will pull them all the way down. It will be their undoing."

"Careful. Don't be arrogant. That's when we find trouble."

Kaashif scoffed as the pickup truck moved through the cold, gray dusk settling down onto Philadelphia. "They thought I was actually scared." He sneered. "I am never scared."

"Did you tell them anything?" the driver asked. At thirty-four, he was ten years older than Kaashif. "Anything at all?"

Kaashif smirked. "I told them only that I will need to make up my high school calculus test. Which, I guess, I will have to do." He rolled his eyes. "What a joke. I could take that test in my sleep and get one hundred percent."

"You will definitely make up the calculus test."

"Whatever."

"Do you think he believed you were in high school?"

Kaashif chuckled caustically. "I *am* in high school."

"Do you think he believed you were seventeen?"

"Absolutely."

The driver pursed his lips as he checked his mirrors. He wasn't as confident that things had gone smoothly in the interrogation. He had extensive experience with U.S. intel, and he knew how good they were. And he'd heard of a man named Wilson Travers who could supposedly see into the future. But if Travers was the interrogator and he could see into the future, why would he have allowed Kaashif to go free? It didn't make sense. The driver checked his mirrors again worriedly. Still, he saw nothing.

"Everything must seem real. The illusion can never be discovered."

"You worry too much," Kaashif chided. "Enjoy life a little."

"I don't have time for that. Neither do you. That is not why we were put on this earth. We will enjoy ourselves in the next life."

"Ah, you don't know what you are talking about. So, how are my 'mother and father' doing?" Kaashif asked sarcastically.

"They went to the police this morning and filed a missing persons report. Just as concerned parents would do. As I said, the illusion must seem real. We will arrange for a reunion scene tonight. The story will be that you ran away from home for a few days because they are so strict. Everyone will believe it, most important the agents who interrogated you. They will believe you are too afraid of them to tell anyone the truth about what happened. It will be good."

"They said they would be watching me. Well, they will see me go into the high school in the morning and come back out in the afternoon. But they will have no idea what I do at night. And then one morning soon I will go into the school, but I will not come back out. Not the way I went in, and they will never know how I slipped away. It will be exactly the way I did last week to see Imelda. That went off without a hitch, and no one ever knew I was gone from school for most of the day." Kaashif laughed again, this time very loudly. "And they will *never* find me after that. I will be gone forever." He nodded. "I will have beaten them, and hell will be raining down by that time. I can't wait. I can't wait to trample them. I only wish I could see their faces when the hour is upon them."

"Just do your job. Don't look at this as a competition."

"Everything in life is a competition."

"Keep your focus, Kaashif. Don't make me—"

"Do you think the U.S. authorities will arrest the two who are playing my parents?"

The driver's eyes narrowed. "I would, if I were they."

Now it was Kaashif who checked his mirror. "And the attacks?" he asked. "What of the attacks?"

The driver smiled for the first time since he could remember. "As we speak, Kaashif, as we speak."

Kaashif glanced over at the driver as his eyes widened. "The hour is upon them?"

"Yes. The decision was made this morning. Hell is already raining down."

"I'M SORRY for all that, Bill." The president nodded at the door Baxter had just slammed shut. "Stewart can be downright unfriendly sometimes. I know it. But he's what I need right now."

"I understand," Bill answered solemnly.

Troy had never seen his father like that. For a few seconds it had looked like Bill was going to come out of his chair at Baxter when the COS hit him broadside with that thing about Jack—and then piled on with the Rita Hayes reference. If Bill had, Baxter would have been sorry. Even though his father was more than three decades out of the Marine Corps, he was still in excellent shape. His father didn't get angry often. But when he did and his temper was unleashed, things didn't go well for the object of Bill's fury.

"I did not ask him to run G-2 lines on you guys," Dorn said. "In fact, I didn't even know he had. You are obviously both above that kind of thing," the president said, gesturing at them. "It won't happen again. I promise you."

"It doesn't make me comfortable that your chief of staff is so against Red Cell Seven," Bill said stoically. "But what makes me even more uncomfortable is that he knows about it at all. You promised me—"

"Don't worry about Stewart. He doesn't get this. And *that's* putting it politely."

"What have you told him?" Troy asked.

"Nothing. And I will tell him nothing. I made a promise to your father," Dorn said, gesturing at Troy, "and I intend to keep it."

Troy glanced at Bill. He didn't want to be disrespectful, but there were people risking their lives out there every minute. They had to come first no matter what.

"I'm serious," Dorn continued when he saw doubt in Troy's expression. "Basically, all Stewart Baxter knows about RCS is its name. That's all I told him." The president hesitated. "But remember, he's been around Washington a long time. Knowing Stewart as well as I do now, it wouldn't surprise me if he had another source. He seems to have sources on everything."

That didn't sound good. In fact, it sounded like an easy way for Dorn to absolve himself of any guilt for giving Baxter information he wasn't supposed to. There wasn't any way Troy or his father could confirm or deny it, either. Baxter certainly wasn't going to admit it if they asked him.

"Any chance Baxter could have set up listening devices in here?" Troy asked, looking around.

The president smiled wanly. "You guys really are para—"

"Any chance?" Bill interrupted. "I'm going out on a very long, very thin limb just by being here. I am violating procedure, and believe me, there are people watching this meeting from the cheap seats who question my view on this. But I'm confident it's the right thing to do."

The president shook his head. "No chance of any bugs. The Secret Service swept the office thirty minutes before you got here as part of their new routine since the assassination attempt. They found nothing, and I've been in here ever since." Dorn began coughing hard, and Bill started to get up to help. But Dorn waved him off. "I'm okay," he said as Bill eased back into the chair. "I need to know everything about Red Cell Seven. If you guys are more comfortable getting out of the West Wing and going into the private residence to talk about it, I understand."

Troy and Bill glanced at each other and nodded.

"Let's do that," Bill said. "I'm sorry if that seems like overkill, but we have to be very careful."

"No, no, that's fine. I understand." Dorn grinned. "Can one of you guys give me a push?"

"LET'S GO, HARRY," Travers urged as he climbed back into the passenger seat. He and Boyd had stopped to fill up the van at a gas station outside Wilmington, Delaware, on their way back from Philly. "If we hustle we can make DC by seven."

"Relax," Boyd retorted as he opened a three-pack of Reese's Peanut Butter Cups and gulped the first one down whole. "Man, that's good," he muttered, licking his lips as he reached forward to turn the key.

"You better cut down on that stuff, Harry. You're starting to get a little heavy in the—"

Travers cut his jab at Boyd short. Something didn't seem right. It was nothing he could put his finger on, but his sixth sense was suddenly going crazy. *Trust your instincts.* Then, through the windshield, he saw two young men sprinting for the van.

CHAPTER 6

"ISN'T THIS one of the places President Clinton brought that intern?" Bill asked. The large room was piled high with cardboard boxes identified by country name with black marker.

The three of them had ridden an elevator up to the third floor of the White House—from the kitchen on the ground floor—and then headed to this storage space, which was in a corner the building. Troy had pushed Dorn's wheelchair from the West Wing to the residence with three Secret Service agents hovering around them the whole way, including the ride up in the elevator.

The Secret Service agents were gone now. They were waiting in another room well away from this one. Bill had insisted on their leaving as a condition of talking to Dorn further about Red Cell Seven. The president had agreed, much to the intense aggravation of Richard Radcliff, the agent in charge.

In this room were stored many different china patterns, silverware sets, and crystal used for formal state dinners. The elevator the three men had just used ran directly between the ground floor and the little-used third floor. It didn't stop on the state floor or second floor and was used mostly as a means of transporting the formal dining room ware. However, the still-lingering rumor was that, during the Clinton administration, it had also transported a covert human cargo named Monica, so she could come in through the kitchen mostly unnoticed and meet the president on the third floor, bypassing the other residence floors where she might run into someone she shouldn't.

President Dorn shook his head. "I'm not commenting on that, Bill. Mr. Clinton was a tremendous president and a great man. It's not for me to speculate on innuendo."

"So, how much have you told your chief of staff about Red Cell Seven?" Bill asked.

"For the last time," the president responded in a steely tone, "Stewart Baxter knows nothing important about RCS."

"What exactly does 'nothing important'—"

"Look," Dorn interrupted sharply, "I can't keep the FBI blindly looking for my assassin for much longer. I'll have to let them know Shane Maddux was responsible. I won't say that directly, of course. That could bring Red Cell Seven into it, and none of us want that. So I'll whisper it to them anonymously somehow. The thing is, I'm going to have to do it soon. I can't keep them tied up this way."

Bill had told the president that Maddux was responsible for the assassination attempt, Troy knew. And he'd told Dorn that Maddux was involved with the LNG tankers that had been heading for Boston and Norfolk. He'd explained that Maddux had done all that to push Congress to give the U.S. intelligence infrastructure broader surveillance and investigative powers at home and abroad, and to incite the American public against terrorism at a time when Maddux believed the population was losing touch with 9/11. With people forgetting the devastation, Maddux believed the country was becoming vulnerable to another attack.

"It's too much law-enforcement manpower to lock up indefinitely," Dorn continued, "and they're going around the clock."

"Of course," Bill agreed. "The public demands that the shooter be caught and punished. It terrifies people to think someone could get away with shooting their president."

"Exactly."

"Just give me a little longer," Bill said. "Let me find Maddux and deal with him myself. I don't want the FBI taking him into custody and giving him any incentive to talk about Red Cell Seven. I can't have him rolling over on us."

That made no sense to Troy. Maddux was guilty of terrible things, but he was a patriot. In Maddux's eyes, Dorn was the traitor because he'd been planning to eliminate Red Cell Seven, as well as seriously limit what "official" U.S. intelligence agents could do to fight terrorism, including the torture of suspects to gain information—which Maddux believed was an essential interrogation tool. Therefore, Maddux didn't consider it a crime to assassinate David Dorn. Maddux believed that the assassination would save Red Cell Seven and, by extension, the country.

Troy seriously doubted Maddux would ever give away RCS secrets. Even if he thought he could make a deal by doing it and avoid or lessen jail time.

More to the point, Troy doubted the FBI would ever catch Maddux—not alive, anyway. So RCS secrets were safe with Maddux. Troy couldn't understand why his father would think any other way. But then, Bill was privy to much more information than he was.

Troy doubted anyone would ever take Shane alive. And if somehow his father managed to catch Maddux, he certainly wasn't going to turn the man over to the FBI—which Dorn had to know.

"All right, Bill," Dorn agreed, "a little more time."

"How much are we talking?"

"I'll let you know before I leak any information about Maddux to the FBI. But that's all I can promise. Let's just leave it at that." Dorn's eyes narrowed. "Bill, how many individuals defected with Maddux out of RCS?"

"Only a few, and I have people searching for them as well. But when we find Maddux, we'll find the rest of them."

Troy disagreed with that, too. But he kept his mouth shut.

Dorn eased back into the wheelchair. "Okay, guys," he muttered after taking a deep breath. "Tell me everything I need to know about Red Cell Seven."

Bill glanced at Troy. "Go on, son."

And Troy glanced at the president. "I want to be as efficient as possible, Mr. President. What do you already know?"

"Your father gave me some information to review while I was in the hospital. It described certain of Red Cell Seven's activities over the past four decades. And of course, over the last year, since my election, Roger Carlson would report to me face-to-face from time to time. On average, that was about once a month. But he never told me much. He was a crafty man."

"Experienced," Bill countered.

"If that's what you want to call it."

"I do."

The president shrugged. "I made the mistake of telling Roger I wanted very specific information. And that I was going to put a buffer between us."

Bill shook his head. "I doubt that went over very well."

"No, it did not. He was furious."

"Knowing Roger, he probably took that as a signal that you were going to shut RCS down."

"Probably," Dorn agreed. "And that's probably what initiated the plot to kill me."

"I doubt it, sir," Bill disagreed. "In my opinion Roger Carlson would never endorse a plan to assassinate the president of the United States. I believe that all originated with Shane Maddux, that it was his idea alone."

"Don't you think Roger told Maddux what I said?"

"Maybe, but I think Maddux was already planning it before Carlson would have said anything to him."

"How would Maddux have known before Roger told him?"

Bill shot Troy a knowing look. "You don't know Shane Maddux the way we do."

"And I'm very glad of that." Dorn gestured to Bill. "Did Roger tell you what I said to him?"

Bill pushed out his lower lip then shook his head deliberately. "No."

"Mmm."

It seemed obvious to Troy that Dorn wasn't convinced by his father's answer.

"Roger died of a heart attack," the president said, "didn't he?"

Bill nodded. "He was found slumped over the steering wheel of his car outside his townhouse in Georgetown."

Troy and Bill had talked about Carlson's death on the way down to Washington. They both suspected Maddux of somehow being involved. The thing was, the coroner had confirmed the cause of death as a heart attack. Despite that, they still weren't completely convinced. But they'd agreed not to say anything about their suspicions to Dorn.

"How many agents does RCS have?" the president asked.

"Ninety-two," Bill answered.

Interesting. A month ago Troy had heard the number was ninety-eight.

"Are they divided into units? I mean, how does that work?"

"We call them divisions," Troy explained. "They include out-of-country terrorism, counterterrorism, interrogation, communications, and assassinations." President Dorn seemed to have suddenly lost the little color he had in his face. "Are you all right, sir?"

"For a man like me, it's hard to hear a word like 'assassinations' when it comes to activities carried out by people I'm ultimately responsible for. The word 'interrogation' doesn't sit well with me, either, if I'm going to be completely honest. I'm pretty sure I know what that really means." He glanced at Troy. "Do I? Do I know what it really means?"

"What exactly do you—"

"Do you guys torture people?"

"Yes, sir," Troy answered candidly, "when we need to, when that option is appropriate."

"Lord. When can that option ever be *appropriate*?"

Troy and Bill glanced at each other uneasily.

"Don't worry," the president spoke up quickly, "I get it. I get the whole lowest common denominator thing. At least, I do now. We have to fight them the way they fight us. Down and dirty."

"That's right," Bill replied firmly. "But Mr. President, the beauty of Red Cell Seven is that you aren't responsible for us in any way. It's even better than plausible deniability when it comes to RCS. It's *genuine* deniability. With all due respect to Stewart Baxter, RCS cannot get you in trouble, no matter what it does."

Dorn shook his head. "In the end, Bill, I'm responsible for everything and anything that goes on in this country. I can't use ignorance as an excuse."

"Yes, you certainly can."

"No," Dorn snapped, "I *cannot*." He nodded at Troy. "What division are you in?"

"Communications." The president seemed relieved by the answer, though he shouldn't have been. Troy had killed a few men. Everyone in RCS did, sooner or later, and so far it had been six years inside for Troy. "My division's also called the Falcons," he continued. "We deliver instructions and cash to other RCS agents around the world. We never use electronic messages or phones of any kind to communicate the most sensitive data." He hesitated. "Why did you want to know what division I was in?"

"And what is your role in all of this, Bill?" Dorn asked the elder Jensen without responding.

"I'm a Red Cell Seven associate. Actually, I lead the associate pool."

"What does that mean? What are associates?"

"We're a network of RCS support," Bill explained. "We're not actually considered agents."

"Be more specific."

"Unlike the CIA, the NSA, or any other U.S. intel group that I'm aware of, Red Cell Seven receives no support at all from the federal government, funding or otherwise," Bill explained. "We're completely autonomous. We operate that way so there are no opportunities for our enemies, foreign or domestic, to prove we exist."

"How would they do that?"

"Money trails. An organization like Red Cell Seven, with ninety-two agents constantly on the move around the world, requires a lot of cash to operate. If we took cash from the federal government and the link was discovered, some ridiculous liberal, left-wing Congressional investigation committee might use the evidence to put an end to what has been *the* most effective intelligence group the United States has *ever* operated. But we don't. We're autonomous. That's why you can never be blamed."

"What gives you the right to operate?"

Bill stared back blankly at the president for a few moments.

Troy's eyes moved slowly to his father. He wanted to hear this, too. He'd always wondered the same thing.

"He didn't tell you?" Bill finally asked.

Dorn raised both eyebrows. "He *who*?"

Bill cleared his throat. "You really don't know?"

"Answer the question, Bill."

"Your immediate predecessor, Mr. President. He had a meeting with you immediately prior to your inauguration, on the day of, in fact. He communicated several extraordinarily sensitive things to you just before you took the oath. It's been that way for many years. That tradition is little known, but it happens every time a new president is inaugurated."

"What did he tell me, Bill?"

"How would I know, sir? The subjects of that conversation are some of the most closely guarded secrets in the world. You were there. You tell me. If you can," Bill added ominously.

"What did he tell me about Red Cell Seven? You know about that specific agenda item. I know you do."

It was fascinating for Troy to watch this play out. Neither man wanted to blink. But one of them would have to.

"If you think I know, then—"

"What did he tell me about Red Cell Seven?" Dorn repeated sternly.

Again Bill stared back blankly for several moments. Finally, he gestured at Troy. "Troy's my son, but he shouldn't be in here if—"

"*What did he tell me?*"

Bill took a deep breath. "He told you that Richard Nixon founded Red Cell Seven by signing Executive Order 1973 One-E. He informed you that the Order established the cell and empowered Roger Carlson by name to move forward without any constraints whatsoever and without any threat of prosecution for anything he or agents reporting to him did. He was to protect the security of the country any way he saw fit, and he was given total immunity from any prosecution."

The tiny hairs on the back of Troy's neck stood up. Total immunity. Amazing.

"How many originals of that Executive Order did President Nixon sign?" Dorn asked.

"Two."

"Where are they?"

Bill shook his head slowly. "I don't know."

"You must."

"I don't."

"Who does?"

"I don't know."

President Dorn's eyes flashed. "Without those two originals, the cell could be vulnerable, Bill."

"Agreed, but if someone tried to prosecute anyone inside the cell for actions taken on behalf of the cell, and one of those original Executive Orders was presented at the right time to the chief justice of the Supreme Court, whoever had tried to prosecute the agent would be in deep trouble. For instance, it would be an impeachable offense if the president of the United States were involved. And there would be no question about it. The chief justice is aware."

When Bill finished, the succeeding silence seemed deafening to Troy.

"You need to find those two originals," Dorn finally spoke up. "I do not want Red Cell Seven vulnerable in any way. Do you understand me?"

"Yes, sir."

"When you have located them, you will let me know."

"Yes, sir."

Dorn eased back into the wheelchair. "Tell me more."

"Since 9/11, Red Cell Seven has detected and derailed six major terrorist plots against the United States. Those plots weren't mentioned in the information you read while you were at Walter Reed. All six attacks would have been catastrophic and would have caused major loss of life within United States borders. Two of them would have made 9/11 look small in comparison. And both of those attacks were being planned by groups who absolutely had the human assets, the financial capability, and the operational experience to execute them." Bill paused. "No one outside RCS ever knew about them or what we did to stop them. Until now."

"Do tell me about those . . . attacks."

Troy heard cynicism in Dorn's voice again.

"No," Bill answered stubbornly.

"Why not?"

"I want you to maintain that genuine deniability I mentioned earlier."

"Telling me about the attacks won't jeopardize that. Last I heard it's pretty tough to get me to testify."

It seemed to Troy that the president was pressing his father because he didn't believe him. Nothing had been said to that effect, but Troy could tell Bill also figured that was the impetus behind this line of questioning.

The room went deathly still again as Bill and Dorn glared at each other.

"There's a town on the west bank of the Hudson River called Nyack," Bill finally continued. "It's about twenty-five miles north of New York City."

"I'm familiar with it. Its nickname is 'Your Gem of the Hudson,' and it's actually a village, Bill, not a town. It's in the town of Orangetown."

"Anyway," Bill continued, "there's a nuclear power plant north of there—"

"Which is actually in Clarkstown," Dorn interrupted. "That's the town north of Orangetown."

"Thank you for the geography lesson, Mr. President, but—"

"Are you telling me terrorists were planning to attack the Nyack nuclear power facility?"

"And destroy it in a way that would have created an immense and deadly radiation cloud."

"When was this attack supposed to have happened?"

"Two summers ago. If the terrorists had succeeded, they would have put twelve to fifteen million civilians at risk. It would have been far worse than the situation at the Fukushima plant in Japan in 2011 that was caused by the Tohoku earthquake and the subsequent tsunami. It would have been even worse than Chernobyl."

"Do you really expect me to believe that—"

"In August of last year," Bill interrupted, "seventeen Somalis were placed in solitary confinement at a top-secret prison the CIA maintains outside Athens, Greece. I know you're familiar with that prison, sir. The Langley boys told you about it during your second meeting with them. That would have been the trip you took across the Potomac immediately after you were elected to 'tour the CIA facility,' as it was termed, I believe." Bill gestured at the president. "Ask Wes Dolan about those Somalis. He'll tell you. When he's done confirming all that, ask him how I could know about those men being sent to Athens. They were the ones who were going to attack the nuclear plant."

"That still doesn't—"

"Last spring we discovered three nuclear silos in the Ukraine that still had active SS-19s in them. There was a plot under way to fire them. I know you heard about that."

Troy's gaze shifted to Dorn. He figured the president was going to come back at his father even more strongly on this one. Instead, Dorn slouched in the wheelchair, as if he were giving in.

"The Russians were supposed to have made certain the Ukrainians had all those nukes out of the silos and destroyed back in 1996," Bill continued, "weren't they, Mr. President?"

"Yes," Dorn agreed quietly. "Red Cell Seven discovered those silos?"

"You're damn right we did," Bill said proudly. "And we kept it out of the press. If reporters had found out that several senior Ukraine officials had been bought off by certain wealthy rogue elements in the Middle East, we would have had a public relations nightmare on our hands."

"And I would have had a political hurricane on my hands," Dorn admitted. "It would have set U.S.–Russian relations back twenty years."

"More like fifty."

"Are those the two situations you were referring to earlier?" Dorn asked. "The attack on the Nyack nuclear facility and the issue with the SS-19s in the Ukraine?"

"Yes. Now, there have been other situations. Planes coming from Europe and Asia that were targeting skyscrapers and other facilities in the United States; embassy attacks; a dam on the Wind River in Wyoming that was going to be blown up and would have drowned an entire town. We took care of those situations as well as many others during the last decade. But none of them compare to what could have happened at Nyack and in the Ukraine."

"For certain," President Dorn agreed. "Of course, there was that LNG tanker headed for Norfolk as well." His eyes narrowed as he gazed at Bill. "That would have been *because* of Red Cell Seven. That would have been on Shane Maddux's shoulders."

"Yes, it would have. But at least one good thing came out of that near-disaster."

"Which was . . . ?"

"No LNG tanker leaves any port in the world and heads for America without a United States naval escort. Not from Malaysia, not from Algeria, not from anywhere. And two hundred miles off the U.S. coast, all those ships are boarded by Marines. And they get fighter jet escorts from a hundred miles in, so nobody can fly a plane into the ship and blow it up. Rogue LNG tankers will never again be a threat to the United States."

"Okay, I hear you."

The room went quiet for a third time as everything Bill had described in the last few minutes sank in. It was the first time Troy had heard most of this. Information was disseminated only on a need-to-know basis within the cell.

"People think it's just a coincidence that we haven't had another terrorist attack inside our borders for more than a decade," Bill spoke up after a few moments. "Well, it isn't a coincidence, Mr. President. Not even close. And we must continue what we do exactly the way we do it, which is however we see fit without any interference. We can't have our president trying to shut us down or limit our interrogation powers."

"So you and the other associates provide the money." Dorn's voice was hushed.

"And the houses and the boats and the planes," Bill explained, "along with doing our regular jobs."

"My God," the president whispered. "I had no idea this thing was so well organized."

"It has to be."

Dorn gestured at Bill. "Now that Roger is gone, are you effectively the leader of Red Cell Seven?"

Bill nodded deliberately after a few moments. "Yes." He paused. "But I can't keep doing it. I can't lead RCS and be the CEO of First Manhattan. I don't have the personal bandwidth, and worse, sooner or later someone's going to figure out that I—"

"Mr. President!"

All three men flinched at the shout coming from the other side of the door and the loud knocking suddenly accompanying it.

"It's Agent Radcliff, sir. I must see you *right now*."

"Come in, come in," the president called.

The Secret Service agent burst into the storage room, followed immediately by two more agents. All three men seemed distraught.

"For God's sake, what is it, son?"

"There's been an attack, Mr. President," Radcliff explained. "It was out in northern Virginia, in McLean at that big Tysons One Mall."

"What kind of attack?"

Troy heard footsteps running toward them.

"Shooters. Two to four of them, according to eyewitnesses at the scene. They had automatic weapons. Eight dead and twelve wounded so far. The men just walked through one entrance of the mall and opened fire. The place was jammed with people."

Dorn cringed. "My God. Were they caught?"

"No, sir. Fairfax County Police and the state people found a couple of vehicles that were suspicious, but no persons in or around them."

"How long ago was this?"

"Ten minutes."

Stewart Baxter pushed his way past the agents into the middle of the room. "Mr. President, you need to get back to the Oval Office immediately."

"Yes, of course, Stewart."

Troy heard more footsteps hustling toward them.

"We don't know if—"

"Mr. President!" Another agent burst into the room. "Sir, we have reports of more attacks. It's the same thing as Tysons Corner. Huge malls. Houston, Los Angeles, St. Louis. Shooters opening fire at crowds with automatic weapons. Seven attacks so far."

The president glanced from Baxter to Bill and then back at Baxter. "Gentlemen, we are under attack." He motioned to Radcliff. "Get me back to the Oval Office."

As Radcliff wheeled the president out, Baxter pointed at Bill and Troy in turn. "Where were you pricks on this one?" He stared hard at them for a few moments, eyes flashing accusingly. "Nowhere, obviously," he hissed as he stormed from the room. "Nowhere!"

CHAPTER 7

As TRAVERS raced down the railroad tracks through the darkness, bullets strafed past. He turned and darted into the dense forest lining both sides of the double main line. Going into the trees was his only chance.

Three minutes ago he and Harry Boyd had been ambushed at the gas station. Boyd had been shot dead through the windshield by one of the men who'd attacked them back there. But Travers had escaped by hustling out the back of the van, then racing onto the tracks that lay at the bottom of a steep ravine at the edge of the gas station's parking lot.

Now he was running for his life.

KAASHIF AND the driver glanced at each other when a DJ broke into the rap song playing on the vehicle's radio to announce in a trembling voice what was unfolding across the country. Huge high-end malls were being attacked in big cities all over the nation.

When the announcer finished, they high-fived each other—just as they pulled into the short driveway of Kaashif's "parents'" house.

"STAY WITH ME," one of the EMTs said loudly as they rushed the young woman toward the mall entrance where the three assassins had opened fire on the crowd eleven minutes ago. "You're gonna make it," he said as they guided the gurney around the security guard's dead body. "Don't give up."

Jennie could barely make out the features of the man above her. Everything about him seemed out of focus, and she couldn't feel the pain anymore. Had they given her drugs, or was her body shutting down? She couldn't remember them giving her anything. That couldn't be a good sign.

"The little girl," she whispered. "Is she all right?"

The EMT leaned down. "What?"

Jennie couldn't say the words again. Her strength was gone, and her eyelids slowly slid shut.

The EMT shook her shoulder gently as they guided the gurney through the outer doors of the mall lobby. But she was unresponsive.

"We've gotta hurry," he urged his partner as they raced her toward the ambulance, "or we're gonna lose her."

"Looks like we may already have," the other EMT responded dejectedly.

"NO DOGS," Major Travers muttered thankfully as he dodged the trunks of leafless trees coming at him through the gloom. Unfortunately, most of them weren't wide enough for a man his size to hide behind. "That's good. A couple of Dobermans would have been a problem."

Travers hurdled a wide stream, clawed his way up the steep bank on the other side, and then hustled into the trees. He had time—though not much. Still, that narrow window provided an opportunity. If they'd sent dogs out on him, the odds of success would have dropped drastically. And life was all about odds.

He stayed in top physical condition with the kind of insane workouts other men his age would have died from. But when it came to physical ability and stamina, working out was no match for youth. He knew that as well as anyone. Despite the heavy workouts, he knew he'd lost a step.

The key difference between most other men in their fifth decade and Travers: He accepted timeless truths and used experience and cunning to turn those truths to his advantage.

Sooner or later the two men chasing him like wolves—steadily and relentlessly—were going to catch up. That outcome was inevitable. He'd seen their faces back at the gas station during the chaos in which Harry had been killed. They were much younger, and they could certainly go longer and farther than he could. More important, they were hungry with much to prove, like most men their age.

And that would be their downfall. He would use that hunger against them.

THE TWO ASSASSINS raced through the leafless forest of oaks and poplars with their pistols drawn, then on into the dense pine forest and the gathering dusk. They were closing in on Travers, the primary target of their mission.

"Don't stop until both men have been neutralized, and bring me back the right forefinger of Harry Boyd as proof of your success." That was the order from their superior, Shane Maddux.

The young man running second had Boyd's finger stuffed in his pants pocket. Now he wanted Travers. Dropping that dead finger on the table in front of Maddux was going to be a proud moment. But snaring Travers was much more important because it would absolve him of his failure in Los Angeles.

As THE two pursuers broke into a secluded clearing, Travers dropped down from above and slammed his right knee directly between the lead man's shoulder blades. Most men would have crumpled to the ground out cold, but this kid was in tremendous shape. He remained conscious.

Travers could feel that natural, youthful energy and strength surging through the young body as he wrapped his arm around the assassin's head so the face was buried in the crook of his elbow. Then he twisted wickedly, fast and hard. It was a shame to do this to such a valuable asset, but he had no choice. This fight was to the death.

The sound of the neck breaking was loud, like a dead branch cracking beneath a boot, and the kid died instantly without even a groan.

Travers dropped the lifeless body to the leaves and whipped around, then lunged immediately to the right just as the other young man fired his pistol. The bullet blew through Travers's jacket and grazed his left side. But with all the adrenaline pouring through his system, he didn't feel it. He lunged again as the young man aimed. But he beat the second bullet, too, and then chopped down like a sledgehammer on the wrist of his attacker so the fight became a hand-to-hand struggle when the weapon flew off into the woods.

The younger man caught Travers flush on the cheek with a brutally fast left, but Travers was leaning away when the punch landed, so the impact did minimal damage. Travers retaliated with a sharp elbow to the Adam's apple, a powerful chop-kick down onto the right patella, and a knee to the groin. It was over that fast, and now Travers had a willing witness—though the kid didn't realize *how* willing he was about to be.

Travers splayed the victim on his stomach on the wet ground like a deer carcass. Then he quickly broke the man's right shoulder by straddling the lower back, grabbing the right wrist with his right hand, pressing down on the right shoulder with his left hand, and then rotating the young man's arm all the way around on the axis as he held it straight out until the joint snapped as loudly as the other man's neck had. Travers repeated the technique with the left shoulder and left arm, and now there was no risk of counterattack or escape. The kid was done. He wouldn't even be able to make it to his feet without a herculean effort.

"You shouldn't have fired at me so fast," Travers hissed as the man beneath him cried out in terrible pain. "You should have taken your time. You always have more time than you think. And you shouldn't have run so blindly into good cover like this." Travers nodded respectfully and thankfully to the thickly needled limbs of the pine trees above him. Then he leaned down so his lips were close to the ear of the young man, who only now did he see was also African American. Up until this moment he'd been too focused on survival to notice. "Tell me who sent you."

"I can't," the other man gasped. "You know that."

"What's your name?"

"No."

Travers stood up, spread the man's legs wide, and then kicked the scrotum again with the steel toe of his boot, as hard as he could. He'd popped at least one of the testicles with that strike, no doubt.

"Just kill me," the kid moaned pitifully as Travers dropped his full weight down on the lower back once more. "Let me die."

The pain was excruciating, Travers knew. But unfortunately for his victim, he knew how to keep it going, to keep him just on that edge, without letting him pass out. And he fully intended to do just that until he received the answers he sought.

"Please," the man begged as he struggled for every breath. "I can't take any more."

"What's your name?"

"I can't— Okay, okay," he yelled as loudly as he could when Travers started to stand up again. "I'm O'Hara."

Travers eased back down onto the kid's back. "O'Hara?" he murmured. "*Ryan* O'Hara?"

"Yeah," the young guy gasped.

Travers hadn't trained O'Hara like he had Nathan Kohler. Typically, he was only involved with one of every three new recruits. So it wasn't like he'd recognize the kid. But he'd heard of him. "You shot the president in L.A."

"Yes."

"Shane Maddux sent you after me," Travers muttered as his eyes darted around, as he tried to see anything through what little remained of the late afternoon light.

O'Hara had joined the RCS Falcon Division only recently, Travers knew, but he'd defected almost right away to join Maddux's small gang of

mutineers. That was what Travers had heard through the grapevine, anyway, and it was absolutely believable because that was the thing about
Maddux: He had this way of convincing subordinates of *anything*, even
something as insane as defecting from Red Cell Seven.

"You're still working for him, aren't you?" The realization rocked
Travers. "Jesus Christ."

O'Hara didn't answer, didn't confirm, but that was irrelevant. Travers took one more panic-stricken look around, then snapped the kid's
neck and took off.

As he ran, he skinned his pistol from the leather holster at the small
of his back, chambered the first round, and let the smooth black composite barrel guide him through the forest. He hadn't bothered to use the
9mm to take down O'Hara and the other kid, even though the odds had
been two-on-one. He hadn't wanted to kill them both right away so he
could draw information—as he successfully had. But knowing Shane
Maddux was involved in this made Travers draw his weapon even though
he had no idea if Maddux was anywhere close or if he was half a world
away. It felt as if he was close, and that was enough.

Trust your instincts.

So maybe it had been an instinct to draw his pistol, Travers realized—a
survival instinct. Because once Maddux put you in his sights, he never
stopped coming until the hunt was done and one of you was dead. Maddux
had been involved in many hunts during his two decades in Red Cell
Seven, and as far as Travers knew, the guy was still very much alive and
free out there despite his defection—which meant all the other guys involved in those past hunts were dead. Travers had no intention of being
Maddux's next trophy.

He put his head down and ran faster. Shane Maddux was the only
man in the world Wilson Travers truly feared.

CHAPTER 8

"Go, go, go!" shouted the leader over his shoulder as the van skidded to a stop at the outer edge of the strip mall parking lot.

Twelve minutes ago the three men in the back had opened fire with automatic weapons inside a huge Minneapolis mall that was now two miles away, spraying the holiday shopping crowd with a deadly hail of bullets. They'd killed nine people in the assault and wounded fifteen more, four critically.

When they were done, the three assassins had raced out of the mall and into this brand-new white van that the driver had waiting for them at the curb just outside the entrance.

"Come on!"

The three men piled out of the van and into the back of another van, which was parked in the spot immediately adjacent to the one they'd just pulled into, while the driver, who was the leader of the squad, raced from driver's seat to driver's seat. This second van was old, rusted, and painted a faded robin's egg blue. The leader figured it would make for perfect cover with its dented sides and the ladder on top. He'd added that detail this morning just before the attack. He'd stolen the ladder from a painting company down the block from the Eden Prairie ranch house they'd been using for the last three months.

As the leader revved the engine of the second getaway vehicle, he glanced through the windshield. Two boys were straddling their bikes less than fifty feet away. Neither of them was more than ten years old, he figured. But they were both aiming cell phones directly at the two vans, obviously taking videos. They would die for it. And their parents would regret giving them such expensive toys at such young ages. Having so much money wasn't a good thing. Flaunting it was worse. This population needed to understand that.

"Kill them!" he yelled, stabbing his finger wildly at the boys.

Two of the men jumped out of the back and fired. Job finished, they climbed into the van again as the leader sprinted to where the boys lay, grabbed their phones off the blacktop, and sprinted back to the van.

THE CHAOS at the edge of the parking lot had attracted attention. A man coming out of a dry cleaner's in the middle of the strip mall had witnessed the horrific scene of the boys being shot off their bikes. He'd called 911 immediately, contacting the emergency service as the leader was running back to the van after scooping up the boys' cell phones.

Fortunately, a local policeman who hadn't been called to the shooting two miles away was emerging from the post office beside the dry cleaner's just as the witness was connecting with the 911 operator. The witness alerted the policeman to what he'd seen, and the cop made it to his squad car before the van had even exited the strip mall parking lot.

The chase was on.

AGENT RADCLIFF burst into the Oval Office without knocking. "Mr. President," he called loudly as he stopped just in front of the eagle woven into the carpet. "Sir, it's important."

"What is it?"

President Dorn sat in the wheelchair behind his desk, studying a piece of paper inside an open folder that Stewart Baxter had just placed in front of him. Baxter stood on one side of Dorn while Jane Travanti, secretary of Homeland Security, stood on the other. Travanti was tall and angular with straight blond hair cut short in a pageboy so it fell to just above her slim shoulders.

Next to Travanti was Wes Dolan, the director of National Intelligence. He was short, nearly bald, and had an all-business air about him.

A television sat on a table beside a wingback chair off to Radcliff's left. It was turned on, but the volume was low, and no one seemed to be paying attention to it.

"You need to see something, sir," he said, pointing at the TV.

"We're about to go down to the Situation Room, Agent Radcliff. Can it wait a few minutes? I can watch whatever it is down there."

Dorn looked exhausted, even more so than he had when Radcliff had wheeled him down here from the residence, and that had been only a few minutes ago. There were deep, dark circles under his eyes now, and he had a gaunt look about him, like he'd quickly gone from predator to prey. Or he had the weight of the world on his still-weak shoulders.

Which, of course, he did.

The president's nurse stood near the table littered with medical supplies. She didn't look much better. There was fear in her eyes, too, though it was a different kind. It seemed like she'd finally gotten the responsibility she'd been wishing for all her career—and now she was wishing she hadn't.

Radcliff hustled to the wide-screen TV in his purposeful, ex-military stride and boosted the volume. The TV was already tuned to an all-news channel, so he hadn't needed to run through the guide. Every news channel in the world had to be carrying this, he figured, as the sound from the two speakers grew quite loud. It was the story of the millennium.

"No, Mr. President, you need to see this *now*," he called out over the newscaster's voice.

"What are you doing?" Baxter demanded indignantly as he looked up from the folder. "We don't have time for—"

"Minneapolis police are chasing a van they believe is carrying the terrorists who just attacked the Mall of America," Radcliff explained in his most formal voice as he pointed at the screen and the view from above of a light blue van racing crazily around and past cars on a double-lane highway. "The Twin Cities airport is close to the MOA, and a chopper that flew over to cover the aftermath of the attack peeled off when they heard about the chase. They picked up the van's trail a few minutes ago heading north. This is happening as we speak."

"My God," Travanti whispered as she moved slowly away from Dorn and toward the TV. "We must take them alive, Mr. President. We must be able to interrogate these people. All the others have gotten away. This could be our best chance to stop any more attacks."

Dolan grabbed a phone on the president's desk. "This is DNI Wes Dolan," he barked at the White House operator. "Get me Rick Burns in my office immediately." Dolan nodded to Travanti as he slipped a hand over the mouthpiece. "Burns is from St. Paul. He'll know how to get to the cops out there fast."

"LOOK AT THIS, DAD." Troy gestured at the TV. Through a Secret Service agent, the president had asked them to stay, so they were using a small room down the corridor from the Oval Office. Bill was speaking to someone over the landline in the room, and Troy had turned on the flat-screen bolted to the wall. "Jesus."

Bill ended his call quickly. "What is it, son?"

Troy was standing beside the TV, and he pointed at a light blue van that was racing down a highway, weaving dangerously in and out of traffic with police cars in high-speed pursuit. The view of the chase was from above. "They think the guys in this van are the ones who just attacked the Mall of America in Minneapolis. They shot more than twenty people."

"Sons of bitches," Bill muttered as he rose and moved to where Troy was standing. "They'd better take these guys alive. I mean, they haven't caught anybody else so far, right? Have they mentioned anything about that?"

"All the other shooters got away from the scenes. No reports of any arrests yet."

"Yeah, we've got to interrogate at least one of these guys. What's the latest count overall?"

"Eleven malls were attacked," Troy answered. "All in big cities, and the attacks all happened within a few minutes of one another. No announcement from any terrorist group claiming responsibility, and no official confirmation yet. But there's no doubt they were coordinated. Everyone agrees on that." Troy glanced at his watch. "It's been twenty-five minutes since the last one. Hopefully it's over."

Bill shook his head. "Maybe for today, but not for good. This is obviously not a suicide thing. Which means the plan is probably for these squads to carry out more attacks. Flying airliners into buildings is shocking, but this is much more effective. This is the nightmare scenario," he added quietly.

"It shuts the country down," Troy agreed. "No one's going to leave their house if they think death squads are going to attack the mall they're headed to."

"Or the Exxon or the Ruby Tuesday or the Home Depot. See, that's what they do next. They go to smaller, more specific targets. Maybe they hit nothing but Ruby Tuesdays for a few days and basically shut the chain down because no one will go there. And if they're smart, they'll take it to small towns, too. They show the country that no one is safe. The killings are obviously the worst part of the attack, but—"

"But it tears the economy to shreds, too," Troy broke in, anticipating where his father was going with this, "especially at the holidays. Every mall in the country will be a ghost town." He glanced from the screen to Bill. He was thinking about that accusation Baxter had hurled at them as Radcliff was wheeling President Dorn out of the storage room. "Had you heard anything about this?" he asked. Bill had been the de facto head of Red Cell Seven since Roger Carlson's death a few weeks ago. He'd admitted as much to President Dorn a short time ago. "Anything at all?"

Bill watched the van dodge several cars. Then his eyes moved deliberately to Troy's. "Had you?" he asked without answering.

After twenty-eight years of dealing with his father, Troy was accustomed to that habit of answering a question with a question. "I'm a Falcon, Dad. I don't hear as much as you. The division heads seem to do a pretty good job of compartmentalizing. There's some crossover as far as info goes, but not much. And remember, my leader was Maddux. He was especially good at that. He didn't tell us anything."

"Still."

Troy shook his head. "Nothing."

"What about a mutiny inside the ranks?" Bill asked. "What about some of the guys in Red Cell Seven defecting to go with Maddux?"

Troy nodded this time. "I've heard a little along those lines since everything went down, but I thought it was just crap. I figured Maddux was out there on his own with only that kid Ryan O'Hara." He hesitated. "Is it true? Did more people go with Maddux than just O'Hara?"

Bill was about to answer when the van clipped the back of a tanker truck and veered left toward a railroad bridge abutment. "Look at this, Troy!"

"Oh my God."

THE LEADER struggled frantically to regain control of the van as it hurtled toward the concrete bridge abutment. He'd been distracted for just a split second as he searched on his iPhone for the best way to exit this road. But that single second had been enough. He'd nicked the back of the tanker truck with the van's front bumper. He figured cops would be throwing down spike strips on the highway somewhere up ahead, no more than a few miles or so. So he had to get off fast or face the unpleasant prospect of four flat tires and almost certain capture—which was not an acceptable outcome. That had been made very clear by his superior many times.

He cursed loudly. He'd barely tagged the tanker, but it was enough to send the van careening to the left, out of control.

At the last moment he swung the vehicle to the right, narrowly avoiding an impact with the abutment, which would have disintegrated the van and killed them all. They raced beneath the railroad bridge, still out of control. The sudden twist in direction sent him and the other three men barreling back toward the truck trailer they'd just clipped. He wrenched the steering wheel back to the left. He had no choice. Otherwise they would have smashed directly into the trailer, which could be carrying thousands of gallons of gasoline.

The van fishtailed wildly for a hundred feet and then went up on its right two tires, beside the truck. For a few seconds the leader believed he could bring his vehicle back under control. But then it tipped over and everything turned to chaos. Bodies, weapons, and ammunition flew everywhere inside the van. However, the vehicle didn't tumble. And that was key, the leader realized even as the crash unfolded. That gave them a chance.

The van slid along the highway on its passenger side as the truck driver jammed on his brakes. The big rig jackknifed, careened off the road, slammed into a wall—and exploded.

The van burst through the fireball and continued to slide down the broken white lane markers, finally coming to a halt several hundred feet farther along the highway than the still-burning truck, screeching to a stop amidst a cloud of smoke and sparks.

"Everybody all right?" the leader yelled.

His left wrist was bruised and bloody, but he ignored the pain shooting all the way up into his shoulder. *Capture is not acceptable,* he kept telling himself. They had to do anything to avoid it, because he wasn't at all confident that one of the men in back—possibly two—would hold up under the scrutiny he knew they would quickly be subjected to. Some people were under the impression that United States agents went the torture route only in rare circumstances. Some people were sorely mistaken.

"Hey! Back there!"

"Saafir is gone," came the groggy reply. "But Gohar and I are all right."

"Are you certain he's gone?" the leader yelled, slamming his shoulder against the jammed door to open it. "Give him a bullet if you aren't."

A gun went off immediately.

"Follow me," he called, gratified that they were still obeying his every order. "Come on."

As he tumbled to the pavement outside the van, a police car burst through the fireball and skidded to a stop twenty feet away. As the other two followed him out of the van and jumped to the ground, the leader calmly reached inside his jacket, pulled a grenade from one pocket, and tossed it at the police cruiser.

The cruiser exploded instantly, and the cop who'd just climbed out of it was engulfed in flames. The man staggered around for several seconds, arms outstretched in front of him as the blaze torched his body. Finally he dropped to the pavement on his knees, and then fell forward on his chest and face. His flesh began to boil on the asphalt as it peeled away from the bones in smoking chunks.

CHAPTER 9

"OKAY, SO maybe Shane Maddux is a little crazy."

Troy was watching the tense standoff outside Minneapolis on the flat-screen. He'd seen a lot of gruesome things during his six-year career as an RCS Falcon, but the image of that cop's body falling to the pavement, engulfed in flames, would stay with him forever. Just as the image of Karen kissing Jack's coffin this morning would.

"I'll give you that, Dad."

"Oh, thanks," Bill acknowledged sarcastically. "But I wish we'd found that out a long time ago. At least then we'd have a president who could deal with these lunatics at full strength."

After killing the cop, the three terrorists had abandoned the van, raced past the still-burning tanker truck, and taken refuge beneath the railroad bridge. They were holed up behind a three-sided concrete barrier that gave them excellent cover, even against the army of law-enforcement authorities who had them surrounded.

"Looks like the cops out there got the word."

"You mean about taking these guys alive?"

"I'm sure that's why nothing's happened yet. They could take out these guys in thirty seconds if they really wanted to, if they didn't care about interrogating them. And they saw the one guy throw that grenade and kill one of their own. We all did. So everybody knows they've committed murder, even if they can't be absolutely linked to the Mall of America attack yet. The authorities would certainly be justified in moving on them. But they're waiting. And whatever's going to happen probably won't for a while. They'll probably wait until dark to finish it." Bill checked his watch. "It'll be light in the Twin Cities for at least another hour."

Troy was getting edgy sitting around waiting for President Dorn. With all that had happened and given how exhausted Dorn looked, Troy figured the odds were pretty low that they'd see him again today. At any moment some aide would come in to tell them to go home. Because Dorn had to focus solely on the "Holiday Mall Attacks," as they'd already been tagged by the media.

He felt like a caged animal in here. He just hoped he never had to take an office job. He'd probably kill himself. Troy hated walls even more than he loved the outdoors, which was saying a lot.

"I *get* Shane," he said quietly. "I mean, you have to be a little crazy to do what we do, you know, Dad? I think he deserves some understanding from us on that."

Bill looked over like he figured Troy had suddenly gone off the reservation as well. Not as far as Maddux, but still off. "Have you lost your mind, too?"

"Maybe."

"Easy there, son. I've got enough problems."

"Maddux loves this country more than most people can possibly understand, Dad. He's dedicated his entire life to protecting it. That objective drives everything he does."

"According to you, he shot your brother. Does that deserve our understanding?"

"Well, I—"

"And he probably shot the mother of your child," Bill added.

It was frustrating to argue with Bill, because he was damn good at making points. People always said his father could have been a top litigator if he hadn't gone the investment banking route. "Maddux shot Jack because in his mind, Jack weakened the country. Killing Jack was simply getting revenge for America, and more important, making sure Jack never did anything again to weaken the country. If you think about it, it was actually a compliment. Maddux was worried Jack would strike again. It's the same way Maddux looked at killing President Dorn. For Maddux, Jack and President Dorn were traitors. Neither one of those shootings was personal. It was only about protecting this country."

"If I find out Shane Maddux really did kill your brother, one way or the other I'll make him pay. That one's personal for me. I'll tell you that right now."

"Dorn was about to destroy Red Cell Seven. You said it yourself, Dad. If not for Red Cell Seven, this country would have been hit by two major terrorist attacks that would have made 9/11 look small by comparison." Troy glanced up at the ceiling. "No disrespect to the 9/11 victims." He looked back at Bill. "Maddux thinks we've got to have RCS or we'll be vulnerable to terrorists. He figures the other U.S. intel arms are so weighed down by bureaucracy, chains of command, and political correctness that they can't move fast enough to be effective against enemies who can move at lightning speed and do whatever they want with no moral or ethical limitations. And that it's becoming a bigger problem every day as Congress tries to dig deeper and deeper into what's going on with us in the shadows. In Maddux's mind, President Dorn might as well have been destroying our military." Troy was fascinated to see how his father reacted to this one. "And believe me, I heard all that stuff about Executive Order 1973 One-E signed by Nixon and how we operate outside any laws or constraints. You and I both know that in this society, without that Order, Red Cell Seven would be vulnerable. Maybe even with it. He's just doing anything he can to keep the cell safe."

"He brainwashed you."

"Hey," Troy shot back resentfully, "that's not—"

"I know, I know," Bill said, backpedaling quickly. "Sorry, son, it's just been a bad day. The older I get, the less I seem able to deal with the stress."

Or the guilt, Troy figured. If Jack hadn't wanted to prove he was part of the Jensen family so badly, he probably wouldn't have gone to Alaska. Then he wouldn't have gotten involved in a dangerous deal with a dangerous man—who'd ultimately killed him. And the reason Jack felt like he wasn't part of the family and needed so badly to prove he was? Bill had lied to him all these years about who his mother was—lied to everyone.

"Look," Bill spoke up, "when Red Cell Seven starts doing the same things terrorists are doing, that's a problem for me. It's that simple."

"Shane has dedicated half his life to RCS," Troy said again. "He was the leader of the Falcons; he was my leader. He knew Dorn had told Carlson it was over for RCS."

"You know more than you've told me . . . don't you, son?"

Troy shrugged.

"Why won't you tell me everything?"

"Why won't *you*?"

"Who says I won't?"

They both knew how absurd the answer to that question was, so Troy didn't even bother acknowledging the response. Bill couldn't tell everyone everything—not even his son.

"All I really know, Dad, is that Maddux would do anything to protect this country. And on some basic level, I have to respect that conviction."

"How can you say that? I mean, what about that LNG tanker?"

"That's exactly what I mean, Dad. He'd do *anything* to make this country strong."

"If that ship had made Norfolk, Virgina, half a million people would have died."

"But Maddux was convinced Capitol Hill had forgotten how bad 9/11 was. He figured they needed a wakeup call. You know as well as I do he didn't want to kill half a million Americans. He was sacrificing some for the greater good of the whole." Troy glanced out the window. Night had fallen on Washington. He pointed at the TV screen as his eyes moved away from the window. "Apparently he was right. We were vulnerable. And now we're paying for it."

"Killing half a million innocent civilians isn't the way to send a wakeup call," Bill shot back. "Even with what happened today at those malls. Jesus, son, you should—"

"I know, Dad," Troy interrupted angrily. "And I did something about it. That's how I got myself thrown off the *Arctic Fire* in the middle of the Bering Sea. Remember? I figured out what was going on with Maddux, and I tried to stop him. Just like Charlie Banks did. And I ended up in thirty-seven-degree water who knows how far from land without a life preserver. Just like Charlie did. The only reason I'm here is that one of the crew took pity on me. And Jack came to save me."

Bill nodded solemnly. "Right."

"That's why he's dead."

"I know. I'm sorry, son."

"So maybe I have to share some of the guilt for that, too," Troy said, sending Bill an accusatory glare.

Bill glanced away after a few moments.

"All I'm saying," Troy continued, "is that in a very small way, I understand where Shane's coming from. Especially now that I know how many attacks RCS has stopped over the last decade."

"We didn't stop what happened today at the malls," Bill muttered dejectedly.

"No," Troy agreed quietly, "we didn't."

"And I can't endorse Maddux's vigilante brand of justice, either. Roger told me about that little sideshow."

"He only took out people who deserved it," Troy argued. "He eliminated the scum who'd worked the system and dodged prison on a technicality. Murderers, rapists, pedophiles—and only ones he was absolutely sure were guilty. I don't have a problem with that."

"But how do you know that's all he did? How do you know he didn't take out a few people who didn't deserve it along the way? People he had a personal beef with."

"I don't know, Dad, and I don't care. Look, if you were so hopped up about what Maddux was doing on the side, and Carlson had told you about it, why didn't you stop it?"

"Who says I didn't try?"

Troy gazed at his father, wondering—about a lot of things. "I still don't understand why President Dorn changed his mind about Red Cell Seven. I don't get why he wanted to destroy it a few weeks ago and now he wants to keep it. Why all of a sudden he wants to make it a cornerstone of the U.S. intelligence program." Troy hesitated. "And I especially don't understand the one-eighty when it was one of the senior guys inside RCS who tried to assassinate him."

"I can think of a couple of reasons."

"Okay. Spin that out for me."

"Over the last few weeks, he did find out how valuable the cell has been. He read those files I gave him, and he probably had his people do some more digging." Bill nodded toward the Oval Office. "He probably knew about at least some of those attacks we stopped before we went in there today. And maybe he figured that if a senior guy inside it is willing to assassinate him to keep it going, maybe it *is* that valuable."

"Maybe," Troy said, still unconvinced. "What else?"

"Simple. He doesn't want to get shot again."

"So he's trying to convince a rogue element he's on their side?"

"Keep your allies close . . . and your enemies closer."

"Yeah, yeah, but Shane's smart enough never to trust Dorn no matter what he said or did."

"Maybe we should be so smart. Maybe President Dorn is being more careful about getting rid of it this time. Maybe that's what this is really all about."

Troy raised an eyebrow and nodded. "See, now you're on Maddux's side."

"I'm on the country's side, son. That's all. If that means I have to deal with shades of gray, so be it."

"Why do you think President Dorn asked you where the two originals of Executive Order One-E were?"

"He was curious."

"Come on, Dad."

"It's like he said. He knows Red Cell Seven is vulnerable without the original documentation President Nixon signed."

"Or he wants to get his hands on the documents so he can destroy them. That's why you mentioned impeachment possibilities. You wanted to scare him."

Bill didn't respond.

"Do you know where the documents are, Dad?"

Bill shook his head.

"So, how many defections did you hear about?" Troy asked after a few moments. His father would never tell him where the original Orders were, even if he did know.

"How many what?"

"Do I really have to—"

"Five," Bill cut in. "I heard five RCS agents defected with Maddux.

"There were three from the Falcons, including Ryan O'Hara," Bill continued, "as well as two from other divisions. You?"

"I heard—" Troy interrupted himself as the news anchor began speaking quickly in an animated tone. "Look at this," he said, gesturing at the screen on the wall. "The guys under the bridge are shooting at the chopper."

"Here we go," Bill mumbled grimly. "This is it. I just hope the cops on the front line are ready for anything."

"What do you mean?"

"These people are crazy, and they're well-equipped," Bill answered. "They aren't like the normal idiots who shoot up places. Most local law-enforcement units around this country are completely unprepared for this kind of capability . . . and commitment."

CHAPTER 10

"ALL RIGHT, all right!" the leader shouted at the other two men, who were still shooting into the air. The helicopter was moving off quickly. The eye in the sky had gotten the message. "Hold your fire."

"What do we do now?" one of the men yelled, panic-stricken. "We can't stay here forever."

"We'll be fine." The leader smiled confidently. He nodded over their shoulders. "You see, help is coming already."

The two men turned in unison to look, as if their chins were connected, completely convinced of the sincerity of their leader's gesture. However, it was nothing more than an old playground trick.

The leader shot both of them in the back of the head as soon as they glanced away. As they lay sprawled on the ground, he put an extra bullet into each man's brain.

When he was sure they were dead, he burst from behind the wall toward a line of police cars. He knew why the authorities had waited so long. He knew what they were doing, and he was too committed to the big picture and the greater good to allow them to derail it this quickly.

He'd been tortured once before by U.S. intel, and he wanted no part of another interrogation session like that. He much preferred a quick death over what would undoubtedly take many painful days to die. Besides, what was waiting for him on the other side was much more beautiful than this world. That's what he believed, anyway.

He dropped his weapon and threw his arms up in the air in full view of the authorities. Then he began to jog straight at the center vehicle in the line of cruisers. He could see the faces and the expressions of the policemen who were stationed behind the line of cherry tops. They were confused by his actions. Where were his compatriots? What in the hell was going on? They had no idea how to react.

They should be shooting me now, he thought as he ran. *I would be shooting me. But they are not trained well, and the chain of command has failed them. Some idiot five levels above these street soldiers still hasn't made a decision on how to deal with this emergency, probably because it was being broadcast live for the world to see and they don't want to be perceived as vicious and insensitive. So they are paralyzed.*

Their hesitation allowed him to make it all the way to the center of the line before they finally raised their weapons and ordered him to stop. By then it was too late—and he pulled the cord.

The bomb in his backpack unleashed its fury, releasing a terrible blast that took eight policemen and women with him.

AS KAASHIF watched the man jog toward the line of police cars on television, he actually felt the exhilaration his brother in arms was experiencing. It was taking the form of a great rush in his chest and a tingling sensation that extended from his heart all the way to his fingertips and toes. The man on TV was doing the right thing. He was sacrificing himself rather than take any chance of giving away something during an interrogation. Of course, the cops had no idea what they were dealing with. They would in a second.

The bomb exploded, incinerating this brother as well as several police officers.

As the sound of it faded from the TV, Kaashif allowed his face to slowly fall into his palms, and he began to sob. They'd been planning this attack for almost three years. Now the first stage was complete, and its success had been nearly perfect. The Minneapolis squad was gone, but they hadn't been apprehended, and every other team was back in hiding and accounted for. Seventy-three civilians were dead, and more than two hundred had been wounded. Even better, the United States population had run for cover. Reports were already coming in that with a week to go to Christmas, malls across the country were empty.

It was the greatest gift he could have received, and the tears would not stop coming. There were others in the house, and he could not have them see him like this, so he moved quickly to the bathroom and locked the door.

Then his tears flowed in earnest.

THE RUSTY hinges creaked as Major Travers pushed open the wooden door of the tiny house he'd built deep in the woods of Virginia's Appalachian Mountains.

It wasn't really a house. It was a shack, and not much of one at that. It didn't have running water, electricity, or heat—not even a fireplace. The stove was nothing more than a crude burner that was fired by a natural gas cylinder, when he remembered to buy one. So he usually ate the soup cold out of cans, when he remembered to buy them. And not many of the up-and-down planks that formed the four exterior walls of the relatively square floor plan rested flush against each other, and he'd never bothered to install insulation, so the place was drafty as hell. But it served its purpose. It was remote out here in the George Washington National Forest, as remote as any place could be within a hundred miles of Washington, DC.

Most important, as far as Travers could tell, he was the only person on the planet who knew about the place. The closest farm was several miles away, at the bottom of the mountains, so it lay outside the national forest. And hunters weren't allowed to take game within the forest's boundaries. Which didn't preclude poaching by the locals, of course, but he'd never had a problem with anyone using the place. He always set up a few inconspicuous indicators when he left so he could tell if it had been used or inspected when he returned. But they'd never been set off, just as he'd seen tonight when he'd gotten here. He'd checked even though he was exhausted after the steep climb through the cold, dark, wet forest.

He built the shack himself five years ago. He'd snared the lumber and other materials from a construction site down in the valley along the river. Then he'd lugged the stuff up the side of this mountain in the dark, without even a path to follow on his trips back and forth to the pickup he'd left on the logging road that night. He'd robbed the site so there wouldn't be any record of him buying anything at a store. Even if he'd paid cash, someone might still have remembered him. He was ultimately paranoid, he knew. But that had always proven to be one of his most formidable weapons.

Roger Carlson would have built him something out here if he'd asked, Travers knew. Carlson would have done anything for him. But then at least one other person would have known about it. As sad as it was for Travers to understand and accept, he couldn't completely trust anyone, even Carlson. And that hadn't been the old man's fault. Travers just had a terrible time with it. The only person who'd come close to that level of trust was Harry Boyd—now Harry was gone, too.

Travers stepped inside the shack, flipped on the tiny flashlight he'd dug out of his pocket, and played the beam around the small, mostly bare room. It was chilly in here, but it wasn't wet. A cold, soaking rain had begun to fall on the Mid-Atlantic an hour ago, as he'd been driving around DC on I-495—and he was glad to be in a dry place after hiking up the mountain in the dark. He didn't use this place very often, only when he desperately needed to go underground. Given what had happened three hours ago in Wilmington, this was one of those times. Shane Maddux wouldn't be happy when he found out his two young soldiers had been killed.

Travers stripped off his boots and the drenched poncho he'd worn up the mountain, tossed everything in a corner of the shack, and grabbed a rolled-up nylon sleeping bag off the table by the burner. He untied the bag and shook it hard to get rid of any black widows or brown recluses that had decided to make it home since the last time he'd been here—which was six months ago. Then he spread the bag out on the wooden floor.

It wasn't going to be comfortable, but then maybe he deserved some discomfort, maybe even some pain. He'd failed miserably in his job today. The United States was under attack. Hundreds of people had been killed and wounded, and the population was terrified, much more so than it had been after 9/11. People were cowering inside their homes with their doors and windows locked. Families who owned guns felt only marginally more secure than the ones who didn't. The men who'd carried out the attacks today were maniacs, but they were good. Only one team had been stopped—and they'd committed suicide. His gut told him this was going to be a long, hard campaign that might never end unless the country took unprecedented actions. Despite the brutal and ferocious nature of the attacks, Travers still wasn't certain the federal government would take those unprecedented steps, which would delve deeply into the personal privacies America's population held so dear.

When he was wrapped inside the sleeping bag, Travers flicked off the flashlight. As he lay on his side and listened to the rain falling on the roof, he stared into the darkness above him. Was Kaashif involved with what had happened today? His instincts told him yes. At least that gave him a place to start. He needed to get in touch with an associate. He needed cash and a secure location. This shack had its purpose, but he couldn't conduct operations from it. It was too far from anything to be effective.

Travers shut his eyes and forced himself not to think of all the issues facing him. There would be plenty of time to think—and act—tomorrow. But right now he desperately needed to recharge his body.

Moments later he was unconscious. It was a technique he'd learned in the foxholes of Iraq and Afghanistan from an older Marine vet. The guy had taught him to force himself to get sleep in any situation. An exhausted soldier was a poor soldier, and the trick to the technique was turning off the mind and all the bad thoughts it fired at him when there were no distractions.

But Travers never turned off his mind completely. It was always there to warn him of danger.

He bolted upright in the darkness and peered around the shack's interior. He couldn't see anyone, but he sensed a presence. Unfortunately, the warning had come too late.

Before he could draw his pistol, someone stepped on his wrist, immobilizing it and his ability to draw his weapon. Then a brilliant light bathed his face, and he shut his eyes tightly against the powerful rays.

"We meet again, Major Travers."

Travers recognized the voice. "How?" It was all he could think of to ask.

"Turnabout's fair play, don't you think?"

"I don't know what the hell you—"

He didn't finish. The dart was fired from nearly point-blank range, and it dug deeply into the side of his neck. Electricity flooded through his body as he dribbled around the floor.

CHAPTER 11

"ARE THERE any RCS associates who would help Maddux even though he's gone rogue and they know it?" As the private plane eased down into the thick cloud cover toward Westchester Airport, it shuddered slightly. Troy buckled his seat belt when the turbulence hit. "And would they do it without telling you? Maybe do it even when you specifically told them not to?"

It had happened exactly as Troy anticipated. A few minutes after the situation outside Minneapolis ended with the last terrorist igniting a suicide bomb in his backpack and taking several law-enforcement people with him, a young aide had knocked on the door and informed them that the president would not be able to meet with them again after all. The guy apologized halfheartedly and then left the situation to four Secret Service agents, who had immediately escorted Troy and Bill off White House grounds. Because of the Holiday Mall Attacks, security had been tightened another notch around the president, and all visitors were being escorted out. Even some of the regular staff had been told to leave and not return until they were contacted.

"I hate to say it," Bill admitted, "but all those things are possible. Maddux was smart about getting to know a few of the other associates even though Roger and I tried to block him from doing that. And I'm pretty sure he did them a few favors to entrench himself."

"What kinds of favors?"

"One of the associates was having a problem with his daughter's fiancé. The guy was abusive. He was beating her almost every night, and—"

"Don't tell me," Troy interrupted as the plane broke through the low clouds. He glanced out the window. It had been raining in Washington when they left, but it was snowing here in New York, he could see in the plane's lights. "The guy went missing."

"No, they found him all right. He was floating facedown in the East River. They pulled him out of the water down off Alphabet City in Lower Manhattan. It was ruled an accident, but nobody has any idea how he got in the water or what he was doing in that part of town. It's a rough area, and he lived up in White Plains."

"Jesus," Troy muttered. Maddux had pushed the vigilante deal for his own purposes after all. After promising Troy he never had, the liar— if Bill was telling the truth. *Mind games,* Troy thought as the plane rocked again. *Always the mind games in this profession.*

"Another one of the associates was having a problem at one of the companies he owned. He was pretty sure the chief financial officer was defrauding him, but he couldn't prove it." Bill looked out at the thin layer of snow on the ground as the plane touched down. "What do you know— one day, out of the blue, the CFO walks into the associate's office and voluntarily admits everything." Bill glanced from the window to Troy with both eyebrows raised. "I wonder why."

"Damn."

"The guy's face was badly bruised. He claimed he'd been in a car accident the day before. That's what I was told, anyway. I was curious, so I checked. There was no record of a car accident where the guy said it happened."

"Well, at least you know which associates they are. You can monitor them."

Bill shook his head. "That might not be all of the associates who are helping him, and I can't do anything about the ones I suspect are. These are very wealthy people, son. Each of the twenty associates has a personal net worth of at least a hundred million dollars, and most of them are much wealthier than that. It would be impossible for me to figure out what was going on in their personal finances without a SWAT team of forensic accountants analyzing and dissecting every wire and money transfer they've made in the last two years. And of course, that won't be happening. I won't ever get that kind of access even though I know them all very well."

Every associate has a net worth of at least a hundred million dollars. The words echoed in Troy's mind.

It was the first time he'd heard his father even vaguely put a number on the net worth. It was no secret that the family had serious money. His parents' mansion outside Greenwich was over ten thousand square feet, and it sat in the middle of five hundred acres of pricey Connecticut real estate along with a stable full of expensive Thoroughbreds his mother loved to ride. The mansion's back porch, which they were sitting on when Jack had been shot, was a hundred feet wide and thirty feet deep. And the family maintained several other homes around the world. Troy had used two of them when he was on missions—so had other Falcons.

He glanced around the beautiful interior of the plane. This was the family's G450 they were flying on tonight. No wonder Bill could afford it.

"Can't you just tell them not to help him?"

"I wish it were that easy," Bill answered. "These people respect me as the leader of the associates, but they aren't accustomed to being told what to do. And they're very loyal when it comes to someone who takes care of a problem they're having. Particularly like the ones I just described. They don't like getting their hands dirty, if you get my drift. So they appreciate people who will and who will stay quiet about it."

"Of course."

"Which means Maddux has at least somewhat of a support system," Bill continued. "When it's only a few agents Maddux has with him, two or three associates would be plenty to support him. He's smart. He probably wouldn't have defected without arranging it. He's a front-line guy, but he understands and appreciates the need for logistics."

That was true. Maddux had always preached to Troy about the need for warriors to be well-supplied. How heroics and grit only went so far.

"There's someone I want you to work with on the Mall Attacks," Bill said as the plane turned off the runway and headed for the terminal. "Maybe you've run into him before on one of your missions."

"Who's that?"

Bill leaned toward Troy, as if he was concerned about listening devices on his own plane. "Major Wilson Travers," he said quietly. "He's in the Interrogation Division."

Troy shook his head. "I might have met him, but those guys are pretty careful about not using real names around anybody they don't know. Even Falcons."

"He's the best interrogator we have, other than Maddux, of course. Unlike Shane, Travers is completely trustworthy, and he's a big, good-looking African American guy."

"Agent Walker," Troy murmured.

"What?"

"I think I know who you mean. Last spring I took cash and instructions to a guy over in Athens, Greece. I think that was Travers. He was with another guy. They called each other Agent Walker and Agent Smirnoff."

It took three men to get Travers into the tiny cell. They'd tased him again several times on the ride to keep him subdued, but he was already recuperating. When they dropped him roughly on the wet cement floor, he tried to crawl after them. So they'd secured him to an iron ring that was affixed firmly to a wall of the room. One end of the chain was locked to the ring in the wall while the other was attached to a collar that was locked around Travers's neck. They were taking no chances.

"That's one tough bastard," the man who'd tased Travers muttered as he locked the cell door.

Nathan Kohler nodded. "Yup." He chuckled as he admired the bars of the cell. "I'm glad I had this thing made so strong. And I had that ring sunk into the wall."

BAXTER HURRIED into the Oval Office. He'd just finished a briefing with Homeland Security. The news wasn't good. "Mr. President?" He stopped with the toes of his black leather tasseled loafers resting on the eagle's tail. Dorn hadn't even looked around when Baxter opened the door. He just kept staring out the window into the dark, rainy night outside. "Sir?"

"Yes, Stewart," Dorn finally answered, slowly turning the wheelchair back toward the desk.

"I just finished my briefing with Jane Travanti and her staff."

"Let me guess," Dorn responded stoically. "We have no leads on any of the death squads. They all evaporated into thin air, except for the ones we think attacked the Mall of America in Minneapolis. And even though we have the remains of those men, we don't know anything about them."

"Not yet."

"We never will, Stewart."

"We've taken DNA samples and—"

"Did we at least confirm that they were the men involved in the MOA attack?"

"Yes, sir. Spent ammunition found at the mall matched the guns in their van."

"But other than that, we have nothing. Correct?"

Baxter nodded. "Yes, sir."

The president gestured at Baxter, then at Connie. "Will you two give me a few minutes alone?"

Baxter didn't like the sound of that. "Mr. President, I don't think you should be—"

"Enough, Stewart." Dorn glanced at Connie. "Please go. Take him with you. I'll call you in a few minutes. Don't come back until I do."

Connie looked quickly at Baxter for guidance. He pointed subtly at the door and nodded.

When they were both outside the office, Baxter took Connie's hand in his. "Stay right here," he ordered. "Wait two minutes and then go back in. I need to get something from my office and make a few calls. Then I'll come back."

"But, Mr. Baxter, the president said—"

"I don't care what he said. You go back in there in two minutes. And when I get back, we'll take him up into the residence together. In fact, I'll call Mrs. Dorn on my way to my office. She'll help us convince him. If the president doesn't get some rest soon, he'll die of exhaustion. I can't have that." He hesitated. "I mean, *we* can't have that."

TROY STARED at the tombstone as snow fell on the graveyard, covering the freshly turned earth above the coffin. It was just before midnight, but he knew he wouldn't be able to sleep well. So he'd come out here after saying good-bye to Bill at the Westchester Airport. He rarely needed more than five hours a night, and tonight wouldn't have been one of those nights even if he wanted it to be. He was tired, and tomorrow was going to be a long day. But he had way too much on his mind to get that kind of rest.

"I miss you, brother," he whispered.

"I miss him, too."

"Jesus." Troy whipped around at the sound of the female voice coming from behind him.

"Sorry about that," Karen said as she moved up beside him. "I didn't mean to scare you."

"I'm fine." Troy glanced up through the darkness at the bare trees towering over the graveyard like sentinels—or ghosts. His heart was still pounding. He didn't like graveyards to begin with, and hearing that voice out of nowhere had shocked him. "What are you doing out here?"

"The same thing you are. Trying to say good-bye to Jack."

Troy reached out and took Karen's hand. She'd been engaged to another Falcon—Charlie Banks—who'd been a close friend of Troy's. Until Banks had been thrown into the Bering Sea from the *Arctic Fire* for the same reason Troy had—discovering that Shane Maddux was doing things he shouldn't have been. Unfortunately, Banks hadn't made it out of the water alive after he'd been tossed overboard by the four-man crew of the *Fire* who worked for Maddux. Banks hadn't been lucky enough to have a brother race to Alaska to save him. His body had never been recovered.

Jack had begun his quest to find out what had really happened to Troy that night on the *Arctic Fire*—he hadn't believed the official story—by contacting Karen. She lived in Baltimore, and Jack had shown up unannounced at her waitressing job in Fell's Point on his way west, the night after he left Connecticut. When she understood how the same thing that had happened to her fiancé had happened to Troy, she'd made it clear to Jack in no uncertain terms that she was going to Alaska with him. And they'd fallen in love.

"I'm sorry for you more than anyone else," Troy said, squeezing her fingers gently. "You've already gone through this once before, and it wasn't that long ago. No one should have to deal with so much."

"Thanks." She smiled sadly as she nodded at the headstone. "He loved you very much, Troy."

"I know. We had our challenges, but all brothers do."

"He wanted to be your brother so badly."

"He *was* my brother."

"I think that's why he went to Alaska when everyone else said you were dead, when everyone else told him he was crazy and to just leave it alone, even your father." Karen shook her head. "He knew you were alive. Even I tried to convince him he was crazy, but he wouldn't listen. And thank God, right? I think that's why he figured you two were brothers even when your father had told everyone you weren't. Jack figured only a brother could know that." It was Karen's turn to squeeze Troy's fingers. "He was jealous of you."

"No, that's not . . . I mean, that was all overblown, Karen. He wasn't really—"

"Oh, yeah, he was. You were the star of the family. You played every sport, and you were the go-to guy on every team. You were everyone's All-American in high school and at Dartmouth, especially Bill's. Jack lived in your very long shadow for a very long time."

"Yeah, well, I—"

"How's Little Jack?"

Troy shut his eyes tightly.

"Sorry," Karen murmured. "I didn't mean to—"

"L.J.'s doing great."

"L.J.?"

"That's my nickname for the baby." Troy grinned. "Mom doesn't like it much, but she'll get over it. She's been a big help. L.J.'s living at the house in Greenwich with her and my father."

"I know. She told me today at the funeral. It's meant a lot to her to have Little Jack around during this time. She loves taking care of him."

During the last six years Troy had rarely made it home. But once in a while he had returned. Last year, on one of those infrequent trips, he'd met a woman from Brooklyn named Lisa Martinez while he was with friends at a club in Manhattan. A few months ago Lisa had given birth to Troy's son and named him Jack because Jack had been the one who'd taken care of her during her pregnancy. Then she'd been murdered, and the Jensen family had taken in Little Jack.

"I should have taken care of Lisa while she was pregnant. It shouldn't have been Jack."

Karen shook her head. "How could you, Troy? You were always thousands of miles away keeping this country safe. You were an RCS Falcon. I get that. Everyone does."

Troy glanced over at her when she uttered the word *Falcon*. "Charlie told you everything about RCS, didn't he?"

She shrugged. "I don't know. Did he?"

"He wasn't supposed to tell you anything."

"We were getting married, Troy. Come on."

"It doesn't matter."

"Look, I'm not going to tell anyone anything Charlie told me about—"

"It's not about you telling anyone voluntarily," Troy interrupted. "It's about you being forced to tell people. It's about you knowing anything that makes you a target for other people who want to know. And that makes Red Cell Seven vulnerable."

"Thanks so much for your concern."

"I am concerned, Karen, believe me. You have no idea what certain elements would do to you if they thought they could get information out of you."

"I'll be fine," she said firmly, letting go of his hand. They were quiet for a while. "What's going to happen?" she finally asked.

"With what?"

"The attacks."

Troy shrugged. "I don't know. No one does."

"Oh, come on. I know where you and Bill went today."

"Who told you?"

"Nobody. It wasn't hard to figure out."

Of course, he realized.

"It's crazy," she murmured. "The newspeople are talking about how these death squads could start shooting people anywhere, anytime, maybe even invading homes. I don't think anyone will ever go outside again. Everyone will stay barricaded in their houses and shoot anyone who even steps on their property."

"Yeah, it's gonna be—" Troy interrupted himself when his phone rang. "Sorry, I need to take this," he said, turning away and walking several paces off into the darkness. "Okay," he muttered when he heard the bad news and the dangerous instructions. Tomorrow was going to be a *very* long day.

THE PRESIDENT gazed steadily into the darkness outside. This had been the hardest day of his administration, the hardest day of his life.

Even harder than the day he'd been shot. Once he'd gotten onto the operating table after taking the bullet, there was a definitive solution to the
problem, and everyone was working to achieve it.

He let his face drop into his hands. No one seemed to know what the
solution was here. No one even seemed able to tell him where to start.

PART 2

CHAPTER 12

Troy followed the doctor into a private room of the Fairfax County Hospital in northern Virginia. He stopped just inside as the door to the busy corridor outside swung slowly shut behind him. He glanced at the young woman who was lying on the bed with her eyes closed and her arms at her sides as the sounds from the corridor faded away. Then he checked the room carefully, as though something sinister might be lurking.

He hated hospitals as much as he hated graveyards. But it was the prospect of death that got to him here, not the finality of skeletons in the ground beneath him. He'd dedicated himself to protecting lives, often risking his own in the process. Death winning was always extremely personal for him.

He understood that it was all an exercise in delaying the inevitable—that death eventually conquered everyone. But it was the length of that delay that was crucial. He was committed to keeping good people alive as long as possible, any way he could. It was what mattered to him most.

He'd tried explaining all that to Lisa once, but it hadn't come out exactly right. Still, she'd cried and hugged him when he was finished.

That was the night she'd gotten pregnant with L.J. He was convinced of it.

The irony of his resolve was that he killed people in order to prolong life. And he'd do it again if the situation required it. He had no problem killing evil to preserve good. He didn't see that as a conflict—which was how he could relate to Maddux in a distant way.

Troy took a deep breath and immediately regretted it. He hated the smell of hospitals. It wasn't the odor of antiseptics that hung everywhere that so offended him. It was the occasional stench of sickness and death overpowering the antiseptics.

He'd only gotten three hours of sleep last night, but he felt fine. He'd decided on taking this detour to Washington last night right after Bill had ordered him to go to North Carolina.

He took one more careful look around the room before refocusing on the young woman. Bill had tried talking him out of coming here, but Troy was glad he'd come.

The woman's body was connected to a web of tubes that led off in different directions to several machines, and it was eerily noisy in here with the beeping and whirring of the devices. Despite the noise and the seriousness of her wounds, she seemed to be resting peacefully.

She was very pretty, and as Troy gazed at her features, he noticed that she strongly resembled Lisa. She had the same sharp, sculpted facial lines; beautiful light-mahogany skin; and long, wavy jet-black hair. She probably had that same wonderful smile, too, he figured as he looked at her high cheekbones and full lips. Hopefully, she'd recover from this tragedy so she could smile that smile again.

He missed Lisa, he realized as he stared down at Jennie, more and more each day. The hole in his heart her murder had left wasn't healing the way it was supposed to, but he couldn't tell anyone. He was the tough brother. Jack was the son who had worn his heart on his sleeve.

Though Troy couldn't prove it, he believed Maddux had killed Lisa execution-style in her Brooklyn apartment a month ago. Since Troy had heard the stories yesterday of how Red Cell Seven had saved the nation so many times, he better understood Maddux's unwavering resolve to do away with anyone who got in the cell's way—including the president.

But none of that could make up for Maddux ripping Lisa and Jack out of his life. He would avenge their deaths if he ever had the chance. He'd sworn that oath to himself on the way down here this morning on the plane. Bill was right. Those two murders were personal.

At least Maddux hadn't been a total monster, Troy figured. He hadn't murdered Little Jack after killing Lisa. There was at least that measure of loyalty.

"How many times was Ms. Perez shot?"

"Twice. Once in the shoulder," the doctor explained, reaching over his shoulder to show Troy the spot, "and once in the middle of the back." This time he reached beneath his armpit and around his torso to point out the location of the entry wound—which was just to the left of the upper spine.

Doctors and nurses did that a lot, Troy had noticed. They pointed to body parts as they spoke. It seemed like they were constantly reminding themselves of the human anatomy as much as they were showing others what was going on. It was probably something they picked up in medical school. He'd been stitched up enough times to recognize the habit, and maybe that was another reason he hated hospitals—because he'd been in them so often. Sometimes to heal his own wounds but more often to visit others who'd fallen victim to something he'd been able to avoid.

"She's lucky," the older man continued. "It's a one-in-a-million wound."

The doctor was tall and silver-haired. He reminded Troy a little of Bill, but his tone was more amiable. So was his manner. "What do you mean?" he asked as he moved close to where Jennie lay.

"She'll live despite the bullet she took in her back. Somehow no vital organs were hit. She was very lucky." The doctor grimaced. "The shooter didn't know what he was doing."

"I doubt the shooter was actually aiming," Troy countered. "If I've read the preliminary reports on these attacks correctly, it was a spray-

and-get-away deal. It was like that with all eleven attacks, from what I understand. I doubt any of the death squads were in the malls for more than fifteen to twenty seconds before they split."

"I think they were on the scene for longer than that at Tysons."

"Was there a witness who said that?" Troy asked. "I didn't hear about one."

"No."

"And the cameras set up to watch the entrance were shot out early, so those tapes are worthless."

The doctor held his hands up. "Believe me, I agree with the spray-and-get-away theory as far as her shoulder wound goes. But it doesn't jibe with the one in her back."

"Why not?"

"There was gunpowder on her jacket."

Troy glanced at Jennie, then back at the doctor. "Are you saying the assassin put the gun right up against her body with that shot?"

"Yes. And she was lying thirty feet inside the entrance when the EMTs got to her. Whoever shot her in the back would have had to run into the mall where she was lying. You know, *after* she'd been hit in the shoulder from the initial burst. That alone probably would have taken longer than fifteen seconds."

"Are you saying the shooter was making sure she was dead?"

"When the authorities get the ballistics report back from the lab concerning the bullets that were found at the scene, I think the evidence will show that at least several of the rounds were fired from a pistol. Probably a twenty-two, judging by the wound. I've seen enough of them to recognize it," he added ruefully.

"A twenty-two? Are you saying these guys used pistols to carry out the attack, Doctor?"

The doctor shook his head. "No, I'm saying they used automatic weapons initially, probably small machine guns. Most of the wounds in the other victims are consistent with those kinds of bullets." He nodded down at Jennie. "However, the one in her back isn't. And two other victims at Tysons had wounds that I believe were inflicted by the same pistol."

"So after they mowed people down, at least one of the guys went farther into the mall and executed people he thought were still alive."

"Yes. He was making absolutely certain those people were dead."

"Because they didn't want to be identified."

"I assume."

"But there were others who were wounded and weren't executed."

"They were farther from the entrance, much farther. Maybe whoever it was got nervous. Maybe he knew there were other survivors, but he realized he needed to get away and figured the ones farther in couldn't ID him anyway."

"Right," Troy agreed. "It just seems so crazy that the wound in her back didn't kill her, that it didn't hit *anything* vital."

The doctor shrugged as if he couldn't believe it, either. "Like I said, it's a one-in-a-million wound. Now let's get out of here before she—"

"Did the assassin shoot the others the same way from close range?" Troy reached around his back and pointed to the spot the doctor had. "Did he put the pistol barrel in the same spot on the other two?"

The doctor hesitated. "Um . . . yes, I believe that's right."

"And those victims died."

"Uh, yes."

Something didn't sound right. "Is that strange? Does that—"

"She's a real hero," the doctor interrupted, smiling wanly.

"Why?"

"She saved a six-year-old girl's life."

"How do you know?"

"The little girl told us. She lost her father in the attack, and Jennie saved her after he was shot right in front of her. Fortunately her mother wasn't at the mall at the time, and the little girl's with her now."

Troy glanced down at Jennie. The more he looked at her, the more she reminded him of Lisa. "How long do you think until I can talk to her?"

The doctor bit down softly on his lower lip as he thought about it. "I'd say a couple of days. Probably," he cautioned after a few moments. "She's coming around really well so far. But it might be more."

"Okay, well, I'm going to have a team of bodyguards up here in fifteen minutes." Troy was worried that if the word got out she'd lived, someone might try to finish her off. She'd been closer to the attackers than any other survivor, and if he could jog her memory effectively, he might get something vital out of her. "They'll be with her around the clock," he continued, "until I say so. If you need to move her to a quieter area of the hospital, Doctor, I fully understand. In fact, I recommend it." Troy pulled his pistol from the shoulder holster beneath his jacket and chambered the first round. "But let's wait until the team gets here to do that," he added, slipping the now-battle-ready gun back into its leather cave and then pulling out his cell phone and pressing the number of a contact on his list. "Until then, I'll stay with her."

The doctor's eyes narrowed. "Who are you, son?"

"I'm with the National Intel—"

"I know what they told me before you got here. I got the official story." He paused. "But who are you *really* with?"

CHAPTER 13

SHANE MADDUX moved down the basement steps quietly. Even though she knew he was close, he still wanted surprise on his side. He always wanted surprise on his side.

But what he really wanted was shock. Shock had the power to paralyze, mentally and physically. That paralysis made his victims weak and engendered honest responses. And in this case, he could get that shock because she had no idea who he had with him.

At five-six and 140 pounds, Maddux was a small man. But he wasn't bitter about it. He had been, as a kid, when the class studs smacked him around for kicks in the hallways of his public high school, then ran all over him on the athletic fields in the afternoon. He could admit it now that his place in the world was rock solid and he couldn't be more certain of himself and his objectives.

In fact, at this point he regarded his lack of size as an advantage. Being slight enabled him to slip through life undetected, like a specter sliding through the shadows. His uncanny ability to do that had done nothing but bolster his reputation as a coldly efficient killer—which he'd become over the last decade. To mythical proportions in some circles of the intel community, he knew.

His natural stealth convinced others he was close when he was far away. It scared them to death even when they swore it didn't, which gave him an advantage at the moment of truth. They were already so terrified of him by the time he was actually upon them that they froze like deer in the headlights. For Maddux, for anyone in this line of work, success was all about having as many advantages as possible.

He was the ultimate survivor, too—which ran his spook reputation even farther up the flagpole. Intel people everywhere swore up and down they'd seen him die in a hail of bullets or pushed from a plane at twenty thousand feet without a parachute or go below the surface of the water somewhere and not come back up. But then they swore they'd seen him alive *after* that. So he was like a cat, they'd rant. Except that it seemed he had a hundred lives, not nine.

Maddux knew all this from personal experience, not just from hearsay. He'd been sitting in the back room of a Paris café one night a year ago with two Russians he'd recognized as low-level intelligence officers. They kept telling him about an American Special Forces agent they referred to as "the Ghost" or "Le Fantôme" over and over as he conversed with them in perfect French. And he kept buying them vodka, getting them drunker and drunker and convincing them he was only a boring *avocat* from the town of Angers who had come to Paris for holiday to enjoy time away from a nagging wife. He told them he was fascinated to hear as much as they would tell him about the wild world of international intrigue. So they'd told him all about Le Fantôme as he'd gotten them drunk. Very quickly he'd recognized that the man they were talking about was him.

When he grew tired of talking, he'd shot each of them in the heart with a twenty-two pistol from point-blank range. He'd done it during a particularly loud song being played by a band out in the main room, after wrapping a thick cloth napkin around the barrel of the gun to make certain no one heard. After shooting them, he'd slipped out the back without anyone knowing.

He'd read about the murders in *Le Monde* the next morning. And he'd realized from the article that he was completely insulated from discovery. The inspectors were appealing to anyone who might have any information about the killings to come forward. So they obviously had no leads. No one did.

Not even the waitress who'd served them. She hadn't because she couldn't. Maddux had killed her later that night as she was walking home, just to be safe. He'd strangled her in an alley and enjoyed it. He was self-aware enough to realize that he was a psychopath. But he believed that sickness only gave him another advantage. He'd justified her murder as simply a necessity for keeping him, and therefore the United States, safe.

Maddux moved into the bathroom at the bottom of the stairs and glanced into the mirror above the sink. He grimaced and looked away quickly. This was the only part he didn't like. His was a face only a mother could love. He'd gotten over his small stature—but never that face. It was twisted and ugly.

He washed his hands, slipped into a pair of rubber gloves, then moved back out of the bathroom and approached her. She was in her mid-thirties, slightly overweight, and had light brown wavy hair. Two hours ago he'd lashed her to an uncomfortable wooden chair in the middle of this room and left her here to soften up. Apparently it had worked. She was already sobbing beneath the gag and the blindfold.

He ran the backs of his gloved fingers gently down her cheek, and she jumped at the unexpected touch, shocked by his presence—exactly as he wanted. She hadn't heard him coming, and now he knew that her heart rate had spiked into the stratosphere. And the major shock was still to come.

It was eerie how good he was at sneaking up on people. It was a natural talent he'd possessed ever since he could remember. Since even before high school when, only a few days prior to graduation, he'd snuck up on this one stud who'd been particularly evil to him in the hallways—and killed him at dusk with a knife in the dimly lit parking lot after baseball practice.

That wasn't his first murder. And even then, he knew it wouldn't be his last. He liked killing bad people, and that was the key. They had to be evil. As long as they were, he had no conflict. He couldn't admit to himself in high school how much he enjoyed killing, but he could now.

Maddux moved behind the chair and untied the knot of the bootlace at the back of the woman's head that secured the gag—an orange practice golf ball. It was made of hollow plastic and had holes in it so it resembled Swiss cheese. He'd run the long lace through two of the ball's holes that were opposite each other, and the combination had made a perfect gag. The lace had left two raw marks at the corners of her mouth that were probably causing her great discomfort. But that was none of his concern.

"Where will the next attacks come?" he demanded as he put his hands on the arms of the chair, leaned down close, and stared into her almond-shaped eyes from close range. "Tell me, Imelda Smith. Don't make me ask twice."

"How do you know my name?"

"Answer my question."

Tears spilled from Imelda's eyes as she looked up at him helplessly. "What attacks are you talking about? I don't know anything."

Maddux had been torturing people for more than two decades, and at this point he quickly recognized the veracity of the responses—or lack thereof. Based on what he saw in her eyes and what he heard in her tone, she was lying. This woman was directly involved in what was already the worst terrorist attack the United States had ever suffered. And it was still going on.

He'd snatched Imelda yesterday afternoon from the kitchen of her small home in Manassas, Virginia—less than thirty miles from the attack in Tysons Corner. Then he'd transported her two hundred miles to this beautiful, remote home built in the hills of central Pennsylvania. So far she seemed to be quite the actress, and incredibly committed to the cause.

Imelda was going to have that commitment tested this afternoon. She was about to face a sacrifice far more excruciating than her own death.

"Don't lie to me," he warned. "I'll go easier on you if you tell me the truth and you do it quickly. Time is important to me."

"I'm not lying," she sobbed. "I *swear.*"

"Are you telling me you don't know anything about what happened yesterday?"

"I don't even know what you're talking about. What happened yesterday?"

Maddux rose up slowly. "All right, if that's the way you want to play it."

"I'm not playing anything. Please let me go," she begged. "What are you going to do to me?"

Maddux walked out of the room and into the next without answering. When he returned he was clutching the hand of Imelda's five-year-old son. This was the shock factor Maddux had been waiting to spring.

He wasn't disappointed with her reaction.

PARKVIEW ELEMENTARY SCHOOL was nestled into a quiet, blue-collar suburb of Springfield, Missouri, in the south-central part of the state about two hundred miles from St. Louis. The school was attended mostly by the sons and daughters of parents who worked at the Chrysler plant a few miles from the school. Or for the Union Pacific Railroad, which operated a large freight yard close to the Chrysler factory.

It was a few minutes after noon, central time, and the cafeteria was filling with kids. Kindergarten classes let out for the day before lunch, but the first and second graders were in the big room enjoying their brown-bag meals or the hot lunches that had been prepared by the cafeteria staff. Third and fourth graders would be coming in at twelve-thirty to eat, thirty minutes after the younger children, as they always did. It was the next-to-last day of classes before school let out for the holidays.

Today's hot lunch was pizza and fries along with a packet of sliced apples and a pint of whole milk. It was a popular lunch, and many of the kids had convinced their parents last night to give them money to buy it when it was posted at five p.m. yesterday on the school website.

The room was noisy. Kids were happy because they were at lunch. It was always a highlight of the day. And they were looking forward to their vacation and the toys they were hoping to get.

As the joy of the season rolled through the cafeteria, three men slipped through a side door of the building that opened onto the playground. Once inside, they pulled gray ski masks down over their faces as they hesitated in a short, narrow hallway just outside the big room. When they were ready, they drew their automatic weapons from beneath their coats, burst through the hallway door, and sprayed the room with bullets.

Thirty seconds later they were sprinting across the playground to their initial escape vehicle and its waiting driver. Three minutes later they'd switched vehicles at a nearby strip mall, ten minutes after that they'd switched again, and within half an hour they'd made it back to the apartment complex on the other side of town where they had been holing up for the last three months.

Yesterday the team had opened fire on an unsuspecting crowd at a huge mall in the suburbs of St. Louis and thrown the city into chaos as part of the initial, coordinated attack at that and ten other malls around the country. Now the team was independent, as were the other nine death squads still operating. They were much like a wolf pack roaming the landscape for the next kill—which they'd found in the elementary school. There were so many "soft" targets to choose from, it was like shooting fish in a barrel. But they had to be careful, too. They wanted to remain free to kill for as long as possible. So, for the next few days they'd be eating fast food and playing video games at the apartment complex. Then they'd hunt again.

Sixteen people at Parkview Elementary had died immediately in the terrible attack. The body count included twelve children, two teachers, a cafeteria staff member, and a security guard who was armed with a 9mm pistol. Forty-two had been wounded—seven critically.

One young couple had lost both of their children in the attack—a boy in the second grade and a little girl in first.

IMELDA'S FACE drained of color when she saw her little boy, and she began straining wildly at the ropes securing her to the chair. "If you touch him, if you so much as scratch him, I'll kill you!" she shouted as despair morphed into rage. "I swear to God I'll kill you!"

Unaffected, Maddux handcuffed the little boy to a vertical pipe leading to the house's water heater, and he began to cry. "You won't have that chance."

"Then they'll kill you!" she screamed as her rant turned maniacal. "They'll rip you apart limb from limb for this!"

When the little boy's wrists were snapped tightly to the copper pipe, Maddux's gaze rose triumphantly to hers. "'They'?" he asked as he stalked to where she sat and leaned down close again. "Who do you mean, 'they'?"

"I didn't mean it," she hissed before she spat in his face. "I misspoke, you animal."

"I don't think so." He smiled sadistically even as he calmly wiped her warm saliva off his skin. She probably assumed he'd strike her after spitting on him that way. So it would scare her more when he didn't. "I know exactly what you meant. You meant the men who killed all those innocent people at the mall in Tysons Corner yesterday."

"What people?"

He chuckled as he moved back to where the little boy stood. "Don't give me that, Imelda. Talk to me, or your son dies."

"Get away from him!"

"Mommy!" the boy shouted as Maddux skinned a long knife from the sheath hanging off his belt. "Mommy, help me, *please*."

The long, serrated blade glistened in the light of the lone bulb dangling from the ceiling. Maddux stepped behind the boy, grabbed him by the hair, pulled his chin up, and placed the blade at his tiny throat. "Talk to me, woman. Tell me what you know."

Her rage evaporated as the tip of the blade punctured her son's soft skin. "Don't kill him." Blood seeped from the wound and dripped down his neck. "Oh, God, don't kill him. Kill me instead."

"Mommy! Mommy, help me!"

"Talk to me!" Maddux shouted, raising his voice as his predatory instincts reached the surface and his blood boiled. "Tell me everything."

"I can't tell you anything. I don't know anything."

"I'll give you one more chance, Imelda."

"Mommy, Mommy. I'm scared!"

"I swear I know nothing."

"Mommy, I—"

Maddux drew the razor-sharp blade deliberately and deeply across the boy's throat. The boy gurgled for a few moments as he mouthed words soundlessly. Then he exhaled heavily one final time, his tiny chin fell to his chest as Maddux let go of his hair, and his body crumpled to the floor—twisted in an awkward way around the pipe.

The woman's tears began to flow like swollen rivers running to the sea. "You, you . . . you are the devil." It was all she could gasp. For several moments she hyperventilated, unable to speak as she barely maintained consciousness. "I hate you."

"Get in line."

"You will pay."

"We'll see." She probably wished she could pass out, but she wouldn't. Her breathing was already turning more regular. "Now you'll talk to me," he whispered as he moved behind her, bent down, and put his lips to her ear. "Now you'll tell me everything I want to know."

"You can do anything you want to me now." Imelda sobbed loudly. "I don't care anymore about anything."

"Yes you do, sweetheart. Oh, yes you do."

"You really are the devil," she whispered. "No person could be this evil."

"The term is committed," Maddux said. "No one can be this committed. And yes, I am. Now, who carried out those attacks yesterday? Who killed all those people in Tysons Corner?"

"I will tell you nothing."

He moved in front of her again. "You know, don't you?"

"Maybe," she whispered, "but you'll never get it out of me. You think you're committed to your way of life, but you have no idea." She glanced down at her dead son. "I won't trade what I know for anything. Nothing you could do would change that." She nodded at the boy's body. "I've already proven that."

For a few moments Maddux stared at Imelda in complete and utter awe. The mother-child relationship was the strongest bond in nature as far as he was concerned. No other came close in terms of loyalty and sacrifice. But she'd watched her son die—her most critical life's work had been snuffed out in front of her, and she could have saved him. But she hadn't.

Maddux's awe turned to fear. It was an emotion he rarely experienced. Now he knew how committed these people were to their objective; now he understood what they intended to do. They meant to change America's way of life forever, to reverse the freedoms its people had enjoyed for hundreds of years. They meant for everyone to fear for their lives every moment of the day. They wanted to turn the idyllic American existence into a nightmare ruled by paranoia, and they didn't care what it took to do it.

What made this all so powerful for him was that he suddenly realized they might succeed. These were people of unprecedented will. They would do anything for their cause. The proof of that had unfolded right here in front of him. They would sacrifice their sons and daughters for the cause, even watch as they died. For them the whole was so much more important than any of the pieces.

In America that wasn't necessarily true anymore. Many of the pieces believed they were infinitely more important than the whole. Perhaps that incredibly selfish me-first and live-for-the-moment attitude that seemed to dominate American society was the bellwether signal of the nation's ultimate and unavoidable demise. Maybe now he understood what the country was up against. Maybe the enemy wasn't these people. Maybe the country's true enemy was itself. He blinked several times. And how did you fight that?

"Have you ever heard the name Jack Jensen?" he asked as once more he leaned down with his hands on the arms of the chair so his face was very close to hers. It was time to end this. He had to get to North Carolina.

"Maybe." Her tone was hollow now, almost robotic.

"Tell me the truth and I'll make sure you die quickly. You won't suffer."

"I've heard the name."

"Did your people kill him?"

The woman stared straight back into Maddux's cold eyes. "I won't tell you. You can do anything you want to me, but I won't tell you."

CHAPTER 14

"Hello, Dad." Troy was just pulling away from the hospital in the backseat of a cab headed for Dulles Airport. He needed to get back on the G450 and get farther south. The other two men accompanying him on tonight's mission were probably already in North Carolina. "How are you?"

"Busy."

The number that had come up on Troy's phone was his father's private cell—Bill carried two at all times; however, not many people had the digits to this one. Still, Troy assumed Bill was calling from his corner office that overlooked Wall Street from ten floors up. He had a First Manhattan board meeting later this afternoon.

Last night on the flight up from DC, Bill had admitted that the funeral and all that was going on with Red Cell Seven hadn't given him much time to prepare. He was worn out, physically and emotionally, so his drive to prepare wasn't what it should have been. After they'd taken off from Reagan Airport, he'd reviewed a few files covering the bank's performance but then quickly closed the laptop and shut it off. Typically,

Bill used every spare minute to get things done, so it was unusual to see him do that, especially with the board meeting looming.

First Manhattan meetings weren't chummy, softball-question-only affairs like they were at some big, publicly held companies. Bill had packed the board with tough independent thinkers. And the culture of striving for perfection from the top down was reflected in the firm's consistently strong earnings. First Manhattan had become Wall Street's gold standard, and Bill had driven the firm to that level with his unparalleled work ethic and steadfast determination. But the quarterly meetings were still stressful. He was held accountable by that board.

"I'm sure you are busy, Dad. I know those board meetings are tough."

"Thorough," Bill said tersely. "Did you hear about the latest attack?"

Troy grimaced. "No." What was it this time? "I just left the hospital in northern Virginia. I saw that young woman who survived the Tysons attack. Now I'm heading for—" Troy stopped himself. "Well, you know."

"Uh-huh."

"So, what happened? They hit another mall?"

They'd discussed this possibility last night on the plane after Bill had turned off his computer. They'd both assumed the death squads wouldn't wait long to strike again. Apparently, they'd been right.

"No. This time they attacked an elementary school in a quiet suburb of Springfield, Missouri."

"Bastards," Troy whispered. "They're making a statement, Dad. They're telling the world that everyone in America is vulnerable."

"This is as bad as it gets."

"What happened?"

"First and second graders were eating lunch when three guys in ski masks entered the cafeteria from a hallway and opened fire with automatic weapons. It was the same story as the malls except this was a school."

"Was there a guard?"

"He was killed, shot through the back."

"He was running away?"

"Yes."

Troy gritted his teeth as he imagined the terrible chaos and the carnage. These were well-trained killers with automatic weapons. Some poor security guard with a pistol was no match for them. You really couldn't blame the guy for running. "Anyone caught?"

"No. Apparently, these guys aren't just excellent killers. They're escape artists as well. Every individual attack is meticulously planned. They have lots of vehicles they're willing to abandon, which don't give us any clues when we find them. They must have plenty of places to hole up, too. My guess is they aren't using hotel or motel rooms, because they'd be easy to spot at those places. They're using apartments or, more likely, stand-alone houses they've been living in for a while, so people around them don't notice anything different now that the attacks have begun. They may even have families with them who have no idea what's really going on, or are plants and are in on it. Either way, it helps these guys camouflage themselves. The only positive I can come up with in all of this is that it's a fairly big operation, which means there's a meaningful money trail somewhere. There has to be."

"There always is with something big."

"And I'm in a uniquely good position to find it," Bill pointed out. "I've already got people on it."

"Have you talked to the chairman again?" Troy asked, using the code they always used—on landlines or cells—to refer to President Dorn.

"No," Bill answered curtly. "And I don't see any reason to. As always, we'll go our own way. If he wants to talk, he knows how to reach me. Otherwise we stay independent, as we always have."

Troy wanted to push. He wasn't convinced David Dorn had really changed his view on Red Cell Seven the way he claimed, especially after Stewart Baxter had slammed them so badly yesterday in the residence right after word of the initial attacks had come down. Plus, Dorn had pushed so hard on the specific whereabouts of the original Executive Orders Nixon had signed. Dorn had claimed he wanted to make sure the cell wasn't vulnerable. But his agenda could easily be exactly the opposite.

Troy wanted to push, but he held off. His father already had a full plate today. And cell phones could never be trusted.

"I bet the chairman's meeting with his guy right now. I bet he's telling his guy everything you told him yesterday. That guy's a snake. Truth be told, I'm not so sure about the chairman, either."

"Easy," Bill cautioned. "We don't want to assume anything."

"Dad, I—"

"I hear you, son, and I'm running some deep-water G-2 lines as we speak. He did it to us. Now it's our turn to do it. If anything's down there in the depths, we'll find it—and at the appropriate time, use it. I promise."

"I don't trust that guy or the chairman. I know I should because of who he is and where my loyalties should lie, given what I do. But I don't, Dad. I fully understand and appreciate the oath I took six years ago. But I've got a bad feeling about all this, and I trust my gut."

"As you should, son. What about your visit to the hospital?" Bill asked, switching gears. "How'd that go?"

Troy glanced out the cab's window at the airport tower in the distance, aware that he'd hit a sensitive topic for his father. You were *always* loyal to the president as far as Bill was concerned. Full stop—which was what made that question he'd considered asking a few moments ago so compelling.

"It was kind of strange, in a couple of ways."

"How?"

"The doctor said something interesting."

"What?"

"He said the woman was shot in the back from point-blank range."

"That's ridiculous. Those attacks were spray-and-away deals. We know that."

"That's what I told him."

"But?"

"She has two bullet wounds, one in her shoulder and one in her back. The doctor figures the wound in her shoulder was caused by a bullet fired from an automatic weapon during the initial burst. But he thinks the second one, the one in the middle of her back, was made by a bullet from a pistol that was literally pressed against her body when it was fired." Troy waited for a response or a reaction from the other end of the connection, but nothing came. "Dad?"

"Yeah, was there anything else?"

"The doctor said the wound in the middle of her back came from a one-in-a-million shot."

More dead air from the other end. What the hell?

"What did he mean by that?" Bill finally asked.

"That the wound should have killed her. Several vital organs are located right around the area where the bullet entered her body, but it didn't hit any of them. It was like the bullet had eyes in terms of avoiding anything life-threatening. Hell, he said I'll probably be able to talk to her in a couple of days."

"Huh."

"I put bodyguards outside her room. I don't want the terrorists sneaking into the hospital to finish the job."

"Good idea."

"Who knows, Dad? Maybe she saw something that'll help us catch the bastards."

"Did you tell the guys you put in there to shoot to wound if there's an attempt?"

"Absolutely. They get it. We'll want to interrogate that guy immediately, and they understand that."

"Did you tell them to get the guy out of there fast? We don't want local authorities or any of the Feds getting him, because they won't use the right techniques to assure answers."

"The guys I put there to protect her understand, believe me, Dad. They've got a van in the hospital parking lot, and they know exactly who to call and where to take anyone they snare."

"So, what's his name?"

"Who?"

"The doctor."

That was an odd question. "Uh, I think it was Harrison. Why?"

"I may want to talk to him."

"Why would you want to—"

"You said there was something else," Bill kept going. "You said your visit to the hospital was strange in a couple of ways. What was the other thing?"

Troy hesitated. The airport was getting close. Maybe now wasn't the time to go into this.

"Son?"

"The woman who was shot," Troy answered hesitantly.

"What about her?"

"She . . . she reminds me of Lisa." Troy took a deep breath. "She actually looks like Lisa."

"Don't beat yourself up, son. I know where you're going with this."

Troy hadn't expected that. He'd been ready for a tough response or no interest at all. "I'm not. It's just—"

"There's nothing you could have done for Lisa. You were on a mission for your country. You were thrown off the *Arctic Fire*. You were fighting for your own life. You couldn't have saved hers. You were thousands of miles away when she was killed."

"She was killed because she knew me, Dad. I can't ignore that."

"We don't know that for sure."

"I do."

"She could have stepped in front of a bus on Fifth Avenue, Troy. People die in many ways for many reasons. It was her time. I know you think it was Maddux, but it might not have been. We simply don't know for sure, and you can't assume anything. It could have been just a random act of violence. Her neighborhood wasn't great."

"Come on, Dad."

"You can't get mired down in the emotion of it. It wasn't your fault. You have to put it out of your mind."

"Yeah, but . . ."

"But what?"

Troy heard impatience creeping into his father's voice for the first time, but he had to say this. He had to hear himself say it. "I loved Lisa."

"You barely knew her."

"I barely know anyone, Dad." The words had come from his mouth without his even thinking about them. "I don't have time. I never stay in one place long enough."

"Son, you've got to—"

"We had a connection. It was real. I . . . I was actually thinking about asking her to marry me, and not just because of L.J." The cab slowed down as it pulled up to the Dulles main terminal. This was the hard part. "I told her I was completely committed to her before I took off. But I . . . well, I was with a woman in Mexico before I went to Alaska." He hated himself for that. "I can't believe I did that." The silence was deafening. Maybe he shouldn't have said that.

"I know how you feel," Bill finally spoke up quietly. "I understand. In fact, I more than understand."

Unbelievable. Troy had *never* gotten that kind of compassion out of the old man—or that kind of subtle though clear admission to committing a wrong himself.

"Troy?"

"Yes, sir?"

"Don't get killed tonight. You hear me? You come back safe."

"I will."

"Your mother couldn't handle it if you were gone, too. She just lost one son. She can't lose another."

Troy smiled wryly. He'd never heard this kind of worry from his father, either.

"Troy?"

"Yes, sir?"

"I couldn't handle it, either." Bill paused several seconds. "There, I said it."

After climbing out of the cab Troy was still distracted by the conversation with his father. For a few seconds he didn't notice anything unusual as he walked into the terminal. Finally it hit him, and he stopped to take it in. The show of force inside the terminal was incredible. He'd never seen so many police and military personnel in a U.S. airport at one time. Many of them had their weapons drawn as they moved about the huge building, even though there was no immediate emergency.

Life in the United States had changed forever.

MADDUX HAD taken nearly an hour to thoroughly clean up the basement of the Pennsylvania house. Not that anyone official would ever come looking for anything, but he wanted to make certain the place was spotless out of respect for the associate who'd made the site available. The man wouldn't have been very happy if he'd known what had happened here today. But fortunately, he hadn't asked, so Maddux hadn't needed to lie. Besides, Maddux had taken care of an abusive fiancé for the man—permanently—so what was he really going to say? He had the man by the balls, and they both knew it. And the man had to know Maddux wasn't using the house for R&R.

Maddux chuckled. That was always a problem with getting into bed with the devil. It felt good at first, but there was no such thing as divorce when it started feeling bad.

He liked being the devil. He always had. And you had to like a job to do it well.

Imelda's interrogation had ended up yielding nothing of significance except the fascinating revelation that she'd recognized Jack Jensen's name. What she'd said was irrelevant—that she did recognize it. She could easily have been lying. It was the look in her beaten eyes that was important. They couldn't lie, and they told the same story. Imelda *had* recognized the name.

She hadn't told him anything more, and he'd done everything in his power to get her to talk. He'd done things to her that most men he'd tortured hadn't been able to stand up to and had quickly begun to babble information to try to stop the horrible suffering they were enduring any way they could. In some cases, those men had been tough intelligence officers, even battle-tested terrorists.

He admired her for that—just as he admired her for allowing her child to die in front of her rather than yield information. Too bad she was on the wrong side of this fight. She would have been a valuable addition to his team.

In the end he'd strangled Imelda and stared deeply into her eyes as her life's light faded while she'd strained pitifully against the ropes binding her to the chair. He always stared deeply into his victim's eyes at the end. He thought maybe he'd see the answer to it all as the last breath left the body. He hadn't so far, but he wouldn't stop looking.

This house was two hundred miles from Manassas, Virginia, where Maddux had kidnapped the family. And it was completely isolated in a dense pine forest. So he was confident that the odds of anyone showing up here as part of an investigation into the disappearance of Imelda and her child were zero.

Despite Maddux's confidence that tonight's murders would remain forever unsolved, he'd taken extra precautions to ensure it. He'd cleaned everything twice and buried the bodies in a pre-dug grave forty miles to the west on a lonely ridge before returning to the house to make absolutely certain everything was perfect. He wanted it to shine when the associate arrived next time with his wife. The man was showing amazing loyalty by continuing to support him even though Bill Jensen had put out the word to stop. And the man's wife was obsessive about neatness. He definitely didn't want her finding anything down here.

Three of the twenty associates were still supporting him, despite Bill's warning. It was the pinnacle of loyalty as far as Maddux was concerned. Of course, he'd done those personal favors for two of them, so their loyalty couldn't be held in the highest regard. There had been quid pro quos in those instances. But he hadn't actually done anything for the third associate who was remaining loyal. That man just believed everything Maddux told him—probably because he was too scared not to.

The great thing was that the three associates who were still secretly supporting him had homes in enough places around the world to keep him operating efficiently and effectively. More important, they were supplying him with cash as well. There'd been a suitcase waiting for Maddux in an upstairs bedroom with ten thousand dollars in it. That would tide him and his followers over for a while. And there would be more money to follow, he'd been assured.

He pulled his cell phone from his pocket and made certain the incoming number was familiar before answering.

"Are you serious?" Maddux clenched his jaw. "All right," he muttered angrily. "I'll call you back in a little while."

He slid the phone back into his pocket, grabbed the suitcase full of cash off the dining room table, and hustled for the door. Ryan O'Hara was dead. The bodies of O'Hara and the young man who had accompanied him had been found in a clearing in the Delaware woods outside Wilmington. The clearing was a mile from where Harry Boyd's body was found alongside a white van.

Suddenly Maddux needed to get to North Carolina quickly. A leisurely drive south from Pennsylvania had turned into a sprint. If he pushed, he might make the farm by midnight.

CHAPTER 15

NIGHT HAD fallen on central North Carolina some time ago. Even though Troy and the two men who were with him had been here for a while, they continued to watch and wait. They wanted to be as sure as possible of the enemy's numbers before they attacked. Being outnumbered wouldn't stop them—unless they determined that the defending force was overwhelming. They simply wanted to be as prepared as possible.

The location they'd chosen for their reconnaissance was a large, flat rock atop a slight ridge just inside a tree line several hundred yards west of the sprawling horse farm's main house. Cover and visibility were good. Unfortunately, so far, their recon wasn't paying dividends. They were ninety percent certain the mission's target was on the property. But that was the extent of what they knew, and there were several buildings to consider as objectives. Two vehicles had come and gone since they'd taken up this position beneath a grove of tall oak trees several hours ago, but they'd gleaned little from the activity. People had gotten out of the vehicles and gone into the main house. The same people had come back out a few minutes later and driven off.

After reboarding the Jensen G450 at Dulles Airport outside Washington, Troy had made the short flight south to Raleigh, where he'd met the two men who were with him tonight. They were also RCS agents—from the Counterterrorism Division. Bill had arranged everything after assuring Troy that both men were loyal to Red Cell Seven and nothing else—that there was no risk whatsoever of their being somehow secretly allied with Shane Maddux.

Troy had never met them before, didn't know their names and didn't want to—just as it was clear they didn't want to know his. These men were members of a different RCS division; it was safer to partition sensitive information such as real names as much as possible, and all three of them understood that. It was how they'd been trained from day one.

Tonight Troy's code name was Agent Montana, and the other two men were Agents Idaho and Wyoming.

The main house was a large, three-story brick structure ringed by a halo of tall maple trees. A hundred yards to the other side of the house from where they were hiding were two barns and a guest cabin. Between the tree line and the house were open pastures with blanket-wrapped horses grazing beneath what was a star-laden but, as yet, moonless sky. Once they left the cover of the trees and started crossing that pasture, they would be vulnerable to anyone watching the open ground with night-vision capability. And it wasn't a stretch to suspect that people in the houses or the barns would have that capability. In fact, it was almost a given.

Another vehicle—the third of the evening—moved quickly up the long, paved driveway from the left and skidded to a stop in the circular driveway before the house. The headlights remained on and the engine continued to run while Troy watched through his night-vision glasses. Two men climbed out of the older SUV and hurried inside. A few moments later what looked to be the same two emerged from the house, climbed back into the SUV, and drove back down the driveway.

When the taillights disappeared, Troy scanned the shadowy horizon before him from left to right. The nearest house that was not part of the farm was a mile away, and behind him were fifty thousand acres of national forest. The sounds of gunfire wouldn't be audible to neighbors if a battle broke out, which was good. Red Cell Seven did not want interference from local law enforcement.

He glanced up at the sky. A full moon would be rising within the hour. Yesterday's storm had cleared out of the East Coast and been replaced by a high-pressure system that had fallen out of western Canada. Temperatures had dropped along with it—drastically. Gusts accompanying the system had nighttime windchills in the low twenties as far south as Georgia. They were a day late, Troy figured. The gusts and the cold didn't bother him, but clouds and rain would have made much better cover for tonight.

"All we really know is there's been no net increase in manpower," Troy said quietly. "Of course, we still have no idea how many people were on the property when we got here." He gestured at the sky. The horizon off to the left was already starting to brighten. "We're gonna have a lot more light on the matter very soon."

"I say we go," Agent Idaho suggested.

"Absolutely," Agent Wyoming agreed.

Troy hopped down from the rock and grabbed the Heckler & Koch MP5 submachine gun leaning against a tree. It was the same type of weapon the other two men would be carrying. He'd brought all three guns and plenty of extra clips with him on the G450 into Raleigh. That was another advantage of flying private, along with coming and going whenever you wanted. You could carry guns on board and not have to worry about it.

The MP5 used 9mm rounds, which would be largely ineffective against body armor. However, Troy and the other men were not trained to shoot at center mass—between the throat and waist—as most law-enforcement and military personnel were. RCS agents were trained to fire at the head, because most individuals didn't wear helmets in situations they were involved with. A head shot was obviously more difficult, but also much more effective.

All three submachine guns were outfitted with sound suppressors, which slightly reduced the velocity of the round and therefore its effectiveness, but Troy was willing to give up a certain amount of firepower in exchange for stealth. Hopefully they could neutralize the individuals inside without using guns. But if it turned out otherwise, these weapons outfitted as they were would enable them to pick off enemies one at a time without alerting others. All three guns were also equipped with dual magazine clamps.

"All right, let's go."

As the men broke from the trees and approached the tall, four-slat fence, they spread the distance between themselves to make for more difficult targets in case they were being glassed.

"Just confirming we have full license from COC tonight," Agent Idaho called over in a low voice as they dropped down off the fence and began jogging toward the main house. "Is that correct?"

"That is correct," Troy confirmed. "If you acquire a target and you believe you are in danger, shoot to kill. Don't bother asking about intentions."

"Roger."

Troy motioned to Agent Idaho by tapping his right ear. Then he veered off from the other two men until he was fifty feet away and then flipped a switch on his belt that engaged the mobile intercom system they were using tonight. "Testing Idaho, come in, Idaho."

"I got you, Montana."

"Testing Wyoming, come in, Wyoming."

"I got you too, Montana."

Troy veered back toward the other two men as they headed across the field past three horses grazing peacefully on the scraggly grass. He glanced at his watch. It was after midnight.

THE FORD EXPLORER was ten years old and looked every bit its age. The fenders were rusty, its dark blue paint was chipped and fading, and the front seats were in desperate need of reupholstering—the cloth covers were ripped, coffee stained, cigarette burned, and smelled like mildew. But the truck could flat-out fly. Maddux kept the engine and the transmission in perfect condition. He always kept pristine what couldn't be seen. It was one of his "live by" rules. He believed that things that couldn't be seen were much more important than things that could. Image was unimportant. Effectiveness was everything.

Too bad he couldn't fully take advantage of the vehicle's speed tonight, he thought as he came out of a long, gentle left-hand curve in the middle of the North Carolina countryside east of Raleigh. He couldn't risk being pulled over. Not with all the guns in the back. Some bored hillbilly cop might want to search the vehicle for anything he could plunder. Then there'd be an ugly incident. Maddux didn't have any problem with killing a cop if he was getting in the way of what the country needed. It was the time being pulled over would take up that would be the problem. As far as he was concerned, time was life's most precious gift and was never to be wasted.

It had been a long trip from Pennsylvania, and his interrogation of Imelda seemed like days ago now. He couldn't shake the fact that she'd watched her child die without giving up any important information. He had no doubt that she was involved in the mall attacks somehow, or at least knew a great deal about them. But she hadn't said a word. She was an amazing patriot—for the enemy.

Maddux glanced at his watch. It was after midnight. He'd make the Kohler family farm in ten minutes.

A SOLITARY individual, tagged Agent Bridger for the evening, knelt in the thick brush beneath the tree line fifty yards north of where Troy and the other two men had been watching and waiting. Agent Bridger grabbed the nightscope off the ground and watched as Troy and the other two men jumped the fence and headed across the field past the horses toward the main house of the farm.

Troy had no idea he was being watched, but that was for the best. Hopefully there would be no need to intervene. Hopefully everything would go smoothly and Troy would rescue Major Travers without incident.

Agent Bridger stowed the night-vision glasses. It was time to follow Troy and the other two agents. Staying here wouldn't help them if things got hot in one of the buildings across the pastures.

TROY AND the other two men had searched the cabin and the first barn. There was no one in the cabin and nothing in the smaller barn except two horses. After rapidly overpowering a lone individual in the second, larger barn, they'd hog-tied and gagged him. Troy was fairly sure the guy had no idea what was going on. But it was better to neutralize him and come back later, after the fireworks were done, if there were any. So they'd stuffed a rag in his mouth and left him in a corner of a stall with a big mare who looked terrified, too.

Now they were headed for the main house.

A covered porch wrapped around all four sides of the huge home. As they burst out from behind three old maple trees and raced up the wide set of stairs at the back of the structure, a silhouette appeared at the door and fired. The lone bullet missed, and whoever had just fired disappeared. Surprise was no longer in their corner. The sound suppressors on the MP5s had quickly become irrelevant.

Shrill, muffled voices rose from inside as Troy pressed himself against the bricks beside a window. With the butt of the MP5 he broke out several panes of glass. Then he unloaded his first clip of twenty-five rounds into the darkened room beyond with an across-and-back motion. He had no desire to be shot at, but, in a way, he was glad that person at the door had fired first without yelling out for any ID. They were completely justified now. No question.

As Troy quickly switched clips on his gun, Agents Idaho and Wyoming crashed through what was left of the window. When the new clip snapped into place on the underside of the barrel, he dove through the window and rolled, following the other men into what turned out to be a large formal dining room. He scrambled to his feet and quickly glassed the area. It wasn't much of a dining room anymore. Everything was basically shot to hell.

He motioned to the other agents and then stabbed in the air at the curving double staircase to their right. They nodded and, with their submachine guns leading the way, raced for the steps. They had to make certain the upper floors were clear first. They couldn't have enemies trapping them in the basement, where they figured the target was—because as far as they could tell from the recon there were no exterior steps leading out of the basement and back up to the ground.

Troy pressed his back to the wall outside the large kitchen as Agents Idaho and Wyoming sprinted up opposite staircases, came together on the landing at the top, and then disappeared. Troy quickly became aware of how alone he was. For the next few minutes, as Idaho and Wyoming made certain the two floors above were clear, things could get dicey down here depending on the number of adversaries in the house. Because they definitely knew they were under attack now.

Troy kept the barrel of the gun swinging back and forth in front of him as he listened intently for any sounds of a battle breaking out above him.

MADDUX COULD feel the coming combat. He'd always had that sixth sense about battle. He figured any warrior worth his weight in gold on the field did.

He had no reason to believe anything was amiss. He'd received no alerts from the farm. But Bill Jensen must be aware by now that something was wrong, and had probably put three and three together.

As if on cue, Maddux's cell phone pinged. He grabbed it, scanned the SOS message, tossed the device back on the seat, swung the truck left into the farm's driveway, and jammed the accelerator to the floor. He'd made it in the nick of time.

CHAPTER 16

"MR. PRESIDENT?"

Dorn glanced away from the darkness outside the Oval Office. He'd been staring into it sadly for the last five minutes. "Yes, Stewart."

"Sir, it's after midnight." Baxter was leaning into the office from the corridor through the open door. He hadn't bothered knocking. After all, he was the chief of staff. There was no need for him to be bound by rules others had to obey. At this point he made most of the rules when it came to dealing with the president, and in many instances knew more about what was going on than the president. In fact, Dorn would be lost without him. No, the president wasn't going to say anything about violating protocol. He'd better not, anyway. "Why are you still awake? You need to get to bed."

"You sound like my mother, God rest her soul."

"Nevertheless."

The president shrugged. "I couldn't sleep. I didn't want to keep the First Lady up. I'd just toss and turn."

"You need your rest, sir. With all due respect, the First Lady can rest anytime she wants to. Maybe it's her duty to stay awake with you and keep you company once in a while if you need that." Baxter hesitated. "She wasn't shot in the chest a few weeks ago, either."

Dorn shook his head at Baxter's audacity. "Come in, Stewart." He motioned at the chair in front of the desk. "Sit down. I can't believe I'm saying this, but I could actually use your company right now."

As Baxter walked across the eagle, he glanced at the pretty, young African American nurse who was sitting in a chair beside the president's temporary bed, reading a magazine. She looked up and smiled sincerely, but he didn't acknowledge her. He didn't have the bandwidth to get to know everyone in Washington, DC.

"What's bothering you, sir?" Baxter asked as he eased into the chair.

"What do you think is bothering me, Stewart? Christ."

"Of course, but what part of it is bothering you so much that you can't sleep? Which," Baxter continued quietly after he'd leaned slightly forward so the nurse couldn't hear him, "I feel it's my duty to inform you, could ultimately affect your judgment very negatively. And therefore negatively affect the lives of three hundred and sixty million people in the United States of America. Not to mention another six-point-four billion people outside this country."

Dorn gave Baxter a prickly grimace. "It's been nearly a day and a half, Stewart, and we have no leads. Law-enforcement departments around the country have gotten thousands of tips about suspicious people in hotels, motels, apartments, houses, schools, and malls, but none of those tips have led to anything, much less arrests. We don't know who's committing the attacks, we don't know who's behind the attacks, and we don't know what they want."

"Begging your pardon, sir, but we know exactly what they want. In the short run, they want to disrupt our way of life. In the long run, they want to destroy it."

"The point is, Stewart, Americans are terrified to leave their homes. People are dying, our economy is grinding to a halt, and I can't seem to do a damn thing about it."

"Patience, sir."

"Patience?" the president asked incredulously. "Are you serious?"

"We're doing everything we can, Mr. President," Baxter said confidently. "Everyone's involved at the federal level who should be involved, and they're all completely focused. The FBI, Homeland Security, CIA domestic assets, and the DNI are all putting everything they possibly can into this crisis. My staff and I are making absolutely certain of that on a minute-by-minute basis. My staffers are constantly in touch with those people."

"It's not getting us anywhere."

"It hasn't even been thirty-six hours, sir. We will find the people who are responsible for these crimes quickly and bring them to justice. I promise."

"You do? Really?"

"Yes."

"Quickly?"

"Yes."

"Oh, now I feel better."

"Sir, I—"

"'Quickly' would have been today, Stewart."

"You can't expect miracles, Mr. President."

"Why not?" Dorn snapped. "The taxpayers spend over a trillion dollars a year on defense and homeland security at the federal level, and who knows how much more on local law enforcement. Damn it, I have to expect miracles." He was seething. "The American public demands that I expect miracles in this situation. And they should."

"Easy, sir." The strain had to be incredible, and Dorn was just letting off steam. That's all this was. "We're doing everything in our power. No one can second-guess you."

Dorn slammed his open palm down on the desk so it banged loudly and the nurse jumped. "I don't care about being second-guessed," he said. "I don't care about perceptions or using this situation to our advantage politically or blaming the Republicans for it somehow. I just want arrests. I want this to stop."

"I'm doing everything I can for you, sir."

Dorn shut his eyes tightly. "I know you are, Stewart," he agreed softly. He moaned and ran his fingers through his dark hair. "I'm sorry. I didn't mean to come down on you so hard."

"It's all right. I know it wasn't personal. I know you're feeling it."

The president shook his head forlornly. "Those bastards shot elementary school children today, Stewart, six- and seven-year-old defenseless *children*."

"It doesn't get any worse than that, sir."

"And we didn't catch the bastards."

"No we didn't."

"There was an armed guard on duty."

"Those kinds of guards aren't equipped to take on what hit that elementary school today. That man had no chance."

"Children were mowed down at that school by submachine guns."

Baxter nodded. "I know," he agreed quietly. "It's . . . well, it's just awful."

"And do you know what the worst part of it is?"

"Well, I—"

"They didn't shoot themselves when it was over because they felt so horrible for what they'd done. This wasn't some kind of onetime, wild-rage event uncorked by years of bullying or mental illness or a fight with a spouse. This was a cold-blooded, calculated attack by assassins who right now are probably picking their next target, which might be a home, a store, even a church or a synagogue."

"I hear you, sir."

Dorn glanced at his laptop, which sat on his desk. It was still open to the page he'd been studying before he turned around in his wheelchair to stare out into the darkness out of despair. "Do you remember the DC Snipers, Stewart?"

"Of course. That happened in 2002. I believe it was in October of that year, specifically. I remember it very well. I was down on K Street doing the lobbying thing. It was my last year doing that." Baxter prided himself on his steel-trap memory. He worked at it, too. In what little spare time he could find, he finished crossword and Sudoku puzzles with a passion because a neurosurgeon friend had told him the brain was like a muscle in a way and puzzle workouts were very good for the memory area. "And if I'm not mistaken, you were a junior congressman from Vermont who was excessively worried about global warming, the spotted owl, and rain forests in Brazil."

"Bravo, Stewart." The president clapped several times slowly. "You have an amazing memory."

"Thank you, sir."

Baxter appreciated Dorn's recognizing that, even if he was being sarcastic about how he did it. The president wasn't nearly as effusive in his praise about it as Baxter believed he should have been. He wasn't as effusive in his praise about a lot of things his COS did as he should have been. But he was getting better, and they'd only been working together for a few weeks. Another week or two and the president would be acting more respectfully.

"There were two of them," Baxter continued. "John Allen Muhammad was forty-one years old, and Lee Boyd Malvo was just seventeen. They were basically a couple of coward drifters who murdered innocent civilians with a hunting rifle from long range. They shot people in Maryland, Virginia, and the District of Columbia as the victims were coming out of restaurants and stores, filling up their cars at gas stations, or just sitting at a bus stop. They used Muhammad's car as a moving sniper's nest. The kid would lie in the back of the vehicle on his stomach and shoot through a hole in the trunk where the keyhole was. They cut away part of the backseat so he could do that. Then Muhammad would drive away as soon as Malvo had shot someone."

"Yes, that's right."

"Muhammad was executed by lethal injection in 2009," Baxter continued, "and Malvo was found guilty of multiple murders and is in prison for life with absolutely no chance of parole. He was spared the death penalty because of his age at the time of the killings." Baxter shook his head sadly. "What happened to their victims is terrible, Mr. President. But at the end of the day, the system worked."

"Did it?"

"What do you mean?"

"You said it yourself."

"What? What did I say, Mr. President?"

"You said they were a couple of coward drifters."

"So?"

"Do you remember how long it took to catch them?"

Baxter pushed his lower lip out as he thought about it for a few moments. "It was no more than a week."

"It was twenty-three days, Stewart."

"Oh." Baxter glanced at the young nurse. She was staring down at her book, but she didn't seem to be reading. Her eyes weren't moving. They seemed locked on one spot on the page in front of her.

"And," the president went on, "right up until the end, right up until a concerned citizen called the police about two guys he happened to notice sleeping in a rest stop on Interstate Seventy, eighty miles west of here, late one night because he thought they looked suspicious, everyone believed those maniacs were riding around in a white van. Well, it turned out they were driving a blue Chevy Caprice." Dorn gestured at the laptop. "The point is that two drifters with no money and very little sanity completely avoided capture for twenty-three days while they murdered ten people and critically injured three more in a fairly small and congested geographic area of this country. And all that time the FBI, the Virginia state police, the Maryland state police, the DC police, and who knows how many other county and local law-enforcement personnel were looking everywhere for them." He paused. "But they couldn't find them. The cops set up roadblocks, they went door to door in some neighborhoods, they begged for the public's help. But they still couldn't find them. It took a lucky glance by a concerned citizen. Otherwise those two might still be out there killing people." The president put a hand to his chest, to where the bullet O'Hara had fired had entered his body. "The men who attacked our country yesterday and today are members of well-trained, well-supplied death squads. I'm convinced of that. They aren't drifters with a few dollars left in their wallets." Dorn's voice was shaking. "If it took George Bush more than three weeks and a lucky break to find the DC Snipers, how in the hell am I *ever* going to find the assassins who shot up eleven malls and killed all those children in Missouri?"

Baxter glanced at the nurse again as Dorn ended his speech. It was obvious she wasn't reading her book anymore. She wasn't even trying to fake it. She was staring at the president openmouthed.

"Excuse me, Miss," Baxter said.

Her eyes raced to his. She was mortified to have been caught staring at Dorn so hard. "Yes, sir?"

"Please leave us." The woman stood up immediately and bolted for the door. She didn't protest at all. "Stay right outside the office," Baxter called as she hurried out. "Don't go far."

"Yes, sir," she called back as she closed the door behind her.

"Mr. President—"

"I should have completely backed Red Cell Seven right from the beginning," the president interrupted. "I should have given them everything they wanted."

"No way," Baxter retorted. "They're cowboys. They're going to get you in very bad trouble if you don't do something about them. They're a cancer on your presidency. They could end up bringing you down."

"If I'd shown them more support, this damn thing might never have happened. They might have found out about these death squads and stopped them before they ever got started."

Baxter rose slowly out of his chair. His heart was suddenly pounding. He had to do this. "I must tell you something very important, sir."

"What is it?"

"You need to understand that what I'm about to say comes from a friend I've known and trusted for a very long time. He's been in this town a long time, and he's always been right when he's told me something like this."

"What is it?" Dorn demanded again.

Baxter took a deep breath as he put his hands down on the front of the president's desk and leaned over it. "Shane Maddux wasn't operating on his own in Los Angeles, Mr. President."

Dorn's eyes narrowed. "How do you even know who Shane Maddux is?"

"Don't worry about it, sir," Baxter snapped. "Worry about this instead." He leaned even farther over the great desk and pointed at the president. "The order to assassinate you came from well above Maddux. It came from Bill Jensen."

Dorn gazed at Baxter for several moments. Finally he shook his head slowly in total disbelief. "You're wrong, Stewart. Bill Jensen is a fine man, a man of principle. He would never be involved in something like that. That's ridiculous."

Baxter rose back up off the desk and raised one eyebrow. "Is it, Mr. President? Is it really that ridiculous?" He hesitated. "Or does it make perfect sense? Is that what's really bothering you tonight?"

"What are you saying?"

"I gave you those background checks covering Bill and Troy before they got here yesterday. I know you read them. You read everything I send you."

"So?"

"So you saw that section in the report about Rita Hayes, Bill's executive assistant at First Manhattan. She'd been with him for a long time before she disappeared a few weeks ago. And they had been intimate. They had sexual relations, and the information I have is that she was about to tell Bill's wife, Cheryl, what was going on. And then she disappeared."

Dorn gazed up at Baxter but said nothing.

"Now no one can find Rita Hayes." Baxter leaned back down over the desk. "Are you still going to tell me that Bill Jensen is a fine man?"

CHAPTER 17

TROY KEPT moving through the spacious first floor, swinging the hot end of the MP5 from side to side as he cruised forward. He had to make absolutely certain there was only one stairway to the basement from this floor of the house and that this level was completely clear of resistance.

"Come in, Idaho," he muttered. "What's going on up there?"

"We're going through the last couple of rooms on level three, and then we're good to go. Wyoming's going through the attic right now."

"Well, hurry up. It's getting kind of— *Jesus!*"

Someone darted from left to right in front of him, at the far end of the long hallway he'd just turned down for the second time. The warm body raced through the living room to Troy's right and continued out of the house after bursting through the front door.

Troy had almost fired, but managed to hold up at the last instant. He hadn't tapped the target because he couldn't make out a weapon and the guy wasn't acting in a hostile manner. In fact, he was running away as fast as he could. The red-orange image in the upper left-hand corner of Troy's left lens was quickly growing smaller through the living room window, and they weren't in the business of killing civilians.

It sounded awful, but sometimes that made this job very hard. Facing live-or-die snap decisions was an inevitable part of this life, and you could never be a hundred percent sure of the target's intention if you fired first. Troy had been trained to err on the side of protecting himself, but occasionally the training didn't kick in. Hesitating could cost him his life one day. That was an inevitable reality. Worse, it might cost someone else theirs.

Troy kept reminding himself that they weren't a hundred percent certain Wilson Travers was even here. He'd only been quoted ninety percent, and that terrified expression on the face of the guy they'd tied up a few minutes ago in the barn kept haunting him. The guy had no idea what was happening, it was obvious. Travers might be a thousand miles from here by now—or dead.

Even at ninety percent confidence, this could all be a massive snafu, and the individual who'd fired at them as they were coming up the porch steps might have done so in self-defense, thinking this was a home invasion. It was probably that guy who just took off—which meant the cops were on their way. Unless there were people here who didn't want cops involved, and that guy was a defector.

Troy took a deep breath as he pushed forward. There were always so many possibilities and unknowns—and so many opportunities to make wrong decisions. Wrong decisions here didn't result in getting fired or being docked a week's pay. This was life and death. Civilians didn't understand that—they couldn't.

"You okay, Montana?"

"Yes," Troy answered. "Just hurry up, will you? We're probably on the clock at this point. Somebody just took off out of here like a bat out of hell."

"Oh, yeah?"

"Yeah, but no worries. He was a civilian."

"You sure?"

"Yeah." Troy really had no idea, but they had to finish this thing off. Rescuing Travers was that important, for one crucial reason that he couldn't relate to the other agents—because he didn't know himself. It was that classified. "Just get down here."

"We're close."

Troy suddenly had a very bad feeling. He hated it when that happened, because he was usually right.

He swung around and aimed when he thought he felt a pair of eyes burning into his back—but there was nothing behind him except an empty hallway. He exhaled heavily. "Stay cool," he muttered, "stay cool."

Agent Idaho broke back onto the IC. "All right, all right, we're done. All clear upstairs."

Troy hustled back to the base of the double staircase outside the dining room as the other two agents hustled down the same side toward him, one after the other.

"They've got to be in the basement," Idaho said, "if they're here at all."

"But there's no exterior exit out of the house from down there. No steps from down there back up to ground level. We confirmed that before we came in. And I can only find one set of stairs to the basement here on the first floor. Any overlap stairs up there?" Troy asked, pointing up with his thumb. "Were there any stairs from levels two or three that skip this floor?"

"No, and we checked everything including closets."

Troy shook his head. "Why would they trap themselves down there?" This didn't feel right. Something was wrong.

Wyoming shrugged. "Quid pro quo?"

"Explain that, will you, Caesar?"

"They're letting us come down. They're going to negotiate their way out once we're down there. They're gonna use Travers as trade bait for freedom. We surprised them, and now they have no choice. *He* has no choice," Wyoming added. "He has to negotiate."

Troy shook his head. That didn't sound right, either. "We won't negotiate. He must know that." Troy gestured ahead. "Come on, let's do it, but careful as we go. This could be an ambush. Maybe that's why they're holing up in the basement."

The three men hustled down the hall to the basement door and then descended the steps quickly, spreading out as soon as they reached the bottom of the stairs, ready for anything.

MADDUX SPRINTED UP the porch stairs. As he crossed the wide wooden slats, he marveled at how silent he was, even as he moved quickly. If he'd been a heavy man, the boards would be creaking and groaning and they might hear him down in the basement. Yes, it was good to be small.

He knew they were down there because he'd just gotten another text—the last one he would receive, he was sure. By now his partner had almost certainly been captured and they were in the process of freeing Travers. But that was fine.

Maddux chuckled softly as he headed down. They hadn't planned it this way, but it was working out perfectly. Timing wasn't everything in life. Training, skill, and smarts were the primary keys to success. But timing was still damn important.

THE ONLY thing Troy and the other two RCS agents encountered at the bottom of the basement stairs was Nathan Kohler. He stood in front of a small but solid-looking prison cell with his arms folded across his chest defiantly—unarmed. Behind Kohler and the narrowly spaced, vertical iron bars was Wilson Travers, who was chained to one wall of the cell by his neck.

Troy recognized Kohler immediately. He was an arrogant prick. Worse, he was a bigot. He didn't flaunt his racial hatred, but it wasn't hard to detect if you dug only slightly below the surface. Especially after a few beers, which Troy'd had the unfortunate opportunity to share with Kohler a month after Kohler had joined the Falcons. The only reason Kohler had gotten into RCS, Bill had explained to Troy last night, was because of his father, Douglas Kohler. Until his death a few months ago, Douglas Kohler had been the senior United States senator from North Carolina—and a Red Cell Seven associate.

As in all walks of life and no matter how hard they tried to avoid it, Troy thought regretfully as he stared at the blond young man, a few bad apples managed to make it through into RCS. For the most part it was an amazing crew of good and dedicated people. But over the last six years Troy had met three or four men he could have done without—Nathan Kohler being one of them.

"Open the cell door, Nathan," Troy ordered. He recognized Travers, too. Travers had indeed been the man Troy had delivered cash and instructions to in Greece. "Let Travers out."

Troy gestured at the lock on the cell door. "Come on, hurry up." He wanted to get out fast. They'd leave Kohler locked in the cell and then make an anonymous call when they were far enough away so someone could come and get the kid out. "*Now,* Nathan."

Agent Idaho covered Kohler with his MP5 while Agent Wyoming covered the stairs in case anyone tried coming down from the first floor. Neither of them had fired a shot yet, so each man had a full magazine as well as another full clip in the clamp alongside the active one.

"Why'd you do this?" Troy asked. Time was of the essence, but he wanted to know. "Why'd you turn on the cell?"

"Fuck you and your father. The nigger stays where he is."

Troy shook his head in disbelief. Bill and Douglas Kohler must have been *very* good friends. "We have full license from COC tonight, Nathan."

"You mean from your father."

"Do you understand what that means?"

"It means you can screw me—"

"It means I have the authority to use any and all force necessary to get Major Travers out of here. It means I can kill you if I want to."

"Yeah, well, fuck yourself. Go ahead and shoot me."

Troy moved to where Kohler was standing and held his hand out. "Give me the keys. I don't have time for this."

"I'm not giving you—"

Troy hammered Kohler's gut with the butt of his gun and sent the kid groaning and sprawling to the cement floor. Kohler coiled into a fetal position as Troy leaned down, rolled the kid to one side, and grabbed the set of keys beneath him.

As Troy rose back up, he was aware of Agent Idaho falling limply to the floor, followed immediately by Agent Wyoming. They'd both been shot through the head. Blood was already pouring onto the floor from gaping wounds just above their ears. They weren't even twitching, the shots had been so perfect.

Then there was a blade at Troy's throat.

"Hello, Mr. Jensen," came a calm voice from behind him.

Shane Maddux. Troy recognized the voice immediately. The man had been his superior for six years. Now he knew who had turned Nathan Kohler against Red Cell Seven.

"Hello, Shane."

How did Maddux *do* it? Travers and Kohler had been the only other people down here—Troy had believed. He and Agent Wyoming had checked the entire basement thoroughly—while Idaho had watched Kohler—and there were no stairs other than the ones the three of them had descended from the first floor. Now Troy understood why Kohler hadn't resisted or tried to run. Maddux wanted them all down here.

"No formal address?" Maddux asked. "No more Major Maddux?"

"You don't deserve a formal—"

"Drop the gun, Troy."

Troy allowed the submachine gun to slip from his right hand where it had been hanging next to his leg. It clattered to the floor.

There was no point resisting. Maddux was far too good a killer. If he sensed the slightest defiance, that blade beneath Troy's chin would slice his throat, and nothing much else would matter after that.

"Pick up the gun, Nathan," Maddux ordered sharply. "Get up. Stop feeling sorry for yourself."

Kohler crawled to where Troy's MP5 lay, grabbed it, and groaned again as he struggled to pull himself to his feet.

"Open the cell, Nathan."

Kohler looked at Maddux like he was crazy. "What?"

"We're taking Major Travers with us." Maddux nodded at Travers. "Get him out of there. Make sure he's still cuffed before you let him out of the ring."

"Why are we taking him with us?" Kohler demanded as he grabbed the keys back from Troy and slid one of them into the lock.

"Major Travers has something very special I want. We need him to lead us to it."

Kohler swung the cell door open and moved to where Travers sat on a narrow bench. When he was satisfied the cuffs securing Travers's hands together behind his back were tight on both wrists, Kohler unlocked the metal collar around Travers's neck. The chain that connected the collar to the ring anchored into the wall snaked to the floor.

"Toss me that gun," Maddux ordered as Nathan followed Travers out of the cell.

Kohler bent down and grabbed the gun lying beside Agent Idaho's body, then lobbed it to Maddux. Maddux released Troy, caught the submachine gun, and quickly slid the knife back into a sheath on his belt.

Maddux motioned toward the cell with the gun. "Get in there, Troy."

"Not going to kill me?"

"I would," Maddux answered, "but I don't want to piss your father off now that he's calling the shots."

The explanation sounded hollow. Why would Maddux be worried about that? He'd killed Jack. He must know Bill was already out for revenge. "You killed Jack. You really think you could hurt my father more than you have?" And how would Maddux know that Bill was calling the shots at Red Cell Seven? He might assume, but he shouldn't know.

Maddux stared at Troy for several seconds like a statue, without breathing. Then he nodded subtly as his eyes narrowed. "So that's what you think. You think I killed Jack."

"I know you did, Shane."

"Of course," Maddux whispered to himself.

"You killed Lisa Martinez, too, along with my brother's friend."

"They saw my face. I had to kill them. It was a matter of national security."

It was insane, but for a moment Troy actually understood the explanation. For Shane Maddux that would have been a matter of national security because in Maddux's demented mind he probably considered himself the primary protector of the nation's security. "But you didn't kill my son. You didn't kill Little Jack. I wonder why."

"You know why."

Troy swallowed hard as he stared at Maddux.

"You didn't kill my son because you're loyal to me, Shane. We've been through hell and back together, and that's why you spared L.J. And that's why you aren't going to kill me now."

A sad grin crept to Maddux's lips. "I didn't kill your son because it wasn't necessary, Troy. How I feel about you had nothing to do with that decision. And it has nothing to do with why I'm letting you live tonight. Letting you live is strategic. I don't want to piss your father off." His eyes narrowed. "In fact, Troy, I don't care at all about you. You are simply an individual who served under my command, and that's as far as it goes. That's as far as it's ever gone. You should understand that. For your own good," he added somberly.

Troy started to speak, but Kohler slammed the butt of the MP5 he was clutching into Troy's gut and sent him tumbling to the floor in agony.

Kohler smiled down at Troy smugly. "How's it feel, you prick?"

Troy grabbed his stomach and tried desperately to breathe. He should have anticipated that one.

As Kohler bent down to drag Troy into the tiny cell, a bullet smashed into his chin, burst through his throat, and blew out the back of his neck.

As Kohler collapsed onto him, Troy saw Maddux pull a small silver ball from his belt and hurl it to the floor. The ball exploded on impact, and the room was instantly clogged with thick, pungent smoke. Troy grabbed the MP5 Kohler had just taken from him, hurled the kid's body aside, struggled to his feet, somehow found Travers in the haze, and then emptied the second magazine of the MP5 into the basement all around them. His stomach was still killing him, but adrenaline and the will to live overpowered the pain.

"I'm Troy Jensen," he yelled into Travers's ear from close range as he reached into his pack, grabbed another double set of magazines, and reloaded. "I was sent by COC to get you out of here." If he hadn't been a foot away from Travers when the bomb went off, he wouldn't have been able to identify him. The smoke had gotten that thick that fast. "We gotta get out of here. Stay close. Don't lose me."

As soon as the device Maddux hurled to the floor exploded, Agent Bridger raced back up the steps to the first floor, bolted for the front door, and then sprinted away past the tall maple trees. Bridger didn't stop running until after recrossing the pasture and making it back into the forest that bordered this side of the farm.

The agent was a former city police officer and knew how to handle a gun, had actually fired in self-defense twice on the streets. But Bridger had never shot anyone, much less taken a life.

Bridger rested against a tree and sucked in air while gazing back through the trees. No one had noticed Bridger sneak down the basement stairs with a pistol leading the way, least of all the poor man who was lying on the floor at the bottom of the stairs with blood pouring from a head wound. In the moment there had been no way to know if he was dead, and no way to check.

But the guy Bridger had shot, the blond one who'd hit Troy with the butt of the submachine gun, was definitely dead. Bridger had always pulled excellent marksman grades—and the bullet had nailed that guy who'd belted Troy. Then that little guy had detonated the smoke bomb, and chaos had ensued.

Agent Bridger leaned the MP5 against a tree and holstered the 9mm that had killed the guy in the basement. Bridger had grabbed the submachine gun off the floor before racing up the steps. It had been lying next to the guy with the head wound at the bottom of the stairs.

Bridger knelt down and took a deep breath.

Mentors on the police force had warned that the first kill was always tough to handle. They were right. Taking a human life, no matter who it was, had a powerful impact on anyone with a conscience.

It had been the right thing to do. Killing that guy had saved Troy's life. But somehow that didn't make the death any easier to accept.

Karen wiped the tears from her face, picked up the MP5, and kept going through the trees.

"Why did you leave me, Jack?" she whispered as she moved across the dead leaves blanketing the forest floor. "I miss you so damn much."

PART 3

CHAPTER 18

JACOB GADANZ swung his five-year-old metallic brown Honda Accord into a narrow, unmarked parking space of the Manassas, Virginia, industrial park. This location was twenty miles from Tysons Corner and thirty-five miles west of the White House.

Gadanz came to a quick stop between a pickup truck and an old white van—vehicles he recognized as owned by two of his delivery drivers. He made a point of knowing his employees well. He wanted them motivated, and he found that taking a sincere interest in them helped that cause. Even more crucial, that interest made them loyal. It made them think they were family, though they weren't and never could be.

It was seven o'clock in the morning, but Gadanz had already been awake for two hours. And he'd enjoyed every moment of it. He and his common-law wife, Sasha, had two beautiful daughters—Elaina and Sophie—who were his pride and joy. He fixed breakfast for the girls every morning while Sasha slept in until six-thirty. The girls loved his blueberry pancakes most, but fixing anything for them was always the best part of his day. It was his only time to be with them, because from the time he left the house until well after both girls had gone to bed, he was completely committed to work. So much so that he didn't call them or take their calls unless it was a dire emergency. So they didn't bother anymore. They'd learned.

Sasha took over all parenting duties as soon as Gadanz walked out at six forty-five sharp, and she was in charge of the house until he got home. She did an excellent job, too. He had no complaints. He didn't ask her how she kept the house and the girls in such good order, and she never asked him how he made the money that enabled her to do that. They respected each other, and they had a system. They'd been together for sixteen years, and the passion was mostly gone. Acknowledged or not, their relationship was more of a business partnership now than anything else. But it worked—for both of them.

Elaina, the older daughter, was halfway through sixth grade, and she'd never earned anything less than an A in any course she'd ever taken. She was a bookworm, and that was perfect. It fit snugly into Gadanz's long-term plan.

Sophie was nine years old and didn't care in the least about her grades, which were never very good. But that didn't matter to her—or Gadanz. It wasn't that Sophie was slow, either. In fact, she was quite smart. She'd always scored extremely high on standardized tests, and she usually figured out problems before any of her friends, even before her older sister, which irritated Elaina no end and amused Gadanz greatly.

Sophie simply didn't see the point of spending time memorizing facts and figures. Her natural gift was the ability to influence people, which she seemed to smoothly wield with everyone she came into contact with. Even her teachers admitted that she had an incredible gift for convincing people to do things, the likes of which none of them had ever seen in a girl her age. She seemed able to get anyone to do anything with her charismatic smile and her engaging way. And even at nine years old, she seemed completely aware of how to use her talents to her best advantage and absolutely comfortable doing so.

Ultimately, she would take over the family business, and Elaina would be the chief financial officer. Gadanz already had the line of succession mapped out. The older sister would report to the younger one. If Elaina didn't like it, well, that would be too bad. She'd have to get over it. He'd never admit this to anyone—even Sasha—and he always made certain to treat Elaina and Sophie exactly the same way and never show either of them any favoritism. But Sophie was the diamond of his eye. She would be the CEO of Gadanz & Company. She would be the next leader of the family.

Their husbands would never be allowed to work at the company, which Gadanz believed Sophie would completely agree with when the time was right to tell her. The husbands would simply provide the seed for the next generation and work at menial jobs that were in no way related to or connected with the family business. They would be at their wives' beck and call.

It would forever be a family business, and for Gadanz, family was only about blood. People were simply acquaintances unless they were physically related. He made his top few executives believe they were family in order to get the most out of them, but they were really just acquaintances like everyone else at the company. Just like the lowliest janitor.

Even Sasha had been merely an acquaintance until she'd borne Elaina. Only then had she become tantamount to blood, and she was the only exception to his rule. She'd truly become family when Sophie was born. Sophie was "the gift," and he'd rewarded Sasha with her own generous bank account, though he monitored it closely and forced her to come to him with any expenditure that wasn't a "normal" household cost. The same way he made the company controller come to him with any corporate expenditure that was unusual or nonrecurring.

Gadanz hummed along while he listened to the end of the Rolling Stones song on the car radio—"Jumpin' Jack Flash"—as he sat in the car thinking about how lucky a man he was. He owned a significant business that he'd built from the ground up—a string of twenty-four convenience store/gas stations that were located throughout northern Virginia and stretched from Falls Church all the way west to Leesburg. He'd added three this year; the plan for next year was to add another seven. And he'd never borrowed a dime to expand, so he didn't have bankers constantly in his face thinking they could tell him what to do. He used banks only for depositing cash. His base of operations was the two-hundred-thousand-square-foot warehouse he'd just pulled to a stop in front of. From here he supplied his twenty-four stores and generated well over a hundred million dollars of annual revenues.

Still, he drove a five-year-old Honda Accord, and Sasha drove a two-year-old minivan with a dent in one side. They lived in a modest three-bedroom townhouse in a modest neighborhood that was a short drive from here and was squeezed in between two major strip malls. The girls went to public school and rode the bus. The family dog was a mutt. And summer vacation was a week in Ocean City, New Jersey, in a rented house three blocks back from the beach. He didn't even have a personal parking space right in front of the company entrance with his name on it as the lease stipulated he could. It wasn't that Gadanz shied away from attention and conspicuous consumption—he despised them. Maintaining modesty was his personal religion, and it had nothing to do with God.

Stones song over, he climbed out of the car and headed into the building. The lobby of Gadanz & Company was ultimately plain. In it were six wooden chairs, an old coffee table littered with dated magazines from home, and some cheap wall art. The corporate offices beyond were just as utilitarian.

However, the company trucks and computer systems were the best Gadanz could buy. He spent willingly on infrastructure and paid his people well—again, so they were unfailingly loyal to him. But the aesthetics of the offices were of no concern or consequence. After all, they didn't generate revenues.

He eased into the chair behind his desk, turned on the computer, and picked up his favorite picture of Elaina and Sophie as the CPU came to life. They were smiling their most beautiful smiles and hugging each other adoringly.

"Hello, Jacob."

Gadanz put the picture calmly back down beside the computer screen, and then swiveled in the chair until he was facing the young man who'd just stepped out of the small anteroom next to his office.

"Hello, Kaashif."

CHAPTER 19

"*DECUS SEPTUM,*" Travers muttered across the laminate tabletop as he picked up his mug and took a careful sip of steaming coffee.

Troy took a careful sip from his mug, too. "Honor to the Seven." God, this coffee tasted good. Maybe it would have tasted good even if it was mud after what had just happened on the Kohler farm.

Troy always made certain to appreciate being alive after a close call. He'd actually take a few breaths and consciously consider the wonder of life when death ran close to the line—as it just had. He'd taken those deliberate breaths in this booth a few minutes ago, as soon as they'd sat down.

"Protect the peak," Travers said.

Troy glanced across the table. Travers was still studying the menu even though they'd already ordered breakfast.

He'd asked his father about those words the other night on the plane ride back up to New York. He'd asked Bill specifically what "protect the peak" meant. The old man had shrugged and claimed it was already a custom to say it when he'd signed on to run the RCS associate pool thirty years ago. And that he'd never asked Roger Carlson what, if anything, it actually meant.

Troy doubted that answer but hadn't pushed. Bill Jensen would always be a secretive man, even to his family. Even to a son who was inside Red Cell Seven.

"Yeah," Troy murmured as he looked around the Denny's. It wasn't crowded in here for this time of day, and he found that odd, given it was morning and the place was best known for breakfast. "Protect the peak."

After spraying the basement with bullets, he and Travers had sprinted up the steps through the smoke and burst through the door to the outside. Then they'd raced back across the pasture beneath the moonlight, jumped the tall four-slat fence twice within a few seconds—Travers with Troy's help each time—and hustled into the protection of the forest. When they were certain they weren't being followed, they'd stopped only long enough to catch their breaths—and bust the handcuffs still snaring Travers's wrists. Then they'd taken off again.

They couldn't return to the car Troy and the other two agents had driven to the farm from the Raleigh airport. They'd parked the car on the side of the road that passed the driveway leading to the farm, a few hundred yards south of the entrance, and then hiked into the spot on the ridge they'd used to watch the place. He'd tried to hide the car as best he could—he'd pulled it a little ways into the woods through a slight opening among the trees—but he was worried Maddux would still locate and watch it, figuring Troy would return at some point. He wasn't at all confident he'd killed or even wounded Maddux with that burst of fire he'd sprayed the basement with.

Troy didn't want another knife blade to his throat. He'd never experienced that before, and it was much more terrifying than having a gun leveled at him, which he'd already experienced several times. A bullet was fast acting; a knife, not so much.

An hour ago they'd finally come out of the trees onto a twisting country road. Fortunately they'd quickly hitched a ride from a passing farmer who was headed into a Raleigh suburb for supplies—Troy hadn't wanted to stay out on the road long, vulnerable to being seen by Maddux out there. The guy hadn't asked any questions, not even "Where're you headed?" and they'd ridden into town in the bed of his pickup. Starving, they'd come into this Denny's for a big breakfast as soon as they'd jumped out of the vehicle and waved their thanks to the farmer.

"Thanks for getting me out of there, man," Travers said. "I figured I was done."

"It wasn't very graceful. And we lost two of our own." He'd have to tell his father about Agents Wyoming and Idaho. He wasn't looking forward to that. "They were good men."

Travers nodded solemnly. "There's been a lot of that going around lately. I lost my—"

"I know. You lost Harry Boyd in Wilmington. You two were close."

Travers gestured at Troy with his mug. "How the hell did you find me anyway?"

"My father had it figured."

"Your father's Bill Jensen?"

"Yeah."

"That's how you know about Harry Boyd being my partner."

According to Bill, Travers was intensely loyal to RCS. And it was very possible that he held the key to everything—which was the reason Troy had led the rescue mission to get him out. They were going to be partners through all of this, and they needed to forge strong trust quickly. Being completely transparent about everything would help that process along.

"Yup. And he told me that as close as you and Boyd were, you and Kohler were the same distance apart."

"He was right."

"Why. What happened?"

"Nathan and I got into it bad during his first training sessions last summer, one time in particular. I was hard on him, but I'm hard on all new recruits I train." Travers shook his head. "He never got over it. More to the point, he wasn't very fond of us black people."

"I heard, but that makes no sense. His father, Douglas, was—"

"A senator. I know."

"And a huge civil rights advocate," Troy added. "It was one of his passions on the Hill. How does that work?"

Travers shrugged. "I know Nathan and his father didn't get along. Maybe it's as simple as that. Everything Douglas loved, Nathan hated. It wouldn't be the first time a father-son story exactly like that's been written."

Absolutely true, Troy thought. In a way, that was how Jack had been with Bill—until recently, until he'd finally felt like a true member of the Jensen family.

"My father mentioned that," Troy said. "He also heard about Nathan and Maddux getting close."

Douglas Kohler was one of the few associates who had a direct relationship with Shane Maddux. However, Bill had made clear to Troy that he had no knowledge of Maddux doing any personal favors for Douglas. No taking out abusive fiancés or influencing fraud-committing CFOs. As far as Bill knew, the senator had kept his relationship with Maddux strictly professional. Of course, the nothing ever being a hundred percent certain rule *always* applied.

"All that led us straight to the Kohler farm. That's why my father sent me down here. It was a guess, but it was a damn good one." Troy hesitated. What he was about to say was tricky. "You know why I came after you so fast, don't you, Major Travers?"

Travers stared at Troy grim-faced for several moments. Finally, he broke into a wry smile. "Well, since we've never met, I know it wasn't because you liked me so much."

"It was because my father says you have something—"

"Or because I'm so damn good-looking."

Troy chuckled. "No, not that either." Travers seemed to be taking this the right way. "My father says you have something very valuable."

"I figured it had something to do with that," Travers mumbled as their waiter approached the table, carrying a large tray stacked with food.

"So what is it?"

"Can't tell you. Not without your father's permission. Sorry."

Troy wanted to know badly. But he knew Travers wouldn't say anything if that violated a direct order. So pushing for an answer would prove futile. "Okay, well, I'm glad we got you out of there. My father has a lot of respect for you, Major. He says you're the real deal."

It took the waiter thirty seconds to serve all the food. They were both famished. They'd ordered heaping portions of eggs, bacon, hash browns, sausage gravy, biscuits, pancakes, and fruit.

"Where is everybody?" Troy asked the waiter as he refilled their coffee mugs.

"Those death squads have people spooked," the kid answered in a heavy southern drawl as he glanced quickly over his shoulder at the entrance. "Everybody's staying home."

"Is everybody worried because of the mall shooting in Charlotte?" Travers asked. One of the squads had hit a major mall in Charlotte, 170 miles west of Raleigh. "That's pretty far from here, isn't it? And that was the closest one."

"I think it was more them hitting that school in Missouri that's got to everybody," the kid answered. "Ain't nobody safe when they go out now, you know? And they killed little children. *That's* what really has everyone going. You guys need anything else?" he asked when he'd finished refilling Travers's mug.

"This is fine for now," said Troy as he looked at all the food hungrily. "Thanks."

He watched the waiter walk away, and glanced at the entrance. How horrible would it be to look over there and see several men come in wielding submachine guns? Mostly it would be the desperation of knowing you were helpless, especially if you had children with you. For a moment he pictured Little Jack sitting beside him. It was just like the waiter said. The baby would be so vulnerable. But the bastards wouldn't give a damn.

As he picked up a piece of bacon, Troy thought back to that comment Maddux had made about Jack. It seemed as if Maddux was saying he hadn't been the one who'd shot Jack on the back porch of their parents' home in Greenwich. But he was probably just trying to fool them, worried about Bill coming after him, and using the opportunity to raise doubts about being guilty of the shooting. Maybe that was actually why he hadn't intended to kill Troy in the basement. He wanted the lie about not killing Jack to get back to Bill fast.

"Why do you think Maddux shot Kohler back there?" Travers asked through a mouthful of biscuits and sausage gravy.

"Maddux didn't shoot Kohler," Troy answered as he glanced warily at the restaurant's entrance once more.

"What do you mean? He was the only one who could have."

Troy shook his head. "Somebody else was down there. I heard a pistol go off, and Maddux didn't have a pistol. He had one of the submachine guns."

He'd been thinking about that bullet tearing through Kohler's throat ever since he and Travers had raced from the house. Who the hell had shot Nathan Kohler?

THE MUSLIM family of six climbed out of their minivan and began walking leisurely toward the mosque to attend morning prayer service. It was early, but the temperature had already reached sixty degrees, which, for December in this area of the country, was quite warm. Tomorrow it was supposed to turn cold and possibly snow. But today they would enjoy the beautiful weather.

The mosque was located in a quiet suburb of Cedar Rapids, Iowa. It was a beautiful building with an imposing minaret rising from the center surrounded by several smaller spires. The mosque was only a few miles from the Mother Mosque of America, which had been built in 1934 and was the second oldest mosque constructed in the United States as well as the oldest still standing. But this one was much larger than the Mother Mosque, and the family admired the towering spires in the morning sunshine as they strolled leisurely toward them.

The couple had four children. The girls were fourteen and twelve, and the boys were eight and seven. They laughed with each other and waved to friends as they threaded their way through the large parking lot, which was filled with cars even at this early hour. At the door the boys would go with their father and the girls with their mother. Muslim men and women prayed in separate areas.

The two boys were tussling with each other in front of the rest of the family when a pickup truck pulled slowly out of a parking space fifty feet ahead and then stopped in front of them. As the boys ceased their pushing and shoving, a man wearing a soiled John Deere cap, a checkered flannel shirt, and dirty jeans climbed out of the vehicle. He smiled and waved, then pulled an over-and-under twelve-gauge shotgun from inside the truck and began firing.

By the time he climbed back into the pickup he'd killed the mother and father and mortally wounded the two girls.

"That's for those kids in Missouri!" the man shouted at the two little boys, who were cowering between cars as he roared past them. "I hope you're next, you little bastards."

CHAPTER 20

JACOB GADANZ leaned forward and pressed a button on his desk that triggered the office door's magnetic lock. It did so with an audible thump, and now he was comfortable that they had complete privacy. He didn't want anyone barging in and interrupting this meeting. That could prove problematic for both of them. Of course, he had more to lose if that happened—much more. Perhaps that was how Kaashif was able to rationalize what he was doing and stay so calm. He had nothing to lose.

"Sit down," Gadanz ordered gruffly, motioning toward the wooden chair beside the desk.

"I am always so impressed by the physical beauty of your operation," Kaashif said sarcastically as he eased into the uncomfortable chair and gestured around the starkly furnished room.

"And I'm always so impressed with your gratitude," Gadanz replied tersely.

"Why should I be grateful?"

Gadanz scowled at the younger man. "How can you even ask me that?"

"You are not doing this for me, Jacob. That fact cannot be more certain."

"But I'm doing it."

Kaashif pointed at Gadanz. "You only do what you do for blood, Jacob. We both know that. And you are doing this specific thing because you owe a large debt to that blood."

Gadanz glanced at the photograph of Elaina and Sophie. So Kaashif knew more than he was supposed to. At least, more than Gadanz was told he would know, which surprised him and wasn't a good sign. Not everyone was as loyal to the family as he, apparently. But he couldn't raise the issue. It would not be well received if it got back—and that was an understatement.

"Did your people have to attack that school in Missouri?" he asked. "Was that really necessary?"

"Absolutely. In fact, I believe that school attack has had more of an impact on the United States population than all eleven mall attacks combined. People are terrified now."

"And furious," Gadanz snapped.

Kaashif scoffed. "They would have been furious anyway. By attacking malls we took away their beloved shopping. But they would have gotten over that, especially in today's world." He laughed loudly. "By attacking that school we took away something much more precious. We took away their freedom. Now they are afraid to go anywhere. They are even afraid while they are in their homes. And if they are not now, they soon will be." His eyes gleamed. "I love it, Jacob."

"I know you do, Kaashif."

"There will be more blood soon. There are so many small towns with so many soft targets to choose from." Kaashif closed his eyes and smiled like he was having a good dream or he was inhaling a wonderful aroma of food that was wafting to his nostrils from a gourmet kitchen. "Homes, movie theatres, gas stations, grocery stores, more schools, churches, and they are all protected by pathetic local police who have no chance against our superior weapons, training, and planning. We will change the way this country lives. The public will begin to order everything 'in,' and then we will start attacking the delivery people so they are scared to supply the population. It will be chaos." His smile grew. "It already is, to some extent. It is beautiful."

"He's using you. You know that, don't you?"

"And we are using him. It is symmetric, which is how any important partnership should be constructed." Kaashif gestured impatiently at the anteroom to this office where he'd waited for Gadanz. "I brought two suitcases, Jacob. Inside them is a total of one hundred thousand dollars, which is the two-week burn for what are now ten teams of four men each, thanks to that unfortunate occurrence in Minneapolis." His eyes flashed angrily at the admission of losing one team already. "You will wash the cash through Gadanz and Company as agreed and as you have before. Then the teams will access the money through the corporate accounts with their cards."

"This can't go on."

Kaashif winced as he changed positions in the chair. He'd been bothered by an upset stomach for the last few days, but it wouldn't slow him down. Nothing would. There was too much momentum to let anything slow them down. "What do you mean by that?"

"First of all, I have to pay taxes on all that money."

"Why?"

"I put that cash in my registers at my stores so you don't have to deposit it in a bank and risk that deposit being reported to federal authorities."

All cash deposits over ten thousand dollars were required to be reported to the Treasury Department by the receiving bank. The government couldn't realistically investigate every cash deposit over that amount, because there were so many on a daily basis. However, computer programs enabled agents to quickly hone in on deposits that were more likely to generate criminal leads than others. Large cash deposits made by stores that normally received large amounts of cash on a daily basis were not typically investigated. Gadanz & Company was the perfect washing machine for the cash the death squads needed.

"So it looks like I received it from customers who are buying items from my stores," Gadanz continued. "And then it goes into my bank as though I earned it. But then my accountant must declare all of that cash as revenue at the end of the year. So I must pay taxes on it."

"So what? I still do not understand."

Gadanz clenched his jaw. Kaashif was incredibly arrogant, but he was smart, too. These questions were being asked simply to annoy. But Gadanz would finish this out. He wanted his objection heard and noted.

"So if your teams use all one hundred thousand dollars I've deposited for you in my company accounts, I'm being shorted. With state and local income taxes, my total rate is nearly forty percent. That means I have to pay another forty thousand dollars on each hundred thousand you have me launder."

Kaashif waved. "Deal with it." He chuckled. "Consider it your contribution to the greater good."

Gadanz clenched his jaw again, harder. "And I hate them withdrawing amounts all over the country from random ATMs." That was what could really get him in trouble. That was what could land him in jail forever, maybe even get him strapped to a gurney waiting for a lethal injection to cascade into his arm.

"I'm not sending cash through the mail, Jacob. The Feds are getting too good at spotting that and following it. People don't know it, but even Federal Express and UPS must notify the Feds of large cash mailings when the machines identify them."

"But I—"

"If anyone asks," Kaashif interrupted, "tell them you are paying suppliers. Tell them you buy things for your stores from many different locations."

"Yes, I'm sure that will convince everyone and there will be no blowback. Come on. You know that won't work."

"Think of something else, then. I do not have time to deal with your issues. I have many of my own."

"What you mean by that is, if this thing is uncovered then I get screwed while your people have time to scatter with the wind."

Kaashif rubbed his stomach again. He really needed to get something at the store for the pain. It was getting bad. "I may need you to get even more involved, Jacob."

"What are you talking about? This is all I agreed to do."

"My team here in northern Virginia may need another place to hole up. They have been in the same apartment complex for a while, and they are getting nervous. I want them to stay around here because I want a team causing chaos at least somewhat in proximity to Washington, DC. It will get much play in the press." Kaashif nodded to Gadanz. "Yes, I definitely want you more involved. I want you to rent them a new place through the company. Do it today."

This was getting out of control, Gadanz realized. The problem was he was already in so deep. That rule about only blood mattering wasn't working out as it was supposed to. It was what he had held on to as the saving grace of everything when this had all been initially proposed to him, and what he had hoped would see him and his family through all of this. But it was now obvious that his hope had been hollow at best.

"Imelda has been taken, along with her child," Kaashif spoke up.

Gadanz's eyes raced to Kaashif's. "What?" he whispered.

"She's gone."

Gadanz felt his chest tighten and his breathing go fast. "Maybe she ran."

Kaashif shook his head. "No chance. She would never have done that. She was completely committed to the cause."

"Well, I—"

"You will take her place in everything," Kaashif ordered, "and there will be no further discussion about it. Do you understand me?"

The little bastard. He would kill him right now with his bare hands—but that would be suicide. Worse, it would mean the end for his daughters. There would be no mercy.

CHAPTER 21

"WHO SHOT Nathan Kohler in that basement?" Travers asked directly as he scooped up a forkful of scrambled eggs. "Who was the other person down there?"

Troy shook his head even though a possibility had actually just occurred to him. "I don't know." He wasn't trying to dodge Travers. It was just such a wild guess it wasn't worth saying anything. At this point he needed to build credibility with Travers, not blow it.

"It had to have been someone on our side. Otherwise, they would have shot us."

Once more Troy thought about suggesting who it might have been. But again he held off.

"Unless Maddux got that smoke bomb off before whoever it was had a chance to take out the rest of us, too." Travers hesitated. "And wasn't necessarily on either of our sides."

Troy wanted to make sure of something before this conversation went any further. "You know Maddux defected, right?"

Travers nodded. "Oh, yeah."

"How'd you find out?"

"And I know he and Ryan O'Hara tried to kill President Dorn a few weeks ago in Los Angeles," Travers kept going without answering. "O'Hara's the one who tried to kill me in Delaware."

Troy glanced up. He was aware that Travers had dodged the question, and he wanted an answer. But he'd get to it later. "What?"

"O'Hara and another young gun were the ones who ambushed Harry Boyd and me in Wilmington two days ago."

That didn't make sense to Troy. "But they aren't the ones who brought you down here to the farm. I thought that was Kohler."

"It *was* Kohler," Travers confirmed. "I took out O'Hara and the other guy after they got Harry. Kohler got me later, at my place in the Appalachian Mountains." He stopped gulping down food for a moment. "Hey, you think you got Maddux when you shot the basement up?"

"I doubt it."

"Me too. I always heard that guy basically survives everything."

Something else occurred to Troy. "You know, I don't think O'Hara was trying to kill you in Delaware. I think he was trying to do the same thing Kohler actually did. Maddux wanted you under his control. He didn't want you dead. He made that clear in the basement. I think O'Hara was trying to bring you to Maddux, not kill you."

Travers had been about to eat a mouthful of hash browns, but he stopped the fork's progress in front of his mouth for a moment. "Maybe." He shrugged then ate the bite hungrily. "How was I supposed to know? I didn't even know who they were when they killed Harry. I was just trying to survive at that point. And they were shooting while they were chasing me."

"From what I've heard about Ryan O'Hara, if he was trying to hit you he would have, even if you were a moving target."

"He missed the president in Los Angeles."

"Well—"

"He didn't kill him. That's what I meant. He hit him, but he didn't assassinate him."

"Only because Rex Stein deflected the bullet at the last second by diving in front of Dorn on the platform."

"How did Stein know? Who tipped him off? I never heard an explanation of that in the media."

Troy hesitated. "My brother Jack called him on the stage."

"Your brother's in RCS, too?"

"No." He quickly explained to Travers what had happened—about Jack going to Alaska and stopping the LNG attack, about his calling Stein on the stage, and then about Maddux shooting Jack.

"Now I get what you and Maddux were going back and forth about in the basement. Sorry about that."

"Yeah, thanks."

"So who was Lisa?"

Troy gave Travers an even briefer explanation about her.

Travers shook his head. "You must really hate that guy."

Troy glanced at the entrance. A Middle Eastern family was standing there waiting to be seated. The man and two small boys were dressed in casual pants and shirts. But the woman wore a full-length black cloak along with a traditional abaya over her head and neck, which left only a thin space for her to see.

"How'd Maddux get down into the basement?" Travers asked as he took another big bite of food. "You guys checked that place out hard. I watched you. It was like he came out of nowhere."

"Like a ghost," Troy agreed as the hostess led the family to a booth near the back of the restaurant. The booth was well away from where anyone else was sitting. "I don't know, Major. There had to be a hidden access from outside or from another floor. I know there was no other stairway down there from the first floor."

"I guess."

"How did Kohler find you?" Troy asked. Other patrons in the restaurant were watching the Middle Eastern family closely. Troy could feel the hatred building around him. It was almost palpable. It wasn't right; it was totally misguided. Unfortunately, it was human. "Where were you?"

"I've got a place in the mountains west of Washington, DC. That's what I was telling you before. It's where I go when I need to hole up. It's in the middle of nowhere in the woods. It's really just a shack." Travers shrugged. "I don't know how in the hell he found me there."

Troy gestured to Travers without looking at him. He was watching two men on the far side of the restaurant who seemed to be taking more than just a passing interest in the family, which had just sat down in the booth. "Check this out."

Travers followed Troy's gaze. "What's up?"

"Maybe nothing, maybe something." A moment later the two men they were watching stood up from their table and headed toward the family. "Christ," Troy muttered. "Here we go."

Words had already been exchanged by the time he reached the table.

"You people ought to leave," one of the men was saying to the family, "before one of you gets hurt."

"And don't ever come back," the other man hissed. "Or one of you will definitely get hurt."

The two little boys were terrified, and their father seemed paralyzed. The woman was holding one hand to the thin opening of the abaya.

"What's the problem?" Troy asked evenly.

The men spun around toward Troy and stepped a few paces back, obviously surprised. But they collected themselves quickly.

"Don't get involved, boy. This ain't your fight."

"Yeah, it is. When you treat someone—"

One of the men reached inside his jacket. Before Troy could react, Travers had cut in front and put the man to the ground with a single, vicious right to the jaw. Travers grabbed the pistol the man had been going for—it had clattered to the floor beside him—and leveled it at the other man, who threw his hands in the air.

"Don't shoot!"

Troy stared at Travers for several moments, then glanced down at the man, who lay prone on the floor, not even moving. That was impressive.

"Come on, Captain," Travers said with a thin smile. "Let's go."

Troy nodded, still impressed by what he'd just witnessed. "Yeah, right."

THAT AFTERNOON Jacob Gadanz left the office at three-thirty. It was the first time he'd left his business before eight o'clock at night in three years. He was waiting for Elaina and Sophie when they got off the school bus, and he hugged each of them tightly before holding their hands as they walked on either side of him all the way back to the family's townhouse.

Sasha knew something was wrong. If everything had been all right, he never would have come home so early this afternoon and then gone right to the bus stop after asking her where it was.

But she was too afraid to ask him what was wrong. The only reason Jacob would have come home this early was because he was scared. And that frightened her more than she could have ever anticipated. In their sixteen years together, she'd never seen Jacob Gadanz even remotely scared. He was the bravest man she'd ever known. Perhaps because of who his brother was. And what difference did it make?

But Jacob was terrified today. She'd seen it all over his face as soon as he'd walked in the door—which was why she was sobbing uncontrollably in the bathroom off the bedroom with the door locked. His terror had petrified her.

And then there was that other thing that was driving her insane and making the tears flow like rivers. She knew a little about what was going on—by accident, of course, but she knew. She'd stumbled on it so now she understood a shred of the terror she'd seen on Jacob's face. She wished to Almighty God she didn't, but there was no denying it.

The soft knock on the door interrupted a harsh sob, and she held her breath. Now she knew what it felt like to be hunted.

"Sasha."

"Go away, Jacob." She didn't want him to see her like this. "Please."

"The girls are wondering why you're in here."

She pressed a tissue to the bottom of her eyelids. "They're wondering why you met them at the bus stop, too."

"Please open the door, sweetheart."

Sweetheart. He hadn't called her that in years. "Please go away, Jacob," she begged through the bathroom door. *"Please."*

CHAPTER 22

IT SEEMED strange to Troy to have to sneak into his parents' house in Connecticut. He never had before, but Bill was requiring it this time. He'd made them wait until nightfall, too, so they had the cover of darkness. Because Travers was with Troy, Bill had claimed—he was taking absolutely no chances on anyone seeing that.

But Troy had a feeling Bill would have been this cautious even if it had just been the two of them meeting tonight—which meant his father was worried about President Dorn monitoring everything they were doing. That was the only explanation he could think of for this intense level of stealth.

It also meant Stewart Baxter was probably operating behind the scenes on Dorn's behalf, which made it likely that Dorn had told Baxter everything he knew about Red Cell Seven. Bill's gamble of letting the president get his nose even farther under the cell's tent wasn't paying off. Bill was trying to be reasonable, but Dorn was showing his true colors, even in the face of the Holiday Mall Attacks.

Once a dove, always a dove, his father had always preached. The mantra had been drilled into Troy's head over and over as he was growing up. Even about Jack, who always banged the liberal drum—sometimes just to irritate their father, Troy believed. Still, it begged the obvious question: Why would Bill violate his own mantra now, especially when the fight involved the president?

As ordered, Troy and Travers had taken a roundabout route to the Jensen property outside Greenwich. An hour ago they'd hopped a cab at the Westchester Airport after flying in on the Jensen plane from Raleigh. And Troy had directed the confused driver to drop them off in the middle of nowhere, in the woods on a lonely country road several miles from the house. They'd hiked the rest of the way through the forest.

Finally, they'd come through the tree line and into the open at about the spot where Troy thought Maddux had been when he'd shot Jack. Then they'd jogged the last few hundred yards across one of the pastures to a back basement door Bill had unlocked after ordering his five-member private security force to stand down for a few minutes and take a quick break from watching the perimeter.

The three of them had then gone directly to the card room of the large finished basement after Bill had resecured the door and turned the alarm back on. It was an interior room that had no windows. His father was being careful about everything. Troy had never seen him this uptight or worried. Usually, you couldn't tell from his face what he was feeling. But the grim, stony expression was an obvious tip-off.

"What happened in North Carolina?" Bill asked as they all sat down around the six-sided table covered by soft green felt.

"We got this guy out," Troy answered, gesturing at Travers. "Unfortunately, we lost the two agents who went with me to rescue Major Travers."

Bill winced. "I'll check to see what the family situation is for both of them. We don't have many married men in the cell, but there are a few. If they were married, I'll take care of their families." He drummed the felt tabletop with his fingertips. "So what happened?"

"Maddux showed up," Travers answered for Troy. "One second he was nowhere, the next he was right in front of us. It was like he stepped out of thin air right in front of us. He shot the other agents in the head before they even knew what was happening. Real clean shots, too, dead-on-impact accurate. Then he had a knife at Troy's throat."

"Crazy," Bill muttered under his breath. "That guy still amazes me even after twenty years."

"Agents Wyoming and Idaho cased the grounds and the other buildings with me before we went down to the basement looking for Major Travers," Troy explained. "Maddux was not around, Dad."

"There's no way to know for sure," Bill said. "And it isn't your fault you didn't find him if he actually was there. Sometimes I don't think Shane Maddux would show up on an infrared camera after running a marathon in the dark."

"Maybe not even on a regular camera on a sunny day," Travers cracked.

"Maybe not."

Bill was preoccupied and hadn't even come close to a smile at Travers's remark. "He'd definitely recruited Nathan Kohler out of RCS," Troy said. "Now Kohler's dead, too."

Bill looked up from a pad of paper he'd been writing on. "Oh?"

He'd been penning a note about checking on the family situations of the two dead agents, Troy saw. "Someone else showed up in that basement in North Carolina while we were down there."

Bill put the pen down. "Who?"

"Don't know, Dad. But whoever it was shot Kohler dead and then bolted when Maddux dropped a smoke bomb for cover. I didn't get a look at the guy's face. It all happened too fast."

Father and son stared at each other for several moments across the green felt before Bill's gaze shifted to Travers. "How did Kohler find you at your place in the mountains? How in the hell did he know you were even there, Major?"

Travers shrugged. "I have no idea, sir."

There was a soft knock on the door. All three men sat straight up in their chairs as they glanced quickly at the door.

"Yes?" Bill called as he stood up.

"It's me, dear."

Troy recognized his mother's voice as Bill pointed at Travers and then to a closet in a corner of the room. When Travers was inside with the door shut, Bill let Cheryl in. She gave him a quick kiss and moved to where Troy was standing after he'd risen from his chair as well.

"Hello, Mother."

Cheryl Jensen was tall and slim. In her late fifties, she looked much younger than that to Troy. Every time he saw her he thought that.

"What do you have there?" he asked, pointing at the bundle in her arms.

"Someone who misses you," she answered. As she leaned in to give Troy a kiss on the cheek, she carefully handed him the blue knit blanket and the baby wrapped inside it. "Someone you need to spend more time with."

Troy smiled as he glanced down at Little Jack. He was damn cute even if he was only a few months old. Most babies looked the same to Troy, and not cute at all. In fact, some of them were downright ugly, even when everyone was oohing and aahing over them.

L.J. was different. He was definitely cute, even handsome already with his shock of straight black hair, distinctive features, and beautiful light-brown skin. Of course, Lisa Martinez had been a beautiful woman.

And the little guy seemed to have a glint in his eye other babies didn't, Troy noticed. He seemed already aware of all that was going on around him. Troy chuckled softly. Of course, maybe L.J.'s father was a little biased.

"Thanks, Mom," he said as he took the baby.

Cheryl smiled lovingly. "You're welcome, dear."

Jack's death had torn her apart. She'd been a wreck at the funeral the other day. But Karen was right. Having Little Jack around seemed to have boosted her spirits. She had a glow about her when she gazed at the baby.

"I guess I can give him up for a little while," she murmured as she touched L.J.'s chin and smiled again.

"I'll take good care of him while he's down here." They couldn't continue until she left, and Troy could see that Bill was getting impatient. "Don't worry."

"That's my cue," she said as she turned to leave. "I get it." When she made it to the door she stopped. "See you later." She smiled up at Bill. "Do tell whoever's in the closet I said hello."

"What?"

Cheryl pointed at the table and the chairs around it. "Six chairs at the table, and three of them are pulled out. I only see two of you." She gave Bill another quick kiss. "I've been around you too long. I've learned to analyze everything. Don't ever forget that," she called good-naturedly as Bill closed the door after her.

As Travers emerged from the closet, Troy eased back down into his chair and gave Little Jack his finger to squeeze. The baby had a nice strong grip and a wave of pride surged through him. Then the guilt fell in behind the pride. Cheryl was right. The little guy needed a father, every little guy did. But that was going to be very tough if he stayed with RCS. Maybe trying so hard to please his father shouldn't be as important anymore. Jack had spent his whole life doing that, and where had it gotten him? Six feet under.

"Where were we?" Bill asked when they were all seated again.

"Who's that?" Travers asked, pointing at L.J. with a wide grin.

"We were talking about what happened in North Carolina," Troy said, avoiding the question. "One thing you should be aware of, Dad, is that Maddux knows you're running RCS now. He made that clear."

"He doesn't know. He was just guessing."

"It didn't sound like he was guessing," Travers spoke up respectfully but firmly.

"It sure didn't," Troy seconded. "The other interesting thing about that whole deal in the basement down there was that Maddux wasn't going to kill me. He was going to leave me locked up, but he wasn't going to take me out."

Bill grinned thinly for the first time. "Think he's going soft in his old age?"

"It had nothing to do with personal loyalty, Dad. He made that very clear. He said the reason he wasn't taking me out was that he didn't want to piss you off. It had to do with his personal survival and nothing else."

Troy and Travers had covered a great deal in the plane on the way up, including what had happened in Alaska; Maddux killing Lisa Martinez; and how Jack had died on the porch of this house. Troy had told Travers about Lisa but not about Little Jack. He was still getting used to being a father, and he hadn't mentioned the baby. Well, he wouldn't avoid the subject ever again, he promised himself as he gazed down into his son's bright eyes. "And Maddux claimed he didn't shoot Jack."

Bill raised one eyebrow triumphantly. "I told you."

"Just because Shane says he didn't kill Jack, I don't think we should necessarily—"

"Tell me about the young man you recently interrogated," Bill interrupted, pointing at Travers.

Troy rolled his eyes. He hated it when Bill cut him off like that.

"I believe you told me his name was Kaashif when we spoke about him." Travers nodded. "Yes, sir, that's right."

"Did you find out anything important while you had him in custody?"

"Well, I—"

"First off, why were you suspicious? Who put you onto him?"

Travers stared at Bill steadily for several moments, then glanced at Troy. He started to say something—twice—but stopped each time.

"What's the problem?" Bill demanded.

"I can't give you my specific source, Mr. Jensen. I don't want you to get angry, sir, but I won't give my sources up to anyone. Mr. Carlson and I had an understanding on that."

"That's fine, Major. Just say what you're comfortable saying."

"Look, we all know people, right? I went into the Marines in 1991, and since then some of the guys I was in with landed on different boxes of the intel game board, you know? All the usual destinations you'd figure. CIA, NSA, ONI, and a few others I'm sure you two would suspect. Maybe one or two you wouldn't as well."

"Go on."

"I keep in touch with those guys," Travers explained. "Like Carlson always said, work every relationship we have to find out anything we can."

"We emphasize that from day one," Bill agreed. "So, what did you find out?"

"Six months ago one of my guys who reports into Langley tells me about this kid, Kaashif, who's a high school student up in Philly. Says I should check him out. That's it, that's all he says, just check him out. Claims he tried to get his superior up the Potomac to do the same thing, but the boss wouldn't listen. The guy told him they don't have time to chase down leads on teenagers because there's too much else to do. So he begs me to do it, because he's got a feeling something's there, and he's usually right. I trust this guy with my life. In fact, he saved it one time in Iraq, so why wouldn't I?

"So I try doing some prelim back-channel work on the kid, but it all comes up empty. I don't mean negative, I don't mean the kid's all innocent or anything and my guy was wrong. I mean I can't find anything about Kaashif before he enrolled in that Philly high school last September. There's *nothing* on him before that. It's like footprints ending in the snow in the middle of a field. So I try getting information on his parents, but nothing comes up on them, either. It's weird, just another trail ending in the middle of nowhere.

"He's got a social security card and a birth certificate. He's got a driver's license, so he had to have them. And I got copies of them. But get this: They're completely phony."

"How do you know?" Troy asked.

Travers gave him an ironic smile. "Kaashif's birth certificate says he was born at Point Pleasant Hospital in Point Pleasant, Wyoming."

Bill nodded as if he knew where this was headed. "And there's no Point Pleasant Hospital."

Travers snickered. "There's no Point Pleasant, *Wyoming*."

"Jesus."

"Anyway," Travers continued, "I figure I'll just turn their names over to immigration. Those people can be an epic pain in the ass for a family like this, and hey, maybe that's as far as it goes. A family getting into this country that shouldn't have, and I'll do something about it by putting immigration on them. But right before I make the call, the kid's name shows up in a transmission a contact of mine in London calls me about. It's a message the Brits skimmed from a group in the Middle East our government isn't fond of, to put it mildly. So I follow the kid a little, when I have some spare time."

"And?"

"And nothing happens for a while. But then it all breaks loose. One morning the kid walks into his high school through the front door and then two minutes later comes out the back. I'm lucky I see him, too; it's completely by chance. I mean, I'm driving away from the building when I catch the kid duck out. I'm not even sure it's him at first, but then I see it is.

"So he climbs in his car and drives off with me in his shadow. I figure he's going home, or he's meeting up with some girl, but that's not it. He gets on I-95 and heads south down to northern Virginia. I follow him all the way down there past DC, all the way to a house in Manassas, which is about forty miles west of the White House. An hour later he gets back in his car, and I follow him all the way back up to Philadelphia.

"A few days later the son of a bitch's name comes up in *another* transmission from that crew in the Middle East we don't like. It's going to somebody in Los Angeles, who isn't at the apartment when our guys crash the place. It's pretty obvious the United States is about to take a terrorist hit, if you believe the transmission. But we intercept a lot of those messages, I'm told, so it's not that unusual. What's unusual is that the kid's name comes up again.

"So Harry and I grab him, and we take him in and rough him up at one of our interrogation sites outside Baltimore. He whines like a little baby the whole time, like he really is in high school and he doesn't know what the hell I'm talking about. But I'm convinced he's playing me. I've been doing the interrogation thing long enough to recognize the act. I'm convinced he's not seventeen, either, and I figure high school's his cover. Pretty good cover, too, right?"

Troy and Bill nodded, fascinated by Travers's story.

"So," Travers continued, "I zip him the TQ Haze and then plan on monitoring him real closely for a few days after I turn him back out. I figure that's the best strategy." The major grimaced sadly. "But Harry and I get nailed in Delaware on our way back from dropping Kaashif off in Philly. Harry's dead, and somebody's obviously going to be real pissed at me, because I take out the two guys who got Harry. It turns out one of them is Ryan O'Hara, who I know is with Maddux. I'd heard through the grapevine he was the one who shot President Dorn in L.A. for Maddux. And believe me, I know well enough not to be on Maddux's hit list. So I go underground. I figure I'll lay low for a week or so.

"But then Kohler shows up out of nowhere at my shack out in the mountains, tases me, takes me to that place in North Carolina, and locks me up in the basement. I think I'm about to go free when Troy shows up, but then Maddux appears out of thin air. So that fast I go from thinking I'm saved to thinking I'm done. Instead, Maddux wants to take me with him." Travers hesitated. "Then somebody shoots Kohler, Maddux throws the smoke down, Troy and I run like hell. And now you're up to date, Mr. Jensen."

Bill nodded. "Thank you, Major Travers."

"When you said you zipped him the TQ—"

"Who did he meet with?" Bill interrupted Troy again. "Down in Manassas, I mean."

"A woman named Imelda Smith. I checked her out through normal channels while I was following Kaashif back up to Philadelphia. I got her street address off her mailbox and worked backward. I got a picture of her on my phone, too, when she was saying good-bye to Kaashif. She's a divorced mother of a young boy who claims she's a marketing executive on her tax returns. I didn't have a chance to diligence it myself."

"By 'normal channels' you mean you called the people at Fort Meade?" Bill asked.

Travers nodded. "Yes, sir, like we're supposed to. Specifically, I contacted that group we've always been told to use."

Troy glanced from Travers to his father. That was a new wrinkle. But as a Falcon, Troy wasn't charged with interrogating, so it made sense he wouldn't have heard about this way of checking on people.

"What about Kaashif?" Bill asked. "Did you run him through normal channels too?"

"No, I kept him out of Fort Meade. I did my own stuff on him. I was worried that group in Maryland might cross the lines and figure out who'd told me about the kid. I couldn't have that." Travers glanced across the table at Little Jack and grinned when the baby shrieked. "I'm not sure they would have found out anything about Kaashif, anyway. He's a damn black hole. But I'm pretty sure I'm on to something with him just because of that. And because he was mentioned in those two transmissions."

"What does 'zip him the TQ Haze' mean?" Troy asked loudly. He wasn't going to be ignored this time.

Travers glanced at Bill. "Can we . . . I mean, am I allowed to—"

"It's a new track-and-trace system we're using," Bill explained. "It uses a brand-new technology that relies on a cutting-edge metallic composite that adheres to the stomach and intestine walls when ingested with water. Microscopic shards of the composite are mixed in a turquoise-colored powder that enables the shards to embed, hence the name TQ Haze. Once in place, the shards send out a unique signal based on the DNA of the subject combining with the composite, as long as enough of the shards embed in the target's internal tissue. So, as long as you have a good DNA sample from the subject, you can track his movements. The app's a lot like a GPS tracking device. In fact, it uses GPS technology once the shards have adhered to the subject's body. It matches the sample DNA you've inputted in your tracking device to the signal being emitted from the subject. It's like phone-to-phone except this is device-to-body. The difference with TQ is that even if the subject figured out what was going on, he couldn't turn off the transmission. The shards signal for about a week before the body breaks them down and flushes most of them out."

"Who came up with that?" Troy asked.

"I can't tell you, son. The existence and membership of that group is as sensitive as the existence of Red Cell Seven. What I can tell you is that the president of the United States doesn't even know about those guys. Only a few of us do."

The room went still for a few moments. Even the baby was quiet.

"Well," Travers finally spoke up, "I gave Kaashif TQ during the interrogation. It's the first time I've used it. I checked my phone while he was still tied up, and the trace was already working."

"How'd you get him to take the stuff?" Troy asked.

"I didn't give him anything to drink for almost a day. He sucked down every drop when I finally gave him a glass of water. He was begging for it. I doubt he would have noticed or cared what was in it at that point."

"And he never knew the difference?" Troy asked. "He was that thirsty?"

"It gives most people stomach problems for a while after they've ingested it," Bill spoke up. "It feels like a mild case of food poisoning, I've been told. But it's tasteless going down. He wouldn't have noticed, especially if he was craving something to drink that badly."

"It feels like food poisoning?" Travers spoke up hesitantly.

Bill nodded. "That's the only thing people have noticed so far. Of course, we've only been using it for a few weeks."

Troy had spotted Travers touching his stomach just then. "What's up, Major?"

Travers grinned wryly. "I thought I had a little of that the past day or two."

Bill leaned over the table. His expression had turned from grim to intense. "Really?"

"Yeah, I—"

"How did you get the stuff you gave Kaashif?"

"Nathan Kohler delivered it to our interrogation site outside Baltimore."

"Did you drink anything after Kohler got there?"

"Yeah, I'm pretty sure I did have a drink of water, now that you mention it. And," he continued as his tone grew stronger, "Kohler got it for me. But how would he have known what was in the package he was delivering?"

"Maddux knew about it," Bill replied. "And Kohler was obviously already working with Maddux at that point. The division leaders all knew about it two weeks ago."

"Damn. If Kohler put the TQ in my water, that means Maddux can—"

"Exactly," Bill cut in, anticipating where Travers was going.

Maddux could be tracking Travers even as they were speaking, Troy realized. "Does Maddux have your DNA?" he asked Travers. So it meant Maddux might have followed them up here to Connecticut from North Carolina. "Spit, blood, anything?"

"Probably. I don't know. Maybe Kohler got it for him."

"You've got the TQ trace app on your phone, right?" Bill asked.

"Yes. It's like you said. It's just like a GPS tracking app, except Kaashif can't turn it off." His expression turned grave. "Which means, if Kohler really did get the stuff into me, Maddux can track where I've been and," he hesitated, "where I am. Just like I can tell where Kaashif has been."

"Maybe that's why he wanted to take you with him in North Carolina," Troy said. "Maybe somehow he knew about Kaashif, and of course, he'd want to track the guy himself."

"Very possible," Bill agreed. "All right, let's wrap this up and get you guys out of here. I don't want Maddux showing up. What are your next steps?"

"I check on Kaashif," Travers answered. "I see where he's gone and follow up."

"I'm going with the major," Troy said firmly. "And at some point, I'm going to see that girl in the hospital again, the one who survived the attack at the mall in McLean. Jennie Perez. I talked to the doctor while we were on the flight up here. She's doing better. Maybe she can tell me something."

"Don't waste your time with her," Bill advised as he donned his reading glasses and scanned the screen of his phone. "She won't be any help."

Troy watched Bill scroll down on the phone. He'd said the same thing about Jennie the other night, that it was a waste of time. "Yeah, well, I think I'm still—"

"Jesus," Bill muttered. "People around this country are starting to lose it."

"What is it, Mr. Jensen?"

"It says here that a crowd in Dayton, Ohio, attacked two men who they thought were 'acting suspiciously' in front of a strip mall," he answered, tapping the phone. "They beat one of the men to death, and the other's in a hospital in critical condition." Bill glanced up, over his half-lenses. "It turns out they worked at one of the mall's stores and they were outside just having a smoke. Somebody thought one of the guys had a gun, but he didn't."

Troy looked down at Little Jack. This was the world the boy was entering. He'd never thought much about the danger before. All he'd ever had to worry about was taking care of himself, and he'd always figured he was bulletproof. Now he had to worry about this little guy's well-being.

"Here's another result of the attacks," Bill said, tapping the small screen again. "The eleven malls that were hit two days ago are reporting a drop in traffic of between sixty and eighty percent. There's a picture on here of the interior of one of them. We're six days before Christmas, and the place is empty. It's killing the economy."

"Have any of the death squads hit anything since shooting up that elementary school in Missouri yesterday?" Troy asked as he continued to gaze down at Little Jack.

"No."

Troy felt that fear again as the baby squeezed his finger hard and seemed to grin up at him. "You know it's going to happen again soon, Dad."

"Absolutely," Bill agreed. "They aren't going to sit around and wait with Christmas only a few days away. That's why they did it at this time of year, to have the maximum effect on the season."

Troy lifted L.J. up and kissed him gently on the forehead. He and Travers had to get out of here. "You ready, Major?" he asked, standing up.

"Yeah, let's do it."

Five minutes later he and Travers were headed down the Jensens' long driveway in a Jeep Cheryl used to get around the large property to deal with her horses and to run errands into town.

"So check your phone," Troy said from the driver's seat.

"What?"

"Check the app on your phone to see where Kaashif's been over the last two days."

"I can't."

"Why not?"

"The phone's at my place in the mountains. I always hide it someplace when I go to sleep, in case of exactly what happened the other night."

Troy nodded. That made sense. "I guess I know where we're going first."

CHAPTER 23

KAREN STOOD statue-still in the darkness of the lonely cemetery as she gazed sadly at Jack's tombstone. How long had she been here like this, motionless beneath the leafless trees that ringed the cemetery's stone fence—three minutes, five, ten? She had no idea, and she didn't care. She couldn't stop thinking about how both men she'd loved had been killed by Shane Maddux—first Charlie and now Jack.

Tears trickled down both cheeks as Jack's handsome image drifted through her memory. Those dark, rugged features and that haunting and unmistakable honesty always present in his expression, no matter his emotion, which she'd recognized right away and found so attractive. She muted a sob as she thought about how much she missed that crooked smile of his, too.

She leaned down to place a single red rose on the ground in front of the stone, and wiped her face as she lifted back up. But the tears kept coming.

She was thinking about that poor guy she'd shot in North Carolina, too. And the terrible result of the bullet tearing into his chin and neck. How his time left on earth had suddenly gone from being measured in years to seconds. Had it been necessary to kill him? She absolutely believed so in the moment, but having had time to second-guess herself now, wondered if maybe she acted too quickly. Either way, she'd put a man down for good. The finality of the act was still hard to accept.

She sobbed again, loudly this time.

"Stop it."

She shrieked and spun around. Ten feet away stood the same man who'd held the knife to Troy's throat in North Carolina. Her heart was suddenly racing a thousand miles an hour, and she couldn't seem to catch her breath. She'd recognized him instantly even though he wasn't at all memorable. He was small and plainly unattractive, not someone who would stand out in a crowd.

"What do you want?" she asked, trying to make her voice strong.

"First I want you to stop crying," he answered.

He wasn't armed. At least he wasn't holding a weapon. But she was still terrified as she stared into his cold, dark eyes through the dim light. Death seemed to surround him like a terrible aura. "Don't worry about me," she said. Her pistol was in the holster at the small of her back, but, God, what a risk it would be to draw. The man in front of her wasn't physically imposing at all, but if he could neutralize Troy, he was no one to trifle with.

"You did the right thing in North Carolina."

"What do you mean?"

"The guy you shot would not have killed you, Karen. I wouldn't have let him. But you didn't know that. You did the right thing, and I liked that. You had an objective, and you stayed true to it." He smiled thinly. "Don't beat yourself up too much for killing him."

How could he know what she was thinking? "How do you know my name?"

"I know all about you."

"Who are you?"

He chuckled softly. "Oh, that's right, you and I never met. It was rude of me not to introduce myself right away."

"Who are you?"

"Shane Maddux."

For several moments the world before Karen blurred to a haze of nothing recognizable. Shane Maddux. Charlie had told her all about him before he'd been "lost" off the *Arctic Fire*. He'd been a Falcon, Maddux was his superior, and at first, her fiancé had been in awe of the man who he claimed could do anything.

But over time, the bright shine from the star had faded until it died completely the night Charlie secretly discovered a terrible truth. Maddux was using his privileges and immunity from prosecution as a member of Red Cell Seven to further his own lurid agenda—murdering civilians in the name of justice, vigilante-style. It seemed some of the victims weren't as guilty as Maddux claimed.

Not long afterward Charlie had been washed overboard by a storm on the Bering Sea. At least, that was the official explanation. But the tragedy had seemed far too coincidental in its timing. So she'd gone to Alaska with Charlie's parents to get more information. However, the captain of the *Fire*, Sage Mitchell, was not forthcoming, and the authorities couldn't press charges or even continue to investigate because the other men of the crew—all family members—backed up the captain's story.

Troy had met the same fate off the *Fire*. But he'd survived Shane Maddux, thanks to Jack. Still, Maddux had gotten his revenge on the back porch of the Jensens' home outside Greenwich.

"Where is Wilson Travers?" Maddux asked.

The world came back into focus. "Who?"

"Don't play games with me," Maddux warned. His tone took on an icy edge. "Where is Major Travers? The man you and Troy went to rescue in North Carolina."

She hadn't gone to North Carolina to rescue anyone. She had no idea what the mission was. She'd gone simply to back up Troy, at Bill's direction. She'd asked Bill if she could get involved. She'd needed something to distract from her sadness, and he'd agreed, though tentatively. Troy hadn't even known she was following him. At least, Bill had promised he wouldn't say anything.

"I don't know a Major Travers. I didn't go there to rescue anyone. I only went to—"

"Stop it. I know about your cop background in Baltimore. And I know you and Troy are working together. I know what you're capable of. I saw what you did to Nathan Kohler."

"Yeah, and it's the same thing I'd like to do to you."

"I'm sure." Maddux sneered. "But believe me, you wouldn't have time to draw the pistol that's snug in the holster at the small of your back. You'd be dead before you could pull the trigger."

For several moments she stared at him, hating him more and more as each second ticked past. She wanted to kill this man. It was a horrible thing for her to admit, because all of her training had taught her to protect life— which was why she was still having a hard time with shooting the man in North Carolina. But Maddux deserved death. She was certain of that.

He took a step forward, and she took one back. She wanted to draw, but this was a very dangerous man. Charlie and Troy had made that very clear. As she stared into his eyes, she believed he could kill her as fast as he'd bragged.

"Tell me what I want to know or I will kill you, Karen. It's a matter of national security. If you have to be sacrificed, so be it."

"Don't come near me."

When he took a second step at her, she turned and fled. As she sprinted through and around the tombstones, she could hear him behind her, breathing hard. She reached the waist-high stone fence, hurdled it in a single leap, and raced into the forest surrounding the cemetery. She couldn't head back to the parking lot. He had that route cut off. Besides, she wouldn't have time to get in her car and get away. He was too close.

She pushed herself to her absolute limit, dodging trees and changing directions on a dime, doing everything possible to escape. She was fast . . . but he was faster. The inevitable lay only seconds away.

As Maddux's footsteps on the leaves edged nearer and nearer and he closed the distance between them, she screamed in terror. She tried reaching behind herself for the gun, but it slowed her down, and he tripped her. His foot caught her ankle, and she tumbled forward, glancing off the base of an oak tree and sprawling to the cold ground. Before she could make it back to her knees, he was straddling her lower back and had her right wrist lifted up her spine to her neck. Pain knifed through her shoulder, and she screamed again.

"Where is Travers?" he hissed into her ear. "I had him right in my sights, and then he fell off my screen."

"Off your screen? What do you mean?"

"Don't worry about it. Now where is he?"

Maddux wasn't heavy. In fact, he felt light on her back. She should be able to move him, but she couldn't. Somehow he had her left wrist locked beneath his left knee, and she could barely twist her body without feeling excruciating pain.

"Let me go!" she shouted. The pain was almost too much to bear— almost, but not quite. He knew what he was doing. "Please," she begged pathetically. She'd never felt anything like this.

"I will gouge out your eyes one by one. You tell me where Travers is, or there goes your vision."

"I don't know." His lips were touching her ear, then her cheek. It felt almost as if he'd kissed her gently. "I swear to God I don't know."

"Is he still with Troy?"

"I don't know!" she yelled, writhing desperately to move away from his mouth despite the pain.

"I need to save this country, Karen. I need to know where Wilson Travers is!"

She screamed as loudly as she could. It wasn't from pain anymore. It was from the prospect of pain. His finger was crawling slowly but inevitably across her face toward her left eye, about to inflict possibly the worst pain she could imagine. He was going to do exactly as he threatened. He was going to gouge it out with his bare hand. She struggled violently, but Maddux was a human vise.

"Tell me."

His fingertip was almost there. "No. God, no, no, no!"

"At this point you are going to lose at least one eye, Karen," he hissed as his weapon reached its target. "Don't make me gouge out both of them so you never see—"

Suddenly he was gone from her back, and a wave of physical relief surged through her entire body as the pain in her shoulder dissipated. She scrambled to her feet, drew her pistol, and aimed it down at him. Maddux lay on the ground a few feet away, shaking and quivering and slowly but inevitably constricting into a fetal position. He was trying to speak, but the tremors wouldn't allow it. His words were just garbled mutterings. He'd obviously been tased hard.

"Hello, Karen."

Her eyes darted left, toward the voice, and she whipped the barrel of the gun around and pointed it at the shadowy figure standing only a few feet away. "Oh my God," she whispered.

CHAPTER 24

FOR THE first time ever, Jacob Gadanz had spent an entire weekday afternoon away from company headquarters with Elaina and Sophie—he'd even turned off his cell phone while he was with them, which he *never* did. In fact, he'd needed Elaina to show him how. He'd lost that phone for a few hours one morning last month and never felt more naked in his life. But after turning it off today, he'd completely forgotten about it.

He didn't regret being out of touch, either. In fact, he found, after a great deal of trepidation about turning it off, that he loved the freedom. Even more amazing, the company actually survived without him. The only thing he ended up regretting was that he hadn't started doing this a long time ago.

The three of them had gone ice-skating at a rink near the townhouse, and it brought tears to his eyes to see how athletic they were, especially Sophie. She was fast and agile and skated rings around Elaina, who wasn't bad herself but clearly couldn't keep up with her younger sister. It wasn't that Sophie was so much more physically capable. In fact, Elaina was slightly more coordinated, Gadanz judged, and definitely stronger. It was Sophie's daring spirit that enabled her to be so much more entertaining. She was fearless, and it was emotional for him when several people watching from the bleachers clapped out loud and cheered at one of her moves.

Afterward he'd splurged for an expensive dinner at an upscale restaurant near the rink. They'd all laughed until they'd cried as the girls regaled him with story after story about younger days when they'd shared a bedroom and played tricks on each other at night while the other slept. Bygone days when things were much simpler, Gadanz concluded ruefully as he'd sipped on a delicious glass of pinot noir and watched them enjoy themselves so fully, struck by how little he really knew about them and vowing to make it up to them as the wine took effect. It was the first alcohol he'd consumed in three years—since Sasha's brother had married, he'd realized as he wiped the tears of joy and laughter from his eyes, which he wasn't at all embarrassed by.

He came to another, much more important conclusion as he sat there listening to them tell their tales, innocently enjoying himself in a way he hadn't for as long as he could remember. It was time to take control of his life—and theirs—and move everything in a drastically different direction. His girls deserved that, and so did he. He'd been an absent father too long, far too focused on business and not family. There was more to life than numbers on a computer screen and checking per-store sales figures every fifteen minutes. Maybe they wouldn't join the family business after all, he realized. Maybe they should be free to choose their life pursuits—even their husbands—for themselves. Perhaps freedom to go their own way was truly the greatest gift he could give them.

When the girls were asleep, he'd kissed Sasha good-bye on the lips— another first in forever, which had drawn a wide-eyed look of surprise from her and then a nostalgic smile. Then he drove the old Accord to Dulles Airport, parked in the cheap lot far from the terminal, and boarded the last Delta flight out, sitting middle seat in coach. He'd almost paid the considerable extra fare for the last seat in first class, which was available, but then decided against it. Too much change in one day might not be a good thing.

After landing in Miami, he'd rented a midsize sedan and driven into the central part of the state, north of the Everglades and Lake Okeechobee. The coasts were densely populated, but for the most part central Florida was quite desolate until one neared Orlando and the thriving American metropolis a cartoon mouse had created.

Under the cover of darkness he'd moved past the gate of the sprawling compound—after having his license carefully inspected beneath the bulb of a glaring flashlight—and parked the rental car inside a huge barn in between two sleek-looking private jets, as directed. The compound was well guarded, though not obviously so, all in an effort to keep prying eyes in the sky—humans in planes and satellites in orbit farther up—from becoming suspicious.

Unwanted visitors to the property were swiftly and effectively dealt with, but they didn't even know they were in danger until they were within a hundred yards of anything sensitive. Only then were trespassers confronted by an overwhelming force of guards and dogs after being watched by well-hidden surveillance cameras from the moment they'd stepped onto the five-thousand-acre property. And it wasn't as if many people trespassed, anyway—intentionally or accidentally. As far as the locals and migrant workers were concerned, this was just another huge citrus plantation.

"This way," one of the men ordered in a heavy Spanish accent as Gadanz rose from the car and the barn door slid smoothly shut behind it, hiding the planes and his car. "Come on, let's go. Hurry up."

Three men carrying automatic weapons escorted him out of the barn and down a long, narrow, crushed-gravel path lined by tall palm trees that swayed gently in the warm breeze. It was eighty-one degrees here, even at this time of night, even at this time of year—which was nice. What made it unpleasant was the humidity. It made him sweat like a dog, it always had. He would never retire to Florida, he promised himself as he moved quickly along with the gravel crunching loudly beneath his hard-soled shoes. Northern Virginia summers were bad enough as far as humidity went.

"In there," the man directed, motioning at the door of a small outbuilding with the barrel of his gun, which was strapped over one shoulder.

Gadanz moved into the dimly lit one-room building first, followed by the three men. It reeked of mildew, and he grimaced when he caught the first major whiff. He'd always been sensitive to nasty odors.

"Over by the far wall."

He did as he was told. This detour did not surprise or scare him. It was simply par for the course, drama for a man who lived for drama—by a creed of drama, really—and always had. But in the final analysis, perhaps that flair for the dramatic was a key to his success, one of them, anyway. If success was what all of this could really be called.

"Turn and face us."

Again, Gadanz did as he was ordered. It was all bullshit, but he would oblige them as he always had before—though coming in this building prior to the meeting was a first and did set off a faint alarm in the back of his brain, as he thought about it again. But it was probably nothing.

"Now what?" he asked impatiently.

"Take off your clothes," one of the men ordered as an incredibly bright row of track lights illuminated in Gadanz's face from in front of the men.

The blinding rays were coming straight at him, and he could no longer see the men. *"What?"* he asked incredulously, holding one hand to his eyes to protect them. He couldn't have heard right. "What did you say?"

"Strip."

He'd heard them all right. This was absurd. "I will not."

"You will."

"Do you know who I am?"

"We know exactly who you are. Now strip, before we take your damn clothes off for you. We search everyone the same way, no matter who they are. Those are the orders from the top."

A few moments later he stood naked before them, with his clothes lying in a heap on the cement floor beside him. He could hear them chuckling at his doughboy physique.

"Turn around."

Or maybe they were laughing because it only took one hand to cover his genitals.

"Now!"

"All right, all right."

"Hands above you, palms on the wall, legs spread wide."

"Jesus," he muttered as he obeyed once more. That alarm in the back of his head grew louder.

Ten minutes later Gadanz sat in a spacious, starkly furnished room in one corner of the large main house. It was nearly dark in here, and he was wearing just a robe. He'd been informed that he'd get his clothes back when he left. The robe smelled pungently of detergent, and he'd noticed when he'd first entered the room that it smelled almost as strongly of disinfectant. Now that he was getting accustomed to it, it wasn't so noticeable.

Wasn't that always the way with everything? *First impressions were so important,* he thought as he looked around and his eyes became more accustomed to the lack of light. He had to admit he was relieved. He'd thought maybe there was more to all of what had happened in the outbuilding than simply a search of his person. He hadn't been worried about his life, not really. But he'd come to the conclusion that people as a whole were pretty depraved sexually, and he'd been concerned that the search was going to get personal.

Gadanz was sitting in an uncomfortable wooden chair that was decidedly too small for him and felt as if it might collapse beneath his weight at any moment. It was positioned directly in front of a much larger chair that was set on a raised platform such that anyone sitting in it would be several feet above him. It was as if he were waiting for an audience with a king.

Gadanz hadn't visited here in three months. In that short time, the level of eccentricity, arrogance, and delusions of grandeur had clearly reached new, unprecedented, and frightening heights, he realized as he gazed at the platform and the large chair on it. Daniel had to be out of his mind by now—or within a razor's edge.

After fifteen painfully slow-passing minutes, a door on the far side of the dimly lit room finally opened, and a hooded figure entered, followed closely by two more individuals. The lead figure moved deliberately toward the platform, climbed the stairs at the back of it, and eased into the large, comfortable-looking chair. As he climbed the stairs, the other two individuals peeled off on either side of the platform until they were parallel to the chair atop the platform, where they stopped and stood with their arms at their sides.

Only then did Gadanz realize that these other two individuals were women—gorgeous women who were completely naked.

"Hello, Jacob."

"Hello, Daniel," Gadanz replied respectfully as his younger brother pulled the hood back and gazed down from the platform.

Jacob had been completely prepared to lambaste Daniel for the terrible treatment he'd received since arriving at the compound. But now that he was in his brother's presence, he was not so keen to criticize. The naked women were staring straight at him, making him nervous. Worse, Daniel scared the hell out of him. He always had, ever since they were children, despite being the younger sibling. The thing about Daniel: From a very young age he would always do what others would not to get what he wanted. He was always willing to go one step further, no matter the consequences. So at that early age he'd developed a fierce reputation. He'd carried that attitude with him into adulthood and had become fabulously wealthy. Of course, the cause-and-effect dynamic had followed Daniel around, as it inevitably followed everyone. He wasn't immune from the laws of nature just because he was fierce.

"I trust you've been well, brother."

Daniel sniffed as though he had a cold or a nasal infection. "Well enough." But it was probably the cocaine causing his irritation.

"I'm glad to hear that."

Like Jacob, Daniel was tall and swarthy with a prominent belly. They were only a year apart in age, and physically they looked quite similar. But somehow, Daniel managed to cut a noticeably more imposing figure. Even Jacob recognized that. Daniel was naturally charismatic—Jacob not at all. It was just one of those intangibles for which there was no reasonable explanation. But that was okay. Charisma inevitably brought attention, which Jacob reviled.

"How are Elaina and Sophie?" Daniel asked in his whispery, gravelly voice.

"They're fine. In fact, they're the main reason I've come all the way down here to see you tonight. I need to talk to you about—"

"How is the business?"

"It's fine, Daniel, just fine."

"Are you keeping Kaashif's men well supplied with cash?" Daniel asked, sniffing hard twice.

"Yes, but I—"

"It's so important that you do," he said, nodding at the women in turn. "So important," he repeated. "They are doing my most important work."

The women moved to where Jacob sat and knelt down in front of him side by side. They were young, beautiful, and blond, and both of them placed their hands on his bare knees after spreading his robe slightly apart. It quickly became embarrassing for him, but he tried to ignore his obvious physical reaction. Sasha had been reasonably pretty at one time long ago, but never anything like these girls. He'd never been with any woman who was even close to as beautiful as they. Now that they were so near and he could see their delicate features more clearly, he wondered if they were even eighteen.

"Daniel," he spoke up, trying desperately to block them out of his mind, "I can't be involved in that situation anymore."

"You can and you will," Daniel retorted gently but firmly as one of the girls dutifully lifted a small mirror to Jacob's face and handed him a short straw while the other slid her hand far up Jacob's thigh. "You must. I trust you to carry out my work."

Jacob took the straw, placed one end in his nose, leaned down, pointed the other at one end of a thick, caterpillar-like formation of white powder, and inhaled deeply as he snorted all of the powder into one nostril. The effect was instantaneous. Adrenaline began coursing powerfully through his system, and there was a pleasant, numbing drip at the back of his throat, which helped drive the buzzing in his body to an intensely pleasurable level.

"Have you met with Kaashif directly?" Jacob asked, handing the straw back to the beauty kneeling at his feet.

"Yes. It was necessary for planning purposes."

"That puts me in so much danger, brother. How could you do that to me? You told me I would always be the go-between. You told me you would never meet with him."

"Things changed. Don't worry. You'll be fine, Jacob."

"My business must be completely legitimate. No more money laundering for these people. Please, Daniel."

"I'm sorry, Jacob, but you must continue your commitment to me. This is the most important time."

"I've paid you back for staking me. You gave me a million dollars to found Gadanz and Company, and I've given you ten million in return. Let me go. My debt is more than repaid, brother."

"I told you I'd need a favor someday that didn't involve money. This is it. I need your loyalty now more than ever."

The same girl handed Jacob the mirror and the straw again. She'd prepared another huge line for him from out of a small clear package. Once again he did the entire length of it in a single snort, though with the other nostril. He closed his eyes in quiet ecstasy as the powder worked its magic. This was the good stuff. Not the shit the street snorted.

"Kaashif wants me to set the squad up in another location," Jacob explained. He was aware that he was suddenly talking louder and faster, but he couldn't rein himself in.

"They cannot be apprehended. Not yet, Jacob. They haven't created enough chaos yet. I want many more people dead. They need a safe place to hole up. You must take care of them."

"Why has this responsibility to take care of the squad in northern Virginia fallen on me?"

"Because Imelda was taken, and she has not resurfaced. Kaashif told you that." Daniel cleared his throat loudly. "You may need to help me in other areas of the country as well. Kaashif cannot do everything himself. The squads must be supplied."

Jacob licked his lips and clenched his teeth. The girls were kissing his thighs and running their fingers all over him. His embarrassment had grown to epic proportions. Flaccid, he was small. Fully inflated, he was immense. The men in the outbuilding had laughed. They wouldn't laugh now.

"Please, Daniel, don't make me do this. My daughters could be in danger."

"They'll be fine. They're in no danger. I would never let anything happen to Elaina and Sophie. They are my nieces." Daniel laughed softly as he rose from the large chair and moved carefully back down the steps. "You'll do my bidding, brother," he called over his shoulder as he neared the door, "as you always do."

As Daniel exited the room, one of the girls stood up, then leaned over and began kissing Jacob deeply while the other spread his robe and his legs far apart before running her tongue up the length of him. He gasped with pleasure and then allowed himself to be led from the small wooden chair to the large comfortable chair Daniel had just vacated.

When he had relaxed into it, the girls began to please him again. While one straddled him and slowly moved up and down, the other fed his nose the purest cocaine he'd ever experienced. Then the girls switched positions. Over and over they did this, whispering to him that he could do anything he wanted to them—which he did. He'd never experienced anything like this in his life.

For the next five hours Jacob Gadanz took full advantage of what Daniel had unexpectedly made available. Jacob had made his deal with the devil. He knew that absolutely, but he couldn't help himself. He was weak. He knew that, too. This was the carrot—but there was a stick, too. A very big and very bad stick, which would do immense damage.

He would have to run when he got home, he realized as his pleasure reached the tipping point for the first time. It was the only alternative now. His brother had politely but absolutely conveyed to him that if he did not comply, he would be murdered—as would his daughters. Daniel had not said so in so many words, but Jacob knew his brother. The code was clear.

CHAPTER 25

"WHO IS your contact?"

"What are you talking about, Mr. President?"

"Don't give me that, Stewart," Dorn growled as he glanced out the Oval Office window at a cold, clear late-December dawn that was just breaking over Washington, DC. "Don't play your goddamn mind games with me."

"I'm sorry, sir. I really wasn't trying to—"

"Enough."

He and Baxter were the only two people in there, since Connie had gone to get a Coke and a cigarette. He was feeling much better this morning despite the Holiday Mall Attacks and the attack on the elementary school in Missouri. He'd actually gotten some decent sleep, the pain in his chest wasn't as sharp anymore, and he was starting to feel like his old self again—headstrong and convinced he was right about everything. He still had a ways to go to full recovery, but the end of his rehabilitation was finally in sight.

"I'm tired of you doing that to me, Stewart," Dorn kept going. He was thinking about giving Connie the day off, actually *ordering* her to take it off. He felt that good; he couldn't have her listening to a lot of what was said in here today; and he didn't feel like telling her to get lost every time he needed privacy. "Who told you Bill Jensen was the one who gave the ultimate order to have me assassinated?"

"Sir, I don't think that's something you want to—"

"*Damn it, Stewart,* no more. I want to know, and I want to know now."

Baxter drew himself up in the chair. "A man I've known for twenty-three years. He's a friend of my son's. They trained together. They're close." Baxter paused. "His name is Shane Maddux."

Dorn caught his breath.

"Maddux is a member of Red—"

"I know who Shane Maddux is." Baxter seemed shocked by the revelation, which Dorn enjoyed tremendously.

"You do, sir?"

"He was a member of Red Cell Seven," Dorn said. "But he defected after he was told by Roger Carlson that I intended to obliterate the cell. He's a man on the run."

"Well, that's true, but there's more to the story than—"

"Maddux was behind the attempt to assassinate me," Dorn continued. "He didn't actually pull the trigger. He had one of his subordinates do that. The kid's a sniper specialist named—"

"Ryan O'Hara." It was Baxter's turn to interrupt, to show what he knew and confirm his credibility. "Maddux told me that, too."

The president stared at his chief of staff for several moments, wondering who to trust, how much to trust, and when to open up. As he gazed at Baxter, he made his decision. He had to trust *someone.* It was one of the worst parts about being president. Having to work with Congress was a bitch, too.

"Stewart, I want to destroy Red Cell Seven. Even in the face of what's going on in this country right now with these terrible death squad attacks, I want to burn RCS to the ground and scatter its ashes to the wind. I don't care what they've done to save this country in the past, and I don't care how valuable they could be in the future. We cannot call ourselves a great society or a true democracy when we allow a small group of men to live among us who can operate outside our laws and follow their own creed. When we do, they take advantage of it. And I don't care about some goddamn Executive Order that Richard Nixon signed forty years ago as he was going clinically insane thanks to Watergate. Do you understand me?"

"Absolutely, sir." Baxter could barely control his smile. Much wider and it would seem unprofessional.

"I've been playing Bill Jensen for the last few weeks."

Baxter exhaled a heavy sigh of relief. "Thank God." His smile inched even closer to unprofessional. It was teetering on the edge now. "You should get an Oscar for your performance, sir, and I'll be happy to contact the Academy on your behalf. Let me tell you, I was worried there for a while that you'd actually switched colors and gone to the other—"

"And you were exactly right, up on the third floor of the residence the other day," Dorn broke in. "They did miss this one. They didn't short-circuit the mall attacks. They didn't ID the death squads ahead of time. That's exactly what they're supposed to do, and they didn't."

"No, they did not."

The president's expression turned steely. "Or worse, they intentionally missed it. They ignored it."

"Sir?"

"They wanted it to happen, they let it happen. They knew about it ahead of time, and they did nothing to stop it because they want more-invasive and aggressive investigative powers over the civilian population. They want Congress to roll over and play dead when U.S. intel inevitably demands greater surveillance flexibility as a result of the Holiday Mall Attacks. At the heart of it, they want unlimited powers to spy on anyone, civilian or otherwise. I wouldn't be surprised if some very senior people at CIA and NSA were involved in this thing."

"Jesus," Baxter whispered.

"Either way, whether they knew ahead of time or not, Red Cell Seven is directly to blame for the bloodshed this country has suffered over the past few days. It's just another in a long line of reasons to take them down."

"Yes, sir."

Dorn gritted his teeth hard. "On top of all that, it's personal for me, Stewart."

"How could it not be?" Baxter agreed.

"I will destroy the people who tried to kill me. And I will bring them to justice."

"As you should, sir."

"Which presents us with a problem."

"Maybe not as much of one as you think, Mr. President."

"What do you mean?"

"Shane Maddux is a friend," Baxter spoke up, anticipating what his president was about to say. "But first and foremost he is a confidant."

The president's eyes narrowed. "I don't understand why he'd indict himself to you, why he'd admit his guilt, even if he is a friend and a confidant and believed you would keep his secrets."

"He claimed killing you was simply an order that came from above. He was only doing what he was told to do in his capacity as the leader of a Red Cell Seven division. He doesn't look at himself in the mirror as being guilty of anything. He was only being loyal to the chain of command, as he took an oath to always be, long ago."

Dorn shook his head. "He's one of them. He can't be trusted."

Baxter nodded. "Maybe not, but he can be used."

"Spin that out for me."

"Shane Maddux is in no-man's-land right now, Mr. President, and that's a horrible place to be. He's vulnerable, and he's not accustomed to being in this position. We can take advantage of his weakness."

"How?"

"Maddux's defection from Red Cell Seven was cover. Roger Carlson and Bill Jensen believed that Red Cell Seven could not be seen in any way as endorsing the assassination of a United States president. They were worried, and rightfully so, that rank-and-file RCS agents would not accept a course of action that was so drastic and blatantly unpatriotic. They were worried that it could lead to massive defections. So they gave Maddux the go-ahead to create his defection story, whisper it out to some people, as they did from the top as well. And they gave him authority to recruit a limited number of agents to help him.

"Then Carlson died, and Jensen saw his opportunity when Maddux lost his mentor and protector. Jensen turned on Maddux. He ordered Maddux's execution so he could absolutely distance Red Cell Seven from anything Maddux had done, especially after the assassination attempt failed. In the last few weeks he has subtly convinced the rank and file that Maddux is truly a defector of his own doing. And that the man must be taken out if RCS is to maintain its sterling reputation among the few senior intel people in this country who know about it."

"That's why he begged me for more time to find Maddux," Dorn whispered.

"What, sir?"

"Bill told me that Maddux was responsible for the assassination. He'd blamed it totally on the guy, of course. Said he was rogue, operating completely on his own. I told Bill I couldn't allow the FBI to continue searching blindly for my assassin. It was too much wasted time and money, and besides, the country needed to know who'd shot their president and that the assassin would be punished. I told Bill that very soon I'd have to put the FBI onto Maddux, anonymously, of course."

"Of course."

"That's when he begged me for time. We had that discussion when we were up in the residence."

"Interesting."

"Bill did not want me putting the FBI onto Maddux. He was very firm on that. He told me he wanted to find Maddux and deal with the man himself. He claimed he was afraid Maddux might try to cut a deal with the authorities if he was apprehended. He claimed Maddux would spill everything he knew about Red Cell Seven to try and get leniency."

"Sir, I believe that was simply an expertly crafted cover story. A story Bill put forward to mask a hidden agenda, Mr. President."

"What do you mean?"

"Bill Jensen had a more personal reason for finding and dealing with Shane Maddux himself, another reason that was literally much closer to home for him."

"Which was?"

Baxter grinned smugly. "Do you remember when I asked Bill about Rita Hayes the other day?"

"Of course. He was sitting right where you are now."

"He got animated, very upset."

The president nodded. "Yes, he did. I remember that."

"Rita Hayes was his longtime executive assistant at First Manhattan. She's an attractive woman."

Dorn's eyes widened. The code was clear. He understood immediately why Baxter had used the word *attractive*. "Bill was having an affair with her."

"That's right," Baxter confirmed. "And Maddux knew about it. He had a video she'd secretly recorded of Bill and her having sex. You see, Rita Hayes was working for Shane Maddux. Maddux was afraid all along that Bill wasn't loyal to him, so he did something about it. He recruited Rita to be his eyes and ears at First Manhattan. Now Maddux is convinced Bill knows he has the video. Maddux believes Rita might have told him about it if he'd threatened her, and Bill is desperate to eliminate any possibility of the affair coming to light."

"For obvious reasons, Bill wants to make certain that tape is never played, especially because of all that happened with his wife and him so long ago."

"Cheryl has never truly trusted him since," Baxter said. "That's my information, anyway."

"Would you trust him if you were she?"

"Of course not. So," Baxter continued, "the only way to eliminate the tape coming to light is to eliminate Shane Maddux."

"What about Rita Hayes?" the president asked. "She could talk."

"I don't think so. I think that's why Bill got upset when I mentioned her."

"Why?"

"She's disappeared. No one can find her. He was worried about me digging deeper into all that."

"Do you think . . ." Dorn's voice trailed off.

"Do I think Bill had her murdered because he found out she was being disloyal?" Baxter nodded. "Absolutely. And he has plenty of people who'd do his bidding."

Dorn stared steadily over the desk at Baxter for several moments. "We must destroy Red Cell Seven, Stewart, and this is our chance. They are weak."

"I agree, Mr. President. But we have to wipe them out completely."

Had Maddux told Baxter everything? Dorn wondered. "Where is it that you believe we start?"

"You mentioned it earlier."

"What? What did I mention?"

"The Executive Order Richard Nixon signed back in 1973," Baxter replied. "I know you said you don't care about it, but if we're really going to wipe these guys out we have to care."

"I know," Dorn agreed, frustrated by the obvious.

"Maddux told me that Nixon signed two originals in 1973, giving Red Cell Seven the power and authority to exist and to carry out the laws of the land as an agent of the executive branch of the United States government. Apparently, Roger Carlson took both of them after a meeting he had in the Oval Office with Nixon and his two top aides, Haldeman and Ehrlichman. We must get possession of at least one of those original documents, sir."

"We need to get both originals, Stewart. If we do, then RCS has no credibility, no authority to exist."

"Maybe not," Baxter disagreed gently. "If we have one of them, we'll know what we're dealing with, and I believe we'll be able to prove that RCS is effectively unconstitutional. Remember, history has not been kind to Richard Nixon. We may be able to get that Executive Order overturned simply on the basis that it was he who wrote it. Most people around the world regard Nixon as a criminal. I'm willing to bet the current members of our Supreme Court will, too."

The president smiled thinly and nodded. Baxter was very good at this kind of thing. Despite the man's notoriety for being a consummate prick, he was incredibly valuable. Down deep, Dorn didn't like the man very much, though maybe his feelings were starting to change based on this conversation. "You're probably right."

"Here's the other thing, sir," Baxter continued. "According to Maddux, one of the original documents may be lost forever anyway."

"Why?"

"It was the document Roger Carlson kept for himself, the one he always kept close by. According to Maddux, Carlson never told anyone where he kept it, so it may be lost permanently." Baxter held up his hand, indicating that he wasn't finished, when Dorn began to speak. "But we may be able to find the other one."

"How?"

"Maddux told me that RCS agents greet each other with two phrases. One of them, the first one, is '*Decus septum.*'"

"Honor to the seven," Dorn spoke up.

"You obviously took Latin in college."

"It was high school, Stewart, and I saw that phrase penned in some of the files Bill gave me. There was another phrase written in those files, usually just after *Decus septum.*"

"'Protect the peak,'" Baxter said.

Dorn nodded. "Yes."

"Maddux told me that 'protect the peak' is the second part of that traditional RCS greeting."

A chill raced up Dorn's spine so fast and furiously it almost hurt as the meaning dawned on him. "The hiding place of the second original document."

"Yes."

"Where is it?" Dorn asked breathlessly.

"Maddux couldn't tell me."

The disappointment was palpable for Dorn. He'd felt they were suddenly so close. Now they were back to being miles away. "You mean wouldn't tell you. His desire to be your confidant clearly has its limits."

"I don't think so, sir. I really don't think he knew where it was when we spoke."

"Maybe no one does. Maybe that secret died with Carlson as well."

Baxter shook his head. "Maddux believes that one other person knows where it is, which peak the phrase refers to."

"Why does he think that?"

"Carlson told him."

Dorn gazed across the desk at his chief of staff. "It's Bill Jensen."

"Yes, sir."

Dorn shrugged. "What do we do? Arrest and interrogate him?"

"On what charges?"

"I don't know, Stewart. I was counting on you to figure that out."

"And do you really think he'd tell us anything if we did arrest him?"

The president shook his head. "So you're saying we're dead in the water. We're an inch from destroying them, but once again they slip away."

"Not necessarily," Baxter replied.

"Talk to me."

"I have another confidant."

"Who?"

Dorn smiled when he heard the name. He'd definitely made the right choice for chief of staff. "You know, Stewart, maybe we should search Carlson's townhouse in Georgetown just to be thorough."

"His wife, Nancy, still lives there. She rarely leaves."

"So?"

Baxter nodded. "All right, I can take care of that."

Dorn relaxed into the wheelchair for the first time in fifteen minutes. Until now he hadn't realized how tense he'd been during this conversation. "Where are we with the attacks, Stewart? Is there any new information in terms of leads or clues?"

"Nothing credible, sir," he answered in a low, frustrated tone. "Thousands of crazy tips from terrified civilians, but nothing we can use. Not as of an hour ago, and I spoke to everyone before I came in here."

Dorn shook his head and glanced out the window into the sunshine of the new day. His relaxation had been short-lived. "They will strike again," he said as he looked back at Baxter.

"Undoubtedly."

"Why can't we find them? Why can't somebody do *something*?"

Baxter exhaled heavily. "I hate to admit this, Mr. President, and not because you were right but because it's such a terrible reality for all of us to face. I think you were absolutely on the mark the other night. George W. Bush couldn't find the DC Snipers for three weeks even though every law-enforcement official in this area was looking for them. And as you pointed out, the DC Snipers were just two incompetent idiots. What we're facing now in this country is a hundred times worse. These are trained killers with tremendous resources who are absolutely committed to a common cause."

"It's guerrilla warfare by zealots. It's the nightmare scenario."

"Here's something else you should hear, sir."

Dorn looked heavenward for divine intervention—or something that would take the edge off. "More good news, I'm guessing."

"Economists are already estimating that the attacks are taking approximately four billion dollars a day out of the economy. That's one-point-five trillion dollars annualized, and that's three hundred billion dollars in federal taxes. And that's now. The longer the attacks go on, the worse it's going to get, sir. We're already in recession territory, and it's only been a few days. If these guys stay out there much longer and keep hitting us, it'll be catastrophic for the economy. Obviously the loss of life is the most tragic thing, but"—Baxter hesitated—"what's happening to our economy isn't far behind. If things keep going like this, it's going to be far worse than what happened with the real estate and mortgage debacle of a few years ago. It'll make that look like a speed bump, and a small one at that."

President Dorn turned to stare out the window again as Baxter's words faded. He needed a break, and he needed it fast. Very soon the country was going to start wondering about his ability to lead, even though he'd almost been murdered a few weeks ago. The country had a short memory, and in this ADD world the mantra was "What have you done for me lately?" no matter who you were—even a president who'd almost been killed.

He muttered to himself, suddenly furious. The bastards had finally figured it out.

CHAPTER 26

"HOW ARE you feeling?" Troy asked as he moved across the hospital room toward her.

Jennie smiled up at him sweetly and appreciatively from the bed, which had been raised so she could sit up. "Much better. Thanks."

There was a book on the nightstand, he noticed, with a page marker in the middle. "I understand you had a pretty rough trip to the mall the other day."

She laughed softly. "Yeah, I heard there were a lot of sales going on. You know, because of the holidays. But honestly, I didn't think the prices were very good."

Jennie had a sense of humor even when she was hurting. He liked that.

Her smile faded. "Look, a lot of people had a much worse trip that day than I did."

He liked that, too. She kept things in perspective. It wasn't all about her.

"I'm Troy." She reminded him of Lisa. That beautiful smile of hers was a perfect replica. "I'm with the Feds."

She nodded. "I know. One of the guys outside told me you were coming. Thanks, by the way."

"For what?"

"For having those guys posted outside my door twenty-four/seven."

"Well, I don't want somebody trying to finish what he started."

"Neither do I, believe me."

The bandages on her shoulder were obvious, even beneath her pajama top. But he couldn't see evidence of anything on her chest. If the bullet had entered her back where Dr. Harrison claimed, it must have come through her chest somewhere. And it amazed him that she could be sitting up like this so soon after being shot. She was tough. He liked that, too.

He'd confirmed that two other people in the mall had been shot from close range, execution-style, after taking a bullet from an automatic weapon in the initial burst of fire. They'd both died. As Dr. Harrison had said, Jennie Perez was a very lucky young woman.

"How's your shoulder?" he asked.

"Dr. Harrison says I'll be okay eventually." She grinned. "But I won't be playing tennis anytime soon."

Troy chuckled. "And your back?"

"Fine."

"The bullet came out of your chest, right?"

"Um, yeah."

"It didn't stay in there."

"No."

"A one-in-a-million wound." She didn't touch herself anywhere on her chest when he'd asked that. She hadn't even looked down at the spot. Most people would have. Maybe it was nothing. He glanced at the end of the bed, then around the room. No charts anywhere.

"That's what he keeps telling me."

He was so suspicious of everything, a function of being in RCS for six years. "You're a hero. You saved that little girl."

"I just did what anyone else would have done."

Troy gazed at her for several moments. He was attracted to her, he couldn't deny it. "I'm not sure that's true," he said softly, reaching out to take her hand. It was a very forward action, but he liked it when she squeezed his fingers. "I'm not sure everyone would have been that brave. That little girl owes you her life."

"Thank you. That's nice of you to say."

She squeezed his hand again with her warm fingers, even more tightly this time. It felt good. "Did you see the men who did this to you, Jennie?"

She nodded. "I saw them, but not up close. I was facedown on the mall floor when the guy shot me from close range. I was lying beside the little girl. After that I don't remember anything."

"You didn't notice anything at all about him? Shoes, a smell, his voice, something he said?"

She shook her head as she pulled her hand away and glanced at the other side of the room. "No."

She didn't seem comfortable with the question. Maybe it was too hard to think back on those moments. He could understand that. "Well, I—"

"Hello there."

Troy turned quickly. It was Dr. Harrison. And over the doctor's shoulder, he noticed Travers standing by the door. The major had gone to his place in the mountains to retrieve his phone while Troy had taken care of several things in downtown Washington, and then hopped a taxi here to northern Virginia and the Fairfax County Hospital. Troy wondered how long the major had been standing there at the doorway.

"Hello, Dr. Harrison."

"You didn't tell me you were coming," Harrison said as they shook hands. "I would have appreciated that."

"Sorry."

"Ms. Perez is still recovering."

Troy glanced at Jennie and grinned. "She seems to be doing pretty well." She smiled back, but it didn't seem as sincere this time.

BECKY KIMMEL gazed up at the golden dome of the university's main building as she walked across the God Quad—crowded by students at this hour—with her friend Vanessa. One more early class, and she was going home to San Diego for a few weeks of sun and fun. Just like all the other kids around her were headed home today. She couldn't wait to hit the beach. It had been brutally cold in South Bend during the last few days, especially for a Cali-kid.

Becky and Vanessa didn't make it much farther. Three men came around the corner of the main building, in the shadow of the statue of St. Mary that topped the dome, and opened fire on the God Quad.

The bullet that struck Becky pierced her lung fatally. As her life quickly ebbed away, she gazed at Vanessa, who was lying beside her and staring at her with doll eyes. Vanessa had taken a round directly in the middle of her forehead. She was already gone.

Three more universities, four churches, and two more restaurants were hit during the course of the day—including the University of Richmond by the northern Virginia squad. All of the attacks were well away from the big malls that had been hit initially, and they were all in smaller towns. The squads were spreading out, and the country was shutting down completely.

EVERYTHING WAS playing out exactly as Daniel Gadanz had anticipated—and prayed for. His father would have been so very proud.

He nodded to the pair of naked women, and they approached the man who was seated in the uncomfortable chair before his throne. The man would have them for a few hours and then be killed for stealing. The man was in charge of distribution in three southern states, and he was holding back more than his share of the take. His bookkeeper had squealed, and action was about to be taken. But not before Daniel enjoyed watching the women pleasure the man.

Daniel took a deep breath as he watched the scene unfold. If Jacob hadn't been Daniel's brother, he would have been murdered as well. The bloodline had provided him one more chance. But that would be it.

CHAPTER 27

BILL JENSEN eased into the chair in front of the vertical bars, while keeping a watchful eye on the prisoner the entire time.

Shane Maddux stared back unflinchingly from inside the cell.

Bill had made certain that the chair was positioned well back from the bars, well beyond Maddux's reach. He knew better than anyone what Maddux was capable of, and he wasn't about to give the man a chance to take a hostage in case this exchange grew testy. Bill had a member of the new security team at the house watching via hidden camera, too. The guy had orders to get in here immediately if anything seemed even slightly amiss on the screen.

There was a camera but no microphone. Bill couldn't have anyone but the two of them privy to this conversation. Maddux couldn't, either. It was a good standoff.

"*Decus septum,*" Bill murmured.

"*Decus septum,*" Maddux replied. "Protect the peak."

"Protect the peak. You okay?" Bill asked.

"Of course."

"You were tased three times on the way in here from the cemetery."

"What was that?" Maddux asked, putting a hand to his ear.

Bill began to lean forward, closer to the bars, and then stopped abruptly. That had been a subtle attempt to draw him physically closer. He could tell by the smug look on Maddux's face.

"You heard me, Shane."

"So, what are you going to do with me?" Maddux asked.

"First, we need to talk. Karen said you kept asking about Travers after you chased her down. Why?"

"You know why."

"Was it because Travers gave Kaashif TQ Haze at the interrogation?"

Maddux nodded. "And I want to find Kaashif. If I have Travers, I have Kaashif. As long as the Haze is still working on Kaashif, of course."

"But why did you come after Karen? You had Nathan Kohler slip Travers some of the TQ he was carrying. I know you did. Travers said his stomach hurt like he had food poisoning. And Kohler got him a drink before Travers went in with Kaashif again. That must mean Kohler lit Travers up like a TQ neon sign."

Maddux nodded once more. "Very good, and my phone had Travers covered just fine. Then, poof, all of a sudden the track-and-trace app stops working." He shrugged. "Sometimes that happens. I'm sure you've been told. Some bodies flush the micro-shards faster than others, and some do it *really* fast. Travers was one of those; he turned out to be a bad host. The guys who came up with the stuff are still working out the kinks." He shrugged. "I figured Karen knew where Travers was because she showed up in North Carolina the other night."

Bill shook his head. "She doesn't even know who Wilson Travers is. She was telling you the truth when she said that. I was the one who had her go to North Carolina, not Troy."

"Interesting, you putting a woman who isn't even in RCS directly in the path of danger like that. What's your real motive in all that?"

"No hidden agenda, Shane. She's very capable, and she asked if she could help. She can handle herself very well."

"So I saw." Maddux stood up and began pacing slowly back and forth. It was a decent-size cell, so he had room to take several paces in each direction. "Who tased me, Bill?"

"Not saying."

Maddux stopped directly in front of where Bill was sitting and wrapped the fingers of both hands slowly and tightly around separate bars. "Why do you and I have so many secrets these days?"

"You know why."

"We used to work so well together."

"Yes, we did."

"It wasn't that long ago, either." Maddux glanced at a corner of the room behind Bill. "Maybe we should consider joining up again," he suggested, covering his mouth with one hand as he spoke.

Amazing, Bill thought. Maddux had already pegged the camera's location, and he'd covered his mouth so no one looking through it or examining a tape later could lip-read. "How did you find Imelda? What led you to her in Manassas?"

"I got a tip from one of my guys at Fort Meade."

"Did she tell you anything during the interrogation?"

Maddux shook his head. "All she did was scare the hell out of me, Bill."

That didn't sound good. As far as Bill knew, the man standing in front of him wasn't scared of anything. "What do you mean?"

"I know she was in on it somehow. I'm convinced. I can always tell when they're lying."

Bill was convinced, too, and he'd never even seen the woman. "But why did she scare you so much?" He'd heard Maddux refer to the woman in the past tense.

"I killed her son right in front of her. I sliced the boy's neck wide open while she watched."

Bill grimaced and glanced at the cement floor. How had the world come to this? How could a civilized man kill a small child, even in the name of protecting a country?

His eyes raced back to Maddux, aware that he'd let down his guard for a split second, and that was all it would take. But Maddux hadn't moved. A wave of relief rushed through him.

"Imelda didn't blink. I gave her a lot of chances to open up, Bill, but she didn't."

"Maybe you were wrong. I know how good you are at interrogation, but maybe this once you had it—"

"Imelda recognized Jack's name when I said it. When I said Jack Jensen, she showed me her hand. She couldn't hide it."

Bill nodded. "That makes sense," he muttered, thinking about what the woman had said when she'd first contacted him. "How did you get in that basement in North Carolina?" he asked. "Troy and Travers swore you weren't down there when they cased the place initially. Travers said it was like you appeared out of thin air."

Maddux grinned. "I'm a ghost, Bill. You know that."

"Come on, Shane."

"One of the fireplaces down there isn't a working fireplace. The chimney is really a tiny elevator, big enough for one small person. There's an entrance to the chimney from the house's porch. I'd used it before."

Bill stared at Maddux for a long time, then, against his better judgment, stood up and moved close. "Do you have a tape of Rita Hayes and me?"

Maddux stared back. "Did you have her killed?"

"Was she your mole, Shane?"

Maddux nodded. "Yes."

"Do you have a tape of Rita and me?" Bill asked again.

"Protect the peak, Bill."

"Yes, yes, protect the—"

"Which one is it?"

"Which one is what?"

"I know you know, Bill. Where is the Executive Order that Nixon signed? What peak is it hidden on?"

"I have no idea."

"Carlson told you. He swore to me he did. We must move it. The enemies are closing in."

Bill stared at Maddux. He hated and loved this man at the same time. How could that be?

"Let me go, Bill. Let me do what I do best. Let me protect this country."

"I—I can't."

"More people were killed today."

How could he know that? Bill wondered as he glanced at Maddux's knuckles, which were milky white because they were gripping the bars so tightly. The attacks had started a few hours ago. Maddux had been in here the entire time.

"I must be allowed to stop them. Please, Bill. I'll get you the tape Rita made. No one but you will ever see it again. I promise." Maddux hesitated. *"Decus septum."*

Bill stared hard at Maddux, trying to decide. Ending a promise with *"decus septum"* was tantamount to taking an oath. Shane Maddux would never break an RCS oath. Would he?

"There's a deal here, Bill."

Bill's head was pounding. He absolutely could not have that tape out in the ether. He cringed and nearly vomited at the thought of it being played on some Internet site. At the thought of his business associates watching the intimate things he and Rita had done over the last few years. He put his hands to his face and shut his eyes tightly as he thought about Cheryl watching it, after he'd promised her he'd be faithful to her forever so long ago. He was close to the bars, and he wasn't watching Maddux, but he didn't care. For a few seconds, he hoped Maddux would do something. But what would that get Shane? Nothing at all, which meant he was safe.

"If I don't check in by noon, that tape of you and Rita goes viral," Maddux spoke up, his tone turning nasty. "That's the agreement I have with one of my people. You don't want that, Bill."

"No, I don't," he whispered.

"Set me free," Maddux pushed, "and tell me which peak it is. Tell me where that original of the Executive Order is hidden. You do, and you get your tape." He shook his head. "Do I really need to describe all the ways she pleases you in the recording, Bill? Do you need me to remind you that in the opening scene you use your tie to secure her to the bed while you—"

"*Stop it,*" Bill hissed. Why had he been so damn weak? "No more, Shane."

"And tell me where Kaashif is," Maddux demanded. "I swear to God if you don't tell me that right away, your video will grow wings and fly. Everyone from Washington to Wall Street to Greenwich will see it. Do you really want that? Above all, do you really want Cheryl to see it?"

Bill swallowed hard. He'd never before considered suicide. He'd always called people who took that route weak and cowardly. He'd always sworn to himself that no matter how bad anything got, he would never take his own life. Suddenly he wasn't so sure.

CHAPTER 28

"THAT YOUNG woman likes you," Travers said as they hustled through the Tysons One Mall together. It was the first day the mall had been open since the attack, and it was like a ghost town in there when it should have been jammed.

"What woman?" Troy asked.

They were almost to the cell phone store. They'd been inside the cavernous building for thirty seconds, and he'd counted a grand total of nine shoppers, none of whom looked comfortable being here. This morning's attacks obviously had the majority of the population barricaded inside their homes for good, terrorized. No one was coming out now, not until they were convinced the insanity had been stopped and the bloodshed was over.

Travers snickered. "What woman? You know what woman—the woman in the hospital. Jennie Perez."

"Give me a break."

"Give *me* a break. I saw the way she was looking at you. I saw how you took her hand, and the way she squeezed yours back."

Troy grinned as they headed inside the store. He couldn't help it. She'd definitely snagged his interest—which made all of this so much more difficult. "How long were you standing there, Major?"

"Long enough to see sparks, Captain."

"Hey," Troy called loudly as he approached the first salesperson he saw inside the store.

"Hello, sir," the young man answered in a deliberate, bored tone. He glanced up from the *People* magazine he'd been flipping through. "How can I help you?"

The kid was probably wondering what in the hell he was doing here today, Troy figured as he pulled a heavy gold badge from his pocket and held it up. He probably wasn't afraid of the place being attacked again— why would he be? There was no one here to kill.

"I'm a federal agent, and I'm investigating the Holiday Mall Attacks."

The kid had been leaning on the glass counter, which was filled with different phones, but he stood straight up to look at the badge when he heard that. "Yes, sir."

The badge was fake, but it looked heavy and real, and the kid bought in to its authenticity immediately. "I want to know who in here helped this woman," Troy said, stowing the badge before pulling out his cell phone and showing the kid the picture of Jennie he'd taken during his first visit to the hospital.

"Wow," the young guy murmured as he glanced at the picture, "she's pretty."

"She was in a few days ago," Troy continued, "a few minutes before the attack here went down. I have her credit card receipt. She bought a phone in this store. And according to those credit card records, your company is her service provider as well."

"Okay."

Troy skipped to a picture he had of the sales receipt for the phone. One of Travers's contacts had found it and e-mailed it over. Troy pointed to a number on the screen after he expanded the receipt. "That's the sales-man's number on the receipt. Who is it?"

The kid's expression brightened. "That's Chad's ID number. He's right there."

Chad was on the other side of the store and looked over when he heard his name. "How can I help you, sir?"

Troy moved quickly to where Chad was standing. "You helped this woman just before the attack here." Troy showed him the picture of Jennie lying in the hospital bed. "Do you remember her?"

Chad rolled his eyes. "How could I forget her? She's beautiful. I asked her out while she was buying the phone. I thought I was golden, but then all of a sudden she had to go." He shook his head as he glanced at her photo again. "Is she all right? My God, did she get shot in the attack?" he asked as his voice rose quickly.

"She'll be fine," Troy answered, stowing the phone in his pocket and quickly pulling out and flashing the badge again. "According to the records I have in my possession, your company is also her service provider."

"Yeah, I remember. That's right."

"I want to see the record of her calls for the last thirty days."

Chad spread his hands wide. "Hey, man, I can't let you—"

"You can, and you will," Travers interrupted, leaning past Troy and over the counter so Chad had to lean back. "Otherwise you'll be in direct conflict with the federal government's ongoing investigation of the Holiday Mall Attacks. Is that what you want, son? I don't think so," he said firmly, answering his own question. "With what's going on in the world right now, that could land you in Leavenworth doing hard time for ten-to-twenty. Now show us those phone records of hers."

"WE HAVE to leave," Gadanz said into Sasha's ear when he'd made it inside their Manassas townhouse and turned the stereo up loud.

For all he knew Daniel had planted listening devices in the home. Hopefully, the stereo would give them cover if there were bugs in here.

"I need time to get my affairs in order at the company, and then we have to leave."

Forty minutes ago, he'd hurried off the plane from Miami and raced home from Dulles in the Accord, terrified that something had happened to Sasha when he couldn't reach her after calling her number three times on the way. He'd prepared himself to find them all dead, murdered by Kaashif or one of Daniel's men as a clear message not to fuck up and to toe the line.

"Do you understand?"

Jacob had almost been overcome by relief when she met him just inside the door a moment ago. Maybe he'd let his paranoia go too far; maybe the cocaine was still playing tricks on him—he hadn't slept in thirty-six hours now, and it had been so pure he was still feeling it. Whatever it was, he was completely convinced they had to get out fast even though everything appeared to be fine. This afternoon Jacob was going to arrange a move to new quarters for the death squad here in northern Virginia, to make it seem like he was cooperating and doing what he'd been told. But once that was checked off the list, he wasn't doing anything else for Daniel or Kaashif. Once the squad had been moved, he was going to transfer two million dollars out of Gadanz & Company—the most he possibly could—to where it would never be found. He and the girls would have to live on that money for the rest of their lives, because he could never lift his head above ground again and expect to survive.

"We'll pack whatever we can, put it in the minivan tonight, and take off first thing tomorrow morning." Tears were already spilling down Sasha's cheeks. "We'll be all right, sweetheart, I promise we will."

"Jacob," she said as he gently wiped moisture from her face, "does this have anything to do with the Holiday Mall Attacks?"

He gazed down at her for several moments, and then nodded once.

She turned and raced for the stairs to pack.

"JESUS CHRIST," Travers muttered as they pulled to a stop in a parking spot at the Fairfax County Hospital.

"What is it, Major?"

Travers glanced up from his phone and over at Troy with a shell-shocked expression. "Don't get too fond of Jennie."

"What do you mean? Why not?"

"Remember I told you and your father about following Kaashif from Philadelphia down here to northern Virginia?"

"Sure."

"How Kaashif went to see a woman in Manassas named Imelda Smith?"

"Yeah, so?"

Travers held his phone up. "I just got a report back from one of my guys. You're not going to believe this."

"Try me."

"One of the numbers on Jennie's list of calls for the last thirty days is for Imelda Smith."

Troy's heart skipped a beat, and the world suddenly seemed to be closing in around him. And then his phone went off with a text. "Holy shit," he whispered as the words on the tiny screen blurred in front of him. He'd run a detailed background check on Jennie Perez, and the results were in.

Jennie was Lisa Martinez's first cousin. No damn wonder they reminded him so much of each other.

SOPHIE AND Elaina shrieked with joy as they jumped from the school bus and ran for their father.

Jacob scooped up Sophie in one big arm and hugged Elaina with the other. He kissed Sophie several times, then put her down and hugged and kissed Elaina.

He didn't care about money anymore, he realized as he gazed at Sasha over Elaina's slender shoulder. She was doing her best to hold back her emotions, but he knew what she was going through. She wanted to get out of here right away, but he had to move the squad and the money.

He'd been a bastard last night in Florida, he'd given in to terrible temptation and all that Daniel held dear. Well, that would never happen again, he promised himself as he hugged his girls. Tomorrow morning they would drive somewhere, anywhere that was far, far from here, and settle down quickly into an anonymous life. From this day forward he would cherish and do anything he could for the three people he cared most about in the world—his three girls.

And he would kill anyone who tried to harm them.

CHAPTER 29

TROY KISSED Little Jack's forehead and then handed him carefully back to Cheryl. He loved the way the boy smelled; he couldn't get enough of that new-baby aroma. It was so fresh and beautiful—except when the little guy had an accident, like now.

"I'll take care of everything," Cheryl said, laughing and rolling her eyes as she took the bundle from Troy.

"Thanks."

"No problem."

Bill and Troy were sitting at the card table in the Jensen basement. His father hadn't seemed himself tonight at all, Troy realized. It wasn't that he seemed preoccupied; he seemed depressed, which worried Troy. Bill was always the rock. He wasn't always pleasant, but he was always calm and collected at crunch time when people around him were panicking.

Right now was one of those times the country needed Bill to be calm and focused. Ten more attacks today, and once again, none of the guilty had been apprehended. Local law enforcement had arrested two men in Boise, Idaho, where an attack believed to have been perpetrated by one of the death squads had been carried out at a shopping center in the suburbs, killing five and wounding seven. But the arrests had turned out to be false. Just a couple of guys in a pickup truck heading into the mountains to hunt elk and loaded down with weapons and ammunition, pulled over on their way out of town by ten cop cars and a SWAT team.

"You all right?" Cheryl asked as she leaned down to kiss Bill's cheek on the way out of the room.

"Fine. Why?"

"You're not yourself tonight," she said as she headed for the door.

"That's ridiculous. And do not bring that baby back in here."

"See?"

"Stop it, Cheryl."

"I know you too well," she said as she reached back for the handle to close the door behind her. "Something's not right."

When she was gone, Bill muttered a few unintelligible words and then pointed at Troy without looking. It was another sure sign that something was wrong. He always made direct eye contact when he was giving an order. It was a holdover habit from his Marine days.

"Come on out, Major," Troy called toward the closet.

When Travers had emerged from his usual hiding spot and was seated at the table again, Bill took a deep breath. "Where are we?" he asked, rubbing his eyes.

"We wanted to give you an update." He and Travers had been at the house for an hour, but Bill had been on the phone until ten minutes ago, supposedly dealing with an issue at First Manhattan. Troy could tell Travers was starting to get impatient. Taking another roundabout way through the woods to get to the mansion tonight hadn't helped the major's demeanor, either. "It's important."

"Okay, go."

"I know you weren't happy about me seeing this Jennie Perez woman in the first place, but—"

"It wasn't that," Bill interrupted. "I just thought it was a distraction."

"Well, it turns out it wasn't."

"Oh?"

His father's tone just then had seemed odd. It was almost as if he'd been expecting this development, Troy thought. "She knew a woman named Imelda Smith," he explained. "Or was at least having consistent contact with her."

"Imelda Smith is the person Kaashif went to see in Manassas, Virginia," Travers reminded Bill. "It was the day I followed him all the way down there from Philly. Kaashif is the young man who I interrogated last—"

"I remember, Major. How do you know they were in contact?"

"Phone records. Apparently, Ms. Perez and Imelda spoke nine times in the two weeks prior to the attacks. Some of the calls lasted for over ten minutes."

"After we left the hospital the second time," Troy spoke up when Travers was done, "we drove out to Imelda's place in Manassas, but nobody was there. A neighbor told us he'd seen a van out in front of her place a few days ago. He'd never seen the van before, and since then Imelda hasn't been around. He admitted that maybe it was just a coincidence, but he was genuinely concerned, no doubt. He told us Imelda has a five-year-old son. The guy hasn't seen the boy lately, either, and he was worried about it. We went inside after we finished talking to the guy, and it looked like there'd definitely been a struggle in the kitchen. Dishes and pans were scattered everywhere, and there were several chairs overturned. The door to the outside wasn't locked, either."

"That's terrible," Bill said quietly, chin almost on his chest.

"You okay, Dad?"

"I'm fine," Bill retorted angrily, forcing emotion into his voice. "I'm dealing with something at the firm, that's all. You all need to stop this crap."

His father dealt with difficult issues all day long at First Manhattan, and he never acted like this. Oftentimes, in fact, he seemed to revel in problem-solving through confrontation. The explanation about First Manhattan causing his sour mood seemed pretty lame.

"You said you went to the hospital a second time today," Bill spoke up. "Why?"

"I wanted to see Ms. Perez's physical charts."

"Why?"

"I just did."

"And?"

"And we got into a records room, and it turns out she hadn't been shot in the back like Dr. Harrison told me she had. That was all a lie."

Bill's expression remained impassive.

"She's Lisa Martinez's cousin," Troy continued. "I ran a background check on her, and that connection came up right away. Ms. Perez was born in Brooklyn and moved to Virginia when she was ten. But I'm betting she and Lisa stayed close after she moved."

"What are you saying?" Bill asked.

Troy glanced at Travers, then back at Bill. "I think what's going on is pretty obvious." He and Travers had run this logic through their collective gray matter several times today on the way up to Connecticut. "Jennie Perez is working with whoever's behind the Mall Attacks." Troy waited for a response from Bill, but got nothing. "These people must know something about Red Cell Seven, Dad. They must have contacted her to try to get to us, maybe to you specifically. I think they figured out somehow that Lisa and I were involved and that I was in RCS." He paused. This was the key to the connection. "Maybe Maddux had something to do with them finding out—maybe everything, in fact. Maybe Maddux put together the whole thing, like he did with the LNG tankers heading for Boston and Virginia. Maybe the terrorists told Ms. Perez that I murdered Lisa after Maddux told them to tell her that."

"Why would you murder Lisa?" Bill asked, obviously unconvinced.

"Maybe because Troy had told her to get an abortion," Travers spoke up, "and she wouldn't."

"She'd already had the baby at that point."

"Maybe we argued about it," Troy said. "Maybe it was just passion boiling over. Ms. Perez would have been bitter and ready to believe anything if she and Lisa were close. They figured she'd want to get revenge, and they were right. They would have had an easy time signing her up to be their agent if they fed her all that. Look, it could be the same terrorist group Maddux was involved with on the tankers. In fact, it probably is."

Bill shook his head. "I don't think—"

"So what was Jennie Perez doing talking to Imelda Smith? And what was she doing in the mall right before the attacks went down? It's too coincidental." Troy was getting revved up, pissed at Bill's stonewalling. "The sales guy at the cell phone store said Ms. Perez was real calm one second, but when she suddenly realized what time it was, she took off. Why would she do that?"

"It's a stretch, Troy. And you know it is."

"Where there's smoke there's usually fire."

"Usually but not always."

Why was his father doing this? "We couldn't find her new phone anywhere. It wasn't with her possessions at the hospital, and no one turned it in. I think she had information on it that was important to them. The guy at the store who helped her said he transferred a lot of data over from her old phone. It's a natural to think that's what was going on."

"Someone at the mall must have gotten the phone," Bill said. "If she was working with them, why would they shoot her?"

Bill kept putting up roadblocks everywhere on this. Unfortunately, that was the one question Troy and Travers couldn't find an answer to, either.

"What about Kaashif, Major?" Bill asked, glancing at Travers. "Did you get any data on him from your phone, from the TQ app?"

"Yes, sir. We believe Kaashif met very recently with a man named Jacob Gadanz who lives in Manassas. The data from my phone shows us that Kaashif went to the offices of a company Gadanz owns, and then later went to a location very near Gadanz's home. So we assume it was Gadanz who Kaashif was meeting with."

"What kind of company is it?"

For the first time tonight Troy saw fire in his father's eyes. "Gadanz and Company operates a chain of convenience stores."

"So it deals with lots of cash," Bill said quietly. "So it has money-laundering capability and would be able to spread lots of cash around easily."

"That's right," Travers agreed, gesturing at Troy. "That's what we thought, too."

"Did you run any lines on Gadanz?"

"Not yet."

"Do it," Bill ordered. "Immediately. Sounds like you're on to something there."

"PLEASE TELL ME," the man whispered compassionately. "I don't want to hurt you. Just tell me where it is."

Nancy Carlson gazed forlornly at the ski-masked man, her mouth dry from the nasty-tasting gag he'd stuffed in there hours ago. In the end, Roger had told her where only one of the two documents was hidden. He'd told her there were two, but he hadn't told her the hiding place of the other one. She was terrified this man would be furious when he realized that she only knew of the whereabouts of the one document and he'd go into an insane rage. She'd been worried about this day coming for forty years, but her worry had grown to terror the moment she'd found Roger slumped over the steering wheel of his car outside the townhouse in Georgetown. She'd cried for him when she'd realized he was dead—and then for herself. She'd considered leaving immediately, but she'd put it off. Now she was regretting that decision.

Her eyes flickered around the dimly lit room. She didn't know where she was now, but she knew it wasn't Georgetown. He'd stashed her in the trunk of his car, and the frigid drive had to have been at least thirty minutes long.

She finally nodded to him, and he removed the gag. "I only know where one of them is," she whispered, "and that's all I know. I don't even know what the document is. I swear I don't."

"It's okay," he whispered back, smiling through the hole in the ski mask as he patted her shoulder comfortingly. "That's all I need. I'm keeping you here until I get it. When I get back I'll let you go. I promise I will. I just have to make sure you're telling me the truth." It seemed silly to say that. She was obviously so scared out of her mind she wasn't going to lie. But he had no choice. "Okay?"

She nodded back. "Okay."

CHAPTER 30

TROY STEPPED into a large room of the mansion's basement. In one corner was a prison cell. It reminded him of the cell in North Carolina, though it was bigger and didn't have that Inquisition-like ring hanging from a chain bolted to the wall. But the steel bars were the same—vertical, black, and cold-looking.

The Jensen family had moved to this house in the countryside outside Greenwich twenty years ago, when Troy was eight. But he and Jack had never been allowed into this section of the massive basement while they were growing up. They'd tried getting in many times when they were left alone. But the thick, metal door was always triple-locked, and there was an alarm—which they'd tripped twice and paid the price on each occasion, the second time dearly, when Troy was eleven and Jack thirteen. It had been the summer, and for two weeks they'd been allowed out of their rooms only long enough to use the bathroom. They'd even taken meals in their rooms.

Troy had found out what was in here only after he became a member of Red Cell Seven. As far as he knew, Jack had died never knowing.

As he looked around, he wondered whether this room had been used not just to hold human beings but to interrogate them as well. He'd made his peace with the need for RCS interrogations to be thorough—rough, even—but for some reason it would bother him to know that torture had occurred in the house where he'd grown up. Which didn't make much sense, he realized. You were either in or out when it came to the tough calls in life—and he was all-in when it came to RCS agents using any means necessary to protect the United States.

Still . . .

The cell was unoccupied tonight—which wasn't a good sign, and there could only be one explanation for that, only one person who could have allowed the prisoner to go free.

Karen had called Troy to tell him that Maddux was locked in the cell, but she wouldn't say exactly how he'd gotten there. She was an ex-cop, but she couldn't possibly have gotten him in there by herself. Troy wasn't sure he could have taken in Maddux alone. So he'd pressed her on what had happened several times. But she wouldn't divulge anything more about the help she'd received—she wouldn't even confirm that she had—though she'd apologized three times for being circumspect.

It had to be Charlie Banks, Troy figured. That had to be the person who'd rescued her at the cemetery and helped her bring Maddux to the house. Charlie must have survived being thrown from the *Arctic Fire* as well, and then laid low all this time. His body had never been found. It was the only possible explanation. She'd sounded happy when they'd spoken. That was a tip-off, too.

Charlie must have realized Karen had found happiness with Jack and not interfered, not made contact with Karen until after Jack was gone. Charlie was a good man. Troy looked forward to that reunion. He just wished it could have been Jack. It was a terrible thing to think, but he couldn't help it.

"What are you doing in here?"

Troy turned around quickly. "I think you know, Dad," he answered when he'd calmed down after the voice coming from nowhere had startled him.

"How did you . . . ?" Bill's voice trailed off.

"Karen called me. She said she was visiting Jack's grave last night when Maddux confronted her. She said he tried finding out where Travers was, and assaulted her when she couldn't tell him. He figured she was holding out, but she wasn't. At least, that's what she told me." Troy shrugged. "Why was Shane looking for Major Travers?"

"He figured Travers knew where Kaashif was. You were right, son. Maddux is a patriot. He wanted his turn at Kaashif. He figured he could break the young man even if Travers couldn't. He figured he could find out who was behind the attacks. As you are aware, he's very confident in his ability to extract information from anyone."

"Did you tell him where Kaashif was?"

"I gave Shane the address to the house in Philadelphia where Kaashif lives."

"Any possibility there was another reason Maddux was looking for Travers?" Troy asked.

"Not that I'm aware of. Why?"

"Just wondering."

"Troy, if you know anything at all, you must—"

"I don't." Troy nodded at the empty holding cell. "What happened? Why isn't Maddux in there?"

"I let him go," Bill admitted.

"Why?"

"I had to."

"What do you mean?"

Bill stared at Troy hard for several moments. But his gaze dropped to the floor when his son wouldn't look away. "He . . . he had leverage on me," Bill finally said in a faltering delivery.

"What does that mean, Dad?"

"It means if I hadn't let him go, he would have released something about me that I could not have released. It was something that would have hurt your mother very badly. I couldn't have that." Bill grimaced as he finished. "There, I said it."

His father's voice was shaking, and that was unnerving for Troy. The rock of the family was disintegrating right in front of him. "What is it?" It seemed to Troy that whatever Maddux had on his father, his father was more concerned about himself than anyone else. "What does Shane have on you?"

Bill said nothing, just looked away.

This was a shot in the dark, but Troy figured he'd take it. "Dr. Harrison, the man who was taking care of Jennie Perez."

"Yes?"

"You asked me what his name was when I was heading for Dulles to go to North Carolina. But you already knew him, didn't you?"

"Yes," Bill answered, almost inaudibly.

"Why didn't you just—"

"You were right about Jennie," Bill cut in, "in a way, at least. She was approached by people claiming to be terrorists. Imelda Smith contacted her, and they were trying to get information on RCS, as you assumed. And they did tell her Lisa had been murdered by someone inside U.S. intel. But it turns out Jennie Perez is a patriot as well. She told me exactly what was going on when she contacted me. Apparently Lisa had told Jennie about the two of you and that I was your father. I asked Jennie if she would help us by appearing to cooperate with the terrorists. She said she would. She's a brave young woman, Troy.

"And yes," Bill continued, "there was information on that cell phone she bought at the store the other day. She had it transferred from her old one before she left the store. I told her she needed to make certain she had a record of what she gave them, even though the information was useless. It was full of red herrings. It would have seemed important to the people who got it, but it really wasn't."

Troy nodded as it all hit him. "She had no idea about the attacks. She thought she was just meeting her contact that day at the mall."

"That's right, and I don't think they meant to shoot her. She got in the way of a bullet, probably when she was saving that little girl's life. But they still got the phone."

"How do you know?"

"Someone followed up on information on that phone. We set up a couple of data traps, and one was hit."

"So that's why they didn't execute her the way they did the other two people."

"I can only assume," Bill agreed.

"Why did you have the doctor tell me she'd been shot in the back?"

"I wanted it to look real to you because I wanted you to leave her alone. I figured you'd hear about the other two being killed at close range and wonder why Jennie hadn't been."

"That's why you told me it was a waste of time to see her."

"Yes."

"Why didn't you just tell me the truth?"

"I couldn't have anyone else knowing what was really going on with her. It was too big a risk for her and RCS, too covert an operation. I trust you completely, of course, but you could have been kidnapped and tortured, had drugs administered. All the typical stuff, so I was simply keeping to the RCS code. Need-to-know only." Bill hesitated. "Once the attacks hit, I was hoping we could get information on the identity of the terrorists through Jennie. But they haven't reached out to her again."

"Her contact went missing," Troy pointed out. "Something happened to Imelda Smith. Maybe her own people figured she had to be taken out. Maybe they suspected something."

Bill shook his head. "No, it was Maddux. He got a blind tip about her from somebody at Fort Meade, I'm guessing, and he interrogated her. You know what happens to anyone Maddux interrogates."

A sinking feeling rushed through Troy. "What about her son?"

Bill shook his head again. "No."

"Maddux killed him, too?"

"Apparently."

"That's . . . that's awful." Troy glanced back at his father. "Did you know about the plan to assassinate President Dorn? Did you back it?"

Bill stared at his son for a long time without answering.

"Tell me the truth, Dad."

"Yes," Bill finally murmured.

For a few moments all Troy saw in front of him was a fury-wall of red. "When we were at the White House," he spoke up, doing his best to control his anger, "you gave me that whole song and dance about how there could be no excuse for killing the president of the United States." But the emotion was still coming through.

"It was a matter of national security, Troy. David Dorn is making us weak. He and people like him are bringing this country down. Look at the attacks that are happening around us right now. This country is being shut down by a small group of lunatics, and Dorn can't seem to do anything about it. Despite the mayhem, he wants to shut RCS down."

"I thought we were going to be a cornerstone of his intel strategy going forward."

"Come on, son."

Troy couldn't argue with that. Hell, he'd felt the insincerity himself at the White House the other day, even mentioned it to Bill. Dorn had been on a fishing trip, nothing else. And Baxter clearly wanted to do anything he could to destroy Red Cell Seven. "We didn't catch the Holiday Mall Attacks, Dad." Another sinking feeling rushed through Troy. In fact, maybe they had, but his father had another agenda. "Or did we?"

"No."

These multiple shades of gray were hard to deal with. How could he know if his father was telling the truth about anything at this point? What about Roger Carlson? What if his father had known and hadn't done anything? What if he'd known about the LNG tankers as well? "Was Carlson backing Dorn's assassination, too?"

"Yes."

"Jesus Christ."

"Protecting the United States is a complicated proposition, son." Bill had suddenly gone pale. "It's a minute-by-minute ordeal on a global scale, and it's getting harder by the day. You of all people should understand that."

"There has to be a chain of command that's never broken, Dad. This is a democracy."

"Grow up, son," Bill snapped angrily, though his face was still ashen. "Democracy doesn't work anymore. It's a fractured model of government for our country at this point. Our society's too splintered. We've got too many special-interest groups fighting to get a piece of a federal pie that isn't big enough to go all the way around, not nearly. Too many lazy bastards want entitlements, they don't want to work for a living anymore, they want it all for nothing. It's too easy, and worse, too profitable not to steal from the government. Decisions can't be made by the population anymore, son. Congress can't agree on anything. How can you expect the population to? So, in effect, we're paralyzed. A small collection of individuals have to make the decisions that *really* matter. It's the only way we survive. Otherwise it's gridlock that only gets worse and worse. It's a few of us taking matters into our own hands because we have to. It's called leadership."

"I hope you're not serious," Troy murmured. But he knew Bill was. He recognized the truth tone. "You're rationalizing what you've done, you're making excuses."

"When was the last time you looked at one of those old paintings of the founding fathers ratifying the Declaration of Independence or signing the Constitution?"

Troy shrugged. "I don't know." Where had *that* question come from?

"Look at one when you get a chance."

Was this some kind of secret that had been handed down for hundreds of years to a limited few? Was there some kind of code embedded in those paintings, and now he was finally being let in on the secret—like the real meaning of the eye atop the pyramid on the back of the dollar bill?

"Why should I?"

"All those men in the paintings look the same."

Troy stared at his father quizzically. "What?"

"They're all the same, Troy. They're all middle-aged white men. Some are skinny, some are fat. Some are wearing white wigs, some dark. Other than that, they couldn't be a more homogeneous group if they tried. They all basically wanted the same things, and they'd just come off all having a common enemy, which they'd beaten against all odds. They were one. Democracy was easy back then, but it isn't now. We have lots of enemies now, and the worst and most powerful one is ourselves. Troy, every face in that painting of the Constitution signing would be a different color if the signing was today." Bill's eyes were flashing. He wasn't visibly upset anymore. He'd regained his signature calm, and the color was back in his cheeks. "And I'm not saying that's bad. Don't mistake what I'm saying for bigotry. Have I ever once made any remark about Little Jack's bloodline?"

Troy shook his head. "No."

"No, I have not, and I never will."

"I know, Dad."

"I never met Lisa. You've never even shown me a picture of her."

Suddenly Troy felt bad. "I'm sorry, Dad, I just never—"

"But judging by Little Jack, she must have been a very beautiful girl. And from what you and Jack have told me, she was wonderful."

"She was."

"And that's what America should be about at its core. Ethnic, religious, and economic diversity coming together to form the greatest union this world has ever known. It's beautiful and amazing when it works like it did for you two." Bill spread his arms wide. "Unfortunately, the reality of every individual having a vote gets complex very fast when that ethnic and religious diversity broadens as dramatically as it has in our country. We're more diverse than any other meaningful country in the world ever has been, and that's remarkable in and of itself. It's our single greatest achievement. It's also our single greatest problem. It slows our progress to a crawl because we all want what's best for our immediate families and the people we know and care about. It creates that gridlock, which makes us vulnerable to external enemies, and ourselves. And it creates a scenario where the opportunists within our society thrive.

"Sometimes some of us have to take extraordinary measures to make certain that our vulnerability doesn't turn into a situation in which we find ourselves utterly defenseless. Roger and I believed that President Dorn was leading us directly down that path."

The room went still as Bill finished his speech.

As Troy gazed at his father, he realized that Bill had never looked older. He suddenly seemed like an elderly man, a man who'd been carrying around too many secrets for too long. The pressure of it all had finally worn him down. It was sad, and Troy felt heat at the corners of his eyes. For the first time he could remember, Bill Jensen looked weak.

Troy gestured at the bars. "Was that cell ever used for anything other than just to hold people?"

"What do you think, son?"

Troy glanced down. He had his answer. While he'd been sleeping upstairs as a kid, men had been interrogated here in the basement. "I've got to go. I've got to catch up with Travers, and then we're headed to Virginia, to Manassas, to see if we can get anything out of Jacob Gadanz."

"Good. I hope you find something out. We need a break."

"Bye, Dad," Troy said quietly as he turned to go. He wanted to hug his father, but he couldn't. The emotional divide was too wide.

"Son."

Troy stopped and turned back. "Yes?"

"Did Karen tell you everything?"

"What do you mean?"

"Did she tell you who helped her get Maddux in here?"

"No, Dad, she kept the secret. But I think I still know. It was Charlie Banks."

Bill pursed his lips. "Of course you knew," he whispered.

BAXTER REACHED across the desk and handed a manila envelope to the president after waiting for Connie to shut the Oval Office door behind her. She'd given him a nasty look when he'd ordered her out with a gruff "get lost." Two, actually, the second being even more obvious. Well, screw her. She'd better watch herself. He had the ability to punish people now—harshly. And he'd use it again if he felt like it.

Baxter had been nervous about sending the ex-con out after Nancy Carlson. It was the first time in his career he'd ever ordered anything violent like that. But the guy had executed the job perfectly—except for initially wanting to let the old woman go free when she'd given him what he wanted—and Baxter had to admit the power was intoxicating. And he felt no remorse whatsoever for ordering the guy to finish the job because they couldn't risk having any loose ends on this. He'd been a little worried about that guilt thing rearing its ugly head. But it hadn't, not at all.

"Is this what I think it is?" Dorn asked excitedly, grabbing the envelope from his chief of staff and pulling out the contents. "My God, it is," he whispered in awe. "It's an original of the Executive Order Nixon signed back in 1973."

"Yes, it is."

"I hate what it stands for, Stewart, but I'm a sucker for history. This is amazing," he murmured, tapping Nixon's neat, flowing signature at the bottom of the page. "Truly amazing," he repeated.

"More amazing than we'd anticipated," Baxter muttered regretfully.

"What do you mean?" Dorn asked as the enthusiasm drained from his expression. He'd recognized that concerned tone of Baxter's.

"I took the document to two people to confirm its authenticity and to try to determine its potential impact. The first person absolutely confirmed Nixon's signature. He said it was quite extraordinary, too."

"Why?"

"By late 1973, Nixon's signature was illegible, for all intents and purposes. In fact, his signature on his letter of resignation in 1974 is basically nothing but a horizontal straight line. The guy I took the order to showed me that signature. It's as if Nixon didn't want anyone recognizing it, as if he was ashamed and completely exhausted from being president and wished he'd never even considered running. Which is understandable, I suppose, given everything that happened to him." Baxter gestured at the paper Dorn was holding. "But the signature on that document is bold and flowing. It's what his signature looked like back in '68 when he was first elected. The expert showed me that signature as well, and it was very different. You could tell he was excited about being president back then." Baxter pointed at the page again. "He wanted people to know he'd signed that order. He was proud of signing that order, maybe the last thing he was truly proud of."

"Who else did you take this to?" Dorn asked, dropping the page on the desk.

"A man who is a recognized expert on constitutional law as well as on the current Supreme Court justices as individuals. He knows them all very well, and he knows how they would react to something like this."

"And?"

Baxter took a deep breath. He knew how Dorn was going to react, and he wasn't looking forward to it now that the man was feeling like himself again. "And we need to get the other original of Executive Order 1973 One-E. Only then will we feel completely confident of our ability to crush Red Cell Seven," he said, glancing at his watch.

He had a meeting he had to get to, and he didn't want to hang around here. He could see Dorn already starting to boil over.

BILL HUNG up the landline in his home office. It was the third time he'd tried to reach Nancy Carlson, but the ring had just gone on and on. She was a sweet woman, and he hoped she hadn't gotten caught up in all of this. But it made sense that she would. She was the only person Roger had ever completely trusted. He hoped like hell she hadn't paid the ultimate price just for being a good wife.

CHAPTER 31

FIVE-THIRTY A.M. and bitter cold in Manassas, Virginia. During the last few hours another Arctic blast had invaded the Lower Forty-Eight from Canada on the wings of an icy northwest wind. The mercury was plummeting in the Mid-Atlantic.

So far, the three men had been waiting thirty minutes for their fourth team member, and Troy was tempted to go in without him. They had to take advantage of the darkness cover going in—and coming out. If they waited much longer, they'd be risking a dawn exit from the townhouse, which was completely unacceptable.

Finally, Troy spotted headlights coming toward them. Relief and anger filtered through him as the twin beams got bigger and brighter. "You're late," he muttered as Travers came to a quick stop and climbed out of the Jeep. It was the first time since he'd met the major that there'd been a problem. But this was a big one. As far as Troy was concerned, you *always* posted on time in RCS—no excuses. "What the hell?"

"*Decus septum,*" Travers said, aggravated that Troy had omitted the greeting.

"And protect the peak, but look, I—"

"Hey, I hit traffic."

"At this hour?"

"Come on, it's DC. Anytime, anywhere, pal. You know that." Travers gestured at the cluster of townhomes closest to them. "Which one is it?"

"It's not in this area. It's two clusters down." Troy pointed farther along the lane. "I wanted no chance of them spotting us early."

"Two entrances to the place?"

"Yeah, front door and back terrace."

"Floors?"

"Three."

"Do we know how many people are in there?"

"Four. Gadanz, the woman he lives with, and their two kids. I have no reason to believe anyone else is inside the home. I've had the place watched since five p.m. yesterday, and no one's gone in or out since Gadanz got home at seven o'clock last night."

Travers reached back into the Jeep for a pistol that was hidden beneath the driver's seat. They were all carrying the standard Heckler & Koch MP5s tonight, but he was bringing his Colt .357, too. "You say kids are in there?" he called softly over his shoulder.

"They're twelve and nine, and they're both girls. It's nothing to worry about."

"But I assume we're operating under normal procedures," Travers said in a low voice as the four men huddled close together so they could all hear. "Anybody sees us, we take them out, right?"

"We've all got our ski masks with us. It won't be a problem." Troy glanced at the other two men. "Make sure you keep those things on," he said, gesturing at the masks dangling from their belts. "Don't let anyone rip them off."

They nodded.

"Still . . ." Travers said deliberately.

"It's a family in a townhouse," Troy replied. "It's not like we're storming an embassy that's been taken over by hostiles."

"And these guys are *my* family." Travers gestured at the other two men. He'd recruited them quickly for this morning's mission from inside the Interrogation Division. They were Agents Potomac and Shenandoah, as far as Troy knew. "I can't take any chances."

"It won't come anywhere near that," Troy said confidently. "We're grabbing Gadanz, and then we're getting out. We shouldn't be inside for more than five minutes. If we have to secure the other three, we will. Then we'll call the cops after we're gone, to set them free again."

Travers nodded at Potomac and Shenandoah, indicating that they should move off a few paces. When they had, he leaned close to Troy so they couldn't hear what he was about to say. "You're not easing up, are you?" he whispered. "You've got to stay tough."

"What are you talking about?" Troy demanded.

"I don't want to jump bad on you, pal. God knows, you saved my ass in North Carolina the other night."

"Say what's on your mind."

"You've got a little boy up north. I saw you with him. I saw how much you love him. I don't want that getting in the way of what might happen in there," Travers said, nodding down the lane. "Or any other place in the future, for your sake and anybody with you. We gotta stick to procedure. Anybody sees us, and they do not greet the morning light, no matter who they are or how young they are. We clear on that?"

"Major, I—"

"I've seen this before. I've seen guys in RCS back off the edge just a little because they get compassionate when they have kids, sometimes even when they just get married. Something happens when they see that baby or they tie the knot, and they lose our religion. And just a little loss can be plenty. It doesn't happen often, but it does. And when it does, it's a huge risk. That's why Carlson didn't want married guys, especially not fathers, in the cell. We are not in the business of being compassionate. Do you understand me, Captain?"

Troy stared at Travers for several moments, then finally nodded. "Don't worry about me, Major. Do *you* understand *me*?"

Travers grinned and patted Troy on the shoulder, then waved the other men back in. "Okay, tonight I'm Agent Walker." He pointed at the other two. "They are—"

"I know, I know," Troy interrupted, "Shenandoah and Potomac."

"And you'll be Agent Smirnoff."

It was Troy's turn to grin. Travers had told him that Harry Boyd had always been Agent Smirnoff in these situations, and Troy understood that Travers was sending a big compliment his way. "Okay."

For several minutes the four men went over the plan. Troy and Travers would enter the townhouse together through the terrace entrance while Shenandoah and Potomac would cover the front door and cut off that escape route from the shadows until Troy or Travers let them in.

When they were all clear on their orders, the four men checked and rechecked their weapons. Then they donned their ski masks and headed through the darkness toward the target location.

"You get all your errands taken care of?" Troy whispered as they hustled along. Travers hadn't been at all forthcoming about where he was going before meeting back up with Troy.

"Yeah, sure, no problem." He pointed ahead as they jogged. "Any dogs?"

"No."

"Good. I hate it when I've gotta deal with dogs."

"I DON'T know why you are so hating me. It must be because I am a—"

"You're part of a group that's attacking the United States," Maddux cut in, anticipating the card his victim was about to play. "This morning has nothing to do with what religion you practice. But you're right about one thing. I do hate you. Anyone messes with my country and they go on my hate list."

"I am not part of any group doing that," Kaashif replied, moaning when he strained at the chains stretched tightly across his bare back and legs, securing him to the cinder-block wall so he could barely move. A muffled sob escaped his lips as the first tear rolled down one cheek. "I am a high school senior."

"That's your cover, terrorist-boy. It's a pretty good one, too. I'll give you that. And stop crying. I'm not buying it. Besides, even if you really are in high school, you should be a man about this. You chose this path."

"I chose nothing. I should be taking a chemistry test today," Kaashif said through his tears.

"Don't give me that crap," Maddux snapped as he lit a cigarette. "School's out for the holidays. Don't insult my intelligence."

Kaashif glanced over his shoulder fearfully as Maddux took a long drag on the cancer stick, then moved his way. "I just want to go home, sir. Please let me go home to Philadelphia to my mother and father."

"I'll be happy to let you go home just as soon as you've finished answering all my questions."

"But I do not know anything about what you asked me before. I swear I do not."

Maddux chuckled. "Well, we're about to find out for sure now," he said as he pressed the hot end of the cigarette to the skin of Kaashif's bare shoulder . . . and the screaming began.

JACOB GADANZ headed into Elaina's room first. She was the easy one to awaken. As he leaned down to kiss her on the cheek, he could see in the dim light that her eyes were already open and glistening. She was like him, a very light sleeper. In fact, she was like him in a lot of ways.

As he rose back up, it struck him for the first time that perhaps he didn't appreciate her as much as he should, and he vowed to do better at that. He'd have plenty of time, too. It wasn't as if he was going to be working anytime soon. That would be far too risky, especially early on. Besides, they should be able to stretch two million dollars a long way. It should provide them a respectable runway and the chance to settle into their new surroundings with their new names.

He'd moved the money yesterday afternoon. It was hidden and safe but still available. The only good thing about what he'd done for Daniel and Kaashif was that he'd become an expert at cleansing cash.

"Morning, Papa."

"Good morning, angel."

"So, where are we going?" Elaina asked as she slowly sat up in bed and rubbed her eyes.

"It's a surprise," Gadanz answered. He'd told the girls last night that they would all be taking a long trip today. But that was all he'd said; there were no details even though they'd both tried hard to have him say more. "A big surprise." Fortunately, this escape was timed perfectly with the beginning of their holiday from school, so they seemed unsuspecting and excited about what was happening. They believed this was the start of a family vacation. He could ease them gently into the realization that the move was permanent, and he didn't have to explain anything today. "And I want you to help your sister this morning with everything, okay? We have to get going quickly."

"Why, Papa?"

"So we get where we're going faster," Gadanz called back with a laugh as he headed out of her room and into Sophie's, trying to make light of everything. "Good morning, Sophie," he said loudly, "wake up, honey." She was on her side, turned away from the door, which was strange. She'd always slept on her stomach as far back as he could remember. A faint alarm went off in the back of his head as he reached out and shook her shoulder gently. "Sophie, wake—"

"I'm awake, Papa!" she shouted, turning over quickly and jumping up on the mattress with a big smile.

His heart nearly exploded as she leapt from the bed into his arms. "God, you scared me," he murmured as he grabbed her and held her tight.

"I'm excited, Papa. I couldn't sleep, I was so excited."

Now he felt terrible. For not telling them where they were going and how permanent it was; for yielding to the temptations Daniel had plied him with in Florida; for putting his family in this situation to begin with. But he'd needed that money Daniel had staked him with to start the company. Unfortunately, from that moment on he'd been in his brother's debt—which was a bad place to be, even if you were Daniel's brother. It hadn't seemed so bad at the time, but down deep he'd figured this day would come sooner or later.

"Tell me where we're going, Daddy."

"It's a surprise, a big surprise."

As she hugged him again, he thought he heard something downstairs. It had to be Sasha starting breakfast. But he could have sworn she was still in the bathroom, which was off their bedroom on this upper floor.

KAASHIF WAS strong and committed to the cause, but not as strong and committed as Imelda had been. Not even close. As Maddux thought back on his interrogation career, he marveled once more at Imelda's fortitude and thought again about how it would have been good to have her on their side.

"I think I know what your vulnerability is, Kaashif."

"What do you mean, sir?" Kaashif asked respectfully as he continued to sob. "Please let me go."

"I think you're just like me. I think you hate small, confining places." The moment the young man hesitated, Maddux knew he'd broken through the veneer. "You're claustrophobic, aren't you?"

"I do not even know what that word means."

Maddux laughed harshly as he lifted the wooden box off the floor. "You're not a very good liar, Kaashif." The box was hinged in the middle of the front with a hole for the neck in the bottom. It would fit snugly around Kaashif's head and, once closed, very accurately replicate the feeling of being buried alive in total darkness. Maddux knew only too well how hideous that feeling was. It was his only vulnerability, too.

As Maddux began to fit the box around Kaashif's head, the young man began to struggle violently.

Maddux laughed again, louder. "I got it, didn't I, you little bastard?"

"Don't do this!" Kaashif shouted, moving his head about as fast and furiously as he could. "Please, no, no, no!" But he could only resist for so long.

As Maddux snapped the latches at the back of the box tightly shut, Kaashif began to scream much more desperately than he had from any of the five cigarette burns on his shoulders. "Now, tell me what I want to know."

The muffled, panic-stricken screams went on and on until finally Maddux realized he was only seconds away from all the answers he sought.

"YOU'RE NOT touching her," Troy said firmly as he stood in front of Elaina, who was lying in one corner of the bedroom floor, hog-tied and crying into the gag that had been shoved roughly into her mouth. "I mean it, Agent Walker." He'd been afraid of this. If only they hadn't talked about it beforehand, it never would have happened. He'd always been suspicious like that, and he knew how irrational it sounded. But things always seemed to work out more often when he was. "I'm serious."

"Get out of my way," Travers ordered gruffly as he moved farther into the room, pistol drawn. "She has to die. We all agreed on this before we came in here."

Agent Shenandoah stood by the door clutching his MP5, clearly agitated. His black ski mask lay crumpled on the floor beside Elaina.

"Where are the others?" Troy demanded as he brought the barrel of his MP5 up at Travers. Troy had come to respect Travers as much as he could in the short time they'd known each other, and he was not a naturally trusting young man. But he was learning that Travers had a short temper. And he was not a negotiator. "Where are Gadanz, the woman, and the other little girl?"

"They're tied up in the master bedroom," Travers answered, raising one eyebrow as he glanced at the gun barrel. "Agent Potomac is watching them."

"What happened in here?" Troy demanded, gesturing at Agent Shenandoah.

"She was hiding behind the door when I came in," he answered angrily. "She tried to run, but I caught her. She tore my ski mask off before I could do anything about it. This sucks, but it's not my fault."

Debatable, Troy figured, but they didn't have time to argue about it. He glanced at the nightstand and the cell phone on top of it. "Did you—"

"She didn't make any outbound calls. I checked. Not since last night, anyway."

"We don't have time for this," Travers spoke up. "We need to get out of here, but we need to take care of this situation first."

Once again he tried getting at the girl, but once again Troy stepped in front of him. "You're not killing her," Troy said firmly. "She's not a threat to anyone."

"You don't know that."

"And you don't have to worry about it," Agent Shenandoah hissed. "She hasn't seen *your* face."

Troy pulled the ski mask off his head immediately. "There," he said, glancing down into Elaina's petrified eyes. "Now she's seen me, too. You satisfied?"

"Damn it," Travers muttered. "That was stupid, Agent Smirnoff."

"Thanks."

"I don't care," Travers said, taking another step forward, "she's not getting out of this alive. I won't risk one of my men for her. These men are like blood to me."

"No," Troy shot back. He could hear Elaina whimpering pathetically beneath the gag. She knew her life lay in the balance. She'd heard the conviction in Travers's voice. "We're better than this. *You're* better than this, Agent Walker."

Pistol still in his right hand, Travers grabbed Troy by the collar. But Troy flipped Travers to the floor, then backed off and swung the barrel of the gun back and forth quickly between Travers and the other agent.

"I've got an idea," he said loudly as Travers scrambled to his feet and looked as if he was going to make another charge. "Give it a chance, Agent Walker. Please."

JACOB GADANZ groaned as the two men picked him up beneath his arms and dragged him roughly off the floor, sat him on the edge of the bed, and pulled the gag from his mouth. "What's going on?" He glanced down at Sasha and Sophie, who lay on the carpeted floor where he'd been, wrists and ankles lashed together, gagged and blindfolded. His wrists and ankles were still secured, but not tied together anymore. "Why are you doing this to me and my family?" he demanded.

"Who's Kaashif?" Travers demanded right back. "Tell me, or your daughter dies."

At that moment Troy and Agent Shenandoah hustled Elaina into the room. They had put their ski masks back on.

Gadanz gazed at Elaina's tear-streaked face. Did it really matter if he held out on what he knew? As soon as Daniel realized that they'd fled, he would send killers—irrespective of what was conveyed or not. And maybe, if he played his cards right, he could get protection from these people. As much as anyone could be protected from Daniel Gadanz.

He swallowed hard as he made his decision. The life he'd known for a long time was over forever. "Kaashif is a man who helps my brother."

Travers snapped his fingers at Troy and the other two agents immediately, then pointed at the doorway. "You guys get the rest of these people out of here. Potomac and Shenandoah, I want you to stay with them."

"Yes, sir."

"Agent Smirnoff, you come back as soon as you have them in the other bedroom."

Troy nodded. "Yes, sir."

"HEY THERE," Troy called from the doorway.

Jennie glanced up from her book. "Well, hello."

"How are you feeling?" he asked, moving toward her after shutting the door. She smiled that completely unbelievable smile, and he couldn't help thinking about Lisa.

"My shoulder's feeling okay, but that wound in my back is still pretty bad."

Troy chuckled. "Yeah, well, I know—"

"I know you know," she interrupted as she put the book down on the hospital bed. "Your father called. So, what are you doing down here?"

When Jacob Gadanz had made his decision to talk and his family was out of the room, the words had gone on uninterrupted for fifteen minutes. They'd learned a great deal very fast, and now they needed to act on it quickly—to determine if Gadanz had told them the truth, and if he had, to jump all over this chance to stop the bloodshed. But the Fairfax County Hospital was close to the townhouse and basically on the way to Dulles Airport, so he'd taken this quick detour. Travers was waiting outside with the Jeep running.

"I came to thank you."

"For what?"

"You know what, Jennie."

She reached out and touched his hand when he made it to the bedside. "I hear you thought I was a terrorist."

He grinned. "I guess I'm getting pretty paranoid in my old age, huh?"

She gave him a coy up-and-down look. "That's okay. I like older men."

"I'm sorry I thought that. It's just the way I've been trained."

"Lisa cared about you very much," Jennie said after a few moments of silence. "From what she told me, it was a quick romance, but it meant a lot to her. And she was waiting for you. She would have been very devoted."

Troy exhaled heavily. Those were bittersweet words for him to hear. He hadn't been so devoted, and it still ate at him. "Well, I've gotta go. Like I said, I wanted to come by and thank you. What you did took a lot of guts."

"I didn't like the getting shot part. I'm not going to lie to you. But I liked thinking I was making a difference."

"You definitely did, and you should be proud of that." He wasn't sure about this, but what the hell. Sometimes life was all about taking chances. "Um, I was wondering."

"Oh, yeah, what were you wondering?"

"I was wondering if I could take you to lunch sometime." That sounded better than dinner, less intrusive somehow.

She nodded. "I'd like that. I'd like that a lot."

"Good," he said as he turned to go. "I'll call you."

"Troy," she called.

He stopped and turned around. "Yes?"

"Just so you know."

He gave her a confused look. "Know what?"

She gave him a great smile. "You were right."

"What about?"

"If you'd asked me to dinner I would have said no. It would have been too soon for that. But lunch is good." She hesitated. "Don't wait too long to call."

FROM HIS comfortable chair atop the raised platform, Daniel Gadanz watched the two young women please his number three in command, Emilio Vasquez. Vasquez was in charge of all distribution east of the Mississippi River. Since Gadanz had promoted him to that important position two years ago, revenues had skyrocketed in the territory, particularly sales of cocaine and particularly in the small towns. Vasquez was single-minded in his approach to driving revenues higher and higher. Anyone who got in the way was murdered. Competitors, law-enforcement officers, pushers, users—it didn't matter. It was a bullet to the head and on to the next problem.

The man in Colombia who manufactured all of that cocaine was impressed with the increased demand, which was a good thing. Daniel Gadanz feared only one person in the world. That man. Few people knew it, but that man was richer than Warren Buffett and Bill Gates combined—and infinitely more vindictive.

Instead of the wooden chair Daniel had forced Jacob to sit in the other night, there was a comfortable mattress in its place today. Gadanz watched as the two women began to drive Vasquez out of control. They were both voluptuous and absolutely gorgeous with dark features, exactly as Vasquez had requested. In fact, they were sisters, which Gadanz had told Vasquez right before they'd come in here—and that had made the little man with the crooked yellow teeth even happier.

A year ago Gadanz had suffered a terrible injury that had almost killed him. He'd recovered, but the near-death experience had left him physically impotent. So now he took his bitterness out by watching. Perhaps, he mused as Vasquez began to arch his back higher and higher off the mattress, because he subconsciously believed that if he watched enough sex his body might recuperate. Gadanz missed the pleasures of the flesh. It was maddening to have so much money and so much power but be unable to use it on women. The only real pleasure Gadanz took from what was unfolding in front of him involved the fact that Vasquez was married with three children and went to church every Sunday.

He groaned when his cell phone pinged softly. He didn't want to be interrupted, particularly as Vasquez closed in on the critical moment, but he had to look. Only a few people had this number, so the message was important.

Daniel Gadanz's eyes narrowed as he read the brief transmission. "Oh my God," he whispered.

PART 4

CHAPTER 32

TROY AND Travers knelt side by side beneath a fruit-laden orange tree a short distance inside the eastern border of the sprawling plantation, studying satellite images that were spread out in front of them on the dry ground. It was warm down here in Florida in the middle of the huge orange grove, and the heat was a welcome relief for Troy after the bitter cold he'd been dealing with sixteen hundred klicks north in DC.

He closed his eyes, stretched, and took a deep breath beneath a cloudless sapphire sky and a bright yellow high-noon sun. He loved the outdoors. Especially beneath a sun like this, because nature's rawest and most compelling scents were so much stronger inside its comforting warmth. The smell of the earth, the plants, the fruit, even the ocean in the distance were all blending into a single amazing aroma. For some reason his love of life and its basic smells right here, right now, seemed more intense than ever before.

"I say we move," Travers spoke up as he gestured down at the images of the plantation. "It looks pretty straightforward as far as I can tell. We've got a few outbuildings and the main house, and we're done. It'll take our guys fifteen minutes tops to crash and take control of the buildings, even if they are guarded. No one inside can possibly stand up to what we're about to throw at them." Travers tapped the paper on the ground in front of him. "The only thing that could be an issue is a tunnel system. That can always be a problem for an attack like this. But even here in the middle of the state the water table has to be high, just a few feet below the surface, so underground stuff should be a nonissue." He glanced over at Troy. "We don't want to give the people in there any chance to spot us and run. It's time, man."

"Yup."

"I mean, it would be better to wait until dark so we've got more cover, but that's six hours off. There could be more attacks, more civilians could die. I couldn't handle knowing we might have prevented that. We've got to go in now."

"Pull the trigger."

Travers tapped out a message on his cell. "Here we go," he muttered as he pressed the send button. "Battle on."

Multiple personnel carriers were standing by a few miles away, ready to transport two hundred heavily armed special-forces troops to the plantation for the assault—along with three Apache attack helicopters, which would probably break most of any resistance ahead of them before the troops even arrived. The information Jacob Gadanz had provided early this morning in the townhouse, in exchange for his family's protection by federal authorities, had led Travers and Troy directly to this location. And supposedly to Gadanz's younger brother, Daniel, who Jacob had sworn was here and was protected by a decent-size force, though he couldn't give them much on numbers or firepower.

So they weren't taking any chances. They were going to overwhelm whoever was on the plantation and ask questions later, maybe. This mission was far too crucial to the country not to take that approach, for several reasons, it turned out.

"This is pretty amazing," Travers said.

"If what Jacob told us is accurate, I'm with you."

"He was feeding us straight dope," Travers said confidently, checking the satellite images once more.

"Maybe." Some guy who was desperately bargaining for his life and his family's well-being didn't seem like a candidate for a have-faith award.

"I spoke to a friend of mine at the DEA on our flight down here."

"And?"

Travers's phone pinged softly—he had the volume turned way down. "Here they come," he muttered, reading the return text. "Cavalry's inbound."

"And?" Troy asked again, louder this time.

"And my guy at the agency said they've been trying hard to crack a cocaine distribution syndicate that's gone viral recently, particularly in small and medium-size towns east of the Mississippi. He said the ring was already a force in the major cities. But according to a few low-level dealers they've pinched off the streets, and at least one mid-level associate who cooperated in order to reduce a major felony possession charge, the man at the top put a Brazilian guy named Emilio Vasquez in charge of the eastern half of the country about two years ago, and he's tripled revenues in the territory since then. My guy said Vasquez is as vicious as they come and leaves dead bodies wherever he goes. But despite the blood trail they can't catch up to him. He always seems to be one step ahead of them."

"You think Daniel Gadanz is really the head of the syndicate?"

Travers shrugged. "The DEA guy told me a story about a son taking over a Miami drug-smuggling operation from his father back in the early nineties. It sounded very similar to what Jacob told us this morning about Daniel taking over for their father. The names are different, but the city and the years are the same. My guy said it was a small-time operation in Miami back then, just like Jacob told us their father's was. But the son blew it out, made it into a huge deal, just like Jacob told us Daniel did."

"Jacob didn't tell us anything about Daniel and him changing their last name."

"We didn't ask," Travers reminded Troy. "And that's exactly what you and I would have done."

"I guess."

"Here's the most important thing about it. Here's the name that does match. Senior people at DEA believe the man who took over that Miami operation back in the early nineties is now the number-one distributor in the United States for Carlos Molina." Travers paused. "And that was the name Jacob mentioned. Carlos Molina is—"

"I know who Carlos Molina is," Troy cut in. "He's the biggest cocaine producer in all of South America. He wouldn't join any of the cartels down there a decade ago, and now he rules. Everybody else in the blow business is terrified of him at this point. I get it."

"Even the Mexicans," Travers said in a hushed voice. "That's something that ought to make the little hairs on the back of your neck stand straight up."

That *was* an eye-catcher. For a lot of Mexican dealers, beheading rival faction members who they'd captured was SOP. But Molina's people in Mexico were rarely touched. And when they were, hell rained down swiftly on the guilty party.

"I can't wrap my mind around why Daniel would fund these death squads," Troy said. "For me, that's the major disconnect about this whole thing."

"Revenge for his father," Travers answered. "Isn't that what Jacob said? The Feds grabbed his father off the street in Miami one afternoon twenty years ago during a thunderstorm, and the family hasn't heard from him since. Daniel never got over it. It happened right in front of him as the rain was coming down, and the Feds laughed at him as they were driving his father off. He saw what the Feds did to his father, and he feels like he's getting back at them now. He's making them look like idiots because they can't do anything about the Holiday Mall Attacks or all the subsequent shootings."

"Yeah, but I can't believe Carlos Molina would be happy about Gadanz doing that. Ultimately, it brings attention to the syndicate when it's uncovered, even to Molina's operation in South America. I mean, that's exactly why we're here. Attention's the last thing Molina wants. Why would Daniel Gadanz want to piss off his biggest supplier like that, especially a guy like Molina?"

"Think about this, Troy. The death squads are distracting local cops all around the country, not to mention keeping the Feds completely busy, too. It's a huge business opportunity for these blow cowboys. It's an opening that's getting wider and wider the longer it goes on. Street dealers are free to trade, domestic trafficking is easy, even shipments from south of the border are probably being mostly ignored because manpower's been moved away. The death squads are creating a massive distraction all the way around, and the syndicate's taking advantage of it. Think about all the nose candy Molina can skate across the borders with no problem while the good guys are trying to find the death squads."

Troy nodded. "Maybe it is a good idea from their standpoint."

"Good? Are you kidding me? It's brilliant. Gadanz finds and recruits terrorists who are devoted to destroying this country but lack the money and hardware to make any real difference. He brings them into the States on the sly and trains them while he gets everything ready, while he arranges places for them to live, multiple getaway vehicles for them to use, and a way to get them cash, which turns out to be Jacob's company in Virginia. Daniel takes his time so nobody gets suspicious, and he's got plenty of money from the drug business to fund these guys. Then, when everything's set, he gives the order and turns them loose. Eleven super malls are attacked within minutes of each other in big cities across the country. The population is petrified, and the economy grinds to a halt. And the death squads keep attacking, so civilians go deeper and deeper underground. Nobody shops, parents keep kids home from school, workers even stop going in." Travers gestured ahead of them through the orange grove, toward the complex in the middle of the thousands of acres of fruit trees. "Maybe this is where he brought the terrorists initially. Maybe this is where they trained."

Everything Travers had said made perfect sense, Troy had to admit.

"The squads completely distract law enforcement from whatever else they're doing, so the syndicate makes more money. And if the distribution syndicate makes more money, so does the producer. That's why Molina loves it."

"I hear you," Troy agreed.

"Jacob told us this morning that Kaashif is a front man for some very nasty factions in Syria and Afghanistan, some real hard-line extremists who are ultimately committed to destroying the United States. They'd make perfect partners for Daniel because—"

Travers was interrupted by the sound of engines firing up somewhere in the distance ahead of them.

They were jet engines, Troy realized as he rose from his knees, quickly climbed the tree they were beneath, and peered through the branches at the top. He recognized the sound instantly.

"What you got?" Travers called up.

"About five hundred yards west of us, there's a Learjet coming out of a barn with guards all around it." He recognized the distinctive shape of the aircraft's sleek design immediately. "Somebody's getting out of here."

Travers scanned the satellite images quickly. "There's what looks like a runway on here. Maybe whoever it is got a heads-up about us. We've got to stop them."

Troy dropped to the ground, grabbed the MP5 leaning against the base of the tree, and the two of them took off together.

"I saw at least five guys with guns around the plane as it was coming out of the barn. There were probably more. And it looked like they were carrying automatic weapons."

Travers nodded to Troy as they ran through the tightly spaced trees, raising their arms to protect their faces from low hanging branches. He was calling the special-forces commander, who was already heading their way. "Get the choppers in here fast," he ordered as soon as the man at the other end picked up. "And come straight through the main gate with the troops. No need for anything but a direct assault at this point.

We're already headed at them. They're pulling a plane out of a barn. What? No, we didn't see it on the satellite pics because it was hidden in a barn. Look, I'm worried somebody important is hightailing it out of here. I know you got those Apaches inbound, but can you get someone else in the air fast who can keep up with a Learjet? Maybe somebody from Mac-Dill or Patrick with an F-16 they can spare for a little while. Huh? Well, try, damn it. Okay, thanks. And hurry up with those choppers!"

"How long?" Troy asked as Travers slipped the phone back into his pocket.

"Six to seven minutes for the troops, two for the choppers."

"That might still be too late," Troy muttered.

As the barn took shape between the trees, a burst of automatic gunfire rang out, and bullets shredded branches and leaves around them. Both men tumbled to the ground and quickly crawled behind the narrow trunks of different trees for at least some protection.

Troy glanced around, spotted the shooter, who was a hundred feet away along the same line of trees, and fired back as the man aimed. The guy tumbled backward violently before he could fire again.

Troy looked around quickly for anyone else, saw no one, scrambled back to his feet, and sprinted ahead, aware that the roar of the jet engines was now close. The edge of the trees—the last line in the orchard before open ground—was only fifty feet away.

As he raced around a large tree in the next-to-last row, he got a glimpse of the plane and the barn behind it. The jet was only a hundred feet away across the open ground and seemed to be parked even though the engines were whining and whistling loudly. He checked quickly left and right but didn't see Travers.

As he sprinted toward the last row of trees, a bullet grazed his upper left arm, and he tumbled into a clump of tall weeds between two trees. "Damn it," he hissed, checking the wound. It burned like a nest of hornet stings, but it didn't look deep. There was plenty of blood, but the round hadn't hit anything critical. He still had full use of the arm.

More fire from ahead that seemed to be coming from behind several pickup trucks parked near the plane. There was gunfire coming from the left as well, from down the tree line. That had to be Travers.

As Troy rose to his knees and aimed at one of the guards standing behind the bed of a black pickup truck on the left, he spotted a man who resembled Jacob Gadanz climbing awkwardly out of a green sedan that had just skidded to a stop beside the plane. The man wore a white suit and was carrying a large briefcase, and when he finally made it out of the car, he labored toward the steps leading up to the fuselage.

Daniel Gadanz, Troy realized. Big, dark, and extremely heavyset, just like Jacob—exactly as Jacob had described his younger brother. It had to be Daniel, and they could not let him get away, so Troy made the decision. He aimed low, squeezed the trigger, and put the man down even though he wasn't brandishing a weapon. Two guards raced for the man in the white suit even as he was still falling, picked him up roughly off the tarmac, and dragged his limp form up the jet's steps as Troy laced the steps with another burst of fire. The two guards toppled from the stairs back onto the cement like bowling pins. But someone inside the plane reached out and dragged the big man in the bright white suit up the last two steps and into the plane. The twin engines roared, and the jet lurched forward.

Troy jumped to his feet. He was going to try to shoot the jet's tires out. But as he rose up he became aware of a man racing toward him through the trees from the right. He started to turn in the direction of the oncoming attacker, but he realized that the other man was going to have a clean shot before he could swing the MP5 far enough around.

"HAVE YOU been through the townhouse completely?"

"Yes."

Bill had sent another RCS agent to check out the townhome. "Were there any signs of a struggle?"

"No."

He marveled at how the man simply followed orders and answered questions. He must have been intensely curious about what was going on, but he wasn't giving that away at all. He was being a good soldier. "Did you find what we talked about?"

"No."

"Have you heard anything about the woman?"

"Nothing, and I checked everywhere. Her car's here, it looks like all her clothes are here, and the dog's hungry as hell. The thing wouldn't leave me alone, so I fed it. I even called her kids and they hadn't seen her. I told them I was an insurance guy following up on Roger's death and that I must have had the wrong number. Nobody's seen her."

Bill took a deep, aggravated breath. "Okay thanks. Talk to you later."

As he ended the call, Bill realized they had only one option at this point. They had to go to the peak.

He had no idea if Nancy Carlson had given up the location of the Executive Order that Roger always kept. He wasn't even certain Nancy knew where that original was located, if she even knew what Executive Order 1973 1-E was—Roger had never mentioned anything about telling her. But Bill felt he had to operate under the assumption that someone who was unfriendly to the cause now had that original, and he had to retrieve the second one. Without at least one of the originals, Red Cell Seven was in deep trouble.

JUST AS Troy prepared for the awful sensation of bullets tearing into his body, the man racing toward him screamed, spun violently to one side, and then tumbled backward to the ground, throwing his gun into the air with his arms outstretched above his head as he went down into the weeds.

Shane Maddux appeared from behind a tree and then sprinted to where the man lay. He calmly put another bullet into the man's head and then jogged to where Troy was standing.

"What the *hell* are you doing here?"

Maddux grinned. "Not even a thank you?"

"Thank you. Now what the hell are you doing here?"

"I broke Kaashif. He told me all about this place and what goes on here."

Travers had told Troy twice that he was convinced Kaashif would never break. But Maddux had proven that theory dead wrong. "Of course you did," Troy said as he watched Travers sprint toward them from the left over Maddux's shoulder. "You could break anyone."

"Given long enough."

"But how did you know where—"

"Your father told me."

Troy gazed at Maddux steadily as the three Apache helicopters roared overhead. They were no more than fifty feet off the ground, and the rotors created hurricane-force gales beneath them, whipping Troy's long, dirty-blond hair about his face.

Bill had released Maddux from that cell at the house *and* told him where to find Kaashif, Troy realized. Whatever Maddux had on his father had to be devastating, and Troy had a terrible feeling he knew what it was. It sickened him to think about it.

As Travers got to where he and Maddux were standing, the choppers laid down an intense fire on the open ground around the barn in which the Learjet had been hidden, destroying the pickup trucks and killing the guards hiding behind them as the vehicles exploded violently. Then the Apaches moved on toward the outbuildings and the complex's main house in the distance.

As Troy, Travers, and Maddux broke from the trees, Troy headed toward the briefcase on the tarmac. The one Daniel Gadanz had dropped when he'd been shot. After grabbing it, Troy followed Travers and Maddux past the barn toward the main house. As he ran, he glanced up into the sky to the south. He could still barely see the jet's far-off silver shape against the clear blue sky as it streaked away toward the Keys. He wondered if Daniel Gadanz was alive up there. He'd aimed low on purpose, for the legs, not to kill but to wound, because Daniel was worth infinitely more to the DEA alive than dead. Interrogated correctly, Gadanz could convey priceless information that would significantly interrupt U.S. cocaine traffic.

But he'd escaped—for now, anyway.

The two-story mansion was ripped and burning from Apache fire as Troy, Travers, and Maddux approached. Still, someone opened fire from an upstairs window, and they dove for cover behind several large live oaks growing in the front yard.

"No reason to be heroes!" Travers yelled from behind his tree. "We've got two hundred special-forces madmen heading this way. And I'm thinking those Apache flyboys are about to do more damage to the mansion. I don't want to get in their way."

"Agreed," Troy yelled back as the choppers circled back for another pass.

As they maneuvered, Troy and Travers quickly donned bright yellow jerseys they had stowed in their backpacks. They hadn't worn them during the initial assault because they didn't want to make easy targets for the defenders. But now they didn't want to be shot by friendly fire—from the choppers or the troops. The Apache pilots and the special-forces soldiers knew not to fire on anyone wearing yellow. Maddux would be safe as long as he was near one of them.

As Troy finished pulling the shirt over his head, he spotted someone sprinting away from the back of the mansion toward the orange grove. "Major!"

Travers glanced over from behind the tree he was using to shield himself from the sniper on the mansion's second floor. "Yeah?"

"Keep this with you," Troy yelled, tossing the suitcase to Travers from behind the tree he was using. "Do not lose it." Then he turned and took off after whoever was fleeing.

Bullets spanked the dry ground around Troy as he ran, but stopped when he made it to the side of the mansion.

As he raced into the orange grove, Troy picked up the prey's trail quickly. Troy was an expert tracker, and he spotted broken twigs and trampled grass most people wouldn't notice. He could see the trail leading away through the trees ahead of him as clearly as if the person had left footprints in a field of virgin snow.

As he jogged ahead, he noticed the trail of broken flora ending at a tree thirty yards up. So he ducked right, sprinted three rows of trees over, went left, and then headed up this tree line, keeping track of the tree at which the trail had ended by counting trees in this row.

As soon as they'd gotten here to the plantation, he and Travers had noticed that the orange grove was perfectly and symmetrically laid out. Trees were planted in seemingly never-ending straight lines spaced twenty feet apart. And each tree in the line was planted exactly parallel to the tree in the line on either side of it.

Troy moved well past the tree the path had ended under, turned left, counted three rows, turned left again, and moved carefully ahead with his MP5 leading the way. His eyes narrowed as he focused in on the tree. The bottom branches of this one fell almost to the ground, and it was loaded down with fruit. But he could still make out the form of someone hiding in the lower branches—someone wearing a dress. It looked like she was, anyway.

The woman was facing in the opposite direction, in the direction he'd been coming before he'd detoured around this tree. Troy was coming up behind her, and he noticed a blood trail coming down her leg. She'd been hit by Apache fire inside the mansion and taken off. She was holding a gun, he could see as he closed in. Aiming it back the way she'd come from.

Could he shoot a woman? It would be as bad as shooting a child. She was no doubt terrified, perhaps even innocent. But she was aiming a gun, trying to ambush him.

The doubts churned through Troy's mind as he moved forward deliberately, step by soundless step. Had he lost his edge? Would he hesitate at the critical moment? Could he really do this?

The figure in the tree whipped around suddenly—and Troy pulled the trigger, nailing the would-be assassin in the chest. The figure dropped heavily to the ground with a loud groan, and Troy raced the last few yards, burst through the branches, and kicked the gun away from the person's quivering hands.

"My God," he whispered, pulling his cell phone out of his pocket and scrolling quickly to the pictures he'd been sent by the DEA while he and Travers were flying down here this morning.

He gazed at one of the photos for several moments, then down at the face of the person on the ground. He'd just shot Emilio Vasquez. The coward had tried to escape dressed as a woman.

CHAPTER 33

"Congratulations, Troy. You risked everything, and you won. The country will never know what a hero you are." Bill hesitated. "But I do."

"I don't care about the country knowing. I care about it being safe."

Troy and Bill were sitting alone in Bill's big study at the house in Connecticut. Bill was behind the large platform desk, and Troy was relaxing in a leather wingback chair before it. The walls were made of dark-wood paneling, it was night, and the only light was coming from a dim bulb in a floor lamp in one corner of the room.

The tables and credenzas were littered with financial tombstones—Lucite-encased announcements of the many Wall Street deals Bill had done during his career—as well as photographs of Bill shaking hands with politicians and sports stars.

It was like a shrine in here, Troy figured as he looked around. "How many of the death squad members have been arrested so far?" he asked as he glanced at a photo of a young Bill Jensen wearing his Marine uniform and shaking hands with President Reagan. He promised himself that if he ever had an office like this, there wouldn't be a single self-portrait in it.

"Thirty-three," Bill answered. "According to the information that was in that briefcase of Daniel Gadanz's you grabbed off the tarmac in Florida, there were a total of forty-four death squad members. Four of them died in Minneapolis the first day of the attacks, and as I said, thirty-three more have been arrested in the last twelve hours. That leaves seven of them still unaccounted for. But with the data from the briefcase and the pictures of those seven men being flashed constantly on TV, they won't be at large for long." Bill grinned proudly. "The country's breathing a sigh of relief, son. There have been no more attacks, and I don't think there will be. You and Wilson Travers are the reasons why. Red Cell Seven came through again."

"There were lots of people involved, Dad. Those special-forces guys with us today in Florida were studs. So were the Apache pilots. They deserve the credit."

"Not like you and Travers."

"How did Daniel know it was time to run?" Bill was being too effusive with his praise, and it made Troy uncomfortable. It felt forced, like his father was trying to make up for something. "Did Jacob send him a message?"

"Yes."

"Why would he do that?"

"Fear. Jacob knew Daniel would find out sooner or later who the rat was. Maybe he figured his brother would go easier on him if he had at least sent a warning. Maybe he wasn't really trying to save himself. Maybe he was just hoping Daniel would spare his girls, that he wouldn't take revenge on them thanks to the message at the last minute."

"We're going to protect them, right?"

"Absolutely," Bill confirmed. "They are already deep into the program, along with their mother."

"And Jacob's in custody? He's not going free, is he? I sure hope not," Troy said firmly.

"Jacob's dead."

Troy had been gazing at the antlered head of an elk, which was mounted on the wall to his left. That elk had been there ever since Troy could remember, and its presence had always irritated him. It wasn't right to kill animals just to hang them on a wall. He'd known that by the time he was ten years old. Why didn't Bill?

"Dead?"

"He jumped out of a van the Feds were transporting him in from the townhouse in Manassas," Bill explained. "It happened on the Dulles Toll Road outside DC. The van was doing seventy at the time."

It occurred to Troy that perhaps Jacob had help jumping out of the van, but he didn't care. "Jacob got what he deserved. And I'm assuming Daniel got away."

"He did. I understand we tracked the Learjet all the way to Paraguay by satellite. We scrambled two fighters from a base in Tampa, but the Lear was out of U.S. airspace too fast to do anything."

"Yeah, but—"

"And too far away."

"Too bad."

"You got Emilio Vasquez. That was a great catch."

"Is he going to live?" Troy asked.

"You got him good through the right lung, but the doctors say he'll survive. The information he has should prove very helpful."

Troy shook his head. "Vasquez won't talk. You know that, Dad. And the usual channels can't do what they need to do to get him to—"

"I'm working on that. I think RCS will get custody of him soon. The DEA will help us with that. They're very appreciative of what you and Travers did. They don't give a rat's ass about President Dorn's kinder, gentler agenda. They are like us. They understand the lengths to which we must go. They understand that it's a guerrilla war, which cannot be waged with decorum. The war on drugs is very much like the war on terrorism. The people at the DEA laugh at President Dorn."

"Good."

"I heard you saw Jennie before you went to Florida."

"How'd you hear that?"

"I called her. She told me. I like her, Troy. I hope you two keep in touch." Bill turned his head slightly to the side. "What's wrong, son?"

"What do you mean?"

"You seem . . . preoccupied. Is everything all right? You should be a very happy man."

Troy thought long and hard before he spoke. "I'm considering re-signing from Red Cell Seven."

Bill pursed his lips tightly. "Does this have anything to do with Little Jack?"

It surprised Troy when his father zeroed immediately in on the issue. Spending time with his young sons had never been a priority for Bill. "Maybe."

"Take your time with that decision. Once you leave, you can't come back."

"I don't want L.J. to be without a mother *and* a father growing up. Mom's doing a great job, and I appreciate it . . . but still."

"Troy, you shouldn't let—"

"Even if I never have another gun aimed at me, I'll be gone all the time if I stay with RCS, Dad."

"It's a huge sacrifice. There's no doubt."

"I'll never see my boy."

"You have a responsibility to your country," Bill argued gently. "Not many people can do what you can. If you leave Red Cell Seven, this country becomes weaker."

"I have a responsibility to my son as well. He needs me."

"It's a hard choice, Troy. I'm not about to say it isn't."

"I'll never see L.J.," Troy repeated. "Worse, he'll never see me. I know how that feels, and I don't want him knowing."

Bill grimaced.

Troy felt bad for launching that verbal missile, but it had to be said. It had been a long time coming. "You knew about the plot to kill President Dorn all along. Didn't you, Dad?"

"It was Shane Maddux's idea," Bill spoke up sharply.

"But in the end, you and Carlson backed it."

"Yes, we did," Bill admitted. "Let's be brutally honest here. President Dorn's a very liberal politician. But even worse, he's a weak man. Down deep I think he understands what has to be done to protect this country. But he won't do it. The Holiday Mall Attacks are a perfect example. We deal with the chaos, and he still wants to do away with us. And things are only going to get worse from here," he continued. "Today it's drug billions partnering with religious extremists. Who knows what it'll be tomorrow. RCS's survival is essential if the country is going to be prepared for whatever it turns out to be. We can't have a man in the Oval Office who wants to destroy us. Full stop."

"So you kill him?"

Bill stared at Troy steadily but said nothing.

"Are you going to try again?" Troy couldn't believe he was asking that question.

Still, Bill didn't answer.

"Did you cut Maddux loose after the assassination attempt?" Troy finally asked.

"We had to. Roger and I couldn't have the cell thinking we endorsed the shooting. That could have caused dissension in the ranks. It was strategic. Maddux understood."

"Protecting this country rules his life. It's the only thing he really cares about, the only thing that matters. You turned your back on him, Dad. You cut loose your loyalty to him for your own gain."

"No, for the country's gain. And like I said, he understood."

"You made it sound like he alone was responsible for the shooting."

"There was a bigger picture."

"Now who sounds like a politician?"

"Why are you defending Shane Maddux so hard? He killed Lisa. You say he killed Jack. Why do you care about him so much?"

Troy took a deep breath. "He saved my life in Florida this afternoon. I'm sitting here now only because of his talents and his devotion to this country. If not for him I would have joined Jack today."

Bill nodded. "Ah," he murmured, "I get it now."

"Jack died because of you, Dad, not because of Shane. Maybe Shane shot him, but you lit the fuse to that execution. Jack went to Alaska to show you how much he loved this family because you made him feel so terrible about who he was for all those years . . . and who he wasn't. At least, you made him think he wasn't. He's dead because you didn't care."

"And a lot of people are alive today because he did go to Alaska, including you. And because I do care, deeply." Bill hesitated. "There's something you need to know about . . ." His voice trailed off.

"About what?"

"Never mind."

"Come on, Dad. What were you going to say? I need to know."

"It doesn't matter."

"I want to hear what you were going to—"

"No," Bill said sternly. "There's something much more important we need to talk about now."

"What is it?"

"I need you and Major Travers to go on another mission right away. I've already spoken to Travers about it, and he's agreed. You must lead the mission because I can only truly trust you. But I can't send you alone. It would be too dangerous."

PRESIDENT DORN eased into the big chair behind the desk with help from Baxter. It was the first time he'd sat in anything but that damn wheelchair in a long time, and it felt good. The wheelchair had served its purpose well, and it should be saved for its historic significance. It should probably go to the Smithsonian so people could appreciate his courage and conviction. But he had no more use for it than that.

"Feel good, sir?" Baxter asked cheerfully as he sat in the chair in front of the desk.

"Very good." Dorn exhaled heavily. "It feels incredible to have these death squads stopped, too."

"Absolutely. I got another call right before I came in here. They caught two more of them in Missouri. We're down to only five outstanding. I think it's safe to say the danger has passed. People will come back out from their burrows."

"Excellent." Dorn intended to put Baxter's mind at ease quickly. "But it doesn't change my view on Red Cell Seven, Stewart."

"Thank God," Baxter said loudly as relief spread through him like a wildfire through a bone-dry forest. "I was worried you might be rethinking your strategy with those bastards. You know, what with Troy Jensen leading the charge down in Florida today."

"I don't give a damn. RCS must be destroyed. It's the only way." Dorn's eyes narrowed. "Is our plan still in place?"

Baxter nodded. "Yes, sir. I'll be leaving in a few minutes."

"YOU AND Travers are going to Wyoming," Bill explained, "to the Wind River Range in the western part of Wyoming, specifically to Gannett Peak. It's the highest peak in the state."

"Why are we going there?"

"You know why."

"Protect the peak," Troy whispered. "You told President Dorn in the residence the other day you didn't know where the original Executive Orders were. But you did. You lied to him."

"Grow up, son. We all knew what was going on in that room."

"So one of the original orders is hidden on Gannett Peak."

"Yes. And I'll give you its exact location immediately before you leave here tonight."

"What about the other one? The one not hidden on Gannett Peak?" Troy asked. "Where is it?"

"I honestly don't know. I never did. But my gut tells me President Dorn has it now."

"Why?"

"Roger Carlson's wife, Nancy, is missing. No one has seen or heard from her in days, even her children. I believe she knew where the other original was, and Dorn made her pay the ultimate price for that knowledge."

"Do you really think he would go that far to destroy us? I can't see him killing a woman to get possession of something."

"You underestimate President Dorn, son. He is weak, and he is a bad liberal, but he is not above having people get their hands very dirty for him. In the end, he is not unlike us."

"What do you mean by that?"

"He'll use any means he has to in order to get what he wants. But his objectives are not as honorable as ours. He's concerned about himself, and that's basically all."

"Where is Karen?" Troy asked after a few moments.

"I don't know."

"I've called her over and over, Dad, but she doesn't call back. If you know where—"

"I don't know," Bill interrupted sharply. "Now, will you go to Wyoming for me and bring back that original Executive Order? Will you go with Major Travers? It's absolutely essential that you do, if you still believe in Red Cell Seven."

Of course he would. Bill knew that. "If you'll answer one question honestly for me, I'll go."

Bill stared across the desk for a long time before he answered. "All right, one question."

"What happened to Rita Hayes?"

BAXTER PARKED the car in the alley, turned off the headlights, climbed out, checked both ways through the shadows, and then hurried inside the abandoned building through a side door. This was a dangerous neighborhood in southeast Washington, but he couldn't have anyone else do this for him. It had to be him and him alone.

"Stop."

Baxter did so as soon as he heard the voice. Fortunately he recognized it right away. "Okay, I'm stopping," he said, holding his arms up, though he didn't know why. It just seemed like the thing to do. "What's the deal?" he asked when Wilson Travers appeared out of the shadows in front of him. "What's going on?"

"We're going west. We're headed to somewhere in Wyoming, but I don't know any more than that yet."

TROY STEPPED outside the mansion and onto the back porch in the bitter cold so he had privacy. He pulled his cell phone out and dialed Karen again. But once again it went straight to her voice mail.

CHAPTER 34

SNOW AND sleet whipped against Troy's and Travers's unshaven faces. The flakes and pellets were blown chaotically about by powerful gusts, which at times exceeded fifty miles an hour. After a long and grueling backcountry trek, they'd finally made their way to Bonny Pass, which was high and deep inside the breathtakingly beautiful and remote Wind River Range of western Wyoming. Gannett Peak, the highest point in the range—and the state—soared slightly over 13,800 feet above sea level, and was another thousand feet above them. If not for the heavy cloud cover and the snow and sleet lashing the two men, they might have been in its impressive shadow. Despite being so close to the massive mountaintop on this late December afternoon, they couldn't see it through the gloom even though it towered directly above them. Thanks to the awful weather they hadn't seen any of the peaks in the range since they'd arrived.

From here on the Bonny Pass apex, the path to Gannett Peak's narrow, rocky ridge rose steeply up across either the Dinwoody or Gooseneck Glacier. Both of those routes involved treacherous, technical climbs, especially fighting the kind of harsh weather western Wyoming had been buffeted by the last few days. It would have been impossible to make it up that last thousand feet right now—probably for another few days, according to the Weather Channel forecast—but fortunately, Troy and Travers didn't have to go all the way up there to "protect the peak."

Troy knew that, but as far as he was aware, Travers did not. As far as he was aware, Travers had no idea what they were even doing here. His father had sworn he'd told Travers only that he must accompany Troy west on a crucial RCS mission—and that was it.

Maybe Travers had put two and two together by now—he was a smart man. Maybe he realized how this mission somehow involved that traditional Red Cell Seven greeting, and maybe he'd even pieced this thing together further than that. But it had been three days since they'd left the East Coast, and Travers hadn't said a word about it. He hadn't even asked specifically about the mission's objective—which Troy found odd and a little suspicious.

There was probably no reason to worry, Troy figured as they slogged through the snow together. But he couldn't help himself. It seemed like he was overly suspicious, even of people he should be able to trust. It wasn't much of a way to live, when he really thought about it—which made the decision he'd come to, early on in the trek, easier to live with. So had the picture of Little Jack that he carried with him all the time now.

They were forty miles from the trailhead and far from anything remotely civilized as darkness descended on the Wind River Range. They'd flown into Casper three days ago; four-wheeled it west to the trailhead from that small city in the middle of the Cowboy State; been forced to hold at the trailhead for a full twenty-four hours before beginning the ascent, because of a total-whiteout snowstorm; then camped last night ten miles from here at frigid, windswept Lower Titcomb Lake. It had been one of the coldest nights of Troy's life despite being wrapped up inside a North Face Dark Star, which, in turn, was wrapped inside a tent. But now they were finally closing in on their target. It would have been so much faster to take a chopper up here, but the weather had precluded any chance of that—and they couldn't wait for it to clear. Troy couldn't take the chance of someone else getting here first.

Soon after starting the trek, they'd encountered a small herd of elk on the trail. The animals were huge and amazingly magnificent. As he'd stared at them from less than twenty yards, Troy had wondered how his father could shoot one just to put the majestic animal's head on a wall. In that moment he'd made his final decision about whether to stay with Red Cell Seven when this was all over.

Troy checked their position on the GPS device he was carrying on his belt. It was supposed to be accurate to within five feet.

"Decus septum," Travers spoke up loudly as gales whipped through the invisible peaks above them with hair-raising howls. "Protect the peak."

Troy turned slowly back around to face the major. The cave was less than a hundred feet away according to the device. "What did you just say?"

"Protect the peak," Travers repeated, gesturing up and to his left. "Gannett Peak is right up there. I'm no idiot."

"Of course not."

"So, what are we doing here, Troy? What's going on? I think I deserve to know. I've been waiting for you to volunteer the 411 for three days. But now I figure I'll never know unless I ask. It kind of pisses me off, too."

Troy didn't hesitate. "We're here to retrieve an original of Executive Order 1973 One-E signed by Richard Milhous Nixon." Travers was right. He did deserve to know what this trek into a blizzard was about. In the last week Travers had more than proven his loyalty and dedication. Troy's paranoia was unwarranted. "That Order established Red Cell Seven, and it's essential that we recover it. RCS's future may depend on the success of our mission. I'm sorry I didn't tell you right away. I understand why you're angry."

Travers gazed back at Troy through the gathering darkness. "Then let's get it and get the hell out of here. I've had enough snow and wind in the last few days to last me a lifetime. I'm from Alabama. I can't stand this stuff."

Despite the snow, they found the cave easily. The opening was exactly where Bill had described it—between two tall rocky outcroppings that formed a rudimentary arch on the right wall of the cut as they were headed toward the peak. If Troy hadn't known the cave existed and exactly where to look for it, he never would have found it. To access it, you had to go around the side of one of the outcroppings and be within a few feet of the opening to spot it. But with the GPS device, finding it had been relatively easy.

It was only a few feet tall and wide, but once they'd crawled inside they were able to stand up with no problem. The cave was seven feet high and ten feet across. With both of their flashlights brightly illuminating the space, Troy began tracking the left wall, paying close attention to a piece of paper Bill had given him and what was scrawled on it in pencil as he moved deeper into the mountain.

Fifty feet into the cave, Troy's heart began to thud when he spotted two initials etched on a rock at eye level—RC, for Roger Carlson—exactly as the paper and his father's verbal directions indicated.

Troy motioned for Travers to help him, and the two men fought the rock for a few seconds before finally managing to pull it away from the cave wall, revealing a small space and a metal box behind where the rock had been. Troy grabbed the box, opened it, and pointed the flashlight down. Inside was a tightly sealed clear plastic bag, and inside the bag was the original Executive Order. Troy held the bag up so Travers could see it, too, and it seemed obvious what the contents were. Nixon's signature was at the bottom of the page in flowing letters, and the words on the page weren't difficult to read—or interpret.

"Jesus," he whispered as the pounding of blood in his body intensified. He was holding a piece of history. "This is it, Major."

"I'm sorry, Troy."

"What?" Troy called over his shoulder as he continued to stare at the document, transfixed by its importance.

"I said I'm sorry. But I have no choice. I have to do this."

Troy whipped around, and his mouth fell open as he realized what was happening. Travers had backed off a few steps and was aiming a Taser directly at him.

"What . . . what the hell?"

"I need to take that with me," Travers said, nodding down at the clear bag and its precious contents. "But you're staying. I'm going to tie you up and leave you in here. I'll send someone up for you when I'm back to the trailhead. I promise."

"I'll die."

"There's that possibility. It's a bad deal, Troy, but that's the way it's going to be."

"Why are you doing this?" Troy asked incredulously.

"Stewart Baxter told me everything."

Troy gazed at Travers, even more perplexed. "You met with Baxter?"

"Yeah, and he convinced me that your father and Roger Carlson knew about and backed the assassination attempt on President Dorn. That it wasn't just Shane Maddux's idea. It was a whole RCS deal. It came down from the top."

Troy was convinced that wasn't true and that it had originally been Maddux's idea. But did it really matter? In the end, Carlson and his father had definitely backed the plan. "How would Baxter know that?"

"Maddux told him."

"*What?*" That made no sense at all. "Baxter knows Shane Maddux?"

"Apparently, his kid and Maddux go way back. Anyway, Baxter told me all about the two original Executive Orders. Baxter had no idea where this one was, but I figured this was what we were coming out here for. Carlson spent his summers out here as a teenager, and he was a mountain climber. He knew this area very well. I checked it out. It all made sense."

"Does President Dorn have the other original?"

"Yes."

"You know what that means, don't you?"

"What?"

"It means Baxter had Carlson's wife killed."

"I don't believe that."

"She's missing. No one's seen her for a week. Baxter must have had her killed. It's the only explanation, Major. President Dorn may even know about it."

"No way," Travers said firmly, raising the Taser. "I don't believe that, either."

"Major, if you take this original and give it to Baxter, you're destroying Red Cell Seven forever."

"If RCS is trying to assassinate the president of the United States, then that's what I should be doing. That's what my instincts tell me, and they're usually right."

"No," Troy shot back. "Think about what we accomplished in Florida. Think about how many people we saved."

Travers swallowed hard as he gazed steadily at Troy. "It's . . . it's a hard decision. I'll grant you that, Troy."

"Don't do this, Major. Forget about me; I don't matter in all of this. But think about the country. You're putting it in terrible danger if you take this Order to the president."

He was sounding exactly like his father now, but Bill was right. Not about assassinating President Dorn, but about everything else. Troy understood that now. Bill and Carlson should not have backed the assassination attempt, but Red Cell Seven had to survive. It was too important to national security. What had happened in Florida had proved that to him. Maybe RCS wasn't for him personally anymore, maybe he'd lost the edge. But the country absolutely needed the cell. It was a vital piece of the intelligence puzzle. Traditional U.S. intel units might have taken weeks, maybe even months, finding Daniel Gadanz and the death squads. Many more people would have died. More schools probably would have been attacked. The economy would have imploded. The spiral would have been catastrophic. The enemies would have won.

"You're a good man, Major Travers," Troy said. "Don't weaken the country you love so much. President Dorn doesn't understand what needs to be—"

The dart struck Troy in the side of the neck, and he dropped like a sack of dirt.

Travers slid the Taser quickly back into his belt, then leaned down and picked up the bag Troy had just dropped. "I promise I'll have someone come back and get you, kid." He slipped the bag into his coat pocket, grabbed a coiled length of rope from over his shoulder, and began to kneel down next to Troy's shuddering frame. "I'm sorry, Troy. I don't like—"

"Major Travers."

Travers bolted up when he heard the voice coming from directly behind him in the cave. "Who the hell are you?" he demanded, turning quickly to face the person.

A man with dark good looks smiled an easy half smile as he calmly leveled a .44 Magnum at Travers from ten feet away. "I'm Jack Jensen, Major Travers. Troy's older brother." Jack nodded to his right as an attractive brunette moved up beside him. She was training a .44 Mag on Travers as well. "And this is Karen Morris. She's going to be in charge of you for the next few minutes while I take care of my drooling kid brother. I'd advise you to do exactly as she orders. She's the one who saved you in North Carolina. As I believe you saw there at the Kohler farm, she's good with a gun. She's very accurate and not at all afraid to pull the trigger."

"WE'VE GOT to get going," Troy muttered as he sat with his back against the cave wall, right beneath the spot that had hidden the Executive Order for so many years. It had been nearly half an hour since Travers had tased him, and he was feeling better. "Seriously."

"You need a few more minutes," Jack countered with a wry grin as he crouched beside his younger brother. "Seriously."

"What the hell are you doing here?" Troy murmured as he glanced at Karen.

She was a few yards away keeping an eye on Travers. Jack had hog-tied him and put him into Troy's Dark Star sleeping bag. They were going to leave him here—as he had been going to leave Troy. They couldn't trust him on the trail.

"I'm not really here," Jack answered. "You're hallucinating, Troy. I'm just a figment of your imagination."

"Thank God. I was worried there for a second I might have to share Mom and Dad's estate with you." He glanced up into his brother's eyes. They'd already gone through the initial emotional backslapping scene as soon as Troy's tremors had settled enough for him to grab Jack. "Seriously, what are you doing here?"

"Watching out for you. Someone has to. You can't seem to do it for yourself."

"I mean," Troy said quietly, "on earth. What are you doing alive?"

Jack chuckled. "Oh, that."

"Yeah, *that.*"

Jack's grin faded. "It was all Dad's idea. He figured Maddux would come after me, so he beat the bastard to the punch. I was wearing Kevlar on the porch that afternoon."

"But I saw the blood coming from your mouth."

"It wasn't real. Just one of those prop cherries."

"But you—"

"You took off across the field right after the shot to chase down the shooter. I was into the ambulance and gone by the time you got back."

"That's right," Troy murmured as he thought back on it. "It was instinct."

"The plan was for Dad to yell at you to do that, but he didn't even have to."

"No, he sure didn't." Troy thought back on how Bill had been about to tell him something in the office. This had to be it. But in the RCS tradition, he'd kept the secret. "I was sure I could run the bastard down."

"The only people who knew were Dad, the guy who shot me, and the EMTs. Even Mom didn't know."

"They didn't even tell Karen," she called out loudly. Her voice echoed in the cave. "And when everything calms down again, your brother and I are going to have a very long conversation about that, Troy."

Jack laughed. "Sorry, baby."

"You ever do that to me again, Jack, and I'll shoot you myself. And you won't have Kevlar on when I do."

"Good to know, Karen." Jack touched his chest. "I've still got a bruise from where the bullet hit me, even with the Kevlar."

"I bet." Troy glanced up as it occurred to him. "So you were the one who got Maddux in the cemetery. You were the one who took him to the house and put him in that cell in the basement."

"I was keeping an eye on Karen from the shadows, too. I really think he would have killed her if I hadn't shown up."

"I think you're right," Troy agreed.

Jack turned his head to call to Karen over his shoulder. "Maybe because I saved her life that night, she'll go a little easier on me when we have that talk."

"Maybe," Karen called back. "Maybe not."

"You know Dad let him go," Troy said somberly.

"Really?"

"You know why?"

Jack shook his head.

"There's a tape of Dad and Rita Hayes," Troy said quietly so only Jack could hear him.

"As in the Rita Hayes who was Dad's EA all those years?"

"As in that one."

"The Rita Hayes who's missing?"

"Yes."

"Is it the kind of tape I think it is?" Jack asked hesitantly.

"Yeah, and Maddux has it."

Jack grimaced. "Terrible."

"It gets worse." Troy took a deep breath. "I think Dad had Rita killed," he said softly. "He thought she had the tape, but it was Maddux."

They were quiet for a long time.

"I can't believe it," Jack finally murmured.

"You were lucky to be dead."

"I guess." Jack shook his head. "Well, it let me be the one to correspond with Jennie. She didn't know who I was, so it wasn't like she could tell anyone I'd faked my murder." Jack raised an eyebrow. "She's a nice young woman."

"Yeah, well—"

"We're just lucky Lisa never showed her a picture of me."

"True."

"She likes you a lot, Troy."

"I like her, too."

"Good." Jack patted Troy's shoulder, then gestured at Travers. "I feel bad leaving him here. I mean, I understand why he sided with Baxter. But I don't see any other way."

"There is no other way," Troy agreed, making it to his feet with Jack's help. "He's a good man, but we can't take the chance that he'd try to grab the Order on the trail."

"You sure you're okay?" Jack asked.

"Yeah, let's get out of here."

"Maybe we should stay here in the cave tonight. It's already dark out."

"I don't want to wait. I want to go through the night." Troy tapped his coat on top of the pocket that held the bag with the Order inside. "We've got to get this thing out of here and safe as soon as possible."

"Okay."

Jack turned, but Troy caught him by the arm. "Thanks, brother," he murmured as they hugged again. "It seems like you're always saving my ass."

"Hey, what's an older brother for?"

TROY, JACK, and Karen had gone only twenty feet from the cave opening when six forms appeared out of the snow that was whipping wildly through the high rock walls of Bonny Pass. The assailants were on them before they could even draw their guns.

"Get off her!" Jack shouted when Karen cried out in pain from beside him. One of the men had clasped her roughly by the upper arms and squeezed them together behind her back, stretching her shoulders terribly. "I swear I will—"

"You will what?" a seventh man demanded as he appeared in front of them out of the gloom. He was short and wiry, even with the cold-weather gear.

"Shane Maddux," Jack whispered in amazement.

"Wasn't I supposed to have killed you?" Maddux asked sarcastically. "With a rifle from three hundred yards, right, Jack?" He took a few more steps forward so now he was directly in front of Jack and very close. "You're looking pretty good for being dead."

"I guess your aim wasn't that great."

Maddux grinned smugly. "Let me tell you something. If I wanted to kill you, I would."

"How did you know we were here?" Troy demanded.

"Your father told me. I had something he wanted very badly. Two days ago we traded that for the information I wanted. It was a good trade. Here I am."

"You wanted to know where the original of the Executive Order was hidden."

"The one Roger Carlson wasn't keeping on hand," Maddux confirmed. "I told Bill that if he tried to get in touch with you after the trade, I'd kill all of you when I got here. Judging by your reaction to our arrival, Bill kept his word. He's a wise man." Maddux took several steps to the side in the snow so that now he was standing in front of Troy. "Give me what I want."

"You're not getting anything, Shane."

Maddux nodded to the men standing behind Troy. As they tightened their grip on Troy, Maddux reached inside Troy's coat and pulled out the clear plastic bag containing the Executive Order. "Well, that was easy enough. I guess now I can—"

Suddenly Karen broke free. As she stumbled forward, she reached for the .44 inside her coat, turned as she fell into the snow, and fired back at the man who'd been holding her and was now coming at her. She fired once, killing him instantly with a bullet through the chest.

Troy and Jack struggled violently to free themselves as Karen turned her gun on the men holding the brothers. She hit one of Jack's captors in the shoulder and one of Troy's in the side, and the brothers broke free.

As she swung the .44 Magnum toward Shane Maddux, he shot her in the head with his favorite pistol—a Winchester .22.

CHAPTER 35

TROY AND Jack sat in a waiting room of New York–Presbyterian Hospital in Midtown Manhattan. It had been a week since all hell had broken loose on Bonny Pass and five days since Karen had been transported from a Casper, Wyoming, hospital to this facility in New York City on the Jensen G450. But she was still in intensive care. She hadn't yet regained consciousness from the head wound, and her prognosis wasn't good.

"The doctors here are the best in the world at what Karen needs, Jackson," Troy spoke up, using the nickname he'd missed using so much. A nickname he thought he'd never use again. "Mom made sure of that while we were bringing Karen home."

"I know."

"She'll make it."

"I . . . I hope so," Jack said haltingly. "But they're not sure, brother." He was leaning forward with his face in his hands as he sat on a couch opposite Troy's chair. "I . . . I never should have let her come with me to Wyoming. I should have known better, Troy."

"Remember, brother, I've known Karen longer than you have, a lot longer. She's an awesome young woman, but she's one of the most stubborn people in the world. Once she knew you were alive again, she wasn't going to let you out of her sight. She loves you that much."

Jack took a deep breath, rubbed water from his eyes, and then cleared his throat, embarrassed at his emotions, even in front of his brother. "That's exactly what she said," he agreed in a gritty voice after a few moments. "I love her that much, too."

"I know." Troy understood what Jack was thinking. "And if you hadn't followed Travers and me out there with her, I'd be dead right now. Maddux wouldn't have kept his promise to Dad. We both know that. It wouldn't have been in his best interest to let me live, and he always acts in his own best interest." Troy paused. "You saved my life, Jack . . . again."

"Karen saved your life."

"You both did."

"And Maddux got away . . . again."

"There's nothing we could have done. He's slick. We both know that."

"And he has the Executive Order."

Karen being shot was the worst part of what had happened. But Maddux escaping with the bag and its precious contents was a close second.

In the end, Troy, Karen, and Jack had shot three of Maddux's accomplices before the other three had taken off into the gloom. Then they'd gone back into the cave and freed Travers, and each man had taken turns carrying Karen's limp body down the mountain to Troy's vehicle at the trailhead. They hadn't stopped once for food or even rest until Karen was in the Casper hospital emergency room—after which they'd all gotten treatment themselves for exposure and dehydration.

"Where do you think Dad is?" Jack asked.

"I called First Manhattan. The woman I spoke to said he was taking two weeks off for a vacation in the Caribbean with Mom." Troy glanced down the hallway. Cheryl was just coming back from changing Little Jack's diaper. "We know that's not true. He told Mom he was going on a business trip to Europe."

"You think Mom knows it was a lie?"

Troy nodded. "Yeah, she's too smart to be fooled anymore. But I don't think she cares that much. I think she's carrying what she cares about."

"Where do you think Dad really is?"

"I don't know, Jack. I'm not sure *I* care."

PRESIDENT DORN smiled serenely at the television as he and Baxter sat in the Oval Office watching the CNN news report. The anchor had just announced the capture of the last member of the death squads—and Dorn was getting all the credit.

He only had one of the Executive Orders, true. So Red Cell Seven was still legitimate. But sooner or later he'd get the other one. He'd learned long ago to enjoy huge victories in the moment, and this was most certainly one of those victories.

"You're a hero," Baxter said loudly. "The country adores you. You've solidified your legacy."

Dorn's smile grew wider. "I am a hero. And they should love me."

"By the way, sir, Major Travers is—"

"Not yet, Stewart," Dorn interrupted, still soaking in the accolades from the newspeople and from the series of interviews CNN had done in Washington and New York with citizens on the street. Everyone was being effusive with praise for the efficient and effective end to what had essentially been a nationwide hostage situation. When the report was over, Dorn looked over at Baxter. "Now what was that?"

Dorn didn't give a damn about Wilson Travers. That was obvious. He probably didn't even remember who Travers was. "What are you going to do about that other original of the Executive Order?" It was the first time Baxter could remember intentionally leaving off the word "sir" at the end of a question addressed to Dorn. Maybe taking this job had been a mistake after all.

"You're going to find it for me, Stewart, and you're going to find it for me quickly." Dorn raised an eyebrow as he stared steadily at Baxter. "If you don't, I'll fire you." He pointed at his chief of staff. "One way or the other I will crush Red Cell Seven. Do you understand me?"

"ROGER AND I shouldn't have cut you loose the way we did, Shane. I'm sorry for that."

Maddux nodded. "I'm glad to hear you say that, Bill, very glad. But why'd you do it? Why'd you tell the president I was behind the assassination attempt?" Maddux had explained to Bill his connection to Stewart Baxter, and therefore how he knew what Bill had divulged to Dorn. "I understand the cover story internally, for the rest of Red Cell Seven, but why give me away to the president? Why make me public enemy number one in the Oval Office?"

"When Roger found out you were the one behind sailing those LNG tankers at Boston and Virginia, he lost it. In the forty years I've known him, I've never seen him that angry before at anyone. He hated it that you'd gone outside the chain of command. He felt you'd put Red Cell Seven in a terrible position. And he believed that killing half a million people to make a point was wrong, even if your intention was strategically correct. He felt we had to cut you loose, because if it ever came out that you were the one behind those plots, RCS might have been finished despite Nixon's Executive Order. He figured the chief justice of the United States might not care about an Executive Order at that point. But he thought if we could prove you'd gone rogue, we'd be okay." Bill paused. "Red Cell Seven and the safety of the United States was everything to him, Shane. I think you were second, even in front of Nancy on some level. But it was a distant second."

"I know. And it should have been that way. For us, loyalty to country must come before any personal fidelity. But why did *you* give me away to Dorn?" Maddux asked.

"I had to trade something sensitive in order to smoke the president out. He was making all this noise about getting behind Red Cell Seven. I was trying to build a bridge to get at the truth. The same way you were doing with Stewart Baxter. As it turns out, we were right for trying to assassinate Dorn. He was lying about his change of heart. He really *was* trying to shut down RCS. As far as I know, he still is."

"Fine. But you had people looking for me," Maddux said. "You had agents who were ordered to shoot me on sight. You weren't just trading information. You were trying to eliminate me."

Bill swallowed hard. For all he knew, Maddux was considering the ultimate punishment here. Admitting that he'd put agents on Maddux's trail might hammer that last nail in the coffin and push Maddux over the edge. On the other hand, Maddux respected the truth.

"Did you really think they'd find me?" Maddux demanded.

"No." It seemed like the thing to say. And they probably wouldn't have. "What happened to Roger?" Bill asked quickly, trying to change the subject.

"I killed him. Then I drove his body back to Georgetown." Maddux's eyes narrowed to slits. "Did Dorn have Roger's wife killed?"

"I don't know for sure. All I do know is that Nancy's still missing, and I doubt she'll ever be found."

"Bastard," Maddux whispered. "That's as good a reason as any to try again."

Bill understood exactly what Maddux meant by that. He wanted to try again to assassinate Dorn. "What now, Shane? Where do we go from here?"

"You take Roger's place," Maddux said firmly. "You're the natural choice to become the next leader of Red Cell Seven. And I become RCS's Number Two." He laughed softly. "Don't worry. I'm not going to kill you." He laughed a little louder. "Not yet, anyway."

A wave of relief surged through Bill's body. Not until now did he realize how much he'd been worried about exactly that possibility. "We've never had a Number Two before."

"Well, we do now." Maddux gestured at Bill. "You'll have to resign from First Manhattan. You won't have time to lead it and RCS. Besides, you basically have to go underground at this point. Dorn and Baxter will be trying to find you. They know we'll be coming after them, so they'll try to get us first. Us and the Order," Maddux added. "Bottom line, you would have had to resign from First Manhattan anyway. They would have made certain of that, I'm sure."

Maddux was probably right, Bill figured ruefully. "Have you spoken to Baxter again?"

"Only long enough to tell him that I have the Executive Order and that he and Dorn will never get it."

Another wave of relief rolled through Bill. "Thank God," he whispered. Maddux wouldn't lie about having the Order.

"I want this to work," Maddux said evenly. "We've had our differences, Bill, but I think we're the only ones who can completely trust each other in the long run. Now, anyway. I think we finally get each other."

Strangely, Bill understood exactly what Maddux meant.

"The safety and security of the United States is the most important thing to both of us," Maddux continued. "Not many men can say that and truly mean it."

"It's true," Bill agreed. "So what do we do with the last Executive Order, Shane? The physical document, I mean. Dorn will be using every means available to him to find it. If he does, he'll have the ability to destroy us."

"I'll keep it," Maddux said firmly.

"I'll need to know where it is."

Maddux nodded. "Okay, but only on one condition."

"What?"

Maddux pushed open the metal door of the cell they were standing in front of. Its rusty hinges squeaked. "You prove to me you're strong enough to be the leader of Red Cell Seven."

"How?" Bill asked, following Maddux inside the cell. "What do I have to do?"

"This is Kaashif," Maddux said, pointing at the young man who was hanging from the ceiling of the stone-walled room by his wrists.

"This is the one?"

"Yes," Maddux confirmed.

Bill and Kaashif stared at each other for several moments before Bill finally spoke up. "We stopped you, you little bastard, you and all of those people who worked for you. They're all in custody or dead now. I want you to know that."

"There are more," Kaashif replied, "many more. There will always be more. I want *you* to know *that*."

Maddux pulled out the Winchester pistol he'd shot Karen with. "I want you to carry out Kaashif's execution," he said, holding the gun out for Bill, handle first. "The sentence has been passed. He must die."

Bill gazed down at the gun for a long time. Finally, he reached out, took it from Maddux, pressed the barrel to Kaashif's head as the young man began to scream—and fired. "There," he said calmly when it was over and Kaashif hung limply from the rope.

Maddux nodded appreciatively. "I need to ask you one more question."

"Go."

"What did you think about me sailing those LNG tankers at Boston and Virginia?"

I think you were out of your mind. "I understood." Of course there was no way he could say what he was thinking. That would have been suicide. "It was a great act of patriotism." He had to play the game.

Maddux nodded again. "Good. Now we get to work." He glanced at Kaashif then back at Bill. "I have information that indicates that there is a plot in process that will make the Holiday Mall Attacks seem minor. Obviously, we need to get on it."

Bill shut his eyes tightly. Would the bloodshed never end?

TRAVERS STOOD on the very top of Mount Gannett's narrow peak, a thousand feet above Bonny Pass. The weather had been good the last few days, and he'd made the climb with relative ease. It was frigid up here, but the view was incredible. It felt like he was literally on top of the world—which was far from the truth. He'd never been lower.

He'd trusted his instincts. He'd allied himself with Stewart Baxter and President Dorn because that was what his instincts had told him to do. But he'd been wrong. Hadn't he?

He'd come up here to get away from everyone and everything and try to decide. And he'd come up here to conquer the mountain. He hated being so close to a great challenge and not completing it. At this point he'd conquered the challenge—but not the decision.

His cell phone rang, and he chuckled wryly as he pulled it out. He had reception all the way up here. In a way, that was kind of disappointing.

He gazed at the number flashing on the tiny screen. What choice did he have at this point? "Hello."

"Hello, Major. You know who this is, don't you?"

It was Stewart Baxter. "Yeah, I know."

"Come in from the cold, Major."

Travers thought about the irony of the remark as he looked out over the snow-laden landscape from the top of the mountain. Baxter couldn't know where Travers was. No one did. Baxter was referring to "cold" in the sense of a spy coming home.

"This is silly, Major. You did the right thing. And there's still more to do."

"I don't know."

"If you don't come in," Baxter sputtered angrily, "I'll assume you're staying with them, and then you'll be an outlaw. We're going to destroy that organization, Major. It won't be good to be on their side when we do."

Travers glanced at the screen on his phone. It was ringing again. "I'll call you back." He switched lines quickly. "Hello."

"Major."

"Yes."

"Do you know who this is?"

It was Bill Jensen. "Yes."

"Have you made your decision yet?"

"MR. JENSEN."

Troy and Jack looked up at the same time, but Troy quickly realized that the doctor was speaking to Jack.

"Yes?" Jack asked.

"You'd better come with me."

Jack rose unsteadily from the couch. "Is she . . . I mean, should I—"

"Just come with me," the doctor said gently but firmly. "And please hurry."

Troy watched as Jack followed the doctor into Karen's room and the door shut behind him. That hadn't sounded good. He kissed Little Jack on the forehead and carefully handed the baby back to Cheryl. "Could you take him for a few minutes, Mom?"

"Of course."

"I've got to make a phone call."

"Fine, but I think you better hurry, son. I'm afraid your brother's going to need you in a few minutes."

Troy quickly found a quiet corner of the floor not too far away, pressed the digits on his cell phone, and listened impatiently to the ring. Watching Jack go into Karen's room had been awful. Life was too good and short not to live it to the fullest every day with the people you wanted to live it with.

"Hello."

"Jennie?"

"Yes?"

"It's Troy."

"Hey there, I'm so glad you called. I was worried you weren't going to when—"

"Can we have that lunch we talked about?"

She laughed softly in his ear. "Of course, but let's make it dinner instead."

"Great, I—" Troy stopped when he happened to look up. Jack was standing right in front of him. "I'll call you right back, Jennie." He couldn't tell from Jack's expression what was going on. He hoped it wasn't what he feared. "What happened, Jack?"

Jack swallowed hard and then broke into a relieved smile. "Karen's gonna be all right. She just opened her eyes. The doctors wanted a few minutes with her."

The brothers grabbed each other and hugged hard.

"That's awesome," Troy murmured when they finally stepped back from the embrace. "Just awesome."

"Yeah, it is," Jack agreed, shutting his eyes for a few moments as the relief washed over him. "Thanks for being here, Troy. I can't tell you how much it helped me to know you were."

"Of course."

"I'm going to marry her as soon as she's well."

Troy smiled. "Good for you, Jack. Good for her, too. She's a lucky young woman."

Jack grabbed Troy and hugged him again, even harder this time. "You're going to be my best man."

"I'd better."

ACKNOWLEDGMENTS

To the people who have helped *so much* with my writing career and have always been willing to listen: Cynthia Manson, Kevin Smith, Kevin "Big Sky" Erdman, Matt Malone, Pat Lynch, Andy and Chris Brusman, Barbara Fertig, Steve Watson, Jeff Faville, Walter Frey, Mike Pocalyko, Jack Wallace, James Abt, Jeanette Follo, Louise Burke, Peter Borland, Mark Tavani, Marvin Bush, Scott Andrews, Dr. Kurt Butler, and Baron Stewart.

Specifically, to the Amazon team that I've worked with very closely over the past few years, I couldn't possibly have asked for more. It has been a tremendous experience. Thank you again: Andy Bartlett, Jeff Belle, Jacque Ben-Zekry, Daphne Durham, Terry Goodman, Victoria Griffith, Larry Kirshbaum, Danielle Marshall, and Alan Turkus.

And to my daughters, Christina, Ashley, and Gabriella—I love all three of you so much.

ABOUT THE AUTHOR

STEPHEN FREY has spent twenty-five years working in investment banking and private equity at firms including J.P. Morgan & Company in New York City and Winston Partners in Arlington, Virginia. He is the author of eighteen novels, including the first book about Red Cell Seven, *Arctic Fire*. He lives in Leesburg, Virginia, where he writes full-time.